Thirst

KERRY HUDSON

Chatto & Windus
LONDON

Published by Chatto & Windus 2014

2 4 6 8 10 9 7 5 3 1

First published in Great Britain in 2014 by
Chatto & Windus
Random House, 20 Vauxhall Bridge Road,
London SW1V 2SA
www.rbooks.co.uk

Addresses for companies within The Random House Group Limited can be found at:
www.randomhouse.co.uk/offices.htm

The Random House Group Limited Reg. No. 954009

A CIP catalogue record for this book
is available from the British Library

ISBN 9780701188689

The Random House Group Limited supports the Forest Stewardship Council® (FSC®), the leading international forest-certification organisation. Our books carrying the FSC label are printed on FSC®-certified paper. FSC is the only forest-certification scheme supported by the leading environmental organisations, including Greenpeace. Our paper procurement policy can be found at
www.randomhouse.co.uk/environment

Typeset in Goudy by Palimpsest Book Production Limited,
Falkirk, Stirlingshire

Printed and bound in Great Britain by
CPI Group (UK) Ltd, Croydon CR0 4YY

To the people I have loved who helped me tell this story

1

She stood on Bond Street, tourists and shoppers moving on either side of her. A small cluster of young girls left the shop, swinging their handbags, spindly tanned legs wobbling in impossibly high heels, giving the appearance of over-accessorised fawns. Alena ran over the rules; it was good to have rules. Rule 1: always lunchtime, there are less shop girls and the ones who are there aren't looking; they're hungry, resentfully waiting for their sixty minutes of freedom.

Rule 2: the clothes don't matter. Her plain yellow cotton sundress might have been the kind of simple that was very expensive. Apart from the fact that the shoulder straps were very slightly digging into the soft flesh between her armpit and breast, no one would know she'd found the dress in a rag box at a women's shelter. Anyway, she'd seen people in old, awful clothes leave Harrods with glossy bags on each arm and get into Bentleys, as though money excused them of usual standards.

Rule 3: Assume The Face. No matter how nervous she was, The Face was something she could believe in. Something she could conjure and it cost her nothing. Because she was someone without the usual money and entitlement bubbling through her veins like a particularly golden champagne, it confused people; it didn't go with her strangely cut hair, her scrawny, undernourished-looking shoulders. She raised her eyebrows fractionally, along with her sharp chin, set her eyelids to a disinterested half-mast and surveyed the shopfront.

But for all the work The Face was doing she couldn't control her body with its growling stomach, her heart thunk-thunk-thunking enough to displace a rib, her armpits growing sticky; responding instantly to the adrenalin as she pulled the heavy glass door and felt the air conditioning cut through the thick outdoor heat.

There he was; the usual sort of handsome, useless security guard these shops always had. This one, dressed in a smart black suit and tie, looked like he belonged in a whiskey advert, lounging by an open fire, or maybe holding a kitten to his bare, oiled chest like that poster she'd had on her bedroom wall when she was fifteen. She paused just long enough and smiled her best uppity smile, a cold, 'little person' greeting, that she'd once seen a woman in Chelsea use. Rule 4: always draw attention to yourself, never let it seem as though you're sneaking in.

'Afternoon, beautiful.'

Was he calling her beautiful? The Face dropped for a second and the guard made a sound that might have been part of a laugh, rubbed his forehead. Alena thought he might be blushing.

'The afternoon . . . it's beautiful. Sorry, I mean it's a beautiful afternoon.'

She noticed he had a proper London accent, a bit rough. She could tell these things after all this time. Not what she expected from that pretty-boy face. She wouldn't have expected the shyness either, the way he rocked lightly on his heels. Still, she gave him a disdainful stare and swept up to the third floor to commence her long, tense examination of the luxury shoes until she found the ones in the torn-out magazine picture getting soggy in her left bra cup. Rule 5: she must never, ever get caught.

He hated this. Especially hated having to do it at the table in the gloomy basement, the stockroom, where he'd just been about to have lunch; at the same table the girls walked by on their way back up to the shop floor with stacks of shoeboxes balanced up their fronts and tucked under their chins. They slowed as they passed to give the girl hard, disgusted stares as though she had stolen their own shoes from their feet. She was really pretty, and not in the painted, tired way the girls from the shop were either. He knew that would get their backs up.

Her shoulders were uncovered, and he could just see the shine of sweat glistening in the crooks of her elbows when she stretched her arms across the table. He was nervous. Her pale eyes dropped to the open foil of a sandwich between them, right by the offending shoes.

'You eat?'

'No, I was about to –' A stutter crept in, the very slightest fuzziness at the beginning of words, and he tried to disguise it with a cough.

'Do you mind? I thank you.'

He couldn't think what to reply and watched as her bony hands snatched his sandwich from the table – corned beef, lots of pickle, his sandwich that he'd been looking forward to all morning – and took several hungry bites, leaving a red crescent around the ghost of white teeth in the bread.

'What is your name?'

'David, Dave really.' He smiled and then pulled himself up. 'But that's not really the point, is it? What is your name? Yeah,' he nodded, like they were finally on track, 'that's the point.'

'I go tomorrow,' she said, half-chewed sandwich just visible.

'What? Go where?'

'I say, I go tomorrow.' She exhaled through her nostrils noisily.

He raised his voice a little. 'And last night where did you

sleep?' He enunciated every syllable, left large pauses in between the words and she lowered the sandwich for a moment, gave him what his mum would've called 'daggers'.

'I speak English for God's sake. Is houstel in Peckham.' She matched his raised voice and left even bigger pauses.

'Hotel? You're on holiday here?' Now he was getting somewhere.

'No, *houstel*. I *live* here. Tomorrow I go find room to live.'

She'd ripped off a piece of tinfoil and was rolling it into a ball. He couldn't stop watching it.

'Where was your *home* before London?' Dave asked.

'Siberia.'

She was using the palm of her hand to roll the ball back and forth across the table now. He felt stupid and he couldn't stop looking at her hand hovering back and forth like that.

'It is Russia.'

'Yeah, I know that.' Though it would have been a guess at best. 'Can you stop please?'

He leaned across and snatched the tinfoil ball; in return, the slightest raise of a mocking eyebrow, a very slow smile.

'Some people do not.'

The girls kept thumping extra hard up the stairs, whispering to each other. Later those same girls would sit at that same table and gossip about the red-headed shoplifter and how she ate poor Davey's sandwich, the cheeky little bitch. The nearly stolen shoes, silver high-heeled brogues made of slippery, soft leather, lay between Dave and Alena, and as she crumpled the last bit of crust into her mouth she fiddled with one of the shoelaces. Her eyes batted up to Dave; he noticed she had a childish smear of pickle at the corner of her mouth and wanted to reach across and wipe it, almost did, then clasped his hands in his lap.

'Right. Well, I can see there's no straight answers here. It's store policy to call the police. So. Is there anything else you want to say before they get here?'

He couldn't say if it was her mouth, eyes or the tilt of her head, but somehow her whole face changed then. She gave him a single word.

'Please.'

She looked down at her hands and when she looked up her face was softer, one hand brought to her neck.

'I'm apologise to you. I am confused.' As she spoke she counted off each point on her fingers. 'I am new, I try on shoes, I am confusing about taking off.'

The rise and fall of her accent put him in mind of seagulls swooping for scraps. His stomach knotted up. Just his luck to get indigestion from the sandwich she had eaten.

'You tried to walk out of the shop wearing them.' He pulled out a curling pair of dusty blue flip-flops, 'You dropped these because you were going so fast. You set off the alarm and still tried to leave the shop. Honestly, I wish this was my decision but . . .'

She straightened then placed her forearms on the table, looked at him and met his eye for the first time, a jolt, then spoke quietly, so quietly he had to lean forward, and he could smell the curdling sweetness of drying sweat on her skin.

'I am apologising to you. Please. I say I feel sorry. I make mistake. I am new and it is easy to be confusing. This city it is big and people don't like friendly talking and it is so much money for toilet even. 30p in Victoria! I'm asking you to understand. Make this just . . . stupid mistake. Shoes are here still and nothing losing. I am asking. Please.'

His body angled closer and he allowed himself to really

look: hair the shade of old brick, tap-water irises, thin lipsticked lips bitten redder. He saw her nervous hands; her fingers pressing at the soft dip between her collarbones. Dave knew it was no use pretending, he'd do whatever she asked.

He held on to the metal bar above him, his damp grip gently slipping, as the tightly packed bodies swayed one way, then the other, across with the bus. The day-old breath of the person squeezed to his right, the tinny whine of headphones playing 'Simply the Best' plugged into a guy who looked like he sold insurance, and the teen next to him, eyes ringed black, a stud through each fleshy cheek, craning her neck away like she might catch his taste in music. He barely noticed any of them; he'd been walking about like an idiot all day, tripping up the stairs and blaming it on not having had his lunch when the girls cooed around him.

He'd let her go. He'd even held the door open for her as she left wearing those blue flip-flops and a guilty, grateful smile.

Yvonne, smelling of two large glasses of Pinot Grigio, John Paul Gaultier perfume and sweaty tights, had taken him into her office when she got back from lunch.

'I mean, Dave, two years and you've never done us wrong but really! You couldn't wait till I'd given her the once-over? I'm the manager in case you've forgotten and it's for your sake too. How do you think it looks? Might as well be giving the bloody stuff away. There's a policy, you know, and word spreads like wildfire around that sort.'

She took out a compact and lipstick with a heave of breath and a roll of her eyes. Dave stared at a brown patch on the carpet, coffee probably, though knowing Yvonne's filthy temper he wouldn't rule anything out. Blood, sweat and tears. Yvonne told every new girl that was the only way to run a business these days, the only way to turn a profit. Dave scratched his tooth against a dry scrap of skin on his lip and nodded.

'She wasn't one of that lot, Yvonne, whatever that means. And I know there's a policy but that's for shoplifters and she was just a confused tourist, maybe a bit daft but not a thief.'

Yvonne paused, partially lipsticked face sour and slitty-eyed. Dave had never been a talker, never mind one to talk back, one of the reasons he'd lasted so long, and so she waited to hear what he had to say. He thought of those thin fingers snatching the sandwich and took a step towards her.

'But you said it, Yvonne, two years, and I've never done you wrong. Now I'm guessing that after that long you expect I can do my job proper. So why don't you just leave me to it? I know a shoplifter when I catch one. Just like I know a stupid tourist when I see one. And if you're that bothered about how I do my job, maybe you could not lock up the office in future so I can interview them professionally and not in the stockroom with everyone gawping.'

He was sweating, waiting for her paint-stripping response, but she said nothing, simply gave a shocked wave of her lipstick.

'Jesus, alright, no need to get your Y-fronts in a twist.'

Dave stood straighter and nodded, fought the sigh of relief welling up in his chest.

'Right, Yvonne. Right then. I'm glad we got that sorted.' He knew he'd got off lightly and his quick walk towards the door showed it.

'Davey boy?' He turned. There was a small smile on her half-red lips. 'I quite like you riled up.'

He'd maintained a grim, extra-vigilant face for the rest of the day while he thought about her hands, the way she brought one to her throat, her bites of his sandwich. Now, in the crush of body heat and smells of the number 73 he couldn't deny it; he'd been woken up from wherever he'd been, gasping, like someone had taken electric paddles to his chest. He'd been given the chance to save her and he had, gladly, even with the risk. He'd found her, saved her and then she'd walked away from him without looking back and he realised he didn't even know her name.

There was nothing on the telly, just programmes of people doing things; ice-skating, cheffing, ballroom-dancing, learning to be better parents or feel happier through the magic of spray tan and a chin lift. Dave spent all day watching people and he liked it; seeing the way women touched their husbands, a hand laid on a chest or the unthinking brushing away of a speck of dandruff, the way mums bossed their daughters, the whispered rows and silent upsets; he could always spot the ones who thought it was important to be seen Being Nice To The Shop Girls or the ones who could only afford to look but tried everything on anyway. It wasn't that he wasn't interested, it was just that the TV showed what he saw every day, though without the sequins, saucepans and paper knickers.

He bit down on the cushion of his fingertip, pressing his teeth on the smooth nail, letting the small spark of pain register, considered how hard he would need to bite before he'd end up with a purple-pink bruise, the colour of a summer rain cloud.

'Fuck this.'

His 'flat' was two rooms and a box of a bathroom built onto the roof of the Best Turkish Kebab shop. The building work was so shoddy that the reek of grilling meat clung to the woodchip wallpaper. He'd rented this place just over two years ago, thinking it was only for a bit, before the students and some of the braver bankers, with the trendier clothes, had starting climbing their way up from Shoreditch, or down depending on how you looked at it.

Back then Dalston was still a long line of Turkish and Kurdish cafes, neon-bloomed florists' fronts and bridal shops with their frothy, flammable eyeball-assaulting displays, all crowned by a market that sold polyester mountains of three-for-£2 knickers and all the yam and plantain a man could want. He'd been there to witness the basement clubs pop up, with lines of smoking kids in eighties jumpers swigging Red Stripe. It wasn't home, it wasn't the estate, but it was alright.

Down the crackling static of the brown-carpeted stairs and out into the soupy night, he gave his usual 'alright' nod to the thick-armed lads slicing at the glistening, spinning carcass for a long queue of bobbies. There were the usual sirens – the station was just up the road – and some self-important, loud chatter from the groups of kids walking past, though he reminded himself they were probably only three or four years younger than him.

Dave walked his usual route, through the puddle of half-melted ice outside the fishmonger's and the chemist crammed with hair pomade and Palmer's Cocoa Butter, the newsagent's with 'NO PORN' in its window. He was just a bloke in his late twenties, by himself, in tracksuit bottoms and T-shirt, hands in pockets, head down, like he had somewhere to go. Dave did have somewhere to go, but it was nowhere special.

He walked in just as a race was finishing, the usual line of slumped shoulders in jumpers in front of the TV screens, the smell of sweat unmasked by the air-freshener that stung the back of his throat. In front of the hunched-over jumpers, a tall tree of a bloke with dreads paced the floor, repeating, 'You're kidding me, man, you're kidding. Man, you are kidding me.'

The jumpers, they just kept their eyes on the screens, the guy with the dreads didn't think they were the ones kidding him, and the spotty boy inside his glass booth stared hard at his computer screen. Dave walked across the confetti of ripped betting slips to the vending machine and paid his pound for a bottle of Coke. The jumpers, faces slack with the accumulated force of gravity, time and disappointment, gave him a slow nod. Man You Are Kidding Me went and squared up to the roulette game in the corner, whacking his fingers at the screen as though to psych out his competitor before entering the ring.

Dave took his bottle to the very back of the room. Enjoying the first cold, sweet rush of the Coke over his teeth and watched the Sandown 19.45. Watched the horses fly, pushing their strong, beautiful bodies over each hedge with a sharp kick from their bowed over jockeys. In the corner the rhythmic thumps of heavy gold coins being fed into the machine were followed by the tinny computerised whizz of a roulette wheel and that deep, repetitive grumble, 'You're kidding me, man, you're kidding.'

One of the jumpers straightened. There was a winner in the house and he quietly made his way to the window, claimed his money, placed another bet and returned to the line-up. Dave sipped his Coke; he never placed a bet and no one gave a shit. He watched a dog race next, the little scrap of pretend white rabbit a stutter on the screen. He thought about how her hair stuck to the sweat on her neck, the different shape her lips had made when she asked for his help, how a taxi had sped by as she was leaving and the breeze had lifted the hem of her yellow dress. In the corner the roulette wheel kept spinning, the pound coins kept dropping, those dogs kept chasing after something they'd never catch.

The round of her shoulders is what he saw first, recognised it from all the way up the street. He hadn't noticed the bag at her feet though, a bulging, dusty red army bag with a sleeve dangling out of the top. He gave a glance towards the shop, glad that Yvonne made him lock up each night, though he would have kept walking towards her anyway even if Yvonne had been there to see. As he approached he thought he could remember all of her features as though he'd seen them every day, those small, fearless eyes, her thick short hair that today made him think of fox's fur; feral, an urban animal.

Sleep had deserted him in the last few nights as though his mind resented taking a break from conjuring her, and he'd lain baking hot, listening to crap talk radio, feet outside the duvet, the rest twisting around his body. On his break that day he'd eaten five Breakaway biscuits, barely tasting them until he noticed the oily film on his tongue. Now, as he walked towards her, he felt the coat of sugar on his teeth, the sweaty synthetic seam in the crotch of his trousers. He was ashamed, in his cheap suit and thin white shirt, and that was just the beginning of what was wrong with him. But she was there, she'd come back to him, in the same yellow dress, a pink gouge on her shoulder from the strap of her bag, and she was waiting for him.

He was going to get her to turn round, touch her shoulder maybe, but by the time he'd crossed the road, catching her reflection in a shop window, he didn't trust his arms or his hands. Instead he stood, looking at her in the glass, a watery picture, as though a puff of breath would drift her away.

She turned to him in the end. They stood facing each other,

her mouth almost smiling, those fearless eyes staring straight at him. 'I come to ask if you will have a drink with me.'

Her eyes turned hard then and she tilted her chin up, defying him to reject her, to judge the bag at her feet. His hand was half raised, about to smooth the hot skin marked from the strap of her bag with his thumb, until he remembered he had no right touching her.

'OK. A cup of tea somewhere?'

She smiled properly then, a quick flash of those slightly crooked but white, baby shark's teeth. She shrugged and held out her bag for him to carry. 'I don't mind what you drink.'

She led the way towards Oxford Street. He shouldered the bag and watched her walk ahead of him, the tips of his boots just touching the outline of her shadow, as though that was the way to measure a safe distance.

2

At the bright red sign of a bookshop, she turned and motioned him down a side alley with a flick of her hand. Away from the shoppers and tourists, crowds stiff as dominoes ready to topple, he felt he could breathe again. Now it was just the two of them in the shady alley and he rested against the white wall, felt the cold concrete. He'd already taken off his suit jacket, knew he was sweating and clamped his arms to his sides.

She turned round and he gave a weak apologetic smile, straightened up; she frowned and walked towards him and for a moment, from the look on her face, he was sure she was just going to keep going, walk past him and say to the back of his head that there had been a mistake, and he would have to watch her go a second time. Her eyes stayed on his as she approached and he stood completely still, then looked away. Her hand was on his arm, gentler than he imagined it would be, as light as a sweet wrapper blown there by mistake.

'David. Dave? I am sorry. You are feeling tired?'

He wanted to apologise and explain he wasn't really, but his mouth was dry and instead he just looked at her, at those clear, unreadable eyes, the slight creases at the corner of her mouth that made him think she'd smiled a lot once, though he'd seen so little evidence of it.

'Because you have been working! And I make you walk this long way. I am apologising.'

She looked small for a moment, a child frustrated with him or maybe herself, and he was able to find his voice.

'No, no, it's not that. I used to run, you know. I'm fit as anything, or used to be. I used to run thirty miles a week. It's just . . . it's just that I . . .' His words stopped as her features smoothed again into that lopsided, not-quite-smile, the set of her lips suggesting something but promising nothing. He took a breath, considered that he might run away himself. 'I just don't like crowds.'

She shrugged, then nodded, her face serious.

'Well, they are behind now.'

Then she picked up her bag and started walking; he took two long steps to catch up.

'So you are runner? You look strong.' A flirtatious laugh seemed to throb underneath her question.

'Was, was a runner. I haven't run in years. Work and stuff, you know.'

She shrugged again as though it didn't matter to her whether he ran or not.

'Once you are something you are always it.'

And with those words she started down the steps that would lead them through Soho, taking them two at a time.

At Shaftesbury Avenue she slowed her pace, walked shoulder to shoulder with him, her head down. He could feel the heat radiating from her skin; her smell was soap, not perfumed, just normal soap, but with a bitter smell underneath which made him wonder how long she'd been staring into that window, waiting for him. Her bag jostled between them, like it was nudging him into making some sort of conversation.

'Have you seen any of these shows?'

But a passing rickshaw, with a red fur seat, fake flowers and blaring Ace of Base had stolen the words as soon as he'd spoken them and he was grateful. A stupid thing to ask. She gave a small frown at the lost question and he was forced to move closer. He could smell her hair then too; lemons. She looked at him as though he were a sum she was trying to do, and he felt so helpless that he shook and said nothing. He just stood there like a dumb animal, with all the traffic and tourists.

He was so near he could kiss her but all he wanted was to put his face to her hair again. Every word he had ever known evaporated from his tongue. Her face changed again then; a strange, frightened look appeared as if she'd done her sum and the number she'd come up with wasn't at all what she'd wanted. Dave felt his heart bump against each rib as it descended to the soles of his feet.

She put a hand on his shoulder and came close enough to whisper. The heat of her breath on the side of his face made him dizzy, but she stepped back again with the same expression on her face and he nodded before he properly heard what she had said.

'It's Alena.'

He ran; his heart thumping in his ears, the cold air burning in his lungs. His feet thumped across the broken paving slabs, skidded on a crisp packet as he concentrated on widening his stride in time to his heartbeat and the sucking in of all that dirty south London air. He was tall, shot up at twelve and just kept going, strong, and if the piss-taking from his mates and the girls on the estate was anything to go by, not bad-looking. When he ran he felt like he owned this place; Roehampton Estate wasn't much of a kingdom but at least it was his, his and his mum's, and he was only twenty-two, he'd a lot more conquering to do – a whole world's worth. If he could get his front foot just a little further ahead it would feel close to flying.

He ran down from his block towards the bus stop, past

the Co-op where he'd do his shift later that night, the Greggs with the fatty smell of hot sausage rolls pulling at his belly, towards the burnt-out GTI and the group of kids with rocks in their hands, stomach flab hanging over the waists of their trackie bottoms. They were eleven maybe, should have been in that well-meaning, always empty 'Connectionz' centre playing on new computers and drinking free fizzy drinks, if it wasn't so uncool to be seen there. He'd known them since they were toddlers, all filthy faces and bare arses. They could have been him and his mates ten years ago, a pack of estate kids who'd end up fighting each other if no one else came along that night.

Dave was the only one left now, except Mickey, and Deano who worked seasons in Greece or Ibiza and so came and went. Most of his mates had graduated the estate one way or another: from fighting and rock throwing, through drugs and thieving, on to prison then usually to different estates up north and back to drugs and thieving. A few had gone to work in banks, shops, the Forces, and got themselves a 100 per cent mortgage and moved further out to new-builds.

The kids lowered the rocks as he ran by. 'Alright, Dave?' The tallest, Sammy, wore a torn Nike anorak on the hottest summer days. Dave'd chased him out of the Co-op a few times until it dawned on Sammy, just beginning his shoplifting career, that you didn't pinch when the security could outrun you any day of the week. Dave could see which way Sammy was headed, and he wasn't going to be the next Deputy Manager of a Barclays branch.

'Where you going?'

Dave didn't stop running, but slowed his pace, turned with a grin on his face. 'What?'

Sammy looked like he might hurl the rock, hardened his face. 'Where you running to, I said.'

'Wherever I want. Right off the estate, through the park and down into Kingston maybe. Feel like I could run a marathon today.'

'Cool.' Sammy nodded, chucked his rock up in the air and caught it again, the same strength of throw that would wreck a windscreen later when a fancy Land Rover drove through, rather than around, the estate. 'Yeah. Fucking cool. Marathon Dave! Marathon Dave!' The others joined in the chant and Dave held his fist up in salute and kept running, past the tower blocks he'd scrapped outside, the alleys where he'd copped off with Jenni Taylor, the empty, smashed-glass-strewn car park where his mum had taught him to ride his BMX.

He picked up his pace as he reached the metal-shuttered Citizens' Advice Bureau, the Right Plaice fish-and-chip shop with its row of sharp-beaked, dead-eyed crows waiting for scraps. People could say what they wanted. His mum liked a drink, it was true. Dave knew, he fetched the bottle for her each day himself, he even joined her for a drop, sat with her in front of the telly when she said it was lonely drinking on her tod. But she'd do anything for him, had done everything, and all by herself too; he still didn't know where she'd got the money for that BMX.

He turned, ran past the last few tower blocks, in time to watch someone's giant granny pants float down on the breeze from a balcony washing line. That ripe smell of horseshit from the stables on the corner, those nice fancy houses on the edge of the estate, walls the same pink pastel colour as those pants, like crossing into another country; they meant he wasn't far off from the vastness of Richmond Park, the sky behind the rolling scrub turning peach, pinpricked with green parakeets.

He hit the grass, felt his muscles tighten with the change

of surface, ignored the burn and increased his speed; a mob of deer moved into his line of vision, then a crow trying to rip apart a Stella can with its beak. Dave ran, he ran like his life depended on it, until the estate was no more than a dirty fingerprint smudge on the horizon. They could say what they liked, but because of his mum Dave was strong, unstoppable and he was running towards the big wide world.

She dropped off her bag at the cloakroom but not before applying a little more lipstick, rubbing a finger under each eye in case of mascara smears. On the top step she watched him by the revolving doors, his hands clasped in front of him, legs wide apart, just like he would stand at the door of the shop. He really was very handsome, or at least he was when he wasn't taking up as little space as possible like a living, breathing apology. Yes, good broad shoulders, an old-fashioned haircut, but nice thick hair, shiny too. Alena smoothed her dress, took a breath.

A teenager, with brown curls tumbling down to the seat of her denim hot pants, craned her neck to look back at him before her father pushed her along. Maybe it was her nerves that made her walk over and mimic his security-guard pose. For one dizzying moment, when he didn't laugh, she thought she'd made him angry, but then she saw it was the flushed cheeks he was trying to disguise by looking away.

'Sorry, it's habit. The shop, you know.'

She twisted her head to catch his eye. 'No. I think you look very . . . grand.'

He read her face for some sort of piss-take. 'Grand?'

She nodded, placed an arm on his sleeve. 'Yes, you look

like . . .' They had started walking up the wide curving steps of the gallery, it was cool, quieter, and finally she was able to hear him properly; she dropped her words like breadcrumbs as they walked. '. . . a proper man. I can tell you were runner.'

He looked away, gave a nod, to no one, about nothing. Alena reminded herself she could leave, say she needed the toilet and not come back, she'd managed these last few months and she'd keep managing. But then he stepped so carefully out of the path of an elderly couple, walking hand in hand and both hunched towards each other as though they might up and over and tumble right down the stairs if they let go of the other. She saw how his gaze lingered on their clasped hands. He wouldn't turn her away, though the idea that he might pulled at her like stitches in a newly healed wound.

'How come you wanted to come here then?'

Because she always had. Because she'd always been too afraid to come in. Because she'd once seen a couple kiss on the steps outside and thought it was so romantic. Because she'd only just learned it was free. Because she didn't want him to imagine her a shoplifting idiot.

'Because.'

Alena had stood outside the gallery so many times watching people spin through the shining revolving doors. One day, a month on the street by then and the bone-gnawing fear getting just a little better, she'd let herself go on a short walk from the shelter she was in for a few nights, picking the busiest places she could find. Dressed in a shell suit from the rag box, she was too ashamed to try and go inside. Unsure what it might cost, if they would even allow her; as though the shelter followed her like a smell or had dyed her skin a particular colour.

She took a few quick steps into one of the rooms off the

main lobby, and when she looked back, he'd stopped, hands in pockets, and she had the feeling she was pushing too hard, overstepping whatever they'd silently agreed. She was so out of practice, though, that she couldn't be sure.

She offered a smile. Keep smiling. She meant to take his hand but instead just touched the sharp bone of his wrist, surprised by how hot it was under her fingertips. The room was filled with pictures of snowy fields and grassy riverbanks, all except for one blazing in the corner. Alena led him by walking just a few steps ahead – it was amazing how often people would follow you if they felt you were just beyond their reach.

In front of them was a painting of a mother brushing her daughter's hair, the hair so long that the girl, sitting on a wooden chair, had to arch her neck right back and her mother had to extend her arm all the way to get a full stroke in; red, orange, cream and grey. It wasn't peaceful, though it showed a homely moment.

Alena thought it screamed fierce love through the hushed gallery. The mother looked like she was capable of turning the hairbrush and smacking it against the back of her daughter's head, though the girl's stretched, exposed neck showed only trust.

She stepped back to check his reaction. He nodded. He looked embarrassed by the picture.

'This is . . . well, it's a good painting.' She waited for more. 'Well, I mean, it must be good if it's in here.'

She looked at the painting, relaxed her eyes.

'And that girl looks like she could be you.'

'What?'

'She could be you. When you were younger.' He was looking at the picture differently now. 'And the mum, in the apron? That's how I imagine women in old-fashioned countries still dress.'

She let out a small laugh but her eyes were on the girl, her pale neck. 'Russia's not old-fashioned.'

'Sorry, no, course not. My mum still wore an apron until I was fourteen, even though she was just chucking in a Fray Bentos pie and stirring a boiled kettle into a packet of Smash.' His face was softer, calm; he smiled. 'Is that why you like it? Because it's like you or your mum? It reminds you of something?'

She shook her head, spun her flip-flop on the shiny floor about to walk away and then turned back again. She stumbled for the words, real words, not breadcrumbs made of salt and sugar and hot air.

'I think it is like fire . . . no, I am meaning it is . . . fierce. The mother is fierce, daughter is gentle. Protection and love. You see?'

He met her eyes. 'I see.'

'Call me Alena.'

'What?'

'I like it if you say my name. Alena.'

She stared back at the picture and threaded her fingers through the splayed tips of his. He didn't pull away and relief spread as warmly through her as though the painting was aflame. Even so, she kept her eyes on the hairbrush of the mother.

'I see, Alena.'

Afterwards Alena walked them around a few wintery pictures that she said reminded her of home. When they retreated from the milling crowds to the cafe in the basement they were still holding each other's hands, treading the path of the elderly couple before them, and looking no less likely to topple and hurt themselves badly.

She had a single ten-pound note folded in her pocket, what was left of the £20 she'd been given after the shower she'd had at Waterloo Station and a sandwich, and offered to buy him a tea.

'Or a coffee. I am saying thank you, remember.'

But Dave, maybe bold from the hand-holding, from the tinge of red that hovered in his sight, pressed her shoulders down into her seat and came back carrying a tray with three slices of cake and two pots of tea on it. Alena insisted they both have a forkful of each.

'This one is good and sweet,' she said.

'You've a sweet tooth.'

She brought her hand in front of her crooked teeth, mortified. 'No, it's not sweets, they grow in this way.' She spoke from behind her fingers; her neck was hot. Dave reached across and gently lowered her hand.

'No, no, it's an English saying, it just means you like cakes and sweets and stuff. Me too.' He pushed his fork into a nest of meringue and it shattered across the plate. 'But I'm more of a KitKat man.'

Alena wanted to resist after snatching his sandwich yesterday but the cakes were as lovely as the high-ceilinged room filled with dark furniture. Still, she was nervy and she knew she'd regret not just being able to enjoy sitting with a nice man who'd bought her tea and cake and wanted nothing in return. Well, of course he wanted *something* – didn't they all? But she felt he'd at least ask, and probably also listen to her answer. He pushed the last bits of cake over to her side of the table.

'Go on. I've already had five Breakaways.'

'Breakaway?'

They talked until the cafe closed. When they came out of the gallery it had been raining; the air was filled with the warm smell of dirt lifted from the pavements and small fish-scale puddles glinted under the darkening sky across Trafalgar Square. Against everything she should have felt, she still thought London was beautiful. But she was so tired.

'Well, I am thanking you. Is . . .' she hesitated as she considered whether the disabled public toilet cubicle in Paddington, even with the threat of being caught and arrested, was still the better option over this barely disguised begging, '. . . very late for me to find hotel room now. Do you know good one maybe?'

She watched his calm face for any sign of discomfort, she wouldn't force it, knew it would never work if she did. But his face was completely, strangely, still. He put his hands in his pockets.

'You don't have a place for tonight then?'

She gurgled out what she hoped was a light laugh, though her heart was pounding. She hadn't had a place for the last three months.

'My hotel is full tonight.' She paused, but he didn't fill it, and she felt a sharp stab of something behind her cheeks; disappointment or hurt maybe. She picked up her bag then gave a wide, stiff grin. 'But is London. Hundred of hotels! Thank you, David.'

And then he was back with her, his head snapping towards her as soon as he heard the bag being lifted.

'Hey, listen . . . I mean, I wouldn't be offended if you didn't want to but . . . well, I live by myself and I could sleep on the sofa. You could have the bed, I mean. Just since it's so late now. I hate to think of you trying to find somewhere and it's my fault for keeping you so long, so . . .'

She exhaled slowly through her nostrils until all the air was pushed from her lungs, the only way she could make it seem like she was weighing it up.

'But I can't, really. Where do you live?'

Her stomach churning all that cake. Please don't say Clapham or anywhere near.

'Hackney, out east. You're really welcome. I mean, it's just a night.' He turned to her now and met her gaze, held his hands in the air. 'All above board. I mean, I'm serious about the sofa.'

Hackney. Out east. Far enough. And then she nodded, tried to smile and held out her bag to him.

This time it was Dave who took her hand, barely a whisper of linked fingers. He took her for fish and chips and both ate quickly out of the paper, saying little as they leaned on the windowsill of the chippy, their arms just touching. Afterwards, she insisted that they walk to the river and though he was shattered from just having her near he agreed, shouldered her bag and was glad when they reached Waterloo Bridge, hand in hand, as the lights shone and the currents of the Thames surged below, somehow spurring them on in whatever this was between them.

He waved away her ten-pound note when she rummaged in her bag to pay for the bus ticket and accepted it as she would accept everything, with a nod and a shrug which might mean anything but in this case, Dave thought, meant she was grateful.

After they had sat, at her request, at the front on the top deck of the 243, she turned quiet.

'You OK?'

'Just sleepy. I don't sleep very good last night.'

She tugged the spilling sleeve from the bag on Dave's lap, pulled on the lime-green cardigan that emerged, put her feet up on the window's ledge in front and dipped her head towards Dave's shoulder, as though she might nestle into him, but then straightened up and closed her eyes for a moment.

Dave looked at their reflection in the window. He had no idea how she had ended up next to him like this, and pretended to look out at the scatter of lights along the river while he concentrated on remembering the rhythm of her breath so close to his body.

A real Chanel handbag. Just lying limp on the floor next to one of the many cigarette burns on the carpet made by her father who had never understood that one day he'd reduce the whole block to ashes. Her mother seemed pleased to see her old friend, though Alena, sitting quietly in the corner with a book, could feel how shamed she was by the state of the place, how little she had to offer.

The friend was all bright lipstick and large hand gestures, no doubt to emphasise the diamond ring on her wrinkled hands, the thick gold bracelet that clanged against the tabletop. Next to her, Alena's mother was as dumpy and unexciting as the last potato in the sack. It was hard to imagine that her mother, ingratiating, apologising, laying down a sparse meal for the three of them, had once sparkled brighter than that diamond ring. So brightly that she'd won Alena's father's affections from this other woman, driving her broken-hearted best friend off to St Petersburg and then to France. Though, as her mother said each time she told the story, she had done her friend the kindest favour she could imagine. It hadn't been an easy life, bearing her husband's drinking and temper all those years until she fell pregnant with Alena in her forties, long after she'd given up all hope, and at least found a reason to keep going. Her friend had realised this in time. With years the guilt had faded, and so it seemed had the blame, because here was the woman, brandishing her Chanel handbag, stubbing out her cigarette in a half-eaten sausage while eyeing her mother and making promises.

'Lots of work. For good girls with good English like you. Lots of work and a good salary too.'

Alena had wanted to slap her there and then, for coming and exposing her mother's poverty, and satisfied herself with the grim thought that the woman might have her hand cut off walking around here with a diamond like that.

Still, Alena and her mother had hugged each other after she'd left, shared some relieved laughter at the expense of the woman's terrible leopard-print blouse, the first shared laughter in a long time. But before that, her mother's friend with her perfect make-up mask had waved away their thank-yous with her manicured nails. 'For my oldest friend's beautiful daughter? It is nothing. We must share fortune, yes?' She looked for something in that handbag, then her cold eyes looked over at Alena's mother. 'This is nothing. It is simply what I owe. You will not believe, Alena, the things you have in store.'

The woman came back the next day looking tired and grey, easily as old as her mother, saying she would never get used to those thin Russian mattresses again and took Alena upstairs to help Alena pack, while her mother made tea.

'This, this. Not this. Take this instead.'

Alena looked at the pile of clothes, bright summer dresses, denim miniskirts she hadn't worn since her teens, and a strange feeling plucked at her spine. The woman took her hand. 'In London everything is different. None of this Siberian bumpkin fashion.' She nodded to Alena's tracksuits, her thick knitted sweaters, tight jeans. 'Smart girls, they show their figures off.'

Alena looked her mother's friend up and down, her two-piece pale green trouser suit, the string of pearls, the impatient line of her lips.

'But for working, you're sure? Look, I've smart trousers and some good shirts. I bought them for interviews but they've barely been worn and –'

The woman laughed, took a sharp drag on her cigarette, and prodded the pile of clothes with a finger.

'These. Not those.' She gave Alena's cheek a little pat, barely touching her. 'These ones.'

Then she gave Alena all the paperwork for the visa, the forms already completed in someone's tight, efficient black capitals; somehow it didn't seem likely they were the woman's. Alena sat looking at the forms, not just pieces of paper but a future, money, an adventure, a guilty freedom from her fragile mother. She would get a student visa, for studying English, but once she was in London there would be work for her, maybe in an office but probably in a cafe or cleaning at first.

A wad of roubles were pushed into her hand. 'Take your mother for a good dinner, she looks like she could use one. Poor woman.'

Downstairs the older women talked and Alena could feel her mother's embarrassment radiating up through the floorboards; the shabby clothes and chipped crockery. Alena studied the London address on her visa papers and turned it over on her tongue: Clap-ham, Lon-don. Clap-ham. Clapham. She tucked her knees beneath the thick blanket she'd slept under since she was a child and decided she would bring her mother her own designer handbag on her first visit home and would never waste good food in front of her no matter how much she had herself.

The music rattled through her breastbone and their shrieks and cigarette smoke drifted over to the bus stop where Dave was just standing, looking at her and then over at the nightclub, as though he had forgotten where he lived. She pulled her cardigan a little tighter around her.

'Sorry, I was just . . .' Alena followed his gaze to a girl sitting on the pavement outside the club, legs sprawled, knickers showing, her soggy face crying into a mobile phone.

She knew this was the delicate time, imagined herself on a tightrope between the buildings high above the road. She knew once she was inside it would be hard to turn her away. She said nothing, smiled a very weak, patient smile, looked back at the crowds outside the club. It was Tuesday, most of the girls weren't in dresses but wore jeans, the boys vests with low V-necks, and she realised she still had a lot to learn about London. But men she understood, and when he turned to her with a fretful look, gave a harassed nod and started walking with his hands pushed deep in his pockets, she gave a small, sweet candyfloss puff of a giggle so that he was forced to give her a limp smile in return. Another minute, silent promise between them.

The stairs smelt of cat piss and there was a sheen on the woodchip wallpaper she thought might be from the rising fat of the endlessly turning shawarma in the shop downstairs. After the noise and light of the city something snaked down her back now it was just the two of them alone in his living room. Well, living room and kitchen both; two plates on a draining board by the sink, a pile of aluminium takeaway cartons by an overflowing bin, the tiny countertop fridge making a low deep moaning sound. Still, she was in, the hardest part, though she knew there'd be harder things to come.

He put her bag down on the floor, sat to take off his shoes and socks and then looked about the place as if he himself had just arrived. Then he started moving half-empty mugs from one place to another, opening the curtains on the estate opposite then closing them again, looking at her in an angry way that suggested she might be to blame for him having to live there. She smiled a bright smile, the kind that is so false you believe it will shatter your face if you hold it too long.

'You see, my hotel was just for few nights so . . . this is much nicer than that cheap hotel.'

She looked about the bare room for something to compliment but there was nothing except a sagging brown velvet sofa, a table made from that tacky fake-wood everything was made of back home, and – 'TV! I like TV a lot. What do you like to watch?'

But he was sitting on the edge of the sofa scratching at his end-of-day stubble. He had changed his mind, maybe realised what was happening, and with his shoulders hunched in that way, a hand up to his face, with his pale bony feet sticking out from black trouser legs, Alena could almost see a little boy sitting there. A small disappointed boy who hadn't got what he wanted for his birthday. She felt a slow seeping of something warm in her belly, sympathy or guilt she didn't know, but she wanted no part of it.

'Sorry, sorry, Alena.'

He stood and left the room and she picked up her bag. She would leave, leave him to his takeaways and biscuits and hot little room. She could hear him slamming a door shut, swearing under his breath. When he came back he had a pile of greying sheets, a shiny quilted blanket, a miserable expression.

'Sorry.' He nodded down at the bedding, but his voice suggested he might be carrying her dog that he'd just ran over. 'I just wasn't expecting you.'

She shook her head. 'I make mistake. I'm going now.' She

already had the ten-pound note in her hand, though she knew full well that he wouldn't take it. 'Thank you for cakes. This is for them.'

She thrust the note towards him and he looked at her, squinting. She thought for an awful moment he might cry.

'No, no. What? Why?'

'But you are upset? For something I have been doing?'

'Don't go.'

'But you are upset. I am upsetting you. I'm sorry if you did not want me to come home. Maybe I am confusing?'

He slumped onto the sofa, still holding the sheets.

'No, I'm not upset. I'm, I'm . . .'

Alena let her bag drop and sat by him, not too close, but close enough to see a nerve at the side of his mouth twitching, a tiny pulse.

'I just, I'm embarrassed about this place. You can see I don't have people to stay often, well, ever actually. And you can stay here, I really want you to, but I don't want you to think you have to . . . I'm expecting nothing. Do you understand? You need somewhere to stay for a while and I just want you to know you can crash here.'

'Crash?'

'Yeah, sleep, stay. Have the bed for as long as you need and I'll sleep on the sofa and there's no . . . I'm not some sleaze, you know? It's just nice to have company, to be honest.'

And so it was done. Alena felt herself uncoiling, worried he might hear the click, click, click of her spine relaxing.

'No trading?'

'What?'

'There's no trading here. So you say I can sleep here for free?'

He laughed, a small, tight-chested laugh. 'Yeah. I'm a good bloke, decent if nothing else, and it's not much but you can stay here as long as you like.'

'I am understanding. Thank you, sweet man.'

And though she wished she could say it was all part of the plan, another thread to bind his affection to her, when she brushed her lips over the softness of his dark eyebrow she knew it wasn't.

'I'm glad you're here, Alena.'

She brought the palm of her hand to the damp of his forehead. He was a gentle man as she'd guessed, or gambled. Silently, she promised to do him as little harm as possible.

He told her how to use the shower and then left her in the bedroom, with its view right across the city, an electric switchboard of popping lights and tangled wire roads. She changed into her nightie, and imagined his belt buckle falling to the floor, him turning his bulk on the old brown sofa, unable to sleep for thinking about her in the next room. After some time had passed and she knew he wouldn't come, she stretched out, pushed her head into the soft lump of the pillow that smelt a little of him. The sheets were a little grainy, but not enough to spoil the fact she was in an actual bed, a double too. She stretched her legs wide, arched her back, let the mattress mould to her body and slipped into a thick, black sleep that lay itself down upon her and pressed her flat.

3

He woke early and went to the Turkish shop over the road that sold everything: tins of ravioli, shining hunks of feta cheese floating in washing-up basins, hair dye, nappies, specialist porn.

He walked the narrow aisles quickly with the swinging basket nipping at the skin inside the crook of his arm. Bacon, eggs, a wide flat Turkish loaf the size of a small pillow. It was early enough for the all-night shift workers, with their stubble and woollen hats despite the summer, to still be manning the till.

One of them had a slim, drooping face made even longer by a wiry moustache; the other, a round, swarthy moon of a face, his white stubble not able to hide an extra chin. They took turns smoking outside, leaning against the £1 bowls of aubergines, carrots and apples while the other served the customers inside. The art students that lived in the factory conversion next door, the estate crowd, Turkish families and Dave were all met by the same weary smile, 'Alrigh', boss? You good?' and the jutting, jangling Middle Eastern music they listened to, seemingly with no pleasure, on a small pink cassette player by the cigarettes.

Dave, who usually only ever came in for a pint of milk or maybe a bag of crisps, wondered if they noticed his nervousness as he hefted his laden basket onto the counter. He wanted to pay quickly, afraid she might be gone, out the door with that dusty bag of hers, disappeared back into the sun-bleached air she'd just appeared from.

He was shyly taking his stuff out of the basket when he realised she'd need more food for the day.

'Just a minute, mate. Sorry.'

He added tins of soup, frozen macaroni cheese, sausages. He knew nothing about her; she might only eat salads. No, sweet tooth he remembered, and added some packets of biscuits, a tub of ice cream and then, passing the newspaper rack, some glossy magazines, their covers full of shiny hair and teeth and long, toned limbs. By the time he got back to the till Moonface was outside with the *Sun* newspaper spread over a pile of leeks, tea in one hand, a roll-up in the other and Longface was apathetically wielding the scanning gun. He paused at the women's magazines, gave Dave a look.

'Doing some reading, boss? You know we got the proper stuff.' He jogged his head up to the top shelf and showed a few millimetres of his teeth, which passed for a smile. Dave offered a hollow laugh.

'I've got someone staying.'

The smile grew a little wider. Dave thought there was some piss-taking there, good-natured, banter, but still piss-taking.

'Mum . . . or sister?'

Piss-take. Dave widened his shoulders.

'A girl actually.' Then felt like a pillock. 'I mean a friend. She's a girl.'

Longface nodded, shrugged, making Dave feel even more of a twat, and started scanning the shopping again. With each beep, tomato soup, beep, custard creams, beep, strawberry jam, beep, Dave imagined her waking up, looking around at his shithole of a flat, the estate opposite with plastic bags tangled in the single rose bush on the dog-shit-strewn grass, then grabbing her bag and slamming the door behind her.

The price of the shopping was a shock – how could he treat her nice if he couldn't even afford to buy them a day or two's food? The shopping-bag handles pulling at his wrists, he wondered if she realised how little security guards got paid, as if she couldn't tell from the flat, and if that would make a difference.

When Moonface came in from his ten-minute stint, Longface greeted him with: 'This one's got a girlfriend staying.'

'Nice one, boss. About time and all.' Moonface slapped his back.

As the door slid closed behind him Dave realised he was laughing quietly.

But the laugh was soon gone. The first thing he saw when he managed to get in with the two heavy bags was the door of the bedroom open and the flat silent. He left the shopping in the hall. No goodbye then. He guiltily thought to check his stuff then realised he had nothing to steal; she was welcome to his two plates and roll-on deodorant if she wanted them.

What an idiot. Bragging to those two about his friend, a girl, who's staying. What a stupid arsehole. But then there she was, on the sofa, cross-legged in a Snoopy nightie, drinking a mug of black coffee that, judging from the smell of it, was thick as tar, the wide-open window fluttering the pages of the *Hackney Gazette* laid across her bare legs. She looked up and half yawned, half smiled, making her face fierce and childlike.

'David. I think you go to work.'

He put his hands in his pockets and just looked at her, legs tangled about each other, a fuzzy mess of red hair on one side of her head, yesterday's mascara looped in charcoal smears under her eyes. He smiled too and shook his head at the exact moment she nodded down to the paper.

'I find job maybe?'

He said nothing, afraid that whatever words he had would break this, would change her mind. He nodded quietly and when she returned to the paper, gulping from her mug, he still stood staring until she looked up, until she raised her thin eyebrows in question.

'I look for job in Hackney, yes? Staying in Hackney.' She lowered her chin when he didn't answer and her expression changed like a sunny day surprised by sleet. She spoke more seriously, searching his face. 'I stay for a while here, until I find a new place? Is OK?'

'OK. I mean, yes, yeah, good idea. Stay as long as you need . . . I mean, like, as long as you like.'

He unpacked the shopping with shaking hands. He'd forgotten the sickness, right down to the soles of your feet, of wanting. To want and maybe allow yourself to have it and maybe be wanted back. He had forgotten how terrifying wanting and having could be.

He'd thought his mates would laugh, take the piss, when he walked into the pub with her. He'd had no choice really. He'd come through to the living room and there was Shelley, dabbing at her eyes with a wad of toilet roll, his mum's fat arm around her shoulder.

'My first proper date in a year and all.'

'He's a plonker. A hangover; what sort of excuse is that anyway?'

'What a sight, eh? Me all dressed up and no place to go.'

They looked up at Dave stood in the doorway, can of Skol in his hand. His mum looked between them, stood up and came round to Dave. She put on that soft face for when she was going to ask Dave to do something he wouldn't want to do, maybe go and buy Tampax, then took a swig from his can and poked her finger gently in his belly.

'Davey, you're out tonight. What is it again? Deano's birthday?'

He stood, silent, took back his Skol, and stared into its hole. When the silence got too long he took a swig and grabbed his freshly ironed shirt from the back of the sofa. His mum tucked her crossed arms in the dip between her boobs and belly with a huff so he knew he wouldn't be getting off lightly.

'Mickey's, it's Mickey's birthday. I've got to get ready, but yeah.' He sighed, tried to eye Shelley in a way that said, 'Isn't my mum losing it? – thinking of you coming out with me and my mates, as if,' but then, a nudge from his mum, 'Come along if you fancy it, Shelley.'

'No, don't be daft. You don't want me cramping your style. Do you? You'll be out on the pull.'

It was a proper, hopeful question, Dave knew that much, but he took it as he wanted.

'Yeah, fair enough.' He shrugged, off the hook. 'Alright.'

Which left Shelley no choice but to laugh, as if her not coming was her idea, and Dave felt his mum pissed off at him, hot as the flame she held to her fag now, giving a quick, impatient puff in his direction.

Usually her and his mum listened to Celine Dion or watched a weepy video and when it got too late for Shelley to squeeze back into those heels and stagger her way through the few blocks of dark shadows back to her flat, she curled up right there on the sofa, a cross between knackered kid and husband in the doghouse.

That night, after Shelley had cried herself out and they'd given her absent bloke a good tongue-lashing, their tired slightly drunk laughs rang hollow over the *EastEnders* theme. The walls were so thin, cardboard and paste his mum used to say, Dave could hear them even over his Discman. He imagined Shelley pulling out a tiny perfume tester and spraying her stockinged feet and then curling them under her, relighting her fag, and all the while his mum sitting smiling at her, giving her knee a little rub. 'You work so hard. You deserve a bit of fun, a good fella to give you some love.'

'I know it, Pat.' She'd blow a long column of smoke here, Dave thought. 'Don't I bloody know it.' From the sound of it they'd had a few drinks themselves, maybe more than a few. 'But if we don't deserve it, Pat, who does, eh? Hard-working girls all by ourselves?'

'Except for Davey.'

'Except for him. So yeah, if we don't deserve it, who does? OK, I'm no spring chicken, Pat. Keep myself looking nice, but I wouldn't get a second look from someone like, say, someone like your Dave.'

'If he'd a good head on him he would. Stunner like you.'

'Us girls,' Dave had heard her say to his mum, 'we should know better.'

And they'd rolled about. Dave, in his bedroom, couldn't work out what it was all about; he'd turned up Eminem and stared at his map. Then Shelley was knocking on his door, wobbling on her too-high heels.

'Your mum sent me in to see if you want a toastie before you go out. Line your stomach and all that. Can I come in then?' And she stepped in, pulling down her little black skirt over her thighs. Dave looked up from his book and she sat down on the bed next to him, pushing herself back so they sat, side by side against the wall. 'What you reading?'

Dave turned the cover towards her.

'South America? On a shoestring? Why do you want to do

that when you can just get a nice hotel, hire a villa or something?'

Her shoulder gave his a nudge; she smelt of a perfume, a perfume like the penny sweets they had in the Co-op, a little of his mum's fags too. Dave cleared his throat, looked towards the map.

'It's not about the money, is it? It's about the experience. Travelling, eating like the locals. It's an adventure. Besides, it's just the beginning.'

She stood and walked over to the map, bending over and tracing her nail across the route he'd marked out in biro.

'That's really cool, Dave. You're really going to do that all the way around?'

'Yeah, I'm going to travel to every continent. Surf in Australia, safari in Africa, ride elephants in Thailand. There's more to life than just this little patch of estate, you know?'

And though he expected her to get the huff, tell him not to be a dick, that he'd break his poor mum's heart running off around the world, she just smiled. 'Cool, Dave. That's really cool.'

Dave sat up straighter. She hadn't asked any of the usual idiot questions – 'How much will it cost?' 'What's the point?' 'Why not just go live in Spain like Tina Howell did?' 'What will your poor Mum do without you?'

'Yeah, I'm saving for the trip now. Mum knows. I mean, she doesn't want me to go but she gets it, why I need to. Then, when I've enough, a round-the-world ticket – first stop New York.'

'I've always wanted to go to New York. All that shopping.' She ran her finger back across the map, 'You know I never miss an episode of *Holiday*? You wouldn't think it, to look at me, but I would've liked an adventure too. Good on you, Davey, for getting out there.'

'You still could. Buy a map, mark out your route, save a bit each week.'

She looked round at him.

'This year I should be ready, that's the plan. America, New Zealand, Oz, Thailand, Africa and the rest, and then back here to start thinking about training up, sports science or leisure and tourism or something.'

She had her hands on her hips now; it pushed her boobs forward, he noticed.

'That's so cool, I mean amazing, Dave. You've got it all planned out, haven't you? Your mum'll be so proud.' She walked the few steps towards the bed. 'I bet you'll leave a few broken hearts behind, though?' She bent down to him – he could see right down her top. 'All the girls fancy you. I've seen you running around the estate, all the women have. You make a lot of the married ones very happy.' She stood up. 'Anyway, your mum wanted to know, cheese and ham or cheese and pickle?'

Dave let out a breath, looked up at her, her hands smoothing down her dress.

'Dave? . . . Toastie? Do you want one?'

She sounded a bit impatient, maybe a bit like she was laughing at him. He picked up his book to cover his beaming cheeks.

'Jesus, Shelley, I don't know, it's a toastie, isn't it? So, whatever. I'm just trying to read this bit before I head out actually.'

She kept that amused sliver of a smile on her face, held up her hands. 'Alright, alright! It'll be ready in ten.'

She was half out the door but turned back when he called her; she wasn't smiling this time.

'Thanks for asking.'

She let out a short laugh. 'About the toastie?'

'About the trip and not just taking Mum's side and . . . everything.' Dave pulled at a loose thread on his sleeve. 'Come tonight. I mean, if you like. You're all dressed up and that.'

When he heard the living-room door shut he put down his book, unbuckled his belt, thought about the shape of her in that dress, the way her finger traced the outline of the Sahara.

His mates hadn't laughed when they walked in, though. They'd taken one look at Shelley's long legs in her miniskirt, the game-for-anything smile, and given him a nod of approval. It was a 'nice work if you can get it, mate' nod and Dave had shrugged and looked away as Shelley squeezed off through the crowd to get 'Aftershocks for everyone!'

'Shelley love, make mine the red kind. Can't stick the blue,' Mickey shouted after her and she threw him a thumbs up over the crowd's heads.

'Alright, birthday boy!'

When she came back with the six shot glasses of thick red syrup balanced on a dinner plate they necked them, the cinnamon taste burning down their throats and then up again from their bellies, faces twisting, smacking their lips. Mickey had his hand just above Shelley's arse and whispered in her ear, but she just kept looking at Dave, her blue eyes darkened by the cage of her clumpy eyelashes, blackish dust gathering in the fine wrinkles as she smiled.

He could see it. Maybe. Now she was out of his living room, not sitting next to his mum. But she'd always been just Shelley, his mum's mate. Younger than his mum by a good fifteen years, yeah, but still one of her crowd. She'd been coming since he was sixteen. He knew exactly the way she got comfortable on their sofa, kicking off her high heels so that a faint animal smell, like wet rabbit fur, filled the living room. 'Sorry for the guff, Pat, it's the walking. Miles and miles us Avon Girls do – they tested it once, made a few girls wear one of them pedometers, and printed it in the newsletter. And I can't stand to put them back on, what with the bunions.'

Now, she licked the sticky bottom of her empty shot glass, twisted her hips towards Mickey but stared at Dave, already half pissed. He couldn't quite believe it, but he did fancy her a bit, this woman who showed up at his house with New Look bags filled with clothes meant for teenagers, who talked too much about her married ex-boyfriend and Avon moisturisers. Maybe he fancied her more than a bit actually, or maybe it was the three cans of Skol and two Aftershocks talking or even the pub with its sticky carpet, its smoky, not-quite-spoiling-for-a-fight-just-yet-but-I'll-maybe-see-you-outside-later atmosphere.

She was chatting to Deano now, just arrived, and he was loving every minute. That bloke Pete was at the bar but looking back at her, bringing her over a plastic flute of fizzy pink wine with an eager-to-please grin. They were eating out of her hand but all the time she looked right at him, waiting for him to step up. He wondered how much she'd had with his mum before they'd got there.

Deano and Shelley made their way to what counted for a dance floor, past the pool table with a wooden board across the top, dancing a dirty one-man, one-woman conga to 'Girls Just Want to Have Fun'. He felt a twinge, maybe jealousy, maybe just being freaked out by his mates and Shelley getting pissed up together – she was twelve years older than them.

It was his own fault she was up there now with one arm around Deano and the other around Mickey; let them get on with it. They were welcome to her. He took his pint outside and stared into the black windows opposite, thinking of his map, wishing for somewhere else.

'And what's up with handsome today?'

'What?'

'You're in a right dreamworld you are, and don't think I didn't notice you sneaking in late either. I don't pay you to look out the window. You're meant to be watching the customers.'

Dave would have let this go, said he was sorry, but today he stared her down.

'I do my job, Yvonne, and it's half three and I haven't had lunch yet.'

The expression on her face made him think that maybe her too-dark flesh-coloured tights, regulation for the girls even in summer, had wedged up her arse. Her mouth made a soft Oh but her look sharpened up good and quick.

'Off you get downstairs for half an hour then. Tanya! Get over and do the door.'

Dave stuck his hands in his pockets and was just passing the till counter when he felt Tanya's long blue, jewel-encrusted nails stroke up his forearm. If he was being honest, it wasn't unpleasant, that stroking.

'You tired today then, Davey?' She was speaking softly, the pink glossed smear of her lips right in his face; he could see the soft bumps of spots on her chin coated over with thick make-up. She kept her hand on his arm. 'You get some last night, did you?'

There was something rank, too moist but also a bit sexy, about her mouth beyond the shiny fuchsia lips, so close to his ear, and he pulled back.

'Tanya, leave it out.'

She stepped away then, a snappy gesture like someone had pressed a button in her back and made her torso jerk, her arms cross her chest.

'Well, I just thought maybe that was your little deal. You know, as payment for letting her off, that foreign shoplifter, that's all.'

'What?'

'I know your little secret.' Her eyes crawled across his face looking for something and once she'd found it she showed a few teeth and delivered her next words in an Essex sing-song whisper. 'You didn't see me, but I saw you.'

Dave shut his face down as well as he could, looked back to Yvonne, hoped she was out of earshot.

'Like I said, Tanya, leave it out.'

Yvonne came striding over now.

'Tanya, come on, love, haven't I told you I'm the only one who gets to bother Davey boy here? Manager's perks. And, Dave?' Yvonne pushed her huge polyester-clothed chest towards him. 'I don't know what's got into you these last few days but I'm still deciding if I like it or not. So watch it.'

Dave looked at Tanya and shook his head as if to say she was being mental and didn't know what she was talking about. He tried to see what her eyes were doing behind her feathery false eyelashes but she was already walking towards the door.

He knew it was bad when he found he wasn't hungry. He just sat at that table thinking about her sitting opposite him. How she'd bitten that sandwich, the way she bit off the end of his sentences sharply, and then the nervous but good feeling of sitting with her on the sofa that morning, eating eggs and toast as she read the job adverts.

'What is po-uwl-try factory?'

'Chicken gutting.'

'Gutting?'

'Taking out the insides? Cutting them into legs and breasts, that sort of thing.'

He thought of her tilting her head to the side, sticking out her bottom lip, nodding and circling the ad then reading on.

Dave leaned back in the rickety plastic chair, set his feet on the one opposite, sipped his tea and stared at his unopened lunch box; it was his word against Tanya's. It'd be OK. He'd keep an eye on her. But he knew he had to have a job, that that was part of the deal. How else could he keep her?

He had a feeling he would have to learn Alena, like learning times tables or a really hard list of spellings that wouldn't make any sense, wouldn't stick, until you came up with a trick that made it all suddenly seem easier. He bit a cuticle off, tasted blood and wondered how he would get her to stay long enough to work out what that little trick might be.

He stank of garlic. Dave could smell it seeping out of his pores as he barrelled about the kebab shop. He was fast, considering he moved like the joints of his legs weren't quite working. Dave and the lads, they were well pissed, they'd been watching the footie all afternoon, drinking pint after pint of too-fizzy cider. Now they all sat at one of the two tables, no talking, the only sounds their munching through doners and burgers, Mickey's gentle belching after each bite, and that song about an umbrella playing on the radio.

Before this wino there'd been two pretty girls in. They were hammered, but you could tell they were a bit classy too. They ordered falafel, their hair was smooth and natural, just like their faces. You got that type in Putney. When the dark-haired one had tripped coming back from the toilet and ended up on her knees by their table Dave and his mates had given drunken cheers.

'Careful there, princess.'

'Need a hand, darling?'

And Deano, of course Deano: 'While you're down there, love.'

She'd laughed, got to her feet and bowed. 'Break-dancing.'

Then she and her mate had taken their falafel, laughter and their lovely, soft-looking hair off into the night and Dave wondered why they never went to any pubs where there were girls like that.

Now they had this one. He was sixtyish but it was hard to tell with that sort. Shorter than Dave, with yellow-grey hair stringy with grease and a red sweating face. He took a few stumbling steps until his chest hit the front of the counter, started tapping at his head.

'This is no' a melon.' His thick Scottish accent filled the kebab shop like the smell of garlic – he must've eaten whole bulbs of the stuff. 'I'm tellin' yeh, this is no' a melon. Now jus' until tomorrow – I'll cash mah giro an' I'll bring in the cash. C'mon, I'm starvin'. Just a bag o' chips and hot sauce. I'll . . . I've no' my wallet but I'll come in the 'morrow. C'mon, it's just a fuckin' bag of chips, it costs pence.'

Dave's mates were laughing now, mouths showing chewed-up kebab meat and chips; Deano had chilli sauce down his chin. The bloke behind the counter wasn't laughing though.

'I've told you before. No. I'm running a business here.'

'C'mon, just a wee poke. Would yeh see an auld man go hungry then? This is no' a melon. This is prejudice this is.'

'Prejudice against getting paid?'

Deano shouted over now. 'You want us to get rid, mate? I'll do it for a can of Fanta.'

Maybe it was the mention of Fanta but Dave was right back in the primary-school canteen again, eating his roly-poly and custard with Deano next to him and Alex Donnelly opposite him.

'Dickhead.'

Dave had to take the spoon out of his mouth. 'What?'

Alex had kicked at his shins under the table, a rhythm to it. Kick, kick, kick. The kids on either side of them stayed quiet, their eyes hot on Dave's skin. Alex had kept going.

'You stink of shit. Don't you wash your clothes? Why don't you wash?'

Dave had pulled back his legs, but not far enough. Kick, kick, kick. He'd bent his head to his bowl and kept spooning his pudding. Roly-poly, his favourite, but it was spoilt now.

'It's your mum, isn't it? That's why. She was such a fat slag that your dad left and now she's even fatter and she's too drunk to clean you. My mum says she was always a drunken slut but now she's a fat drunken slut she has to give it away.'

Alex was on the floor before Dave knew it, Deano on top of him. He'd gone right over the table sending the pudding bowls flying and Dave, maybe only after a second, pulled his spoon from his mouth and did the same. Pushed his body across the debris of lunch while the kids thumped their fists on the long table.

'Fight, fight, fight.'

It was Dave who gave Deano the black eye pushing him

off. 'She's my mum! Get off. I'll do it.' Then, unsure of what to do, Dave pulled his best Power Ranger move and thumped that little bastard Alex in his stomach until he was dragged off him by the strong hands of the dinner ladies.

'Don't you speak about my mum. My. Mum.'

He'd been suspended for fighting but he wouldn't tell his mum why. She didn't mind, she'd just said, 'Defending yourself, I bet. Good lad. You need to look after yourself. You're the man of the house.'

Now, he could almost taste the grainy yellow custard on his tongue as he watched Deano walk towards the old wino; the guys behind the counter threw worried looks at each other as the old bloke, oblivious, was saying over and over again, 'C'mon, one bag o' chips.' That primary-school afternoon was what had made him and Deano best mates. Deano never grassed about the black eye. But Dave knew well enough now, Deano just loved a scrap, it was all the drugs that did it these days, who knew what it was back then. Dave grabbed his shoulder just before he was out of reach.

'Don't be a dick, Deano. Sit down, finish your food. No one wants your help here.' Deano struggled at his grip. 'I mean it, mate. Sit the fuck down or I'll sit you down. Mickey too. We're eating here.' Mickey carried on stuffing chips in his mouth but Deano sat down. 'Right, you want a fucking Fanta?'

Dave went to the counter. 'Can I get a Fanta, mate?' He turned to the old wino, searching through his pockets for coins Dave knew weren't in there. 'You want chips then?'

They looked into each other's faces for just a second. The old bloke reeked of booze, garlic and piss. He could be my dad, Dave thought. He ignored the next thought: could be my mum too, if she hadn't kept going for me.

'Fuck that shite, son.' He tapped at his head again. 'This is no' a melon. Quarter-pounder an' cheese an' a 7-Up. An' a big poke o' chips an' all'

Dave paid. A few quid further away from that plane ticket, the phantom taste of custard still on his tongue.

Beautiful women, advert after glossy advert, thumped their pretty little fists across Alena as quick as her fingers could turn the pages. She'd sat for a while under the open window in a pale wash of the overcast but already warm day. It had been a long time since she'd just been able to sit somewhere; peaceful and private. Then she had a shower; a long hot one, not one paid for in a train station where the water would run out halfway through. Rinsing away the thick smell of a good night's sleep, she made her hands slippery with a shower gel that smelt, like him, of mint, and made her skin tingle as she ran her fingers over her belly and the jut of her hip bones.

Afterwards, she looked at her sleek, shining body in the mirror and thought about his eyes on her, then she twisted a towel around her, went through to turn on the kettle and started leafing through the magazines. It was only then she felt a black seed of anxiety lodge itself in her stomach. How could she keep it up? Surely he would see how little she had; the magazines showed her everything she was supposed to be, and she found herself lacking.

She counted: three dresses – yellow, blue with flowers, a red one that clashed with her hair – one pair of jeans, two T-shirts that bloomed a sour smell of sweat in the armpits, an ugly jumper that had been vomit-speckled when she'd got it, a cardigan with a hole in the elbow and her Snoopy nightie. All had come from hostel boxes except the cardigan which she'd found draped over a wall and the pair of jeans, expensive ones that hung loose, from her life before. Everything was too big and had to be gathered, belted or hitched up in some way. She had a small rectangle of cracked soap, her toothbrush and mascara, lipstick and eyeshadow; all testers in Boots which was hardly stealing, something she would never risk for herself. She wondered if he thought she had a big suitcase somewhere. She did, a bright green shiny shell of a thing, a gift from people who had loved her, but it was nowhere she'd be going to get it.

Pushing the magazines aside, she placed a tea bag in a mug. She just wouldn't unpack. She could find a job and buy new things. She wouldn't need a lot of money, there were shops that sold second-hand clothes for poor people, she'd seen them. She could look like those glossy women, keep him wanting her, make him proud. No, prouder, because he was already, wasn't he? He would be glad to walk through the streets of Hackney with her naked at his side. Especially if I was naked, she thought, and as she reached for the milk she gave a small reassured laugh which bounced back to her from the inside of the fridge, an icy echo.

She scalded her tongue on the first sip, swore and then reminded herself to be grateful that she was in this small safe flat. He had left her so much food, the magazines, she'd had a shower and could have another after lunch. She'd eaten soup, bread, cheese, macaroni with baked beans all finished with two bowls of ice cream. He'd said at breakfast that he was impressed by how much she could 'put away'. Impressed. She hoped he wouldn't guess that she was frightened it would all be gone too soon, that she knew what it was to be empty and so gorged herself on fullness.

After her second shower she put on her blue dress, the one with yellow flowers, and tied it with a long red scarf she'd found at the entrance to Green Park Underground. She went to the mirror again and inspected herself; she didn't have food around her mouth, anything in her teeth; she had good lips, pretty eyes and beautiful breasts, everyone said so. She checked that her expression wasn't too pathetically grateful, though she was. She was so grateful and very afraid of being sent away, but the trick of staying was to make him the thankful, fearful one. And as she caught herself smiling in the mirror she reminded herself that this was all just a trick, there was nothing real here, and killed the smile instantly, like a small insect under a hard fingertip.

It was better than she'd imagined, the taking off. It really did feel like flying, a weightless feeling in your stomach, your shoulders being pushed into the seat as you rose, rose, rose into the air; forced through the thick pelt of grey Moscow cloud. In one moment clear bright light filled your eyes and then all you could see for miles around was that perfect blue; the blue of a baby boy's hand-knitted booties, of nursery rhymes and hair ribbons.

Alena pulled her thin blanket around her and folded over her tiny pillow against the cold window so her eyes soaked up the sky. She was exhausted. Exhausted from the endless coffees and meetings at snack bars where she dutifully chewed over food she couldn't afford and had goodbyes with people she mostly wouldn't be keeping in touch with.

Mikhail had been one of the hardest, sitting opposite her not touching his food, telling her his plans for St Petersburg; building a world for her with his morose words, saying he'd thought that one day they might get married, but of course, now she was going away that seemed to be over. She'd patiently reached across and ruffled his hair, leaving a few crumbs, and reminded him, as she had every other time, that things had been over for months, since they'd left university, and that he should find himself someone new, someone nicer than her. When his face had flashed with an unfamiliar bitterness, she told him more firmly to eat his pizza, it was costing them enough, and filled her own mouth quickly so she didn't have to say any more.

On her last day she sat with Agnetha, by the river as they always did during the summer, their legs shiny from baby oil, hands still sticky with ice creams eaten hours ago.

'– and then I'll get a job. Maybe something low at first, you know, just waitressing. Maybe I'll be a cocktail waitress in a fancy place, a nightclub. Each night I'll dress up and walk around serving the rich and famous. One of them will fall in love with me. But they'll be too shy to tell me at first and they'll secretly send me flowers and chocolates –'

'Jewellery and lingerie.'

'What?'

'Flowers, chocolates, they're gone in a few days. Jewellery lasts.'

Alena had slapped her friend's sunburnt shoulder, made a face.

'Spoken like a top-of-her-class economist.'

Agnetha lay down with her eyes closed as though bored by the burden of being so intelligent.

'But I'm not the one off to London, am I? It's boring old Tomsk for me and borscht and books coming out of my ears. Carry on, I need a good story, I'm so sleepy. This sun –'

'So he'll keep it a secret and then one day I'll accidentally spill a drink on him and he'll be so important the manager will almost give me the sack and . . .'

Alena chattered on and her friend made occasional hmmmmmm noises. She knew Agnetha didn't mind, that she'd felt guilty about leaving Alena when she went off to study her Magistr's degree at the end of the summer. Just as Mikhail was headed for better things. While Alena, unable to pay tuition and not well connected enough to 'win' a scholarship, was headed for nothing. Nothing before all this came along; a wish come true as bright and unexpected as a large red balloon rising into the sky.

The stewardess brought the drinks trolley and Alena let herself have a small glass of vinegary white wine and sipped it slowly, still staring out of the window. Her mother was the most exhausting; a weathervane, swinging one way and then another. One day, her small fast fingers re-hemming one of Alena's skirts, 'You'll have a time alright. Like when I went to Moscow for those two summers. Boys and shopping and parties.' The next day she'd stand in the doorway of the kitchen, her apron bunched in her fists, watching her daughter carefully pack up food for the long train journey to Moscow. 'Alena, why so far? Are you so sure? If you waited you could find work here. How can we be so certain about this? London is such a big city. Please don't go.' And Alena had wanted to reply, 'You're too old to understand. Stop ruining this,' but instead she bit her tongue, tried not to notice her mother's sudden vagueness, the forgetting of names, her difficulty in asking for the right thing in shops, and suspected her mother of playing the frail old lady. But nothing would have stopped Alena. She wanted to skip, dance, sing in the street, to leave that town behind and never see it again.

As she swallowed the last of her sweet sponge cake from the plastic tray and held out her cup for some tea she worried there would be an extra charge for this meal but she was hungry, Moscow had been so expensive, she couldn't resist, and asked for another glass of wine too.

The announcement woke her from a fretful dream that left a sick feeling in her stomach. The whole journey had been punctuated by being startled awake, when she had been desperate for sleep; on the train, in the Moscow hostel, now on the plane. She hoped to sleep properly that night, or if not that night, if she was too excited, say, the night after when she'd feel a little more at home.

'Cabin crew prepare for landing.'

And then Alena felt it; nervousness sweeping hot over her skin, her heart flying around like a caged bird, making her thoughts fuzzy. She put her nose to the dark window and held her hands either side of her face. Lights, just lights, shining up at her as she'd imagined. She was terrified, she was jubilant. After all the months of waiting for something, anything, to happen for her, it was here. The beginning of her real adult life, her future rising up, up, as though that big red balloon was filled with opportunity lighter than air and it was sweeping across the inky London sky.

She bent over the sink applying a little powder, some mascara. A Mariah Carey song warbled from the speakers in the ceiling and was amplified from the row of empty sinks, making her feel very alone. Outside, the signs, the chatter around her, all of it was in English and she had to concentrate, stilling briefly, the shrill nervousness whizzing around her brain like a child mid-tantrum.

As she stood on the walkway that whirred her resolutely forward she took out her passport from a small pink plastic wallet Agnetha had given her, a drunken picture of them Sellotaped to the front, and looked at her student visa. It seemed so official but she still couldn't quite believe it, even though she had gone to the government office to collect it. She couldn't stand it if she was turned away now.

She thought of all the girls who had made fun of her for wanting more, her mother adding up what little money they had after her father died, making the calculations on a flimsy pocket calculator and then starting again as though re-counting would magically make more appear. She thought of the life she might have had with Mikhail, two red-cheeked children, anniversary dinners and years spent in the tangle of gossip of that town, of asking Mikhail to please not drink so much, to come home earlier at nights. She wasn't like the others, Agnetha had said, implying she wasn't either but she was better at faking it. But Alena had always known it and could never fake it.

She partly stood apart because her father was an especially mean, volatile drunk and had left them with nothing but his feuds with every important person in town, bad feeling towards the family and the bank account of a teenager saving for a new stereo. And partly because she had caught Mikhail, the fish in the sea every girl wanted, and had thrown him back in again. But really it was because she wanted more – the town, even the vastness of Russia, it wasn't enough for her. When her classmates bought their red-and-white Russian-flag tracksuits, declared Russia to be the greatest country on earth and joined Putin's youth movement, Alena sat quiet, unadorned in the national colours, edging herself further away. That wasn't the life for her but this one might be. And now she had something that felt like it was enough in her hands she was going to run with it as far as she could.

As she got closer to the dreary woman behind the passport control desk, with no make-up, thick unplucked eyebrows, Alena stood taller, though her heels were killing her, walked with aggressive clacks of her shoes, and pushed across her passport, visa page open. There was a pause, Alena felt light-headed and waited to be taken into a room as her mother's friend had said she might be and where she was to stick to her story no matter what.

The woman looked at her, then down at her embarrassing passport picture – something about the colours was so Soviet – and then thumped the stamp. As she handed Alena back her passport her eyes were already on the next person. Alena noticed, in her over-alert state, that the woman had a sparkling engagement ring, no wedding band, and that made Alena want to look at this drab woman a little more closely, but she'd already been a fraction of a moment too slow and felt the push of the other person behind her. Alena walked away with a sensation of slight vertigo, as though she was already not following an unspoken set of rules.

Still, her shrieking nerves had become a pop song by the time she reached the luggage carousel, the fizz in her chest a frothing strawberry sherbet. Now her visa was approved, she was in. She had truly arrived. One whole year, even if the job they gave her was no good, she could find another, better, one. That stamp of approval was her golden ticket to a new life.

She saw her bright green, shiny suitcase emerge from the gaping mouth of the carousel and then slam onto its side and make its slow progress towards her. That case was a present from Mikhail, his mother Henka, who had never quite got over not having Alena as a daughter-in-law, and Agnetha, after Alena had complained at length to each of them about the shame of having to take her luggage in a laundry bag like a farmer's daughter.

Now, as she pulled it from the conveyor, and wheeled it across the smooth floor, she swung her hips just a little, brushed her hair out of her eyes. She felt beautiful right then, walking towards her new life. In her favourite tight jeans, not-too-tight T-shirt and high heels, she felt magnetic. She knew enough to know that not everything would be perfect but from now on she'd really be living, having an adventure that she could talk about for years to come, like her mother's summers in Moscow but better, so much better.

She scanned the mostly unsmiling, waiting faces, only an occasional hopeful one pushing itself over the railings. Alena walked purposefully through the crowd expecting to see a sign with her name or for one of the women to shout, 'Alena? Alena, over here.'

She'd emailed them a photograph already, her prettiest, so they would recognise her but also hoping they'd think she was too attractive to be cleaning or waitressing after all. When she reached the end of the barrier, though, she realised there was no one and her confidence started to sputter. She had no choice but to wheel her suitcase over to the seating area and wait, as if that is exactly what she had expected to do. Somehow the whole thing felt like being stood up. As she sat she tapped the heel of her sandal against the side of her case and thought about how much money she had (not much), where she might stay (no idea), how she would even reach the city by herself, if they did not come.

She would find an Internet cafe she decided, and email them, there must have been a mix-up, something to do with the time difference. She was starving hungry.

'Alena?'

Incredibly long, bright blonde, not quite real hair; Barbie's hair; and good smart clothes, almost a Russian style but not quite, all dripping from one of the scrawniest bodies Alena had ever seen. She was so thin that her knees looked like tennis balls in her tights. Alena thought she must be sick.

Alena replied in English. 'Yes, I'm Alena. Good to meet you. I worry when no one is here at first!'

The girl's big, sunken eyes looked into the distance for a moment and she sighed, then gave a death mask of a smile, pulled Alena into a tight, jabbing embrace.

They walked in silence from the airport. Alena was surprised that the woman's spindly little legs in her high-heeled boots could move so fast. But she marched through the airport as though she had spent her teenage years doing military drills. She'd sounded Ukrainian, so it was possible that she had. Alena followed in her blonde wake, but she wasn't able to copy the woman's fierce walk. For each small skipping step she took to keep up, her case either dragged too far behind or banged against her calves.

When they reached the car park the blonde made a phone call – Alena was sure she was Ukrainian now – and after a few minutes of waiting in silence and enduring another of her smiles, chillier than the gloom of the car park, a silver car stopped in front of them, that Queen song about fat-bottomed girls booming from inside. The blonde stepped forward and held the door open for Alena in an oddly subservient gesture before getting in the back seat alongside her.

Alena felt the eyes of the driver on them. A big man with a shaven head, piggish skin, a pale blue T-shirt that was dirty at the collar and even paler blue eyes. He nodded, an only partly interested nod. The woman said something and he turned down the music, locked the doors. There was something about the way they spoke that made her wonder if they were lovers and had perhaps argued.

Alena turned to the woman who was now lighting a cigarette.

'We'll go to Clapham now?'

The woman paused for a moment and then nodded.

'The journey was so tiring but I just cannot sleep! Do you know when I'll find out about my job? Do you know what it is?'

The woman blew a long plume of smoke and the taste of it made Alena want one but she wouldn't ask. 'Very soon. Where's your passport, ticket and things?'

'Oh, they're here.' Alena produced the bright pink wallet. 'Sorry. My friend gave it to me. Is silly leaving present.' Alena pointed to Agnetha, who raised a cocktail glass to her beaming pink cheek in the picture. 'That's my best friend there. It was taken when we –'

And quickly, again quicker than Alena might have imagined, the sparrow-boned hand holding the cigarette reached over and snatched the wallet from her and then zipped it into a black handbag. Another of those cold grins – Alena realised it was scary because the woman's teeth looked loose in her gums.

'We need to make copies of everything.'

'Oh, of course, could I just –?'

Alena was thinking of her traveller's cheques, American Express, but then she felt the driver's eyes on her and the woman was now staring hard out of the window, smoking more intently than ever, so she bit back the words. Best not to make trouble, get off to a good start. These people were friends of her mother's oldest friend, they'd bought her train and plane tickets after all, got her a visa and all the way to London. This was probably the Ukrainian way, this thick silence. She stared out at the ugly squat buildings, a McDonald's, an old man pushing a shopping trolley along a pavement with nothing inside it, a pigeon pecking at something that looked like vomit outside a metal-shuttered shop. Welcome to London.

The windows were all open, letting in a soup of early-evening Hackney air: dirty pavement, exhaust fumes, kebab meat. The radio was tuned to something that definitely wasn't Heart FM. And there she was, sprawled on the sofa, drinking another cup of that thick coffee, her foot twitching, a bead of sweat sliding down from her hairline.

'Is Russian! I was looking for music and I heard. Is Russian comedy.'

Dave listened to the jumble of sounds, the canned laughter, her own joining in. He stood above her, as he had this morning, looking at her long, slim legs folded under her, the way a quick finger reached up and smeared the drop of sweat to a shining line. She caught him looking.

'Sorry.' She switched off the radio.

'You don't have to do that.'

'Is OK. Is on every day, I think.'

'Like the Russian *Archers*.'

Her face was blank and then broke into that lopsided smile. 'I get you drink. You want ice cream? I save you.'

He could only see her back now, the curls at the nape of her neck where her short hair stopped, the creases on the backs of her legs from sitting on the rumpled fabric of her skirt. From the kitchen counter she looked over her shoulder with a proud smile.

'I eat a lot today.'

She was a miracle standing right there in his shitty little flat.

'Um . . . good.'

'Yes, delicious.'

He watched her clank about in the kitchen, not the coffee, please God not one of those coffees, but then she put ice cubes in a glass. He settled on the sofa, eased off his shoes.

'Have you been out?'

She gave him the glass: Ribena.

'How I can go out? I have no keys to get back in.'

He sipped. No water; maybe a drop but no more. 'I'm sorry, Alena. I just didn't think. What an idiot. Sorry.'

She bounced herself down next to him and pushed her feet under his thighs. He wanted to tense them so she wouldn't feel the flesh give.

'Is fine. I had shower, lunch and then I find radio and it is good to watch from this window. Is funny place! I don't watch TV in daytimes, it is making zombies.'

Dave tried another sip. He imagined his tooth enamel thinning out. 'Funny? You obviously haven't been in Hackney long. We'll go out tonight then. I'll just shower, get out of my work stuff. We can have dinner somewhere – you pick.'

He was almost through the door.

'David?' She held the glass of pure blackcurrant syrup out to him. 'Take it with you.'

He did as he was told and heard her switch the radio back on as he flushed the drink away. The toilet water was still pink two hours later.

They walked past the boarded-up 'KFC: Kebab, Fish, Chicken' shop closed by environmental health never to be opened again, beyond the purple sign of the shop selling ear candles, crystals and incense and the Turkish herbalist with its poster of a small boy covered in medicinal leeches. They walked further, past Sardines, the roughest pub in the not-too-rough area, its outside benches packed with red-faced, gristle-nosed blokes, a few quid and a pint glass away from being winos with plastic bottles of cider down the park. Dave felt their blood-bruised eyes all over Alena and noticed she turned away, as though the garage forecourt across the road was suddenly intensely interesting.

When he was a kid he loved this stupid film about a mermaid who gets washed up in New York and she stops and looks at everything, twisting her head this way and that, tracing her fingers across shop windows. Alena was a bit like that but not quite; she was sharp, he knew that already, but she was really curious too. He looked at her bending to stroke the gigantic display bouquets outside the florist's, her fingers pinching the waxy shell of a glitter-burnished blue lily.

'An English flower?'

He shook his head. 'Not like that it's not.'

It wasn't a put-on either; you could see she was really interested in what was in the windows of the Chinese furniture shop and in the Rasta crowd outside the Caribbean cafe.

'So how long have you been in London?'

Her smile dropped. 'A few months, only months.'

'And you were staying in hostels all this time? Didn't feel like getting a room somewhere? A flatshare?'

She said nothing but her pace quickened and he had to take two hurried steps to catch up with her.

'Sorry. I mean, I just mean I'm not, I mean . . . I don't want you to tell me anything. Unless you want to. It's just –' they had stopped now and he looked around him – 'this is pretty bog-standard London around here.'

She gave a smile so small it just raised her cheekbones a bit, her top lip had pinpricks of sweat and he wanted to kiss them away in the hot night, with the traffic going by. He wanted to put his hands around her waist, pull her close so he could smell her skin and tell her it didn't matter, whoever she was, wherever she'd been. He respected secrets, understood running away, didn't want her digging into his dark places any more than she wanted his prying fingers in hers, but instead he gave her a wide, strained smile.

'So yeah, this is it. Hackney. What do you think?'

'I think it's not like Paddington or Southwark or Trafalgar Square. It is maybe like Shepherd's Bush, little bit. I think it is where you are.' And with a smile and a slackening of her shoulders she was off across the road again and into the shop built into the mosque.

He'd never been inside before, though he'd always loved the shining silver dome of the mosque, its blue tiles that he could see for miles among the grey concrete blocks and solid chalky houses of the rest of Hackney, telling him he was almost home, or what counted as home these days.

She was at the counter with a ten-pound note in her hand and Dave, not a betting man and the lads at Paddy Power could back that up, would have put money on it being the only one she had.

He was so busy watching the shopkeeper watch Alena's pale, bare shoulders he didn't get to the counter on time to pay, and felt heat rising through his chest as Alena handed over the money. Outside she gave him a glass bottle of mango juice and a single piece of baklava from a grease-soaked paper bag.

'Is to say thank you.'

She looked down, flicked a fag end with the tip of her flip-flop, and he saw the blush spread up the back of her neck. When she looked up again her eyes were bright and he couldn't tell if she was embarrassed or proud as she took a bite of her own pastry, the oily syrup running down her wrist. 'A very little thank-you.'

'Thank you.' Dave gave a small bow and took a swig from his bottle.

They walked beyond the mosque into the dirty-orange dusk, lit by the shopfronts, yellowish street lights, the white neon cross on the New Blessings From The Good United Church, and it seemed like the most natural thing in the world, when the breeze picked up and she moved in towards him, for him to put his arm around her and kiss the crown of her sweat-dampened hair. She seemed to take shelter in him for a moment, the bare skin of his forearm against the back of her shoulders. But then she looked up at him, a soft look of alarm crossing her face, or maybe more of a question, and she slowly stepped away to look in another window and Dave, who barely knew her, understood even she probably wasn't that interested in the launderette.

4

The bill came, folded over on a saucer, and she could do nothing but sit with her hands in her lap. It wasn't an expensive place, not like the horrible restaurants she used to get taken to. There were no bad memories hidden in the grain of the wooden tables, plastic chairs or wipe-clean menus with sticky ketchup smears. Alena had chosen an omelette and chips, the cheapest thing she could find. Dave had had the same.

He asked her nothing about the past, which meant that he'd been paying attention when she'd warned him gently off that subject earlier. She knew he would train well. Instead he asked her a lot about Russia, what food she liked, how she would say omelette and chips in Russian. Safe things. And she asked him safe things in return, as though they were having a conversation on a rock face and their choice of questions, safe questions, they were their ropes. Where was he was born? What food did he like to eat? She told him how you say omelette and chips in Russian.

'No, you're using your tongue all wrong.'

'Not the first time I've heard that complaint. I mean . . . Jesus . . . sorry, I meant saying exactly the wrong thing all the time.'

They laughed awkwardly together, though she didn't really understand what he meant. They were strangers and it seemed they would stay that way, both too afraid to accidentally stray into the stormy part of the other. Until the bill came, when they were laughing, it seemed she was just a woman and he was just a man and they were having dinner together, like she had with boyfriends back home. It was a feeling she'd thought she might never have again. As though she was not some strange poor woman he was giving charity to, as though he was not a lonely man, as though they weren't trading his safety for her company, though what 'company' entailed she wasn't sure yet. As though, but not quite, Alena, don't fool yourself.

Outside, she linked her arm through his as they walked back towards the flat, that was the trade for dinner she thought. His body was soft but solid next to hers. She felt him pull closer but the feeling when the bill had come and of only having £6.32 clanking in her pocket wouldn't go away. How long would it be before he got tired of her just taking? How long could she eke out the little she had to offer in return, scattering her affection, her meagre trail of breadcrumbs, when she only had a single slice of bread to begin with? They passed the pub again and the old men with deep wrinkles, noses the size and shape of beets fresh from the pot.

'Do you drink here?'

She asked the question to make noise, to have him hear her and to distract herself from the leering men at the nearest table. He looked towards the table and his mouth tightened; he pushed his hands hard into his pockets. It was the bill. She knew she should have offered some money but then she'd be left with almost nothing. He wanted to send her away. He would send her away. He looked at her and for the first time she saw a coldness, a hard glint that she stupidly hadn't expected from him. She spoke again to cover her fright. 'Or to another place?'

'No. Of course I don't drink somewhere like that. You think I'm like one of them old losers?'

Alena reached over and squeezed her hand into the pocket,

beside his. That was the trade for having upset him. 'I understand. I don't go out very much. At all even.'

His fingers, the tips icy cold, curled around hers in the cramped dark space of his pocket. 'Sorry, I don't know what's wrong with me. I just don't want you thinking I'm like them, that's all.'

'I understand, I do. Do you believe?'

They were outside the mosque again now, its windows and doors outlined in bright blue neon against the deep blue of the sky, the sound of the call to prayer just audible, a slow melodic hum from behind the walls. She stopped and bent her head. It was meant to be easy, she was meant to be making everything happen, deciding it all, but she felt raw. This was worse than curling up in the warm disabled toilet in Paddington or tearing off other people's bite marks from stale sandwiches. It hurt more than paying her last few pounds for a shower and then wandering around London until she had blisters. Being with him, having all his hope rest on her, she could feel it and it was too heavy; this was too hard.

She tasted the tears before she realised she was crying them. They weren't the kind that pained the eyes or caused a lump in the throat so she had no time to beat them down, to swallow them away or turn her face from him. He bent to see her more clearly and she twisted away.

'I am sorry. Stupid.'

But the words were lost in her breath as she tried to quell her crying. He took her into him then, smoothing her hair with one hand and holding her close with the other.

'I am sorry.' This time the words were clear enough, and though his touch wasn't a trade this time, it felt good to be close to him. She pushed herself back so he could see her face. 'I have no money. This is all I have.' She held the five-pound note and coins out in her hand.

'That's why you're crying?'

Alena thought about all the reasons she was crying and how she would never say any of them to him, but then saw this was the moment, the time to take another promise from him. 'I have nothing. I think finding job will be hard and –' she looked up at him now through her lashes, shiny as blades of grass after the rain – 'I'm afraid you will send me away.' She felt a tremor of guilt, of disgust, and then consoled herself that at least the tears were real, and what she had said was true too.

'Alena, I don't have much money either.' He was smiling, his own bad mood turned on trying to coax her out of her tears. 'I've got a steady job but it doesn't pay much, you know? In fact, we're probably going to live on beans on toast for the rest of the week. I just wish I could help you more.'

This was the very second, an opening, so she pouted gently, touched his chest. Trade, everything was trade, one thing for another, she mustn't forget. 'I have nothing to give. In a few days where will I be again?'

'I told you, you can stay as long as you want. And I don't mean a few days, I mean a few weeks, months if you wanted. And I'm not after anything; I just want to get to know you. That's enough.'

She felt a wave of heat go over her, a rush of fire that left a stinging, bitter taste on her tongue that she chose to ignore. She could tell his touch wasn't demanding, she knew that other sort of touch well enough, she knew he wouldn't try to take even though he might never be offered. It was a hungry touch, but a hunger that she could choose to feed or not, and she knew that part of this whole thing was keeping him hungry. And he was so good, or at least he seemed to be. She could feel, through the thin material of her dress and his T-shirt, a frightened heart beating. She reached her hands up to his face, took a moment to look into those eyes, sad and uncertain and wanting. It was the moment for a kiss, she knew, but that was a valuable thing to be saved for another time.

Mail-ordered all the way from Moscow. Somewhere, like a small fly buzzing just inside her ear, Alena had a memory. A memory of a package arriving. Inside was bubble wrap, as though the contents were precious, breakable. The pale blue lingerie with lacy panels and dark blue bows.

She had taken the material to her face for a moment and then, imagining her mother's expression, lowered it with a guilty smile. She had carefully folded the items into her suitcase, her skin tingling with all the possibilities of her new life. Just to know I am wearing them, she had thought. She was only twenty and had wanted to be beautiful in every way somewhere as sparkling as London. As she'd zipped up her suitcase and felt her mother's reproachful shadow on her back she vowed that London would be the making of her. A trip that would change her for ever.

And there she was, still just twenty, but so changed. That girl was already gone but the underwear was still with her. She was wearing it when the sedatives started snaking through her bloodstream. An acrid sweet smell had pulled her from the black dream she had been suffocating in, then what felt like ten hands, their dark hairs bristling against her skin, dirty thumbs digging. Those fingers gripped her bones tightly, as though they were scaling a rock face, before those same bones softened under their constraints, probably just one or two pairs of hands in reality. Then Alena was submerged in the sweet honey-slick of the pills.

She could see them; a few smirking men, one woman with a wide smile, shrieking with laughter. She might have at least lifted her arms to cover herself. Instead she stood, slack-armed, dimly aware of the change in atmosphere as the men became serious. Sale had commenced. A heel of a hand in the soft centre of her back. 'Walk.'

But her limbs would not and a clammy hand gripped her elbow and pulled her past the men at the Formica tables in the shuttered cafe, the smell of stale sausages served during the day still in the air. One man reached out to touch her stomach, tracing his fingernail along the top of her knickers. The woman by his side stopped smirking. 'How old?'

'Seventeen. Russian.' The voice by Alena's side.

Alena wanted to tell them she'd turned twenty in February, as though they might then decide to take her to a recruitment agency where they might give her work that she could do with clothes on.

'Used? She looks it.'

'Used? No, this is a good girl. A good Russian girl with sexy underwear.'

The woman gave a short stabbing laugh and then turned to the man and placed her hand on his leg, 'Good girls don't wear this.' She waved her cigarette at Alena, the tip close enough to burn. The man dismissed her, with a lazy flick of his fingers against her stomach, shrugged and stood.

'Hey,' the voice behind Alena, 'the lady knows about bad girls but this is good girl.'

The woman sat back, silent.

'Anyone else for this one?'

Alena was one of three girls that night and there were tensions in the room; currents she did not understand, but would much later, and which went beyond getting a good girl to make into a bad girl.

'Over here.' Alena dared to lift her head; this from the oldest man in the room, the only one wearing a suit and not a tracksuit. He had a neat handkerchief in his pocket, like a dentist or an accountant. Alena was pulled over, clumsy-footed, banging her hip on a table hard enough to have a bruise that stayed long after she had left that place, and the woman unfolded herself in order to laugh harder. Alena stood in front of the man.

'See,' the voice, his breath moist on the back of her neck, 'real nice.'

The man, the dentist, he said nothing, but she felt his cold fingertips on her hips, turning her like a carousel of sunglasses, while the other man held her up.

'OK. Two. No more. We collect tomorrow and no one touches before.'

'Andriy. Two? Are you crazy? Serious. A good girl like this? Two?'

The older man stood up. Dabbed his lips with his handkerchief and said in a low voice: 'I am always serious. You should remember. No touching. No one.'

Then he walked out, leaving a chill that settled in the slats of Alena's ribs. The room was silent except for the beeping of the fruit machine and Alena was pushed towards the door.

'Next one!'

She fell, stumbled towards the floor. She couldn't tell if she was being dragged or carried back to that big dark cupboard piled with giant tins of tomatoes and beans before she was propped against a stack of bread rolls.

There were just two of them in the cupboard now. The other, taken there and then. As the drug wore off, Alena felt the fear creeping, spreading out from the lowest part of her stomach until it accumulated under her fingernails and in the cavities of her back teeth. The cupboard was freezing and pitch black but for the column of light at the edge of the door. Alena reached out for the other girl who scrabbled away.

'It's OK. Please. What is your name. Do you speak English?'

The girl stopped crying, just for a moment. 'Shut up. No talking.' The crack of light around the door frame darkened and the girl dug her fingernails into Alena's foot, then let go, vomited and curled into a ball. Alena counted the beats of her heart and tried to trace a path backwards in her mind. She knew she wasn't strong enough to look to what might lie ahead.

The smell of vomit stung her nostrils. Alena stared at the crack of light and tried to remember her mother's face as they'd said goodbye at the bus station. She had held Alena's hand and begged her not to go. We'll manage, she'd said, you'll find work, or I will. Alena had pulled her hand away, shaking her head, had asked her mother not to spoil it. Her mother had kissed both her cheeks, pressed a tinny little St Christopher into her palm, and Alena had laughed. 'It's only London! I'll be back for Christmas. I'm going to have fun. But not too much, I promise.'

Alena was jolted from her thoughts, from remembering her feeling of elation as the bus pulled off, by a noise. The door opened, light blocked out by the bulk of the man in the doorway. He had a sort of skinhead, shorter at the sides, the kind popular with the young boys in her village. He sniffed the air, stepped inside, and Alena stayed absolutely still while the other girl pushed herself harder against the wall as though it might absorb her. He took another step inside straight into the vomit then picked up his foot in a strangely feminine gesture. 'Ugh. Pigs not women!' Alena saw he was holding bags of crisps. He lowered his face down to her and she closed her eyes; his breath smelt of onions. 'You? Is this you? You little bitch?'

She shook her head. 'No. No, not me. No.'

It was only when she heard the other girl scream that she opened her eyes, saw the man dragging her by her left foot as her hands grabbed helplessly at the concrete floor. Alena pulled her arms around her naked torso. The girl kept on screaming. 'Take her. Take her. Please. It was her.'

She couldn't look away, couldn't turn her head. Another, smaller man quickly knelt on top of the girl's shoulders, and the larger man came back. Alena scrabbled into a corner, felt the concrete burn as she pushed herself backwards. He blocked the doorway and threw in the crisps and a can of drink, which hit her knee, then shut the door. But the door wasn't thick enough to block out the screams, the men demanding the girl sound like she wanted it or the girl's attempts to do as they instructed.

Hours later the girl had still not returned and Alena succumbed to hunger, eating the crisps in rushed handfuls, like an animal. She tried to stifle one memory – that the last thing her mother had said to her was sorry.

She expected these sorts of people to own a shining tank of a car like the ones in Moscow but it was the same car as before. And they seemed to have only one CD, the driver singing along to 'Radio Gaga', drumming his hands on the steering wheel to the beat.

Alena stared at the normality of people looking dragged down by shopping bags and children having tantrums, standing in queues for the bus. Her long-imagined gilded London was not so different from her nearest city in Russia – another McDonald's, rows of shops and bored, poor-looking people forcing themselves from place to place.

But this, this house they'd arrived at, was just as she had imagined London would be for her when she was back in her bedroom in Russia. It wasn't like the first house she'd pictured – that was an apartment in a shining glass skyscraper with floor-to-ceiling windows looking out at Big Ben; in that apartment she drank wine and gossiped with friends from the office. But this one, this was what came next in her fantasy – a big house on a street with other big houses, a shiny car behind electric gates by a neat garden. It was where she would live with a handsome man she had fallen instantly in love with on a London Underground platform. A man she'd eventually marry. This house was exactly the sort of house she imagined – a house with peach, ruched curtains in bay windows, a bird feeder, decking.

They walked her up the path between them, one carrying her suitcase, like proprietorial big brothers. The bell played a long tune she didn't recognise and beyond the stained-glass panel in the door she heard the yipping of a small dog, and the slower, deeper, echoing bark of a much bigger one. She pulled down her skirt, moved her tongue around to moisten her mouth. He was young, the man who opened the door, reminded her of a friend's older brother with his lean face, dark, slicked-back hair and Nike tracksuit.

'You bring her like this?'

And after everything, Alena still felt the embarrassment of his glance prickle right down to the soles of her feet. The man took her wrist while Alena tried again to pull down her skirt with her other hand, thinking of her legs covered in bruises.

'You can leave her then.'

The men stared from him to each other to their trainers, swagger evaporated.

'Go on, into your shit-heap car.'

Alena felt herself briefly pulled between them, unsure of who she belonged to, but, gauging risk and violence and power and all without realising it, she went to the new man's side.

'We . . . ha . . . we need the money today. Big problem if not.'

Even Alena could hear the shake in his voice. The young man looked away, licked and pressed his lips together and then took a Stanley knife from his pocket. He held it carefully by his side, so it would have been impossible to see from the street, but what was clear was that he would use it.

'Do I cut her? Mess her up and send her away with you? Or you two?'

He was so quiet. Alena stayed completely still, watched the knife. Her minders stepped back. Then he was smiling, pocketing the knife again before giving a short steely note of laughter and slapping the bigger minder gently around the face.

'On the doorstep, idiot? Let me get Andriy and you can ask him to hand it over in a big wad, maybe we invite the neighbours and celebrate over a cup of coffee, a slice of cake. Idiot! It will go to you tonight.'

They took a few steps backwards before turning, making long strides to the car, their shoulders broadening as they got further away, then slammed the car doors and sped off.

Then they were alone. She would not move. In just forty-eight hours she had learned – be told everything, decide nothing yourself. He stepped back and put his slightly moist hands on her shoulders, looked at her face and shook his head. 'You are not good.'

Alena felt the tremor of it coming. She nodded, her bottom lip stretching as she fought to gulp down the tightness in her throat.

'Come, you'll change and eat. Come on.'

He pulled her through the doorway and gave her a small, almost playful, slap across the face but still a harder one than he'd given to the man before her. 'You will learn.' He shook his head again, grabbed her upper arm roughly and marched her further inside, put his other hand in his pocket and kept it there alongside the blade. 'I am Fedir. If you try to run I will hurt you – do you understand? If you scream, I will hurt you. I can do horrible things to you and no one will know. No one will care. I have done them before. Do you understand?'

Alena nodded, afraid that if she opened her mouth she might, in fact, scream. The whites of his eyes were tinged pink, he had dried blood on his lips and he spoke with his mouth too close to hers. She could tell he would keep his promises.

The house was spotless, soft and airless. He told her to take off her shoes, those same strappy heels she'd bounded across the airport in. They passed through a living room with a thick pink carpet, cream walls, a picture of Marilyn Monroe, the famous one of her billowing white dress, in a gold frame on the wall. A small white dog, its brown eyes looking like they were leaking blood, poked its head up from an armchair. They walked through the kitchen where a fat older woman in her sixties, just like one of her mother's friends, sliced a huge loaf of bread. There was a smell of toast. She looked up at Alena's bare legs with a blank face and then continued sawing into the bread with the seasoned arm of a lumberjack; that was an arm you wouldn't want a back-hand from.

'Come.' Fedir motioned her. 'After you wash you'll have food.'

He said 'wash', not a bath or a shower, but a wash, something for a car or an animal. He thought she was dirty. They were climbing the stairs now, Alena in front, her hand hovering around her backside in its short skirt.

'They didn't touch me. The other man, he said no touching. They didn't touch me, those two.'

She couldn't turn round on the narrow stairs but she heard the sigh and didn't know him well enough to gauge whether it was impatience or disgust, or maybe, she could only hope, pity. He gave her a push and she almost fell.

'Shut up. Andriy likes a clean girl.'

She wondered if he knew her name and he sent her towards the bathroom with another hard push to the middle of her spine.

'Just a shower not a bath. Use everything.' He jerked his head towards the bottles along the edge of the bath. Still she stood, afraid to go into the enclosed space alone.

'Go.' He gave her another small push, her cheekbone glancing off the door frame, and the door closed behind her.

The taps were gold, the towels white, warm and fluffy like she imagined they were in hotels, the windows were shuttered and locked. There were three types of shower gel but no razor. She wasn't crying but she couldn't breathe. She heard a movement outside the door and so she started the water, forced herself under it and began soaping her body. It amazed her that anything could still feel even a little bit good but she was glad to be clean.

He took her dirty clothes and gave her new ones to change

into, a purple satin knee-length skirt and a transparent white blouse. The sort of thing popular with a certain type of older woman back home, though they wore bras under their blouses usually and she hadn't been given one of those. Downstairs through the kitchen and down another set of stairs, it was colder; the softness had gone and a chill clung to the greying walls and rough blue carpet tiles. He led her into a room with bars on the window. Not bars like a prison but decoratively wrought ones, painted a medicinal-pink colour to match the duvet cover on the tiny bed in the corner. There was a sort of toy lying on the pillow, a white rabbit but with the face of a doll, as though the doll, with its red shapely lips, arched eyebrows and long bristling eyelashes, was wearing a costume. She heard the door close behind her while she was staring at the doll, the key turning in the lock. It wasn't a sharp noise, it was a careful, slow turning, and she wondered whether he was trying to pretend she wasn't locked in.

She took the doll onto her lap and fingered its ears. She sat still and straight. When her vision clouded she forced herself back to anger, imagining her escape. She would be wearing her own clothes and underwear, she would come back with the police and watch the men of this house be taken away to prison, she'd be in the newspaper for her bravery. She stood and went to the window, where she could see a tiny triangle of sky above a privet hedge. She forced her face as far through the bars as they would go, a wave of hysteria running through her. The bile rose as her gullet closed and she found herself panicked and choked.

She had no idea how she ended up asleep. Fedir stood over her with a tray. Not toast, some sort of meat in gravy with a fatty smell that filled the room.

'Sit up. Come on, girl. Sit up now.'

He held the tray in both hands and nudged her in the ribs with the yellowing sole of his sport-socked foot.

'He is coming soon. He likes you to eat. He doesn't like a skinny, sad girl. Sit up and eat and stop crying.'

Alena, blank-eyed, sat up and he set the tray on top of the bed.

'Milk, you see?'

He smiled at her, the smile of a boy answering a question nicely in class before cornering someone in the toilets to piss all over them. Alena stared at him, shook her head. His expression turned and he grabbed her hair tightly and pushed her head towards the tray. Then, just as suddenly, she was released and she felt he might stroke her hair.

'Just eat it. OK. Good girl.'

He strung his words through the room as he stepped backwards, away from her, the anger seemingly forgotten, watching her as intently as if she were an unexploded bomb.

When Fedir next appeared much later on that night, she was kneeling and reading the love poem printed in curlicue writing on the dinner tray aloud, slowly, word by word, while trying to pick a crust of dried gravy from one of the lines. She was going to stand but his face was closed off and he did nothing but hold the door open and jerk his head. Alena walked up the stairs carrying the tray, feeling his eyes on her as she moved.

At the top of the stairs he took the tray and left her to stand while he carefully rinsed the fork, knife, plate, glass and stacked them in the dishwasher, the first she had ever seen in someone's home. There was no sign of the woman from earlier and somehow she knew the man they were waiting for wouldn't be coming that night either. As he wiped the tray she moved towards it and he flinched, looked ready to hit out. She tried to smile through her fear, no good could come of him being angry with her, she knew that much.

'The writing . . .'

He stood with the tray in his hand. She couldn't decide whether he looked more like he was about to bludgeon her with the tray or bring a casserole out of the oven. She forced her smile a little more though it hurt.

'I didn't finish reading. So . . .' She gave a small laugh, the sound of a stick on a rock. She had nothing to laugh about but something in it calmed him and he lowered the tray.

She bit her upper lip, suddenly embarrassed. '*Till a' the seas gang dry, my love*.' She felt the blood hot in her face, and she looked up, saw him looking at her. 'I have it wrong, my English is not so good.'

He shrugged, looking at her face. 'I don't know.' He turned away from her, threw the tray onto the counter. 'I don't read too well.'

Alena made a noise, a sound that might have meant that she understood, or that it didn't matter or that she was frightened.

'We go into the other room now.' Fear pooled in the back of her knees but she did nothing, absolutely nothing, she stayed completely still. He came a step closer so she could smell stale tea on his breath, moved his head until he caught her line of vision. 'It is secret, you understand?'

Something cold ran over the surface of her skin. 'But he . . . he comes soon?'

'He comes home tomorrow.' He gave a small grin. 'So this is a secret, yes?'

Alena gave a small nod as he started walking.

'Come on then.'

What could she do but follow him to the living room, the peach plush sofa, the giant TV, that picture of Marilyn Monroe? 'You'll sit?'

A question with no choice. Alena sat on the edge of the sofa. Pulled the hem of her skirt down, bunching the material in her fists, and he stood in front of her and started to untie the cord of his tracksuit bottoms, grinning down at her while he did it and making a 'Huh? Huh?' noise.

'No, please.' Alena was pushing herself backwards into the plushness of the sofa, 'Please!' When he started to pull down his waistband, Alena could see he was hard and she started shivering. He grabbed the back of her head and then she stopped resisting. Her nose was in the coarse hair above his waistband when just as suddenly he pushed her away by the forehead, back against the sofa. He was laughing now, pulling up his tracksuit bottoms and readjusting his erection.

'Is joke! Ha, you look so scared. Ha! Is just stupid joke.'

He was laughing down at her; she could see dark fillings in his upper teeth. He kept laughing but it seemed forced, as though he were squeezing it from somewhere deep in his gut, and she realised she was meant to laugh too and so, through the shivering, swallowed and tried to do her best. He was smiling again now, playing host.

'Wait! I remember.' And he left.

She stared though the living-room entrance at the front door, with its chrome locks, its chain. She could hear him opening and closing cupboards in another part of the house. She looked at the windows, at the high hedges beyond, and imagined the unknown night streets of London beyond that. She tried to remember any of the streets that had brought her here. She imagined running, knocking on doors, screaming for help, but instead stayed silent and still on the sofa, staring at Marilyn's half-closed eyes, and then he was back at her side.

'Here.' An ice cream, a foil-wrapped cone, the kind they sold at the kiosk by the fountain in her home town, thrown onto her lap, then he went to sit at the other end of the sofa.

Alena stared at the ice cream, the cold spreading through the fabric of her skirt.

'Mint is OK?' He looked at his own and reluctantly gestured it towards her. 'Or strawberry? Is my favourite.'

Alena felt her senses blunt, her inner workings slow. She blinked, shook her head. 'Is fine.'

'Sure?'

She nodded, tiny jerks of her chin. 'Thank you.'

He picked up the remote and turned on the television. 'You like cop shows? They are my favourite. And *Top Gear*. They don't have it in Ukraine. Me, I get crazy about cars.' He grinned over at her, then nodded. '*Friends*? You have seen *Friends*? Ross and Rachel and Joey? You understand, Alena,' – he did know her name – 'that this is a big secret. If he finds out we both get it.'

He pulled a finger across his neck and made a sound to suggest it was being cut, but where she was from that gesture meant you were full. She looked at him, barely older than her. The type of boy who got crazy over cars. She imagined him, just a lonely boy from her high school with a crush on her and no way to tell her, and somehow she managed to smile. 'Don't worry, I understand. A real secret.'

He let out a breath, smiling again. 'Now we can watch *Top Gear*, yes?'

Alena kept the smile fixed and nodded. While he laughed at

the screen she looked again at the doors, the windows, tried to remember the streets she'd been driven along. Then she looked over at him, twitching his feet as the race on-screen came to its climax, mouth open in delight, and she saw a way out.

He walked her back to the room and brought her nightdress and toothbrush.

'I get from your bag. OK?'

Alena felt the laughter rise from nowhere. And before she could clamp her lips it was echoing in the corners of the room, the ridiculousness of him checking it was OK to go in her suitcase. She pressed her fingers hard to her lips and watched his face but he still had his head bent, eyes lowered. 'Sorry.'

She stepped forward and, as she reached for her things, he took her other hand in his. It was softer than she thought it would be, a little damp, and she struggled to keep her face arranged, struggled against the instinct to pull away, pummel at his meaty face with her sharp knuckles.

'First thing tomorrow you change, yes? For him. He is coming back first thing.'

She nodded.

'And this is our secret. Tonight.' His face hardened; as he spoke he squeezed her hand tighter and tighter. 'If you tell him first he will beat you and then I will visit and beat you too. Do you see?'

He stared at her now, his eyes drilling into hers. Not only a question – they were making a deal, an agreement and promise Alena barely understood but couldn't refuse.

'Yes.'

He gave a sharp, leering smile, released her hand and stepped towards the door.

'I'll put the heating on.' He retreated further but kept his eyes on her.

She took off her clothes and got into her nightdress, the same one she had worn back at home less than a week ago, with its giant cartoon print, the same childish choice she'd been so embarrassed by at the Moscow hostel. She clasped and unclasped her aching hand. She would watch and learn. She would be smart, sly. She would get out. She would find a way to swallow down that doped maniac like the violent, dumb animal he was, and then lick her lips if she needed to.

In her own nightdress, in a warm room, Alena woke up. As she stretched and kicked the duvet off, her mind fully awoke, and her panic stole the air from her. He was coming. First thing. She stumbled up and used the tiny toilet attached to the room, washed herself at the sink, dressed in the clothes she had been given the day before and then sat down to wait.

She was folding her nightdress under her pillow, afraid that somehow it might be taken, when Fedir knocked and then opened the door. She forced a smile but there was none of the sick camaraderie of the night before, just a spark of warning in his eyes. 'You'll come now.'

He sat at the dining table in an area leading from the kitchen: the man who had bought her. He still looked like a dentist, or an accountant. Yes, a small-town accountant who took bribes for taxes; short grey hair, rimless spectacles, a grey tweed suit with a pale blue shirt and tie. Fedir pulled a chair out for her opposite the man.

'You'll sit.'

The man raised his eyes from his breakfast, looking only as far as Alena's neck. She saw now he was an old man, older than he'd looked in her sedated daze in the dim of the basement; his bones protruding, lips thin, bloodless. He had three boiled eggs and a plate of toast cut into strips which he ate with deliberation, dipping each piece of toast, chewing, then a swallow of tea, a clean quick movement to scoop out the egg white. Once he was finished the woman from yesterday collected his plate. The man looked towards Fedir, standing behind Alena. 'Go.'

Fedir's expression barely flickered recognition as he turned and walked out, closing the door behind him.

Now there was no clatter of dishes from the kitchen or the crunch of the toast, it seemed too intimate to sit in silence across from this man. He folded his hands and laid them on the table, waited a moment until she shifted in her seat.

'Alena. I am Andriy. And I . . . do you understand what has happened to you?'

His voice was calm, precise and measured; it made her think again about the way he had eaten his breakfast. She shook her head, lowered her eyes from his gaze.

'You know what they do to girls like you who come here the way you came?'

His eyes slid across her body. She wondered if he had picked her clothes himself, surely they wouldn't have been the other one's first choice. He rested his elbows on the table.

'What do they do, Alena?'

She thought of the bag of crisps lying on the vomit-slicked floor, swallowed and whispered, 'They rape them.'

He let out a small yip of a laugh, showing neat, white, presumably false teeth.

'You say: they rape them, Andriy.'

'They rape them . . . Andriy.'

He nodded, shifted his hands to his lap. 'It is not rape, Alena. The girls are paid. Do you understand? Those girls, they want the money, and some of those girls –' the tip of his tongue moistened his lips – 'they like it. What do they do, Alena?'

Alena felt the edges of her vision sparkle. 'They . . . have sex for money and they like it.' He turned an ear towards her, a small smile on his face. '. . . Andriy.'

'Good. Now you, you look like a good girl.'

She felt the smell of toast catching at the back of her throat; she thought she might be sick. The first of her tears fell.

'Are you a good girl?'

'I am, Andriy.'

'OK.' He started coughing, reached inside his jacket pocket for a small tin and took a shiny black sweet from it. 'Because I want you to do something for me.'

She was crying properly now, could taste the salt on her lips.

He pulled out his chair and patted his lap. 'Come sit.'

She could barely control her breath but stood and perched herself sideways on his lap. She felt his legs widen beneath her, could smell the liquorice of his sweet, hear it hitting his teeth as he turned it on his tongue.

'Would you like to sleep with twenty or thirty men a day?'

'No. Please, no.'

'Andriy.'

'Andriy.'

'Do whatever they tell you to? Get diseases and abortions? Take drugs and probably one day overdose and when you do just be thrown into the river like a sack of kittens?'

She brought her hand to her face and he firmly lowered it again.

'Or would you rather just be my girlfriend? Help me with my business?'

She was shaking hard and he snaked his hand from her knee up her skirt.

'You are a very lucky girl. I picked you.'

His fingertips were dry and warm, her skirt straining against his wrist. He pinched her thigh, a sharp pain that made her gasp and stopped her shuddering.

'You know, Alena?'

He released the skin, pulled his hand out, smoothed her skirt down, raised his hand to her breast and took the nipple tightly between his fingers, then he pulled her lips to his and slid the sharp, slippery sliver of his sweet into her mouth.

'Get up now.'

She stood and he led her through the kitchen and the living room where Fedir watched *Friends* with the small white dog with brown liquid streaking from its eyes lying on his lap. He didn't look round but as Alena followed Andriy upstairs she heard the volume go up, the canned laughter follow her through the door and into the bedroom.

Of course he wanted to, had wanted to since he first saw her walk into the shop; not even a handbag on her but looking like she owned the place. But he couldn't ask her to spend the night with him. He was decent if nothing else and, especially in the last few years, he'd clung to that idea. And she looked so young, standing under the bare bulb in the living room, her mascara a bit awry, like one of the estate girls tearful after one WKD too many. She made a wide-eyed expression at him, gulping down a glass of water. The radio was switched to her Russian channel again. The music was some sort of pop, with shouty lyrics and an eighties-style synthesiser. Dave imagined Human League but wearing those tall furry hats.

'I did alright in history at school.'

She looked at him, the glass half covering the bottom of her face, her eyes saying 'what a weird thing to say'.

'I mean, we did Russia.'

'You can change channel. I like Magic too maybe?'

'Magic?'

'On the radio. I listen today. Neil Fox.'

'Right. No, I like this.' The music changed to something with a big guitar intro, maybe he heard pan pipes in there. 'I just meant, about doing history, I want to get to know you. About what it was like in Russia for you and –'

She flopped her arms to her side and laughed. 'Not tonight. Russia is a giant and I am tired. Another time. We have time.'

She shifted so quickly that he was always off balance, knowing that the wrong word, the forcing of anything, he didn't know what, would tip everything. The singer on the radio, a big male voice, probably with a big Whitesnake perm, started up now. She stepped towards him.

'We do still have time?' And she was serious again. 'Yes?'

'Yeah, course.'

In this room, under the glare of the bulb, it was all so much harder. She was looking at his face but hers was blank, what she wanted or needed, what her thoughts were, where he was allowed to stray and at what point she would take fright, hide, he couldn't even begin to guess. Still, he took her by the elbows and kissed her; a chaste, firm pressing of his lips against her cheek.

'Course we have time.'

She said nothing when he took his hands from her, moved

towards the door. She simply slumped down on the sofa and started turning the knob of the radio to try and get rid of the fuzz of static.

'It's getting late so I thought I'd get ready. For bed.'

Her eyes were on the dial, her fingers turning it millimetre by millimetre. 'I just listen to this song.' She looked up. 'It's a romantic song, yes?'

Dave had no idea, but thought that even without the static it was ear-bleedingly painful to listen to. 'Yeah, I, well, I don't understand the words, do I? But power ballads, that's the English for that sort of song, they are, aren't they?'

'Power ballad.' She turned the words over, nodding. 'This music is power ballad type.'

It wasn't a question and he felt a stab of jealousy as he wondered who she was practising that cute little line for. 'You'll be OK in my room again, yeah? I can leave the radio in there for you, if you're not tired yet.'

She was quiet now, staring up at him with that same face. He read nothing from the straight mouth, her clear, curious eyes.

'It's just I've work tomorrow and . . .'

He waited a moment, cheeks burning, for her to say something, but she shrugged, turned back to the radio and switched it off. She seemed upset. He wouldn't ask though. He couldn't.

After they had both taken their turn in the bathroom, him listening to her brushing her teeth as though it were somehow another clue, she seemed recovered, kissed him gently on the cheek and whispered something in his ear. 'Russian for sweet dreams.'

Then they walked to their rooms at opposite ends of the flat. But the flat, so small it could be paced, end to end, in ten of Dave's steps, meant that each could hear the creak of bed, the kicking of blankets, the sound of two people trying to find some peace.

* * *

They huddled from the wind, arms linked to each other: Dave to his mum, his mum to Shelley. Faces shone from the spray of rain. They'd got a good spot though; the chill on their skin felt good and even the scummy Thames smelt clean in this weather. His mum was wearing a bit of mascara and the pink lipstick Shelley had said would go lovely with her eyes, though it bled into her wrinkles a bit. Now Shelley reached over, used the edge of her thumb to wipe a smudge from under his mum's eye, then bent forward and smiled at Dave from inside her furry hood, under her silly hat that was meant to look like panda ears.

Shelley counted down to the klaxon while his mum slipped from Dave's linked arm and Shelley curled around it in her place. Shelley counted, six, five, four . . . pushed her body close to his. He knew he was blushing, hoped the drizzle covered it. He wanted to shake her off but then he looked over to his mum smoking a fag, blowing the smoke away from them, a sly smile on her frosted lips, and stayed where he was. The rowers passed and Shelley gripped tighter. 'You could do that.' The fur of her hood touched his wet cheek. 'Couldn't he, Pat?'

'He could, all the running he does, he could do anything he wanted.'

Dave stared at his trainers, felt Shelley's prying fingertips through his coat, his mum's big body behind them, taking the worst of the wind, the smell of her smoke catching in their hair. The race was finished by the time it took him to realise it felt good, it made him happy, the three of them standing like that. 'Well, you two, flattery will get you everywhere. How about I treat us to lunch?'

They wove through the crowds. Shelley stopped to look in every buggy, pulled faces, cooed, kept her arm fastened through Dave's even when Pat had a coughing fit going up the damp stone steps leading from the river, and he tried to untangle himself to see to her.

'Mum? You alright?' His mum coughed into a scrap of stringy pink tissue, wheezing as though her windpipe were a penny whistle. 'I'll just get us a takeaway, yeah? And we'll get a taxi back.'

She waved her hand – her anorak sleeve dangled where she'd bought it a bit too big in the sales, as though she'd thought she'd grow into it. 'A taxi from Putney! We bloody well will not.' She stopped, gave him a look. 'Besides, I need a drink.'

They didn't stay by the river, didn't want to go to one of the pubs full of booming-voiced, red-faced posh posers, drinking designer microbrewery bitter and talking about the good old uni days and the 'property market'. Instead, they walked up the high street to the Wetherspoons, and Dave saw it, the way those blokes with their expensive leather jackets, bottles of champagne tucked under their armpits, clocked Shelley. She didn't notice, or maybe she was used to it, she was busy looking at him, smiling back at his mum, didn't seem to feel their eyes all over her like schoolboys' fingers over a sticky copy of *Nuts* magazine. She cuddled into him, her hot breath telling him how cold it was.

His mum and Shelley demanded a jug of Sex on the Beach and then ripped him for looking mortified when he ordered it. He drank JD's, tried to forget about the five miles he'd been planning to run that night, how £20 could buy you three nights in a beach hut in Goa. He got them another jug and then they were in their cups and on to gossiping about Sandra who got caught pinching from the chip-shop till.

'And then he says, straight-faced as anything, he thought there was something fishy going on.'

Pat wiped her eyes as they laughed up a gale. That's what

two jugs of Sex on the Beach will do. Dave was on his third double already. He'd lost focus himself, except for Shelley's hand on his leg and the heat of sitting next to her, which made her feel in perfect, humming focus.

'Another? Let your old mum buy you young ones a drink.'

'No, Pat, let me get us some grub. I'm starving.'

At the bar Shelley swayed her tiny little white-denim-covered arse to 'Starship Trooper'. He kept his eyes on it, back and forth, and thought he'd maybe drunk himself sober somehow. His face felt soft, his chest and his neck warm, he was dying for the burger and chips Shelley was ordering him but he was thinking straight enough. She was gorgeous.

His mum was rummaging in her handbag, her chipped nail varnish the colour of starfishes showing up against the cracked navy-blue leather. He could tell her head was a bit loose on her shoulders from the cocktails as she raked a clumsy hand through the jumble – keys, a few chewed-up pens, half-empty perfume bottles, loose Polo mints, lipsticks, probably one of those tattered wordsearch books she liked so much. She nudged her body into his, a bit harder than she might have soberer. 'Look, here it all is.' She took out her purse and unclasped the card section. He would've stopped her but he didn't want to ruin the day. He hated it when she did this when she was pissed.

She was lining them up on the sticky table now. Dave wiped a beer puddle away with his sweatshirt sleeve just before she started laying them down. A locket, two four-leaf clovers sealed in yellowing Sellotape, two photos, a little credit-card-sized creased poem – Dave's handwriting hadn't changed much, he noticed. The sun had come out a bit and cold, pale, early-evening light shone in on his mum and her little row of treasures. In one of the photos she was in a red swimming costume. You couldn't see her eyes properly in the picture but she looked bright, bold, happy. Really happy.

'Look at that figure then. Weekend I met your dad. Honest, I could barely get him to look me in the eye. He always did love my boobs in that costume.'

Dave knew his part. 'Mum!'

'Shame I ever had to take it off. Shame I lost my figure after you. I was never going to keep him, maybe that's why I liked him. I had plenty of offers but he was hard work, a challenge. Led me a merry dance, he did.'

She flicked the locket, they watched it spin, and Dave stared at his own slow, solid writing on the scrap of a poem, an awkward row of hearts and kisses under it.

'Not much to show, is it, Davey? For a whole life? These . . .' She started putting them back into the purse – quick, clumsy. '. . . these nothings. Trinkets.'

And he saw her blink away tears, her double chin wobble before she snapped her purse shut and pushed it deep back down into the chaos of her handbag. She screwed up her mouth, shook her head as though something had landed in her hair. He knew, he'd learned, in all the years they'd been through this routine, what to say.

'I know, Mum. I know, but we had each other.' And he looked away because that was the kindest thing to do for her. Be close but let her have her privacy.

'I miss the bastard, you know that? Over twenty years later and I still miss the way he could make me feel with one of his cheeky lines. It's been a lonely life.' She tried to shift herself but the booth was a tight squeeze and she gave up and just shook her head again. Over at the bar Shelley was singing the last lines of the song to an old booze hound, making his week, lucky bugger. His mum picked up his whiskey and Coke and finished the dregs. 'But you, Dave, you're no trinket, are you? My boy. If you're what I've got to show for it then I'd do all the scrimping and scraping, the lonely nights, being scared sick for us, again. I did my best, you know? It was as good as I could do.'

And though usually he just let her talk herself out, he could see Shelley working her way through the pub again and he just wanted the night to be a good one. So he pulled his poor mum to him and kissed the top of her head. 'Give over, you're the best mum. The best. Let's just enjoy the night, eh? It's just the booze, this. You'll be giving me shit again tomorrow.'

But when he released her he wasn't looking at her, he was looking at Shelley walking towards them, a pissed grin on her face, and Pat looked between them.

'I see, Davey. Yeah, you're right, son, let's enjoy the night.'

And then, just like the sun had parted the grey-lilac clouds and shone in on them, she was good as gold again. Lumbering herself out of the booth so Shelley could slide in next to Dave. He was so busy trying to work out the change in his mum he barely noticed Shelley's hand sliding up his leg.

Later he would wonder how bad she'd felt that day, if he should have noticed the loose folds of skin, or her complexion, grey as the sky, under her make-up, but he was too busy. He didn't see his mum that night just like he didn't really see Shelley, not as she properly was. Later he'd realise he couldn't see straight for thinking about Shelley's warm body, her wandering hands, his mum looking so chuffed to see them cosied up. He couldn't think straight that night either, for thinking about all those other blokes' eyes all over Shelley, and her with her sweet boozy breath hitting the corner of his jaw, wet on the top of his neck. A dirty laugh escaping from between her lips. Her saying 'I'm fucked' as they watched Pat walk, with a gentle rock in her step, to the bar, 'and I want you to be tonight too'. He was blinded.

She wasn't herself, her face going from happy to sad and back again, like one of those flick-books. She didn't even haggle down the price of the taxi to the hospital, though she harangued the driver to let her smoke out the window. 'For the price this is costing us you should be smoking this fag for me. Anyway, doctor's orders, honest.'

She wore her smart coat that she'd got from House of Fraser, and Shelley had done her wispy hair a red-brown colour that reminded Dave of dried blood but that his mum had thought was 'really glam' and she'd liked it so much she didn't say anything about the splashes all up the wall behind the kitchen sink.

'You're a scarlet woman, Pat.'

Dave had sat at the kitchen table watching Shelley's long, thin fingers comb through his mum's hair, then give her a shoulder massage while they waited for the colour to take. He saw the proud tilt of his mum's chin as she turned her head this way and that in the mirror. He wouldn't deny it, how good Shelley was for his mum.

They'd all sat side by side on the sofa, *Coronation Street* on mute. It was Shelley, her hand clasped in Pat's, who told Dave that his mum had found a tumour, that the tests had already been done. His mum sat quiet, gripping on to Shelley for dear life, as the sick, terrified silence had filled everything.

Dave tried to get up and Shelley reached behind her back to hold his hand, keep him there. The three of them quiet and entwined, staring at Roy Cropper serving his five thousandth bacon sarnie, before Shelley said to him, 'It's alright to be scared, you know. Or have a cry.'

And his mum pushed herself forward on the sofa, pulled her hand from Shelley's. 'It bloody well is not OK. We'll fight it. You'll be strong whether I'm here or not, the both of you.'

Their first, and only, cross word. Dave had swallowed down the soreness in his throat and Shelley had pulled a fist of her own hair to the back of her neck. 'You're right, Pat, sorry, what a thing to say. We'll be strong together, whatever's down the road. We're not beaten. Plenty of life in these old dogs yet.'

And that was how they spoke then: we, us, our.

Shelley was in the front of the taxi now, charming the driver. 'Aren't you good, letting her have a cheeky fag . . .'

Dave reached out, about to stroke his mum's soft hair, then thought better of it, imagined her scalp and skull paper-thin. He'd started thinking he could see her wasting away, and him and Shelley too, though not as fast, skin greying, bones sticking out. We, us, our; as though they were sharing the same cells, intestines, had the same globs of poisonous tissue growing inside the chest, behind the throat, now curling around the spine like a venomous snake.

They drank and sometimes laughed together. An early wake. His mum said she wasn't spending her last days not enjoying herself and so they chinked glasses and watched *Jeremy Kyle* then *Loose Women*. They'd all have a sleep about two in the afternoon. Shelley spooning Pat under her yellow candlewick bedspread on the double bed and Dave, not sleeping at all, in his. Still, he'd sober up before his night shift at the Co-op. Not too much though, he still had to put up with the smiles, tuts and questions.

'How's your mum bearing up then?'

'My auntie had it, rotted her inside out it did.'

'You'll be a brave lad for your mum, eh?'

Dave let them squeeze his arm, told them his mum was doing great, she was a fighter. He thanked the girls for putting out the pink loose-change boxes by the tills and doing a 10k run in their bras and counted each black minute ticking over so he could go home. His mum would already be in her bed; a bit of cheap brandy in her tea, Magic FM's 'Late Night Love Songs' down low on the radio. Shelley tucked her in each night.

After he got home and showered, Shelley would knock on his door. He was grateful to her for that, her knocking. Sometimes they didn't make it across the room before he pulled up or down whatever she was wearing, flattened her against the wall or the carpet, lost himself in her pleasing, flexible limbs and soft, begging mouth. When they finished, while she was still pushing her own unspent body against his, he laid his head on her slight chest and, heavy as it was, she would stroke it and repeat again and again, 'It's OK, Dave. It's OK to have a cry, you know.'

The two of them a broken tangle on the carpet and his mum sleeping on the other side of the flat, her soft insides being eaten alive.

Alena slotted into his life. For weeks he disbelieved it, kept his eyes closed when he woke, just to keep the feeling of knowing she was sleeping in the next room. Waiting for the moment when she would come into the living room, her hair a fiery nest, face childlike as though still holding her dreams inside it. Then she would come and sit on his outstretched legs, her nightie riding up, asking him what he'd dreamed and, just like every other morning, if he trusted her to make him a cup of coffee yet.

It wasn't easy though, he was on edge, too grateful, too careful, but even when he was terrified he was about to crush whatever this was he couldn't stop himself reaching for her, even in the times when he could see he was having to reach too far.

He never stopped being grateful for that first moment of realising in the mornings, but inevitably the day wore it away. That day at work had been hot, boring and endless when he just wanted to be back with her. The flat smelt of burnt toast, and Radio 1, Alena's new favourite, blared while she was in the shower. He tried not to look, though the hallway led straight into the bathroom and she'd left the door open. He could see her skin scalded pink through the shower door.

He stood leaning against the hallway wall, nursing a can of Diet Coke, another of Alena's new favourites, enjoying the idea of her being naked, wet, so close to him. He imagined her soaping herself, thought he could see the soap slipping between her palms; underarms first then sliding the soap down, down a little further. She didn't even realise what she was doing to him, had just called him through from the living room to talk with her, lonely as she always was when he'd been at work all day. She raised her voice over the running water.

'There is nothing for jobs. I walk and walk all the way to Liverpool Street. I ask in every shop and there is nothing.'

Dave felt guilty for his thoughts but still couldn't get her naked body out of his head. 'Come on, it doesn't matter.'

'Yes matters! One place, Polish shop, they say they need someone and I get excited and I told her my English is good and I am hard worker but she holds up her hand and asks about visa and then I just walk out and I –'

It was hard to tell with the water, her words distorted by the glass door, softened by the steam, but Dave thought she was crying. 'What do you mean?'

'I mean . . .' She had turned the water off but her voice remained raised. He got just a flash of her glistening skin before she came out with a towel around her body. '. . . I have no visa and no one will give job.'

'Well, we'll get you a visa, Lena. I mean, now you're living with me and you've got a proper address and everything . . .'

And even though he knew nothing about visas, he knew he was just saying words, that it couldn't be that simple. She stood dripping in the hallway, her shoulders rounded, hair slick to her head, eyes wide and chin quivering. *Put down your Diet Coke, idiot.* He did as he told himself, stood and took her wet body into his arms, raised his hands to the smooth wet of her hair as her tears and body soaked his shirt. She sobbed and sobbed. Dave had no words, could only offer her his body to lean on, make a comforting shhh. She was speaking into his shoulder.

'I can never get visa. I don't even have passport any more.'

And because he had seen how quickly she could run from a question, how it could turn an evening stone cold, because he had learned, over the weeks, to take whatever scrap of herself she offered, to stow it away, there and then, like a kid with his treasures in a biscuit tin, he said nothing. But Dave wondered, as he held her small, shaking body in his arms, where her passport was, and then realised, his heart light with fear, that he didn't even know this girl's surname.

5

She cooked on the tiny two-ring stove, her elbows scraping the sink taps, bottom banging the fridge door shut. Earlier she'd picked roses in Clissold Park, returning the tight-lipped stares of the yummy mummies with a wide, easy smile. 'For dinner. Celebration!'

They had no choice but to give her a limp smile, turn back to each other for a gratifying exchange of looks. Even in a pickled-onion jar, with the label carefully soaked off, those roses looked beautiful; a pop of colour in the sparse room. She'd thought they smelt of pink sherbet when she was sawing through the waxy stems with nail scissors, but now that the room was filled with the stink of singed fish she thought she might have imagined it.

She wished she had spent more time watching her mother cook, wished that she were serving *kotlety* or a goulash, a spicy borscht, rather than burnt grilled trout with tomatoes and cabbage and egg salad in plastic cups for want of salad bowls. Dave got in, sweaty, tired-looking, from the journey back and she was waiting; wearing the yellow dress she knew he liked, her wet hair just starting to curl as it dried. In the weeks that had passed since he had held her wet weeping body next to his, she had found herself thinking about him; his arms, his mouth. Today, as she had wandered around the market, she'd found herself imagining his hands on her, thought about his fingers tucked under the straps of her dress, the spot at the crook of her neck and shoulder where he might kiss her.

He sank down on the sofa now and she brought over the plates, two cans of icy Diet Coke.

'I make special dinner, you see?'

His head was bent as he unlaced his shoes, balled his socks, undid his belt. He didn't look up.

'Work was OK today?'

She put the plates down on the coffee table with a gentle bang and he finally straightened up.

'Sorry, looks lovely, thanks, Lena.' They picked up their cutlery. 'Work was alright but the air conditioner broke so the girls were in foul moods. Yvonne went out and bought everyone Magnums but half of them are on this Miami Beach thing with no sugar, no dairy and kept giving me theirs. And there's this girl, Tanya, I thought she liked me, maybe more than liked, but now she keeps –'

'Keeps what?'

He pulled a fish bone from between his lips, shrugged. 'I don't know, just . . . hassling me.'

'Is she pretty? All the girls are pretty there, I saw.'

'No. I mean, I suppose some might think so but she's all fake; boobs, hair, nails, enough slap to sink a battleship. And there's nothing pretty about the mouth on her, I'll tell you that.'

He was quiet then, seemingly concentrating on dissecting his tiny, incinerated trout. Her creeping fear that he would become tired of her returned. He would see she was messy, silly – or worse, damaged. He worked all day with those pretty, bitchy girls and soon he would notice the oily red spots she got on her chin when her period was due, that one breast hung low and heavy compared to the other, that a sharp musky smell clung to her armpits deodorant or not. She thought the more he stared, because he was always staring, keeping her in his sight, the more he would see beyond her outer shell and get to her insides. To her guilt, anger, mostly guilt. But even now he just sat, observing her as he slowly chewed. Just looking, always looking.

She would not let her head ruin this though, for the moment he was still hungry, for her if not the food. She couldn't wait any longer to tell him, toyed with the petal of a rose in a play of nonchalance.

'So, today, I find job.'

'You what?'

He didn't turn to her, just cut a tomato with the edge of his fork. She felt the butterflies in the tips of her fingers, bounced herself softly on the sofa cushions.

'David? Is job. I get one after all this time. I think I will never find!'

His expression was fixed and Alena felt a dull thud of dissatisfaction.

'Right, why didn't you tell me? I mean, that's great.'

'I want to surprise. I meet man in newsagent's, old man, nice, and now I work for him. No passport, no visa, and he says no problem.'

'What guy?'

She was confused, he didn't even seem to care, and she sat back trying to read his face. He looked tired, maybe he was coming down with something.

'What? Old, like old.' She crumpled her face into what she hoped was a wrinkled old-man expression but she could see that he was far from laughing.

'What sort of job?'

'Delivery – I work delivering for him.'

He looked away from her and when he spoke it was in a small tight voice. 'Alena, you can't just go talking to weird men in Hackney and taking jobs from them. You've no idea what goes on. I mean, Jesus, did you give him this address?'

The butterflies shattered, turned to metal splinters. He didn't want her to work, to have her own money, to have a little bit of something for herself, he wanted her to need everything from him. She pulled her knees up, crossed her arms over her chest.

'I know what is like! Hackney, Clap-ham, where is different? You think I am idiot. Stupid girl who give address? Silly, stupid girl who isn't clever to know a bad man? I know bad men but this man is a nice old man. Do you know who a bad man is? You are a bad man for spoiling. I meet tomorrow and then –' She was angry, her heart pounding, voice raised.

He shook his head. 'Come on, I didn't mean . . . I just wanted to . . . but you can't meet him by yourself is all I'm saying, Alena.'

'And delivering newspaper is not very fancy. I don't get to dress up, not like pretty girls in your shop, this Tanya whoever, with her *boobs* and wearing high heels and make-up and her liking you. But is summer and I like walking and I –'

'Papers? You're delivering the papers?'

Tears made her throat feel raw, the disappointment swelling in her chest,

'*Hackney Gazette*. Is free paper, sometimes I do paid papers and leaflets too . . . I say to you, I get job at newsagent's.' She had been preparing the next line all day, imagined telling him, her arms held wide in triumph. She'd imagined him holding her tight, the smell of him. She'd thought he would laugh, would be happy. Now her lip trembled, and she suddenly felt ashamed. 'I'll be best Russian paper woman in east London.'

And then his laugh, as though it had been only temporarily stuck somewhere, came bursting into the room. 'That's amazing, Alena. You will, you will be amazing. I thought, well, well, these days you just don't know. I'll be a kept man at this rate.'

She laughed with him, gave him a teary smile. They relaxed

back into the sofa now, faces turned towards each other, so close that Alena thought she could see the colours within the colours of his iris changing. It was less than a second, but she felt a hot shyness come over her – it made her think of a snag on a jumper that, if you aren't careful, will catch when you least expect it and leave you standing naked. Then she blinked the thought away and gave his shoulder a gentle push.

'Is really amazing?'

'You. You are amazing. And, Alena, just so you know, there isn't a girl in my shop that can hold a candle to you.'

She thought she knew what he meant about the candle and if she was wrong she didn't want to know right then. They sat for a few more seconds with the plates warm on their laps, looking at each other, the smell of their uneaten food clinging to their skin.

They made a strange, unhappy threesome, sawing away at their lamb chops, the only sounds in the chilly room Fedir's open-mouthed chewing and the slow glug of Andriy pouring wine. Alena was only permitted water.

'Wear something nice. A dress or skirt I mean, I know you want to look good for him.'

Fedir had been sent down to her room to get her and had stood in the doorway as she rooted through her case, watched as she pulled off her jeans, put a dress on quickly over her vest and underwear. No smile from him, no word. He just stood. He just stared.

They sat in a triangle at the table with Andriy at the head, his dry-looking cheeks flushed from the wine. He seemed almost cheerful, giving the occasional sharp single note of laughter but saying nothing. Fedir kept his face down, took his food to his mouth in huge forkfuls, but Alena thought she caught a flicker of something cross his face when Andriy chuckled to himself. When he had finished Andriy stretched, took off his glasses and cleaned them on the corner of the cotton tablecloth, so thin you could see the blush of his fingertips through it.

'Alena, we'll be taking you out tomorrow.'

A shot of alarm ran up Alena's arms so hard that she almost dropped her cutlery.

'You can thank Fedir. He thought you might like to go shopping, didn't you, Fedir? A treat. He seems to want to get you out to work.'

Alena resisted the urge to look at Fedir, knowing somehow she shouldn't, lowered her eyes. Suddenly there was something electric, sharp, ready to ignite, in the cold air of the room.

'And if you are good – and why wouldn't you be when I'm going to buy you a nice new dress? – you'll be able to start working for me because we'll have seen you can behave. You can behave, can't you?'

The silence lay heavy on her breastbone until she coughed out some words. 'Yes, of course. Thank you, Andriy.'

He reached over and tilted her chin so she was looking at Fedir. 'I said you should thank him. He wants you. He seems to think he knows you better than I do.' He let go of her face, gave a sharp glance at Fedir. 'She's quite something, isn't she?'

Fedir's cheeks reddened and he tried, and failed, to smile as Andriy brought his sharp-fingered clasp to Alena's breast. Fedir's mouth was stuffed but he nodded, not too enthusiastically Alena saw; this wasn't all boys together. Alena returned to spearing her peas one by one, her hand shaking only a little, and wondered, not for the first time, what had brought Fedir to this house, to Andriy. What had he done that he should have to live in this place? What did he owe that restrained him from beating Andriy to a bloody pulp with his dinner plate as he clearly wanted to? Maybe it was common; perhaps all across London there were bulky security men, living in, taking their fill at the dinner table as their bosses roughly grabbed the breasts of their 'girlfriends'.

'Yes, Alena, he appreciates you, I think. Well, boy, you can have a try when I'm finished, how about that?'

Fedir held his cutlery still, and Alena imagined the blunt knife being rammed through Andriy's chest. His jaw stopped working and a thick silence filled the room until Andriy took his hand away from Alena and laughed, slapping the table as he did.

'Sorry.' He let out another rattle of forced laughter. 'Of course I know you already have your girls. Of course I know about your visits to the houses to "check up" on things.'

Fedir seemed to make an effort to swallow his mouthful, shrugged and started scraping gravy from his plate noisily with the edge of his knife.

'Of course you should. Of course. You have yours and this one is mine.' Still laughing, Andriy shoved his hand hard up Alena's skirt, that old favourite of his. 'But, I wish you could feel how soft her little bush is between these sweaty little thighs.'

Fedir scraped the last of his gravy noisily, licked his knife and left the table without another word.

She spent those first two weeks in her cell of a room downstairs, not yet trusted, or maybe broken, enough to be allowed to work. Even after she had behaved so well, tried on so many dresses, had spoken to no one, in that giant shining palace of a shopping mall, Westfield.

Fedir brought her magazines and meals on a tray. Sometimes

a terrible joke and sometimes a threat she felt sure he would one day make good on. And on two of the sixteen nights – where Andriy was Alena didn't ask – he took her upstairs to watch television and fed her ice creams. He never repeated his first 'joke' but on some evenings he reminded her, whatever Andriy said, he could take her if he wanted her, that he would surprise her in her sleep by putting her pillow over her face, and then he'd laugh, 'Joke, I'm joking,' and go back to his choc ice.

Andriy, on the other hand, simply summoned her to his room, made her work with her hands and her mouth when there was clearly no point. He was too old, anyone could see, it sat in her mouth like a boneless baby animal. He treated her like a child or maybe a doll, every time sure this would be the 'right' one. And when, every time, it wasn't, he spoke to her like a slut and used his hands painfully on her instead and spat his dissatisfaction at her as though she had demanded, had herself asked for, this treatment, though she simply grunted and repeated, 'Yes, Andriy.' She had quickly learned her part.

Afterwards she returned to her basement room, her vagina stinging, stomach sickened, mind racing to blank itself. She would walk past the kitchen, past the woman bent over the work surface in her headscarf, chopping onions.

Andriy was at least predictable. But Fedir was a barrel of petrol sitting still, calm, waiting for the flicker of a flame. One night after they had watched television he stood in the doorway and watched her undress for bed. She didn't acknowledge him, she simply took off her clothes, paused at the moment that she felt he might try to take her, and when she felt nothing but his eyes on her, pulled her nightdress on. When she finally turned round he had his hands in his pockets. She forced a small smile which he didn't return.

'You can't tell him.'

And he looked so frightened, that in spite of everything her instinct was to step towards him. 'I won't. This –' she nodded up towards the living room as though that were the secret between them – 'is between us. I don't tell your boss.'

She felt the exploding crunch of the heel of his hand on the sharpest point of her cheek before she felt the pain ballooning across the right side of her face, singing through her teeth.

'Stupid bitch. You filthy little whore, stinking cunt of a woman.' Alena stepped back, hand to her face, a frazzle of white light at the edges of her vision. 'He's not my boss, stupid whore, he is my father.'

She sat on her bed, arms around her head, waiting for the next blow. It never came. He was standing over her.

'Say that again and I will really hurt you, you know?'

By the time she had wiped the tears from her eyes the door was closed and locked.

The week after that they started taking her out for real. They started small but before every trip Andriy took her upstairs and told her, his fingers inside her, her face pulled painfully back by the hair, that they knew where her mother lived and first she would be killed and then they would find Alena.

Inside that house she believed him. Outside the house, where people still got married, had children, got into debt and went on holidays to the sea, outside, she felt sure no one would believe her.

'So I say, my job is to deliver paper. If I don't then I get in trouble and – ouch – and so she brings her husband, or anyway some man, and he says you cannot read? I say, I read, why does he think I deliver newspaper if I can't – tsh – read and she says, behind him though, hiding, still in her dressing gown even, her hair such a mess – ach – that the job is for reee-tards. Is bad word, David, yes? Insulting word. Reee-tard? Dave?'

She sat on the bed in a T-shirt that said 'No Angel' across the front, a patch of her red knickers just visible under it, plucking her eyebrows. Her eyes flooded. He gave her a mug of tea, his temper rising. 'Where was this then?'

'Up near Tottenham.'

'Lena, you never said. You're delivering in Tottenham now? It's pretty rough up there.'

She kept her eye on the mirror, continued plucking her eyebrows with angry sharp jerks of her hand. 'Near Tottenham I say. I like the walk, does not matter. Anyway, so I throw paper into garden and tell them to read and not be moron, I use moron right, yes? And he shouts after – isk! –' she pulled a clump of eyebrow and drew blood – 'that I am immigrant scum and should I go, go – ouch, that one hurt! – home.'

It was the smell, not the red knickers, waving like a flag at him, or the swell of her naked breast under the thin cotton, that made him do it. She smelt of lemons with something rougher just underneath, leaves only just fallen. He moved closer and kissed the drop of blood from her brow bone. She threw aside the tweezers and stared at him. For a moment he thought she was angry, but then her fingers moved across his chest, her hands lifting his T-shirt to feel the hot skin of his stomach. Her face furious, her tears stopped, leaving shining patches here and there on her cheeks.

'And you hate my cooking.' She spoke quietly, splaying her hands across the firmness of his belly. It felt so good, her face so close to him, he could barely struggle out a word.

'What?'

'You are skinny and is my fault. I am bad cook.'

He was grateful he was wearing jeans. They were speaking in half-whispers now, Alena looking at him like she might take a chunk out of him with her teeth.

'It's since I started running again, Lena. Not your cooking.'

She was even closer now; he thought he could feel the wetness of her breath on his lips and licked them. A small red pinprick had bloomed on her eyebrow again, and just as he had before, he leaned in and kissed it upward and then her hands pushed up inside his T-shirt, and she hooked them behind his neck, moved forward, kissed the centre of his chest and then, with a look that would kill, brought her mouth to his. Just as he was waking up, instinctively putting his hands around her narrow waist, trying to pull her closer, her lips released his and she stood up. Looking down at him, she said in a whisper, 'I just want to be good girlfriend to you is all.'

And then she walked out of the room with her cup of tea, leaving Dave with the word girlfriend, the scent of unspent sex and the ache of that solitary first kiss on his lips.

It was a late night for them, an early morning really. She couldn't sleep any more because of the mouth ulcers, couldn't drink either, so they sat up together eating orange-squash ice lollies made in the freezer. She laid her head on his lap, he couldn't get used to her lightness now, his always big mum, but he still felt pinned there. There was an advert with a few dolly birds telling them to 'Text to Chat!' That's how you knew you were up too late. Those adverts and the feeling the day was waking up outside the drawn curtains.

'Comfy, love?'

Dave reached for the patchwork blanket, he remembered her knitting those little squares for months, and laid it over her. 'Yeah, Mum, you feeling sleepy yet? I'll turn down the telly.'

She made a noise with her tongue, the metallic taste was in his mouth as though he had ulcers too. 'No, I'm not sleeping. But you get off to bed, Davey, you must be shattered.'

He gave her shoulder a rub, thought he heard the click of her bones, and tucked the blanket around her. 'No, I'll stay up, Mum. My sleep's all messed up because of the night shifts anyway; I'm glad of the company.'

'So's Shelley.'

He looked down on her; her eyes were shut. 'What?'

'Glad of the company, Shelley is. More than glad. I'd say that's love, that is.'

He nodded. 'Well, like I say, she's a good girl.'

'She is, she's a catch.'

They went quiet, watched the woman with the big eighties hair, maniac's smile and yellow trouser suit take the rap for killing her cheating husband. When he thought she was asleep, he tried to shift her, roll her body off his thighs, but her eyes opened and he brought the cup of his palm gently to the sharpness of her cheekbone.

'Sorry, Mum, you were sleeping. I was just moving you.'

There was a car insurance advert on now, that little dancing phone that would have him humming its tune all bloody night.

'I'm ready to die, if I know you'll be looked after.'

Cold slid up his wrists; for a single second he wanted to stand up and let her fall to the floor. His battleaxe mum, just giving up, 'Mum, come on. You heard what the doctor said –'

She reached her hand up and put it to his mouth, and

though she was trying to shut him up, he gave it a little kiss anyway. 'I did. Did you? Not wanting to know won't change it . . . Davey, you've done me so proud.'

He bit his cheeks, closed his eyes, let the tears flood them. That tune on the telly was doing his head in.

'You trust me, son?'

He nodded, kept his eyes closed. 'Course.'

'Well, there's something I think you should do, and do before I'm a goner.'

He proposed on Putney Bridge with his mum looking on, a fag in her hand, eyes filling up and a sickly smile on her face. He went down on one knee and Shelley cried and then jumped around; cars beeped, some kids knocked from a bus window and gave two thumbs up.

And he should have put a stop to it. But he couldn't, wouldn't hurt his mum, have her worrying. That's what he said to himself; last of the martyrs. As if some part of him thought it might get her well again, a life for a life. It didn't. But it kept her going alright; shopping for her hat at House of Fraser, picking Shelley's dress out, the trip to the wedding fair in her wheelchair where everyone made a fuss of her, arranging the cake, deciding on flowers. They both went on fast-forward; on the phone the whole time about little pink bags of almonds or having a cup of tea with the bloke who had a video camera, or the other whose brother's little sister's boyfriend had a fancy camera for the pictures. A friend of a friend of the White Hart's landlord who could get them a white Bentley for a couple of hours. Dave had tried to put his foot down over that. 'We'll be laughing stocks, it'll get a brick through the window – great start to married life.' But his mum said she didn't care if they wrapped her in a bin liner and threw her in the Thames; she wanted them to have the wedding they deserved, one to remember. And Dave, mouth stopped up with words about how long she'd have those memories to keep, just nodded and wrote the cheque.

That was his job. Sit quietly, flick through the TV channels, write the cheques with a shaky hand, his heart working out what to do with the loss of a mother, the gain of a wife and his head working out how much money there was left in his travelling pot while the guilt of that thought curdled his stomach.

After it all, the dress, suits, car, pink-jewelled necklaces shaped like shoes for the bridesmaids, chocolate fountains with spears of plump marshmallows, bubbles in miniature plastic champagne bottles, he'd be lucky to have enough for a coach ticket to Skegness.

'You've made an old, sick woman very happy, Dave love.'

He put his arm around her. 'Mum, don't talk about Shelley that way!'

He was wedged between them, Shelley's sweetshop smell and his mum's, TCP and fags and Charlie perfume, and they showed him shiny picture after picture from wedding magazines. His mum jabbed her finger hard at each page, making her opinion heard. She kept saying it was once in a lifetime. For all of them – especially her.

He didn't know what made his blood run thinner, hotter, when she was close to him. Maybe it was the fact that she constantly felt out of his reach even when she was wrapped round him, her knees pushed into the crook of his, or the tautness of her flesh against the curve of her hips, that soft, shadowed dip above her collarbone. He would admit he thought a lot in the earliest days about her full, shapely breasts so completely natural on her small frame; like one of those 1950s Blackpool postcards. Or perhaps it was because she was suddenly just there, bringing colour and noise to everything, holding his hand, running to the bathroom door to kiss him when he came out of the shower.

What he had noticed in the weeks, months, that followed was the fact that she stopped to stroke every dog in her path; ignoring the owner entirely, she got down on her bare knees on the filthy pavement and put her face close to the animal's, so she felt it understood she was saying, 'Hello, darling. Hello, beautiful.'

She did the same with babies but smiled up at the mum and dad. 'It looks like you. Yes you do, beautiful.'

She stunned the local Bengali newsagent by asking, 'How is your day?' and then listening to the answer and asking in return, 'Have you always had problem with the headache? You should leave the coffee off and take a drink of more water,' while people fingered their wallets and refolded their newspapers impatiently in the queue behind her.

She liked their road, a strange sewn-together string of shops selling fried chicken, Turkish wedding dresses, African books and fabrics, baklava and second-hand fridges, that led all the way into the City if you walked for long enough. She liked their road far more than the pastel-fronted boutiques and mung-bean sellers of the posher streets of Stoke Newington. She'd stopped the other day and stared at a Mr Whippy of a wedding dress in a window. 'Like in Russia, for rich girls,' she blushed and looked at the pavement. 'The dress can never be fat enough.'

'You mean wide.'

'Fat!' And she stepped away from him to hold her arms wide as though she herself were walking in a beast of a dress.

She loved the Rio Cinema, stopped still and stared at the black plastic letters lit up from behind, advertising some foreign film.

'Is old-fashioned movie house? Like in black-and-white films?'

Dave nodded, hoped she wouldn't ask if he had seen anything there.

She darted in and out of the string of pound shops, fingered the synthetic flowers, thermal socks, shower curtains with ducks on them and barrels of Danish biscuits. 'For one pound? Everything?' Then pulled him out onto the street and into another shop selling a different jumble of tat.

She threw sentences away without thinking. It seemed to Dave that she wanted him to know everything she was thinking – but only what she was thinking that day, never what had happened before, as though she erased her memory each night. When he asked, 'Remind me, was it summer when you arrived in London?' she turned away, shrugged his arm from her shoulder and said, 'I have bad memory. Besides, I tell you before.'

At the market she bargained so hard, with such a cheerful cheek, that even the local elderly Caribbean ladies nodded their approval, as she drove down the tired-looking fishmonger with a sunburnt neck, for the sake of saving 20p on a slab of cod.

She'd never asked him to buy her a single thing, even before she got her newspaper round, but sometimes Dave had asked, just when it was something he could afford, a dress once in a charity shop, a little cactus with delicate pink flowers in a florist's. 'Will you let me get it for you? As a present?'

She would turn quiet, shake her head and then smile. 'When I get a job I will buy you present. Lots of presents.'

He offered to buy her a cheap mobile phone and she had laughed at him. 'And who will I call except you who I see every day? I have no one else.' And she'd said the last few words so easily he thought it might break his heart.

He knew she took the blanket from over the back of the sofa to the park while he was at work because he'd find strands of the scorched grass on it. And while he watched the girls on the shop floor struggle with the summer sale, the heat-bruised tourists stream in and out of the shop, he imagined her pale limbs shining in the sun, her face shaded by one of those second-hand books she'd taken to buying now she had some money of her own.

When he came home she would be waiting for him, just sitting with her bare feet on the windowsill, window open, her skirt blowing in the breeze from passing traffic below. She would grin, so free with her smiles, as though she had never had a reason not to smile, though Dave knew that couldn't be true. She'd turn down the radio and climb onto his lap, lean over and untie his shoelaces for him.

He'd admit it, he was reckless. Blind to the danger of letting a stranger have everything of him. And though it was her ripe, warm beauty that had made it hard for him to think around her at first, it was all the rest that was the hook that snagged in his insides, never to be pulled out.

He looked at his mum the whole way through, sitting in the front row just beyond Shelley's bare shoulder.

'In sickness . . .'

Her face was a mess but he was glad she was getting good use out of the lace hanky she'd bought specially. She had on a blonde bobbed wig. 'Maureen said I looked like Britney during the bad times but the woman in the shop said it's a tasteful ash blonde.' And it was quite tasteful, considering it was topped by a pink floral and feathered hat.

'. . . and in health.'

Shelley looked like a magazine advert. Not just pretty – she was though – but like she was made of glossy paper and coloured ink. Her deep tan, her doll-like make-up, those red roses in her hair with the same hard, shiny look as the ringlets framing her face.

They'd decided, Shelley and his mum, a small ceremony then invite everyone to the reception at the golf club: free bar, proper buffet, wedding cake with four frothy pink tiers, a spray of carnations on every table and a DJ, the works. In the beige, too-warm hush of the registry office there was Deano, a few of Shelley's old schoolmates and a scattering of Dave's distant cousins looking pissed off they'd had to travel from Colchester. Just like him, all through the vows, they were looking at his wasted mum sobbing into her hanky, her pink feather bobbing up and down.

The registrar spoke in a plodding South African or maybe Australian accent, Dave couldn't work out which and was all too aware he wouldn't be finding out the difference for a while.

'Till death do us part.'

He hadn't seen his mum until the registry office. Her and Shelley had been holed up at the flat while he went for a morning run, drank a good-luck breakfast can of Stella at Deano's and got himself into a nice suit that was going back to the shop tomorrow.

She was beautiful though. She was. Even with her teeth sticking out from her thin lips, mascara streaking behind her glasses, her dress already a size too big. She was beautiful, and she was his mum and he wanted this to be the best day of her life.

They all rode together in the Bentley to the golf club, the

windows wide open, her and Shelley leaning to wave to passers-by like departing royalty. Dave sat with an arm around each of them, still working soggy heart-shaped confetti off his tongue, shouting to the driver, a nineteen-year-old with a shirt collar too big for his skinny, spotty neck, to go easy on the speed bumps. The radio was playing Van Morrison and they sang it together, his mum's lipstick on his cheek as they both cuddled into him.

'It's a wonderful night for a moon dance.'

He stroked the back of Shelley's neck where the hair was fine and soft, and squeezed his mum's bony shoulder. He was a married man.

He'd never forgive himself. For being in Southend. Just an hour or two away but that was far enough. They were playing crazy golf and they'd had a laugh, the wind whipping at their hair and coats, him jostling her from behind every time she went to take a putt, giving her arse a squeeze. They'd even had a good, rough snog behind the Dutch windmill, Shelley's lips still filmy from her bag of hot doughnuts until the attendant bawled them out. 'Come on, mate, we're newly-weds. Have a heart.'

Afterwards they'd gone down to the firm wet sand and gouged out 'S + D' inside the shape of a love heart. He'd always remember Shelley laughing that day, running in her puffy pink anorak like a child towards the shore to find shells to 'pretty it up a bit'. Dave stared past her, at the murky brown water and the long, long Southend pier, feeling like it was going to twist around and sweep him up and away. His mum was dying. His mum. And with the same sea-softened stick he wrote 'Pat Morton best mum ever' into the sand and held the cardboard box of his disposable camera above it and snapped.

The landlady looked pissed off. That's something else he'd

remember. As though he'd brought death in and sat it down at her shitty little plastic-covered tables, scattered with tiny jams, and soft, rancid rectangles of butter. He remembered her watching him, his mobile phone hot against his cold cheek, that red, uneven lipstick bleeding out into her wrinkles, her face acidic, as though she thought she could close up her heart like Southend in the winter and death wouldn't be right there between them on the worn vomit-coloured carpet tiles of the reception.

He'd remember shouldering his way past her and Shelley into the breakfast room, the feel of a rough, sour-smelling bar towel under his wrists, Dolly Parton playing quietly somewhere and the outline of the landlady pressed against the frosted glass of the door. He wouldn't remember pushing Shelley off him, telling the landlady to fuck off or what he did when he left the B&B, returning a few hours after, cold-boned and shattered.

'I've got one of those already, and one of them. Come on, Dave, be sensible, it's a one-bedroom flat. I loved her as much as anyone but there's things that have to be done. We don't just stop because she's gone. Things don't just stop.'

Give her her due, she got things sorted. While he was filled with hot, raging grief, weeping over his mum's toastie-maker, Shelley was bright-eyed and brittle in her own sadness, constantly moving, a list on the go. They were out of his mum's flat in the week. He'd taken no more than a rucksack of things to Shelley's, didn't even sort through the piles she'd made for him, just shoved big armfuls into the charity-shop bin bags, trying not to think too much about the slogan written on the side, 'Your stuff saves lives!' Too fucking late.

Shelley kept aside the little velvet box that held his mum's wedding ring, her locket, the four-leaf clovers, though Dave had told her not to bother with the ring. The little ring so thin and brassy that it made him boil just to look at it; his mum had deserved diamonds, and a husband who wasn't a shit right down to his marrow. Dave took his clothes, a few of his *Lonely Planet* books and his world map which he Blu-tacked up in Shelley's hallway until she ripped it down after a drink too many. He hadn't stopped thinking about his big adventure, though. It would be a different one – not him boozing and shagging and bungee jumping his way across continents now he was a married man – but he kept thinking, kept convincing himself, they could travel together, get to know each other properly away from the estate.

'I was thinking I'll just cut back a bit, so I can save up again. I thought I might do an Outward Bound to Norway next year, just a little trip, you know, to keep me going while we're saving up for the big one.'

'You will, will you?'

'I mean us, we can. We'll just tighten our belts, we could go to Norway together if you like?'

'Well, we will need to save, that much is right.'

'Yeah, just imagine, save up a bit and then you and me around the world. We can still do New York first, just like you wanted, and I'll get some extra shifts, we might need to go out a bit less but no big deal, and then –'

'No, I mean we'll need to cut back because babies are expensive.'

'What?'

'I'm off the pill. I could be pregnant right now.'

'You fucking what?'

'You heard me.'

'Without telling me? What's fucking wrong with you?

This is the only thing I wanted. We talked about us going away and –'

'Well, this is the only thing I wanted. I'm not as young as I used to be and you're not a little boy with big fantasies any more, Davey. You're a husband now, so start acting like it.'

He tried, and failed, not to have sex when she refused to go back on the pill, turned herself away from him if he used a condom. What did he think happened when people got married? She wasn't getting any younger. But young enough, he'd said, to wait another few years, let him have even a crumb of his dream, they could travel together, and then he'd be the best dad ever. But, filled with loss, he couldn't refuse Shelley's body at night, the way she used her fingertips to knead the muscles in his neck, her warmth and wetness. Just like he couldn't refuse a drink as their long evenings, empty of conversation, grew darker, drunker, quietly nastier.

He stopped running for a few weeks, that turned into a few months; the *Lonely Planets* on his bedside table gathered dust and tea stains. But sometimes it didn't matter how badly him and Shelley fell out, what horrible words they'd aimed at each other's soft parts, when he looked at her, what he saw was his mum making them promise to look after each other, saying that Shelley was the only true friend she'd ever had and that by marrying her he'd made them both the happiest women in the world.

It took eighteen months before he was out of the sickening loss, stopped feeling like he was waking up from a bender in a bleary panic, a queasy feeling below his spine. But at least, he thought, Shelley wasn't pregnant. And quietly, as he listened to the chest freezer thrum and the sharp chirrup of the scanners in the Co-op, he started to worry away at the knots he'd tied himself in, looking for a way to untangle himself and live.

Once she thought those three words she was afraid they would jump from her mouth like a jack-in-the-box and terrify him. Alena was good at weighing the balance of things and things had changed. They walked the length of Upper Street, stopping to share an expensive cake and drink a cup of coffee outside a cafe, the pale grey pavement swirling with fallen, pale flowers from a nearby tree. No talking, just sitting, watching people, though he'd nudged her calf with his trainer when a puppy went by, knowing she'd want to try and stroke it.

When they were done Dave stood first and held his hand out to Alena but he pulled her up so fast she stumbled into him and they laughed, but still they said nothing. It was the first rainy summer day and she wore a thin brown woollen coat. 'Is all the way from Japan. Look at the label!' She'd been so happy when she'd found it. But it wasn't warm enough and she pushed her arm through his, held herself snug to the side of his body.

There was a pile of stuff on the street corner; bouquets, cheap-looking ones, all the petals crushed and on their way to rotten, giving off a strong, sweetish decayed smell. Scattered around were soggy teddies, a half-deflated basketball and a few dented cans of Irn-Bru with burnt-out tea lights on top of them. Crowning the small, sad mountain was a weather-beaten, laminated picture of a young black boy, his hair in cornrows. He had buck teeth that his face would probably have grown into and he wore his school uniform, the knot of his tie just a little too tight. In one or two other sodden printouts of him you could just about make out his baseball cap and what might have been a basketball vest, still smiling his goofy smile but looking just a bit cooler than in his school uniform. Not cool enough though. Or maybe trying to be too cool. Who knew.

They stopped. A child had died here. A boy. For no reason, it seemed. Stabbed six times. A boy who must have drunk that orange fizzy drink, probably played basketball. Dave stood a step ahead of her and when she went to him she saw his eyes were shining, the tears yet to be spilled. He turned and smiled at her, looped a single finger through hers. His voice was ragged, quiet.

'Was just thinking. Makes you want to be grateful for every day you get. You never know what's coming. Just be glad for what you've got, you know?'

Alena stood on her tiptoes, but then looked down; she told his feet before she told the rest of him. 'David, I love you.' Then she looked up at his ecstatic, bewildered face.

'Only if you want to. I mean, maybe you don't want to sleep on the sofa. Then we can take you in our car to hostel. Isn't that right, darling?'

Alena took a sip of her cold, bitter coffee and put her hand over Aoise's. Aoise, seventeen, from a tiny village outside Lagos, running from poverty, an arranged marriage postponed by the promise of sending money home; here in London to find some cleaning or childcare work. Fedir moved his chair in towards the two women.

'Of course you're sure, right, Aoise? Why pay for a hostel?'

The girl smiled; she had drawn on her eyebrows too heavily, wore bright red lipstick that showed the yellowish tinge to her teeth. The girl had said she was glad to be sending money home to her mother, and, though it felt as if a sheet of glass was expanding and shattering under her, Alena had managed to keep smiling, noticing how the girl's eyes climbed all over her beautiful handbag, her manicured nails shiny as beetles' backs, and all over Fedir too.

Now Alena gauged a slight hesitation from the girl, a very gentle leaning back as though trying to get more perspective on this good-looking couple who'd met her at the airport, bought her coffee, offered her a place for the night. Alena changed tack, pulled her hand back, acting affronted. 'Come on, Fedir. Of course Aoise wants to be in big city by herself. When I arrive I think meeting new people, new friends is all part of the trip but probably Aoise is braver girl. Clever girl. Anyway, we are going now so –'

Just as Alena had known she would, the girl looked alarmed. 'Oh no. I was just thinking whether I could maybe buy a paper on the way? To be looking for jobs? Yes?'

And Fedir laughed in the too-relieved way that Alena knew meant he was high on the addictive thrill of making a catch.

'Sure, no problem. Let's go, I'm starving.'

And Aoise smiled back at him, a small, sweet pursing of the lips. 'Me too.'

So Alena led the way through the airport with the same fast walk she'd picked up from the too-skinny Ukrainian blonde four months ago.

The worst thing? She was so, so good at it. Not at first. At first the worst thing had been the nerves. And the beatings. Only her body – they needed her face. A beating for every day she didn't get a girl, which was every day for almost three weeks. Fedir stood in the shadow of the doorway popping his knuckles and staring while Andriy gave her sharp kicks and stamps with his pointy, lace-up shoes. He was a true craftsman, she'd give him that; each sickening crunch, the sweat-inducing sensation of skin being twisted until it almost tore, the pressure of the sole of his shoe on her chest just enough to bruise, to hurt worse than Alena would have imagined something could hurt, but never enough to put her out of action for even a day. Instead she was left with a wincing, slow ache when she moved a certain way, and pink, purplish bruises fanning across her arms and legs and across her breasts and torso too.

And so, as the bruises turned greenish and yellow, she learned to be good, and then she just got better and better. She learned to read each girl's face, the oil dripped from her tongue in just the right way, she draped across Fedir, proprietorial and smug. On the first day a girl went with them Fedir drove home through Covent Garden and he told her she could go to a shop and buy something as a reward.

The electric relief of getting a treat. The relief of him being in a good mood and saying Andriy was out that night, that they'd just watch TV and order Chinese takeaway, that was the spark that ignited something in her, a slow mercurial turning of herself. She'd started small that day, a little lacquered green-apple charm on a gold chain, but as the days went on she'd bought handbags, an iPod, shoes, lots and lots of high-heeled, brightly coloured shoes. She grew to love those things, she'd plan what she was going to get the next time she made a catch, had slipped into that language so easily with Fedir on their way to the airports. Alena sat with Aoise in the back seat of the car and chatted about London, her favourite shops, the food, Aoise's intended husband, her favourite sibling. Alena counted off the familiar streets to the house full of the women Andriy owned, in reality not so different from the cafe basement where he'd purchased her, but, like Andriy himself, a more respectable exterior for the truth that lay within.

When they reached the big red-brick new-build, all the girls sat watching TV on sofas in a sparse room in strange summery, skimpy clothes, legs blotched and pasty, feet crammed into cheap heels, all lined up on the grey nylon carpet. One of Alena's first, Magda, sat among them; obese in her red Lycra, dead-faced under her make-up, smiling at Alena, pretending this was all such fun, as though seeing an old friend. Alena acknowledged her with a cold, sharp splinter of a smile. Aoise was looking around her, a polite half-smile on her face as though this might be a joke.

When Alena walked out into the cold night, with its wind that felt like it grazed the skin, she began rubbing her fist in circles hard against her chest, urging her breath to come easier, thinking of the soft red silk dress she wanted to buy that night and wishing Fedir would hurry up so she could make it hers before the shop closed.

As months went by she began to believe that autumn might never come; the sun would be a constant in the sky, a sugary shining ball of too-yellow ice cream, making the creases of her elbows clammy, filling her dreams with long cold glasses of water that never quite quenched her thirst.

Shading her eyes from the light bouncing over Hackney Reservoir, she stared at the tower blocks in the distance, so similar to those back at home. She would have to climb them later, leaving her small trolley at the bottom and lugging her courier bag up the surprisingly clean stairs, guessing what food was cooking from the wafts coming from under doors, greeting the students in too-tight jeans and Soviet spectacles and the terse-faced wide-bottomed African matriarchs.

When she imagined, before, back in Russia, what sort of job she might get in London she would never have thought that a job like this one could make her happy. She'd imagined gleaming office blocks, not tower blocks, wearing a smart suit, not a courier bag.

Instead, she had blisters on the balls of her feet where her flip-flops couldn't cushion, the constant thirst, the dusty black of the streets between her toes, and they were well worth the smiles she shared, the fried spicy food that Mrs Khan forced on her, the paper already slick with fat, that she'd later give to Dave.

And the money; not a lot but she worked two routes now: Stoke Newington, Upper Clapton, Dalston, Hackney Wick in the morning; Stamford Hill, Seven Sisters, Tottenham in the evening. Mr Scannell said she was his best worker and she smiled, proud, though her mother had always warned her pride was something that would blow up in your hands and burn your hair off. She walked for hours, ears plugged into the little yellow tape machine David had bought her. 'It's a bit knackered. I had one just like it when I was a kid but, well, we've no computer so an iPod's useless.' Anyway, iPods were expensive, and this hung heavy and comforting on the elasticated waist of her skirt, made a satisfying whirr when she wound the tape back to her favourite Michael Jackson, Def Leppard or Barbra Streisand song, though sometimes Barbra made the tears come a little.

She bought the tapes in charity shops along the route. She went into every one, couldn't resist the racks of clothes now she had some money jangling in her pocket, and she passed so many. Each week she decided what she wanted: a red skirt, a nice pair of shorts, a matching blouse.

'You look like a supermodel,' Dave would say as she twirled for him.

'Fifty pence from the bucket on floor!'

She had tried, when she had first got that little clear plastic bag of three twenty-pound notes, to offer Dave some rent but he pushed her hand away and walked angrily from the room. Now she bought him small presents between the morning (daily papers) and afternoon (*Citizen*, *Advertiser*, brochures and flyers for pizza and hire-purchase furniture schemes) shifts. Running magazines usually, socks from the pound shop, or a bumper pack of Breakaways.

Mr Scannell gave Alena presents too; bars and bars of chocolate mottled white over the glossy dark. 'Otherwise you'll be a wisp of smoke, all that walking you do.'

When Dave got in from work he showered and she ran to him and kissed his wet lips. She wanted to climb under the running water with him but she was still sleeping alone in the double bed at night. Somehow those few steps from the bedroom to the living room, to Dave, had become a vast distance which she had become more and more afraid to cross, as though it was a dark pocketed forest, patrolled by bloody-toothed animals and wicked witches. Each night as they watched TV and the city outside became more scorched, tempers frayed and people fainted on the Tube in the heat of a summer that refused to leave, she told herself she would be brave, she would make that night-time journey to him.

Sirens blared through the indigo evenings and Alena could smell him, a smell that now pulled at her. She moved her body closer to him on the sofa and wished for the sun to stay high. She begged the unrelenting sky for a bigger hole in the ozone and for the eternal summer to stay just as it was. As if she knew, lurking in the dark parts that had stayed, unbidden, inside her, that as soon as autumn did come, bringing the reek of dead leaves and fires and a cold that whispered across your skin like a lie, her old bad luck would be back too.

She knew what she was doing when she licked the caviar straight from the blini, saw the impatient tilt of his chin, the twitch of his lips that others would have thought was an exasperated smile. She was stoking violence but she knew now how far she could push. Especially at this sort of thing where he was forced to appear calm, benevolent.

She had developed a fearlessness that she knew excited him. As soon as they'd arrived she'd excused herself to the ladies' room, pulled at the tight fabric of her skirt so her pale breasts, dusted with a fine glimmering powder, almost spilled over the strapless dress. As she gulped down her first glass of champagne, she eyed him over the rim.

Of course he needed risk, he needed it more than money or even the status of being invited to something like this. He sought out transgression, wanted the girl he could get to do anything to be among those great men. It was a fine line she walked between exciting him, keeping him wanting and watching, earning her own keep, and offering herself up for punishment.

At the table she stayed silent, played with her food, and Andriy would say as he always did, that she spoke little English.

'And what does the woman in your life do, Andriy?'

Alena licked the acidic white wine from her lips then inched towards the man.

'Well, you see, I am a commodity. Andriy deals in export and import and I am part of a very valuable shipment. I am valuable because I have a body he uses . . . I mean, when he is able, which is almost never, not in the way you, for instance, might use this body, and a face that can tell a thousand lies to girls just like me. Girls just like I used to be. My job, it is a very important job, is to go with his son, Fedir, who isn't as smart as his father but is equally dangerous, vicious in his own way, and we sit and drink coffees at airports and train stations until our stomachs turn bitter. We wait a long time. I read – yes, I can read, it's amazing, isn't it? I like romantic books, love stories, and Fedir plays Tetris on his phone, he is very good now but can't quite reach that top level yet. If we wait long enough a girl will walk past usually with a bulging case, and a look in her eye, they all have it, I know it well, I had it myself once – a mix of terror and hunger and a little pinch of hope. And that is when I'll paste on my smiley-smiley face and strike up a conversation. Strike! These girls aren't stupid, you know, but neither am I, and I know what they want from this journey, what they hope will happen; how frightened they are. I did it in the beginning because I was scared for myself. Now, now I am buying myself back, pound of flesh by pound of flesh – who would have guessed someone so worthless could be so expensive?'

The man, who had a wart on his upper lip, watched her run her finger through the sauce on her plate, the thin hairs sprouting from the wart quivering like sexual antennae. He had said nothing at all. And, of course, neither had she. She had stayed silent in the face of his leering, head tilted, mute and malleable.

'You have to excuse my dear Alena, she doesn't speak English.'

In the car home Andriy kissed her shoulders, pushed a hand with sharp fingernails down her dress, bit her earlobe, earring and all, and told her he wouldn't just stop taking her to the dinners, there was worse he could do. The driver, a fat Lithuanian, watched in the rear-view mirror, his slitty eyes the mix of hate and wanting that Alena had grown to know so well.

Alena looked from the car, into the windows of bars, inside an Indian restaurant, a barbershop with people lounging in the chairs watching a football match. She was tipsy enough to fool herself that tonight she was part of this city. Or perhaps there was another Alena, having a cocktail in a bar somewhere, dressed up and excited about the night ahead, tired after a long week of work, going back to a little room somewhere and dreaming of somewhere bigger. This Alena wore jeans and watched TV while imagining meeting a nice man and having a date. She made it true all the way home, where she was dismissed. 'I have indigestion, the cheese.'

Fedir came that night, to claim her, when the soft darkness lay on her body and sleep had crept into the spaces of her eyelashes and she was ready for rest.

Every time he walked in, he came straight to the bed, pulled himself from his boxer shorts, and then lay above her, pressing himself onto and into her, pushing her nightgown up around her neck and sucking her breast like a boy deprived of his mother. It took a long time for her to learn to be ready for him, to raise her knees, position her pelvis in a certain way to make his hurry less painful, make the shock of it less. He stayed like that, mouth clamped to her breast, pushing himself inside her until he was almost done when he would flip her over, put his big hand around her neck, squeezing at the windpipe, and finish himself. She had learned that he could not mark her, but in that room, in that silence, she could mark him. So she began to bite his salty skin, tear where the muscles were thickest, thrust herself against him and enjoy the sharp pain that followed.

In the beginning she tried to remember, this wasn't real, this was part of the journey she'd started when she kissed him, when she'd started judging the pendulum of his moods and greeting the good ones with gently suggestive remarks, when she inched across to him on the sofa and when she'd been deliberately touching herself when he collected her in the morning. His nightly visits now, her efforts to want him, even a little, in return, this was the road she'd set them both on and at some point she'd steer them towards the destination she was staring at over his shoulder. But it had been months and she became less and less sure of who was steering who.

And when he clasped at her neck that night, whispered that she was his, his, his, as he pushed, pushed, pushed, he was just like his father. Except his father had never carefully untangled her nightdress from around her neck and smoothed it over her legs as Fedir had done once or twice when he was drunk and sentimental.

Afterwards, she let him lay his head on her chest, stroked his hair and waited until his breathing had slowed.

'Fedir?'

She whispered, twisted her head to get close to his ear.

'Fedir?'

'Hmpgh.'

'Fedir, if you wanted we could have this. No hiding. Whole days, all nights, just with me. Just us, away from . . . everything.'

'We do.'

'No, no, I don't mean working, I mean like together. Like boyfriend, girlfriend.'

He said nothing.

'We could, you know.'

She paused for a moment of violence, a reaction that didn't

come. He was silent, his breathing seemed to have slowed. He was listening.

'He couldn't find us. And we could get money, and even if there's no money, I can find work.'

'How?' One word, damp on her collarbone.

'One day we just go and then get on a train somewhere and be gone and be together. Properly together.'

'And my father?'

She could just make out his eyes, black bullet holes in the darkness. 'He would find a new girl to do his work.'

She felt her breath leave her body before she understood his weight was on top of her, his hands pressing down on her chest, enough air being pushed from her lungs to throw her body into panic.

'A new son maybe too? He'd find one of those, bitch?'

'Fedir, please. I'm meaning –'

'He is my father, I will never leave him. I take business. You –' he released the pressure from her chest and she took a burning, gulping breath – 'you are the whore I take because I can.'

He didn't tell his father and of course, of course, he came again to take her body. But it didn't matter; if he didn't want the rest of her too the chance was gone, the other life, her sliver of something beyond this. Now it was time to do nothing because there was nothing left to do.

There wasn't anything special about that girl. She had a flat round nose and a fold of flesh spilling over the waistband of a pair of pale blue jeans with those nineties rips all down the front. Poor girl, she probably thought she was being fashionable for the big city. She was no more stupid or clever than the others, her story no sadder. She made Alena's bones ache the same as the others and her mouth fill with that familiar bitter taste but no more so than usual.

They were in Victoria that day; the sound of the departure announcements and the icy cold working into her muscles. They'd had to stop going directly to the airports, security was tighter, there were cameras everywhere and Andriy, cautious as ever, had forbidden it.

Fedir saw the girl first, it was the clothes that gave her away; those tidy, colourful, dated clothes and rosy cheeks; made in colder climates than England. He spotted her and kicked Alena under the table. She checked her make-up and walked out into the freezing station. The girl was standing at the toilets trying to push her chubby hips through the unturning turnstile. Alena was behind her.

'Do you have English money?'

She asked in Russian, it was so much easier when they were Russian. The girl turned but her mouth was a circle of incomprehension, her eyes apologetic. Alena tried again in English.

'Do you have English money?'

The girl smiled; one of her bottom teeth was chipped. 'No, not yet. I need to change some. I know there is a bank in Victoria Station?'

'Here.' Alena pulled out her purse, made sure to pull out her wad of twenties while reaching for change, and handed the girl a twenty-pence piece. 'Here.'

She inserted the coin and motioned the girl forward. Followed her with the clink of her own silver coin and when the girl came out of her stall Alena was applying lipstick. They smiled at each other; she was probably even younger than twenty.

'Thank you. I like the colour of your lipstick.'

Alena gave her best laugh, a conspiratorial smile, putting her somewhere between an older sister and mischievous best friend. She waved her hand. 'Was so expensive, like everything in London. Where are you from?'

'Gdansk in Poland.'

'Ah, then London is *very* expensive place! I'm Magda.'

Alena told her she was having coffee with her boyfriend. How she remembered what arriving was like and that she'd love to welcome her in the way she wished she'd been welcomed. Couldn't she buy a new girl just one cup of coffee before the journey across to the King's Cross hostel? The girl went willingly.

Fedir, more of a pro than Alena, if not such a natural, had already tucked away his phone by the time they got back to the cafe, took Alena and kissed her full on the mouth. That was how Alena had really kick-started their affair all those months ago, a kiss, a slap and a threat in return, and then more kisses, kisses that at the time she'd been grateful for, but that now made her want to bite down on the soft flesh of his tongue.

'And who is this? Another one of your friends?' He turned to the girl, who started chewing on her thumbnail; it was easy for Alena to forget how handsome Fedir was, though she was sure he never forgot. 'She has so many friends, I don't keep track.'

'Leo, this is Katya, we just met. She is from Poland. Get us some coffees, darling.' She turned to the girl. 'Coffee or tea?' The girl said nothing, just stared at the menu with its exorbitant prices. 'Have the coffee, our treat, it is so good here. And, darling, pastries too.'

When he returned Alena was already part-way through her spiel; it was amazing how little she had to tailor it to each girl, how it was almost as if they knew it too, had been given the script when the air steward handed out immigration forms.

'Yes, when I come from Russia I was scared! I had little money but I was lucky, I make a good friend quick and started working. You have work? Someone waiting for you?'

'No, and no job yet, but I have money until I do, only a little bit but – oh, thank you.'

Fedir placed the coffees in front of them and a plate filled with cakes.

'Well, you will have surprise about how fast money goes. What sort of work would you like? I don't know . . .' She turned to Fedir, who was giving the girl an admiring stare. 'Leo? What was that job Sasha had? In a nightclub, wasn't it? It must pay OK, it's quite a fancy place. Just till you find something else maybe?'

'Oh –'

The girl looked at the cakes and Alena held the plate out to her. 'Please.'

'I haven't worked in a nightclub or even a bar before. But I was a waitress last summer.'

She spoke through a mouthful of chocolate crumbs. She was a child; a blushing, sugar-hungry child.

'There we go. Perfect! Sasha will be happy.' As he spoke Fedir drummed his fingers on the table in triumph. Alena's next job was to convince the girl to come home with them, or get into the car with them; she would talk about how dangerous the hostels were, how they could go and meet Sasha as soon as possible the next morning but if the girl didn't have a phone it would be hard to find each other, how she could stay with them and save the cost of a hostel for the night. But instead Alena said nothing, bit into an almond croissant and filled her cheeks. Fedir looked at Alena and took a bite of his doughnut. They sat eating, saying not a word, the girl's cheeks getting redder as the silence thickened and even she realised something was going on that she didn't understand. Fedir tried to catch Alena's eye and Alena looked out of the window.

It was the girl who spoke first. 'This is good food. Thank you. I thought London would be . . . I was nervous on the plane.'

Alena said nothing, carried on chewing her croissant.

'No, London is not unfriendly, is it, Magda?'

Still she said nothing and Fedir, as stupid as the girl but more practised, picked up the scene.

'So, Katya, where are you staying? I was thinking, we have a spare room, don't we, Magda?'

The lines were the same but when a woman's boyfriend asks you to come stay and the girlfriend looks stony-faced it will never work. Katya was the colour of an uncooked pork chop, from the embarrassment of being caught between two people, somehow having done something but not knowing what that might be. 'Oh no! You have been very nice. I'm sure you two want to be alone.' She was pulling on her rustling anorak now, the one that had a target drawn on the back, pulling out her purse clumsily, trying to catch Alena's eye. 'I mean, really, thank you. It's not English money but maybe if you are in Poland.'

Alena pushed away the money and held the girl's gaze. 'Is fine. I hope you are happy here.'

Fedir pushed the sharp heel of his shoe into the top of Alena's foot; she felt the tiny bones throb. 'But, darling, tell Katya it's not a problem for her to stay. It's no problem, is it? We'd like to have her to stay?'

'Actually, darling, you know is not a good time. Sorry, Katya, I'm sure you are understanding.'

The girl stood mortified, confused, sweating in her outdoor clothes, her lip trembling but she smiled weakly, looked from one to the other. Then she was staggering backwards away from them both. 'Thank you. I'm sorry if . . . thank you.'

She wheeled her giant suitcase through the cafe, bumping chairs and customers, her face a twist of hot, baffled tears to come. Let her cry, Alena thought, and then she allowed Fedir to grip her by the arms and carefully walk her out towards the car as though he were about to try to corral a tiger into the boot.

In the car he raged, threatened to kill her, cut her, put her in a brothel for a day, for a week. Since she stayed silent Fedir smacked her around the head a few times and then said nothing more to her until he came that evening. Then he seemed terrified, tender in a way she wouldn't have imagined, saying over and over that she couldn't do that again, she didn't know what would happen, at least until he broke and finally slapped her hard enough to make her eyes move in their sockets, her jawbone feeling like it was splintering.

After that day she let all the girls go, she even refused to get up and speak to one, forcing Fedir to drag her out. In the empty car park he slammed her forehead against the car bonnet, his temper making him forget both the danger of passers-by and of ruining the pretty little head of his father's doll. As he checked for a dent and Alena checked for swelling it occurred to her that she might have screamed, run and begged for help, waited for the police. But what was there to say? I am a whore, I make young girls into whores, I sleep with the father and the son, but this is not my fault. They said they would hurt my mother, they would harm her, kill her. Perhaps they are lying, but would you take that chance? And how could I face her again if she knew this? She would know in the way mothers do, she'd see immediately how dirty, how ruined, I am. No, this is not my fault, but I am a whore and nothing can change that now.

Instead, she continued her strike of sorts, unsmilingly thinking of it as good old-fashioned socialist action. But it wasn't a strike really, or a call to arms, it was a suicide note, and Fedir looked paler, angrier, more and more afraid of losing the woman he fucked, the woman who held him after they'd fucked, who belonged to his father but made that house bearable for him, the Alena who he wanted to own who suddenly had the stench of chaos and brutality about her.

'Do you understand? My father will not kill you, he will send you to one of his houses and you will be handled like an animal. Imagine it. This isn't so bad, you know.'

But all she could imagine were the girls she had sent to be treated that way and she wanted to say, this is bad, this is so much worse.

He surprised her, though. Despite the fact that each night he whispered promises of violence, he lied to his father far longer than Alena expected him to. Excuses about them being watched, being sick, about girls whose families were meeting them. But after three weeks, when Alena heard raised voices over the furious yapping of that small dog, she waited patiently for whatever would come. Her heart satisfied, she would be punished by having done to her what she herself had done to those girls; an eye for those eyes.

The next morning Fedir sat down to breakfast without a word and Alena knew without looking up from her plate that he had taken a beating for her. He said nothing, crunched through his toast, and Andriy watched them both closely, while he delicately removed the white of his boiled egg.

'Today is the day. Do you hear me? Today.'

Alena dipped her finger in the tepid tea in front of her. Fedir put down his piece of toast.

'I understand, Father.'

In the beginning she was calm. She didn't run on the short walk to the car, didn't knock on any doors to beg for help, just as she had never done before. Besides, she was wearing stupid shoes. Fedir didn't speak, simply pulled the keys from his leather jacket, chewed his gum with a grim mouth.

He put on the radio. There was a quiz with slapstick sound effects and the shouting laughter of people paid to have a good time. She had wondered whether she might be considered too dangerous to go to one of the houses, whether they would simply get rid of her. There had been other girls, she knew. Unmentioned, unknown except for a stray earring found tangled in the carpet under the bed or a splash of foundation on her bedroom wall; one of the girls had had an olive complexion, another liked long diamanté earrings.

She looked at the road spooling away underneath them, then the bumper of the car in front; when the window blurred she wiped away the tears, ignored the seeping terror, and kept staring ahead. And still he said nothing, as they ended up on an unfamiliar road, a desolate stretch of cars, concrete and grey sky.

'You understand this is it now. He thinks, he knows, he can do anything he wants.' He was shouting over the music, some guitar band, turning his face away from her. 'I tried to warn you. You have job and if you don't do he will hurt you. He can't hurt me but he'll hurt you, he'll make me . . . I tell you this already. I've seen girls . . .' He banged his fists against the wheel and the car swerved. 'You know.'

Even in her state of muted panic Alena felt a stab of irrepressible, unwanted sympathy for this man-child who would fuck and beat his father's personal prostitute and then be shocked when it ended badly. Her novels, with their curlicued pink writing, had more of a grasp on reality. It would be just like Andriy to test his son in this way.

They stopped in Shepherd's Bush with its kebab shops, Internet cafes, run-down-looking mums pushing even more run-down-looking prams. He turned round now, his eyes somehow animal-like with raw pink eyelids. Alena sat with her hands on her lap, tears rolling down her neck, her breathing so fast it burned the back of her throat. Still he wouldn't look at her as he spoke. 'This is your fault I have to do this. Yours. You understand?'

He couldn't do it right there surely? With all these people watching.

An old woman pushing a tartan shopping trolley walked painfully slowly past the car and Alena, worried the woman would become an unwitting witness, turned her head, angled her body towards Fedir. He took her chin tightly in his big, sweating hand and kissed her, stopped up her gasping breath. A kiss that would bruise her lips, leave them swollen with the memory of it. As though that mattered.

He reached into his jacket pocket. Alena closed her eyes, cried out: 'No! Please, please.'

She heard the car door before she felt the absence of him, and after a moment, opened her eyes, her heart thudding in her ears, to watch him run away from her. Then she saw the money and the mobile phone on the dashboard.

It wasn't until she was shaking so badly she couldn't get the coins from her purse to buy a ticket at the Tube station that she understood – this was the most brutal, frightening thing Fedir could have done to her.

6

He took the stick, thought of her slim shoulders carrying the newspaper bag, her smiles, of her aching feet that he massaged with the pad of his thumb until she squirmed, and took the stick for her.

'Six. That's not your size, is it, ducks? Secret panty wearer, I reckon. That what you do on the weekend? There's clubs for that sort of thing, you know.' She put her mouth closer to his ear. 'And I'm an open-minded girl. Whatever you like, I can like too.'

'Look, just put them in a box and make sure you do the staff discount.'

'Hold on.' She pressed a long, sharp fingernail on top of Dave's hand. 'These are for your little foreign friend, aren't they?'

He couldn't help it, he looked around the shop to see who was in earshot and got a twisted, pink smile from Tanya in return. He knew he should have waited until she was off the till but he'd wanted to wait until Yvonne was gone; too many questions otherwise.

'You know what I'm into, Tanya? Privacy and a bit of peace. You think you can be into that too? Enough now. You don't know what you're talking about. Ring them up.'

She gave a long yawn and fingered her black beehive. She hadn't stopped flirting with him, bending for the shoes and looking over her shoulder at him, offering to give him a shoulder rub when they found themselves having lunch together and then looking at him, taunting, 'Does this look tarty to you?' as she tugged at the hem of her tiny skirt.

He wasn't sure which was worse, the flirting, or this new tactic, the piss-taking. The other girls had started teasing Dave a bit too, following Tanya's lead. Not that it bothered him, but it meant he wasn't able to just sink under the radar, spend his days thinking about Alena, chewing on the little information she gave him and wondering how he could get her to offer more. He didn't know how it was possible for a woman to drive you mad and make you so happy at the same time. It wasn't just about the physical stuff but the emotions – happiness, love, whatever people called it, he needed more, he didn't want it to ever stop. He looked at the red high-heeled sandals, then at Tanya giving him a deliberate eyeful as she stretched over the counter and swung the till keys around on her finger.

'Oh, you like the view though, don't you, Davey?'

He did, he was only human, and he looked away quickly. The other girls had noticed something was going on now, had drifted away from their stations – evening, daywear, accessories – to watch them wrangle, see how long she could make him wait at the till. She smiled up, rolled her eyes at one of the girls who, thrilled to be sought out to play a part, gave a loud muffled giggle and in turn looked to another girl, who did a variation of the same eye-roll.

It had been dead all afternoon, that was part of the problem, and Dave wished for a Land Rover full of those demanding Saudi women with their headscarves and Versace glasses; so loaded, so good for a commission that the girls pulled their fingers out and kept the bitching to a minimum. At least until the women piled back into their cars. Then they went for a fag break out the back and let rip, Claudia mimicking their accents while Toni shuffled in an impression of the women in their long robes.

But the shop stayed quiet, just an older woman browsing with no intention of buying, the air still and hot, the yeasty, stale-biscuit smell that all the girls seemed to share filling up the place. Tanya pushed her face towards his and stage-whispered, 'So who are they for then, Davey? Your mum?' He flinched and she gave a little smile. 'Cause honestly, these are a bit slaggy. Unless your mum's a goer, an' if she is, well, good on her.'

He bit the inside of his cheeks. The other girls, after a horrified hushed moment, turned away to straighten shoes, to restack the deluxe insole display.

'My mum's not a goer, Tanya. Ring the shoes up.'

'I'm not being funny, Dave, I mean, I hope I'm still a goer at that age, but you know, if your mum's picked these, then she's doing a lot more than going down the bingo in them.'

'Tanya, I mean it. Shut it.' He slammed the note on the counter between them. 'Ring them up and make sure I get my discount.'

'All the trouble I could get into in these. Wonder if they'd be wasted on your old mum or if she's got some trouble to make herself.'

'She's dead, Tanya. Cancer. That trouble enough for you?'

He snatched the box and walked downstairs. He was shaking, there was a metallic taste where he'd bitten his cheek too hard. He imagined Alena's face and managed not to go upstairs and tell Tanya what he thought of her. He had responsibilities now; their future to think about.

More bother than they were worth those shoes; end of season, slashed down to nothing with his staff discount to make way for something more special. But she would love them, she'd look beautiful wearing them. What a soppy twat, he thought, as he wrapped the tissue back around them. It was true though.

Kissing. Soft, warm mouths meeting, the moment you open your eyes and there's a brush of his eyelashes against yours, the smell that makes you want to lick his skin, sometimes a quarter of a second when your partly opened eyes are so close you can't see anything but him, think you can see right inside his head.

His hands, on your waist, cradling your jaw, stroking down the pale smooth skin of your neck, a thumb tracing the collarbone. The solid warmth of his body when you lean against his chest, move inside his strong, circling arms, feeling the hot rise and fall of his lungs, sometimes catching a gentle, irregular thump of his heart against yours.

Alena had forgotten these things. The sweet ache of feeling safe, of wanting another body, craving a scent, the comfort of reaching for that and it being given without the sharpness of fear or cruelty or taking.

They slept together now in the big bed with the grainy, olive-coloured sheets, the slumped-in-the-middle mattress. Getting shyly into the bed, from either side, pulling the covers up around them, rolling towards each other because of the dip.

They were so slow to find each other. The first night he had reached across to trace down the bulge of her naked calf with his big toe and in return her hand had reached across, fingertips whispering against the cleft of his chest through the cotton of his T-shirt. The wanting seemed to lie over her, something hot and weighty that seeped into the spaces between them, making the smell of their desire and their bodies rise up from the bed.

The second night she had rolled a little closer and they lay shoulder to shoulder. Dave had taken off his T-shirt and she could feel his skin on her forearm; he placed a gentle, too gentle, hand on her stomach and, in return, she looped her foot around his, as though anchoring herself in the sea of what she was feeling:

mostly fear, some confusion, murky feelings that made it hard to find that sweet place again.

And so, like explorers, they approached the bed each night, climbing in from their sides, out into a stormy ocean with no lifeboat. Not a word from their lips but sharing the same pregnant, pulsing air as she pushed her back into his chest and he met the crooks and nooks of her body with his. The next night they turned, slept forehead to forehead, knees pulled up towards each other, sharing each other's breath, their skin sticky with the other's sweat.

Each night he asked nothing of her, though she knew, it was obvious, that he wanted to ask for everything. And each night that he touched her only as much as she wanted, something he somehow knew even when she didn't herself, she discovered the shelter, of arousal, sweetness and longing again.

'You can take it off for me.'

She spoke in a near-whisper and he lifted the pale pink slip over her head, his rough fingertips running across her skin, his hands as tentative and gentle as if he were unwrapping a gift that might suddenly shatter. She stood naked in front of him, silhouetted by the chiffon orange haze of the Hackney night, looking down at him. He turned his head away and she moved her arms to cover her chest, then he was looking right at her, taking her hands from around her ribs.

'You're beautiful, Lena. You're so beautiful.' He coughed, looked at his knees. 'I'm just a bit, you know. Nervous. I'm a bit rusty, you know?'

And Alena felt a new blooming of love inside her, for this big, strong, vulnerable man and knelt up on the bed beside him. She kissed the crown of his head, his damp temple, the smooth curve of his shoulder, and then he turned, took her shoulders in his hands, pulled her to the mattress and they completed their long journey towards each other.

Shelley threw away her little white pills, the pack of ribbed condoms Dave had brought home, and left them resting on potato peelings, the bin lid open, for him to see. Later Dave would think he'd gone a bit dead during those months. He worked his shifts in the Co-op and each night they ate, drank, fucked, slept, and did it all again, only sometimes with an explosion of a row.

He tried, but somehow he was never able to save a penny; there was always something they needed for the flat, someone's birthday drinks, a takeaway on Friday and a fry-up on Saturday. Shelley said everyone bought Avon online now. The bottle of vodka, or two or even three a week, that added up too. But at least they took the edge off the long nights when they had nothing to talk about but whatever they were looking at on the telly. He'd feel the insistent vibration on his thigh just before the end of each shift, Shelley texting him to remind him, and he'd finish his shift having a joke with the checkout girls about being a booze hound. After a while, though, they stopped laughing and began ringing through the bottles silently, a stiff smile on their thin lip-linered mouths.

At least Shelley knew how to make a proper drink, took some pride in it too; they might have had charred waffles and beans for dinner but her drinks came in nice glasses, from John Lewis not Ikea, good vodka, real Coke, ice cubes shaped like hearts and fat wedges of lemon. They sat with the heating on high, the only sound the blare of telly and Shelley's glass that she'd set down harder and harder on the glass coffee table with each new drink. He barely felt real, just a jerky shape of a man, as if he was being moved around by a console with sticky buttons that never quite hit the mark.

Shelley lay on the sofa with her feet on Deano's lap, head thrown back and neck exposed as they shared a joke, a joke fuelled by the half-empty bottle of sambuca on the floor. Dave had had a shit of a day; three scallies from the estate tried to buy fags and then got lairy with Bianca when she asked them for ID, and when he'd tried to throw them out they'd knocked over the flowers, water and petals everywhere, and worse than that, they'd called him a fat dick.

Fat? He was the fittest lad on the estate and everyone said so, or used to. What really burned was that he knew they were right. He was completely out of shape now, couldn't catch them and ran out of breath, or any sort of energy to bother, halfway down the street. He had to stand outside the Right Plaice, during the Saturday-night rush, bent over and holding his knees like a geriatric.

Deano, tanned and too skinny from his summer working Ibiza and all the drugs that went with that, inched towards Shelley, really milking the punchline of a story Dave had heard too many times before. He looked up, nodded. Shelley didn't look round.

'So she says, "But, Deano, I can't . . ." she was twatted like, I knew that, fuck knows what she was on, but I was off my face and all. So I said, "Come on, sweetheart, look, you want to, I want to, let's get it on, what's the problem?" And she looks at me, her pupils like fucking saucers and says, "I don't have any holes in my body."'

Shelley threw her head back and gave a shriek of laughter, brought her fingers to her eyes to wipe her mascara and slapped Deano's shoulder.

'Turns out, poor lamb had been on the mushrooms all night. Instead of getting a nice shag with a fittie I ended up making her tea and toast.'

'Bless you. What a gent.'

'Well, she was grateful in the morning, if you know what I mean.'

Dave walked to the kitchen for a drink. As he slammed the ice-cube tray against the work surface he caught a word or two of Shelley's. 'I bet you . . . good . . . I bet, all man . . . I would . . . Dave.' He poured himself a triple and left the ice that skidded away to make puddles on the lino. He walked back into the living room and Deano looked up at him, flushed, maybe a bit smug. 'You've a right one here, Davey. I always said it.'

Shelley didn't look at Dave.

'You're not wrong there. Can I have a seat?'

He stood in front of them, glass in hand. Neither moved until Shelley let out an exasperated breath and swung her legs off Deano's lap. Deano shuffled along with a smarmy smile for Shelley. Dave stared down at them, he felt like shit, he looked like shit and now his wife was treating him like shit as well. His hand tightened around the glass. He felt them both looking up at him in his ugly polyester trousers, stinking shirt straining at a few of the buttons, his upper lip prickling with sweat. They were like naughty, drunken kids. 'I'd like a seat next to my wife if that's OK, mate?'

Shelley rolled her eyes. 'Dave love, stop being an arsehole. It doesn't suit you. Though actually . . .' She started giggling, Deano fell about into her, they were well pissed. 'Honestly, for months I've had to beg him to lay a finger on me and then he gets all possessive.'

'Shelley, I'm warning you, that's enough.'

'Enough? I wish. There hasn't been any, let alone enough. And it's not my fault I'm a woman with needs. Deano, Dave here is petrified of getting me up the duff. As if that would be the end of the world. Don't know why he bothers though –' she pushed her face into Deano's, a sloppy whisper – 'he's shooting blanks.'

Dave allowed himself one deep breath. He'd seen on some telly programme that you should do that when you feared losing control in situations. Stay calm, assess the problem, what was the next move, how can you – the glass shattered against the wall behind their heads. Their faces changed for just a minute before they collapsed into each other again, Shelley's face all red from laughing so hard.

'Fuck me, Dave, what are you like?'

Then Deano: 'Fuck you, Shelley? Don't mind if I do.'

They were pissing themselves now, legs falling over each other's, heads resting on the other's shoulders. Dave stood above them, empty-handed, at a loss.

'Shelley?' but she was too busy re-enacting Dave's face for Deano. Before he realised it Dave had her arm clamped in his fingers and she gave him a strange crooked smile. 'Shelley, you're a fucking cunt.'

He didn't even stop to get his coat. He couldn't stand their laughter hammering at his back.

'Oh, you're a cunt!'

'No, you're a cunt!'

'No, you!'

Their laughter chased him through the letter box and clattered down the stairs behind him.

If you had asked him he would have said it was easier than anywhere else, that he had ended up at Liverpool Street on the

District Line and then thought, why not, fuck it, it's only a few hours, clear my head, leave them at it like rabbits.

But if you'd asked him again, after his whiskey chaser and fourth can, and coming into Norwich, he would probably have been honest; admitted he was going because of his mum. Because they went to Great Yarmouth for a weekend each summer, God knows where she found the money, and they played 2p machines, ate ice creams dipped in lemon sherbet, had one or two rides on the fair.

And once he was in the pub on the corner of Yarmouth seafront, still in his uniform, coloured purple under the neon light, letting the banging music pound down his spine, well, he would have happily told anyone willing to listen that he couldn't stand thinking about that phone call on his honeymoon telling him his mum wouldn't last the hour. How he'd spent the day playing crazy golf when he should have been by her side.

But that was Shelley and Pat, deciding it all. They'd agreed; it was a weekend, they'd see her the Sunday morning.

'You watch me, Davey, I'm going to stick around until you make me a grandma. Don't get rid of me so quickly.'

So as he knocked back a test tube full of a thick, sweet shot of something that made his eyes water, he'd admit it, he'd come to Great Yarmouth because he wanted to remember his mum swinging his hand in hers, treating him to another ice cream though she said they'd be eating nothing but chips for the following week, her sucking a mint after her drink so the locals wouldn't think she was just another tacky tourist.

But Christ, it was desperate there even in his state, and he was looking for misery. November, not a soul about, all the shops shuttered and just the occasional crowd of kids on the streets swigging cider from Coke bottles and passing a single fag between them. And didn't he just fit pathetically right in; in his work clothes, slumped at the bar and swallowing down the cheap booze. Oh, and the fact that his wife was probably shagging his best mate on the sofa right now. The worst of it all was that he didn't care.

Another beer – too fizzy and drunk too fast – collecting like acid in his chest. And what about his mum, who'd thought they were perfect together? Who wanted Dave looked after and wanted to say thank you to her only true friend? Hadn't his mum ever heard of a box of fucking Roses? And where was she now to sort this mess out? To help him get out of this? She wasn't even there to see what she'd done.

'Mate?' The barmaid shouted over the bar, pulling away his glass.

'Yeah?'

'You need to go home.'

'Home?'

'Yeah, the place where you can have a bubble in peace.'

'I'm not at home though . . . and what the fuck's . . . a bubble?'

She sighed; as pissed as he was you could see she was knackered, had had a long night, probably a long life though she looked, if anything, a few years younger than him. A goth, all in black, lots of eyeliner, she patted his hand.

'Crying. House rules, no crying at the bar. Fuck knows this place is depressing enough already.'

Her hand was still on his, he didn't want to go. Plus, he didn't know where to go.

'What about not at the bar, just sitting back there?'

She sighed again, pushed his drink towards him. 'Whatever. You do look like you need it. Pick a dark corner.'

'Yeah, yeah, I did need a drink.'

'I meant the cry.'

Then she turned her back to him, her glassy smile primed and hard for the next punters. She was big but not too big to see the curves, a lovely round grabbable arse, nice big boobs. And the dimples, they were very sexy. You could tell she wasn't really in the mood for smiling but was doing her job anyway and he liked that too.

He went back to the bar after he'd got himself together and ordered an orange juice. 'Thanks.'

'What?'

He moved in closer; she smelt of beer and spearmint, crème de menthe, his mum's Christmas drink.

'I said cheers, for not kicking me out and for getting me to sober up a bit.'

'You all sorted now then?'

He nodded. 'Just this one for the road and then I'll be off to get a room.'

'Good lad. Wait forty minutes and I'll be off too.'

She showed him her dimples, not the dutiful kind either, and went to collect some glasses. As simple as that, Dave thought. As simple as that.

He stayed in Great Yarmouth for a few days. Called into work saying he had a family emergency, though everyone knew it was just him and his mum and not even that any more, and turned off the mobile phone that had been silent since he'd left London anyway. He found a B&B, run by a woman with a long grey ponytail down her back and a suspicious mouth. The hallway had a fountain complete with plastic squirrels, giant ladybirds and flowers climbing a trellis fixed to the wall.

He filled his first day with a six-pack, a half of whiskey and *Jeremy Kyle* on the Freeview, until self-disgust and the stench of cigarette smoke from the wallpaper drove him out. He bought himself a pair of cheap trainers and two tracksuits from the market then pushed himself out on his first run in a year. It was heavy going. It bloody hurt: his legs, his chest, his pride. Still, the first day he managed forty minutes and the day after an hour. He still had it, under the flab and the slumped shoulders.

He ran the length of the seafront, past the arcade machines flashing and bleeping for no one, a gondola canal made out of fibreglass, up along to the dunes and the wind turbines turning ghostly against the sea.

He put one foot up on the boarded-up carousel at the end of the pier, stretched his burning hamstring and watched the scummy water below thrash and bellow. He'd played Shelley at her own game and beaten her by a long way. Because they couldn't stay together now, they just couldn't, and she wouldn't want to.

He stayed off the cans on the train home, though God knows he wanted one. Instead he bought a Twix, a KitKat, Rolos, Skittles, then ate till he felt his stomach swelling with the sugar, pushing up his lungs. He watched the grim colours of the Norfolk Broads and the heavy sky slide across the dirty glass. He did the sums in his head: three years to save what he'd saved before, less if he could get another job, longer if he couldn't find a cheap room to rent. Maybe he could go work somewhere, a cruise ship or a resort, travel and save at the same time.

At Chelmsford a girl got on; she wore a headscarf but didn't look religious, all that make-up, the tight jeans and red jumper.

Her eyes were beautiful, framed by the blue scarf. She slid in across the table in front of Dave.

'You don't mind, do you?' She had a flat northern voice and a way of talking where she tilted her head.

'Eh? No, not at all.' He'd almost never had the chance to speak to a girl like her. He drew himself up, wished he hadn't bought such a cheap tracksuit, felt painfully aware of the sweet packets in front of him. 'Sorry, kids before me, they'll be bouncing off the walls. You all the way to London?'

'Yeah, back to uni.'

'Yeah?' He couldn't think of anything else to say. 'I've never been to uni.'

She was texting but looked up, shrugged. 'Lots haven't. You're not missing anything.' She looked at him a beat longer, then put down her phone. 'But you could if you wanted, you know; lots of mature students on my course.'

He tried to hear some sort of slagging in the word 'mature' but her face was clear, not even a hint of a smile.

'What's that then? Your course?'

'Sports science.'

'Really? Ages ago I was thinking about doing that after travelling a bit. I'm really into running too.' He felt the cast of her eyes down his rounded stomach. 'Well, I mean I was. I'm a bit out of shape, just getting back into it all actually. I mean, that's why I'm in my sports gear.'

His neck was burning at having called his shitty nylon tracksuit 'sports gear' but she laughed kindly, her eyes shifting down to his hand on the table. 'And married.'

'Separated.'

She nodded and said nothing, her fingers returning to tapping the phone's buttons. End of the conversation. It didn't matter though; there were a thousand girls out there. Not just girls; things, countries, places and jobs. He was only twenty-five, he had his whole life ahead of him.

On the Tube back he was sure that Shelley would agree. That one day they'd bump into each other, maybe in the big Asda's, and have a laugh over their daft wedding, the stupid Bentley and the chocolate fountain that made her nephew spew all over the golf club's white carpet. They'd talk about how much they both missed his mum, how she was looking down on them.

And when he walked into the living room, she stood up, took a few steps towards him with a sheepish half-smile on her face, then hung back. He actually thought, this will be easy, we've probably wanted the same things for ages, me and her, just couldn't do it to the other; pair of idiots.

They stood facing each other until she made a small sound from the back of her throat. 'Tea? Or something stronger?'

'No, no, tea's good. Yeah, tea's lovely, Shell.'

She clanked in the kitchen, making tea in her usual order so he could predict how soon the pouring milk would follow the kettle clicking, when the teaspoon would sing against the mug's rim. She gave him his and they sat side by side, on the sofa, staring down into the hot, brown mouth of the mug, elbows almost touching. She gave him a stiff, shy smile.

'Where'd you go then? I couldn't think where. Tried your phone and –'

'Yeah, sorry, turned it off after the first night. Great Yarmouth. Clear my head and all that.'

'Weird choice.'

'Yarmouth? Yeah . . . well, no actually, not really. Mum used to take me there, didn't she?'

A silence fell between them, greasy with unspoken things.

'Listen, Shelley, I'm sorry about calling you that name and then, well, not calling to tell you where I was. I'm sorry if you was worried. The thing is, and I think you'll probably be the first to agree, which is a relief, I mean, not a relief but you know . . . I mean, scenes like the other night they're just poison and if my mum could see how it turned out, well, she'd –'

'Dave?'

'Sorry, yeah, I know I talk about her too much and you know that's part of it because I didn't really have time to think about everything back then, you know? When Mum was getting sicker, and . . . anyway, I think we both know now that –'

'Dave?' She put her hand on his arm. 'Dave. I did a test.'

Her fingers circled his wrist. He fought the urge to shake it off. 'A test?'

'I was late, so I did a test.' She was speaking slowly and carefully, fuck it, she was smiling, he was meant to be happy.

He slumped back, nodded. 'Right then.'

'And I was worried cause you know we like a drink but even the doc, lovely Indian woman she is, so graceful, lovely jewellery, well, she said in the first few months it hardly matters. In moderation.' She gave a little warble of a laugh, clasping her fists to her chest. 'Dave, are you listening?'

'So the other night? Deano?'

'Forget that, we were just pissed. Come on, it was a stupid row. We're not the first husband and wife to have those. Isn't this amazing? Out of the blue after all this time, you're going to be a dad! I'm finally going to be a mum.'

'No, I can't believe it.' He forced himself to look at her, smiling at him, tears in her eyes and he saw his mum willing his dad to want him before he walked out on them both. 'I mean . . . yes, Shell, it's unbelievable. You'll be such a good mum; the best.'

His own fingers circled her wrist now and he felt the skin and bone of the mother of his child and tried to remember if he had ever loved her. She stood up, suddenly full of beans.

'Let's have a drink, eh? Celebrate. One won't do any harm. How do you feel? A shock, isn't it? I was shocked, I mean thrilled, but still, it's a shock.' She walked towards the kitchen rubbing her flat stomach. 'And well, I was frantic when I couldn't reach you to tell you but Daphne from two doors down, she was the one who said, just leave him, he'll come back in time. A good lad like Dave, he'll always be back, he's responsible. So, how do you feel?'

He wanted to answer but his tongue was dead in his mouth and anyway what would he say? He wanted to be a dad. It felt like he was going to do something amazing, just as amazing as seeing Angkor Wat or bungee jumping in New Zealand, and he was going to do it proper. Something his dad had never bothered trying to do for him. A little bit of his flesh and blood, a little bit of his mum really. He would be the best dad, he wanted to be. And he was smiling when she came through with two tall glasses, the fresh fizz still jumping above the rim. When she smiled back he realised, he did, he wanted this. He would be everything he'd never had and they'd have this beautiful, fresh, new thing to keep them going.

She told him to meet her at the ping-pong table by the playground in Clissold Park and watched the kids wield their bats, leaves swirling around their bright trainers; poor players but enthusiastic as their limbs twitched and they made tennis pro-style grunts.

A small boy, Alena guessed he'd be about six, with a shining blond cap of hair and bright green corduroy trousers, threw himself face down and wailed while the winner, a skinny black girl, danced around the table, bat held aloft in victory. Alena slipped off her shoes and pressed her feet into the ground, enjoying the slightly warm bite of the gritty tarmac on her bare soles. It was getting cooler in the mornings and evenings now, though the hot days had lasted all the way until late September, until Londoners looked at the sky and hoped for raindrops.

But Alena wished she could capture it in a small box and turn her face to it in the darker days to come. Still, she had a bottle of Appletiser in her bag, a pack of KitKats for Dave, they would get an ice cream from the van and she would unfurl the Transformers duvet cover she had found at a car boot sale to use as a picnic blanket. It was warm enough for them to lie in the rose garden until dusk, the newly cut parched grass prickling through the cover, her head on his lap.

She had been safe and loved and happy for six months. She felt cleaner than she ever thought she would. Or, no, clean wasn't the word: cleansed. She'd somehow muffled the other Alena, the one who was dirtier than she could imagine now. The one who curled herself around a toilet on winter nights, warmed her numb hands and face on the hand dryer and whose biggest happiness was a hot shower or a greasy cheeseburger and a cup of tea. She imagined that Alena somewhere dark, enclosed, pushing against soft but immovable walls. Now she stood swapping smiles with the mothers of the ping-pong champions, cheering and clapping her hands for them.

That mother with the glossy blonde hair held back with sunglasses and a stylish white summer dress that you could tell cost a fortune, she would never guess. For all that woman knew Alena was watching her own child. For all that woman knew Alena wasn't so different from her. And here was Dave; Alena saw the woman's glance rest on him and then notice him smiling at Alena, and quickly return her attention to the game.

He looked so strong and young. It seemed to Alena he was looking younger each day. He'd changed from his work clothes into a pair of blue trousers, a white T-shirt that showed how brown and lean he was from those morning runs. He came and put his hands around her waist, his mouth right by her ear so his breath tickled. 'What you laughing about?'

'Is . . . you look younger. You look handsome like pop star.'

She saw he was blushing a little and she was sure she felt her heart pop like a filament in a light bulb from too much heat, imagined her raw heart beating faster and faster until it exploded inside her chest in a shower of glittering confetti at the sight of him. She wouldn't let herself think about their argument yesterday. It had been her fault, she'd got carried away and had accidentally told him the town she had grown up in, the maiden name of her mother, a story about chickens and her drunken father and a feud he had started, and she'd tightened her jaw waiting for his questions. He always kept his promise, he asked nothing, but she couldn't do anything about his listening. He'd looked away, his face darkening, and when he'd turned back it was only to kiss her. To cover her own indiscretion she'd asked him about his mum, knowing he always wanted to talk about her, that it made him happy to be asked; he'd launched right into a story.

'Like I say, Alena, my mum was the best mum in the world. She was so good to me. Right up until the end and even getting me together with Shelley, she meant well, just wanted me to be happy. She was the one organising everything, she wanted everything for me, the perfect wedding.'

'Wedding?'

Then his face had changed, how could he be so careless with his secrets, with her. The wolf sleeping behind her ribs had woken, bared its teeth, had circled, the thought of his marriage, of this Shelley, the flat, all of Hackney. She'd stood up, her body unsure if she wanted to cling to him or sink her teeth into his arm, to hurt him in some fast, painful way. And then they'd screamed at each other so loud the downstairs neighbours knocked on the ceiling.

'I did tell you. Anyway, it was only . . . it was just a mistake –'

'You never tell me! About you and Shelley marrying? You never say!'

'I did, when I first told you about Shelley, about me coming here to Hackney.'

'No, you say was bad relationship and because your mum was sick was hard to tell bad relationship. Bullshit you tell me. And you have divorce and I don't even know!'

He'd let out a breath, turned away from her. She wanted to slap him. Her jealous wolf had threatened to go for his throat and taste blood.

'Means she can come and take you any time.'

When he'd reached for her arm she'd used both her hands to give his shoulder a hard shove away from her. 'Alena? Stop this. Stop being so daft. We broke up, we were never even meant to get married. If it hadn't been for Mum . . . do you know what it's like to see that sort of pain? And I wanted to leave, I almost did, but it was so hard and –'

She'd wondered how he could have kept something like that from her, her see-through David, though of course she knew better than anyone how, and the words were in the air before the new almost-good Alena could swallow them back.

'Always about your sick mama. You are fucking liar.'

His face had paled and she'd enjoyed the brief sweet thrill of hurting him.

'Don't you dare speak about my mum. And you? You telling me that I'm a liar? That's a fucking joke, that is. You just walked in, literally off the street. I didn't know your second name until a month after we'd met. I'd do anything for you but I don't get to know a thing about you. I mean, who are you? Where's your family? Who were your boyfriends?'

'I tell you, I don't say, I never say.'

'Well, have you thought I could find someone else? In fact I might like a girlfriend who tells me stuff? One who doesn't make me beg for a bit of history?'

'I don't say because I can't.'

'How do I know you're not the one who's married? That this isn't just some massive scam and you'll sit here and listen to me talk about my mum, her dying, how awful it was and with Shelley, and you let me spill my guts and give me nothing back. Maybe this was never going to work. Maybe I've been fooling myself about this whole thing. I'm sick of it.'

He'd sat on the bottom of the bed and she had crawled towards his back, wrapped her legs around his waist, buried her face in his neck.

'Please, David. My boyfriends were monsters and my mother is somewhere I can't go to her. Please, don't ask me anything. I love you.'

'You love me?'

'I do. I love you so much, David. Please, I –'

She hadn't been able to finish because the words were choking her and, because he didn't want her to cry any more, he had simply let her lean on him, cry her tears.

'I love you too, Lena. I love you so much sometimes I think it will kill me.'

But that argument was yesterday. Today it was all forgotten and now he was standing in front of her, shading the sun from his eyes in the park. He gave her the shoebox, a gift for her, took her by the waist and they held each other as the children chanted and the ball made gentle protests as it bounced against the table. They had known each other for six months, they were in love, and when they kissed, it was as though they had no secrets at all.

She had money. The thick wad of notes she been given to impress the girls, to show them she wasn't a con artist after their purses or luggage; the same money that had bought her and Fedir's endless cups of coffee, crumbling stale muffins that stuck to the roof of her mouth, her silly romance novels and boxes and tubes of smelly things from Boots. Each morning Andriy would slide more notes across the table to her, sometimes demanding a kiss in return, though not so much in those last days. Money hadn't mattered at all and though she'd thought about hiding some somewhere she'd always worried about being caught, told herself she would start the next day. And now that money, plus the money Fedir had left in the car, about £160, was all she had in the world. She would stay in a hotel with a fake name. Then she would leave London, go somewhere far beyond Andriy's reach. She knew that the cheapest hotels clustered around train stations, and Paddington was the nearest, but far enough from Clapham to buy her some time at least.

One of the girls had given her the name of a hotel, she couldn't remember what she was called, only remembered the scabbed-up pimple on the girl's chin, how her jeans had been an inch or two too short. The girl had said the hotel was one of the cheapest in London as though that were a mark of excellence. Alena part walked, part ran down the biggest street, feeling as though the sound of her heels clicking could be the sound of death itself, ignoring the strange looks she drew. She spotted a large grey office block with a laminate printout calling it the Britannia Hotel. At the reception desk was a short, overweight, bearded man with an accent she couldn't place, somewhere in the Balkans she thought.

'Passport.'

'It was stolen. I don't have.' She put £60 on the counter instead.

He sighed, looked away and then at her tiny handbag and her panicked face, full of trouble, and shook his head, raised his arms in the air as though to say 'rules are rules'.

'No passport, no check-in.'

She was exhausted, she put the notes back into her pocket, sat on the steps outside, next to two young girls smoking, laid her face in her lap and wept.

'Come on.'

The receptionist angled his body to shelter her from the girls who were averting their eyes, blowing long 'women of the world' plumes of smoke into the air, as though Alena was an embarrassment.

'Hey, hey, hey, you've got to stop.' He sighed, tucked his stained shirt more tightly into his waistband. 'Come on.'

Alena was just about to tell him that he could take his 'come on', wrap it twice around his scrotum and then swallow the whole thing down with a coating of honey, when he gave her a piece of paper with an address. His voice was lower now and she thought she saw something else, a dark memory of his own perhaps, dancing across his plump features.

'Listen, it's not the best place but it costs almost nothing and it'll do for a night until you can get to an embassy. They'll help you out. It's just three streets.' He motioned to touch her shoulder and then retreated. 'They don't need passports.'

Alena stood and left without looking back or saying thank you, afraid that even wasting a minute might be the thing that got her caught, killed or worse, and so she didn't hear him say, 'Hey, look after your stuff though.' But it wouldn't have been any different if she had. Her, in a nice red coat with her smart high heels, her pale, expensively shiny blonde hair; she had no place there, among those women. A metal-shuttered building, smelling of bleach, with childish, upsetting paintings on the wall. And the women, even the young ones, with lumpy bodies, limp hair, greying teeth, that calculating, fearful look she would come to know well. She had no place there with them.

That night she'd gone to bed as early as was allowed, fully clothed in her bunk bed; not trusting the lockers, she clutched her bag, swearing she would rest her body but wouldn't sleep. But in the morning her handbag had gone and she wondered how she'd slept while it had been wrenched from under her pillow, imagined someone lifting her sleeping head gently with both hands. All she had in the world were the three twenty-pound notes she'd hurriedly stuffed into her pocket back at the hotel, the clothes she'd slept in and no chance of escape after all.

'My bag has been stolen.'

The woman on the day desk had a face glowing with health. Creamy skin, clear, bright brown eyes, a thick ponytail pooling as she bent over a tattered *Metro* newspaper. She looked like she'd only ever done good all her life, drunk hot milk and honey and walked along the coast every morning to catch the roses in her cheeks, and Alena felt suddenly ashamed about bringing trouble to her.

She put a hand on the desk so the girl might see her still nicely manicured nails, the sleeve of her expensive coat bought just a week ago on a shopping trip with Fedir to Harvey Nichols.

'Excuse me, I'm sorry, but my bag. It has been stolen.'

The girl looked up, she had a smudge of biro under her chin. Alena searched for the flicker of irritation on her features but she saw only a quickly smothered spark of surprise, perhaps that Alena should be at the shelter in the first place.

'That's awful. I'm so sorry. OK.' She pulled a battered red notebook out onto the desk and flipped to a free page at the end of it. 'I'll put it in the book. We don't call the police unless you ask us?'

At the words 'police', panic tightened up Alena's throat clearly enough for the girl to nod her understanding. 'You lose much?'

'Everything I had, except a few notes I had in pocket.'

She looked up from the book. 'I really am so sorry, but look, we've got some spare clothes in the back and I'll speak to the duty manager. We'll work something out so you can stay a few extra nights at least, OK?'

And Alena nodded and gulped back her tears and thought that perhaps this girl really had known nothing but warmth and comfort all her life and so it just flowed out of her. And then she thought, if what we had been through was what we were made of, then she was black, rotten; filthy, right to the core.

As they filled in the red book, Alena saw the entry before was for the theft of a 'Mars bar and *Woman's Own* magazine'. The girl, Helena was her name, had got them to let her stay on a few nights, so Alena said she didn't feel well, pushed her three twenties into the sweaty cup of her bra and went back to bed. She turned to the wall, bunched the thick, stinking blankets around her shoulders and closed her eyes to it all.

When she woke it was the middle of the night, a lamp in the corner casting shadows across the room, outlining humps of women in their own bunks. She lay listening to them breathe; one had a snore that was part gentle whistle, another woman let out a slow, relaxed fart in her sleep and, despite herself, Alena almost giggled. She ran her palm down her body, her clothes damp from being slept in all day, felt the softness of her breasts and jut of hip bones and pelvis. Her body, safe here, no one would come tonight to take her. The sweetness of realising this stole in through her nostrils and settled behind her throat. She could be free, in her way. At least for tonight.

Over the coming days she thought about all the movies she'd ever watched with Mikhail where someone is on the run, has to survive with nothing, how there was always a happy ending with the silhouette of the hero backed by bright sunshine as they walked towards the horizon. She tried to turn it into a game for herself, though there was no game about the way her hands shook or her spine jolted at the idea of leaving the shelter. She had raided the clothes box now, had found herself a large grey cardigan and a man's polo shirt to wear with her own dirty jeans. She left her own jumper and her coat behind the counter with Helena and walked round the corner to Boots. She walked with her head down, her heart howling with fear, her steps awkward – feet either too fast or too slow, so anxious she drew glances from passers-by that made her hands flutter up to the back of her head.

In ten minutes she was back at the shelter where Marina,

newly down from Dundee, who said she used to be a hairdresser, left her with a ring of red hair dye all round her forehead and a short jagged cut that looked like it had been done with nail scissors over a sink – because it had been.

The sun scorched the back of her exposed neck though it wasn't yet noon. Alena stood in the shade, under an awning, behind sunglasses that revealed nothing but her small mouth and the bloom of her hot cheeks, self-conscious in her yellow sundress, its shoulder straps too tight, the over-big waist tied with a red scarf. Still, it was amazing what you could find, borrow, beg. That you could look almost clean and decent after curling up for the night on a toilet floor.

She heard the uneven clatter of Marina's heels before she turned her head. Of course Alena knew the shoes well: red patent leather, a little scuffed in places now, the line of gold spikes that ran down the back of the stiletto heel had left marks on her stomach when one of them had almost slipped out from under her coat. They had left marks on many others since that day, she was sure, but that was between those men, Marina and their wallets.

Marina had come a long way, at least compared to Alena, since the Teenage Mutant Hero Turtle sweatshirt and stained Kappa hoodie she'd worn a few months ago in the shelter, though even then she'd worn a perfect mask of make-up covering the grime, and she was so beautiful it was only when she smiled and you saw she was missing two top teeth that you'd see that face did belong to those ragged clothes.

'You're late. I say to you –'

Marina waved a hand in Alena's face. 'Shush, will you? I've a right head on me.'

She still had her Dundee accent, though she once got Alena to try to teach her the sound of a Russian one and occasionally put on a gentrified voice that made her mouth move too precisely and gave her the impression of lip-syncing.

Alena never wanted to meet in Soho but Marina, for everything else, worked her arse off, quite literally she would add, and never had much time. So whenever Marina managed to get a message to Alena at the shelter, where she still stayed when she could afford to, the plan was always Soho. Alena was changed too, with her short chin-length red hair, the ugly clothes, the vulnerable slouch in her shoulders. She'd repeated as she walked there, 'No one would ever know it was me, no one.' It wasn't that she wouldn't refuse Marina, she'd refuse her a lot, but she couldn't refuse the cash or the free breakfast. Or the company.

They sat on one of the tiny circular pavement tables. 'Full English please. Toast, extra beans and mushrooms, tea. And strawberry – no, raspberry jam.'

Alena rattled off the order she had rehearsed in her mind on the long, sweaty walk from Paddington, the sun reproachfully beating down on her head, so risky, it seemed to say, so very risky. Every week she had planned to hitchhike out of the city and each week she had delayed it. She had learned London, or at least her version of it, she knew the streets, which cafes threw out leftovers, free places to go, the safest places to sleep. She was managing, just, and safe, just about, and she had no idea whether another city would be as kind. Still, it was a risk. But the waiter in his striped waistcoat smiled at her, the food smelt good and she was sitting opposite Marina, her not-quite friend which was the most Alena could have hoped for. Even with the smell of toast floating through the air, reminding her of the house in Clapham, it didn't seem such a risk.

'Eggs Benedict, a double espresso. She'll have one too.'

Alena, who often wondered how Marina, formerly a Sandra, managed to get her Dundee tongue to twist itself around things such as double espressos, shook her head at the waiter. 'No. Tea, please.'

Marina lit a cigarette and slid the packet across the table. 'Take a few, they'll come in handy.' Alena blushed but she took them anyway; they were good to trade. Marina had gouges of blusher in her cheeks, and a thumbprint just below the tidemark of her foundation.

'For God's sake, love, take off your glasses. You're no' Nicole Kidman.'

Alena lifted her fingers to her glasses. 'I like to keep them on.' But it was a game and Alena knew it was too late.

'Ah, come on. I look shite, you look shite, what's the big deal, eh? We'll have fried egg down our chins in a minute.'

And Alena laughed, took off the glasses and hung them from the front of her dress. They met each other's eye and they were those two girls back at the shelter again, scraping together enough for some sort of dinner and making big, empty plans. Alena looked at the torn magazine picture: high-heeled silver brogues.

'Really, you want a heel this high? For standing all night?'

'Aye. You think I should wear trainers? Maybe some shin pads an' all? Just get me them an' I'll give you the cash. Here's a bit now tae keep yeh going.'

She threw a twenty-pound note on the table, stubbed out her cigarette and looked at Alena staring at the picture. 'Unless you're not up to it? Fancy shop like that?'

Alena folded the paper in three sharp creases and tucked it behind her bra strap.

'It's hard. But I can do it. You are rich now, why not just buy?'

'Rich my arse! I'm no well off enough for them places after Shaun's cut. And since you won't take any money, or earn yourself . . . well, this way we both get something we need.'

Alena brought her hand to her neck, where the heat had risen. 'But I worry, Marina, customer –'

'Client!'

'I'm apologising – client goes bad and you won't run in these shoes.'

'Well, a girl's got to suffer for beauty, love, worst comes to worst that's a bloody sharp heel. 'Sides, the whole point is that my clients are bad . . . they're bad, bad boys.'

Alena laughed, shook her head. They ate breakfast and when it was time to leave they didn't hug but Marina twisted to watch Alena's back push her way through the busy Soho streets towards the expensive Bond Street department store.

She had to go back to the cafe twice that week, and get one of the younger boys to cover her afternoon round. Finally, amazingly, there was Marina, smoking at a table outside her cafe, upending the sugar shaker into the tiny cup in front of her. She was wearing a black PVC mac and the sort of sunglasses she had once chastised Alena for wearing. There was something about the set of her mouth that made Alena want to turn back, but she didn't. Marina, whatever she reminded Alena of, was the only person who properly knew her. A not-quite friend, but the giver of money that once kept her from harm, the person who had bought her a hot meal and who gave company when she thought she might go mad if another person didn't say her name.

As she approached, Alena saw Marina's legs, bare and mottled with bruises. She wore cheap plastic platforms and you could see, even from a few steps away, her toenails were filthy. Alena stood in front of her, hands in the pockets of her jeans, smiling into the blank of the sunglasses. When Marina finally smiled her never good teeth were greyer still, with a gap now in the bottom too, the lips withered around them. 'Fuck me! Alena? Well, fucking hell. Sit down.'

Her voice was deep, slow, snarky, and Alena sat, suddenly shy. No, not shy. Staring at the new gap in her teeth, the greasy clumped strands of her friend's hair; she was repulsed and then ashamed of herself.

'I thought you'd been nicked. Maybe deported. Maybe that thug of an ex of yours had found yeh at last. Though it would've served you right, stickin' in London. I would have been out like a shot.'

She moved forward as if to hug Alena, but instead just stared right into her face; she had the sweet, stale smell of a few days without a shower. Alena caught the waiter's eye. 'Cafè latte please?'

Marina sat back heavily. 'Cafè latte, is it, madam? You've certainly not been in the nick.'

'No, I'm sorry. I wanted to come earlier, or sooner, but I have a job now and I'm in Hackney.'

'Hackney, eh?'

Marina's hand shook as she lifted her espresso cup. Alena struggled on.

'Yes, Dalston. Well, between there and Stoke Newington. On the High Street, do you know?'

'No. I don't leave Zone 1, love.'

It was the sort of thing that would have made them laugh before, but there was something behind it.

'So how are you? Things . . .'

Marina shrugged, picked at a scabbed-up scratch on her bony chest. 'Och, yeh know, up an' down. I lost a few clients but I'll get some more.' She stubbed her cigarette out in a long streak against the glass ashtray. 'I'd better anyhow. An' you, Miss Smiles, what's the deal?'

'I meet someone. A nice man.' She reached across the table, had misread Marina's hurried nodding for eagerness.

'Got yourself a pimp, lovie?' Marina spat the words but she sounded so tired that they landed between them, reeking of something foul.

Her coffee arrived, she took a sip and scalded her mouth but pushed forward. 'What? No. He has no money really. I do paper round. I love him. I fall in love.'

There was a quiet pleading in her voice that made Alena want to bite her own tongue. Marina pulled off her glasses. 'Ohh I love him! You've a paper round?'

Her voice strained to mimic Alena's, but it was forced, she couldn't quite get the wind up in spite of her anger.

'Why are you being like this? Are you OK?'

Marina looked over the street towards a group of Japanese tourists snapping away at a sex-shop window. She gulped down the last of her espresso.

'Aye, fine. Listen, I'm chuffed for yeh. It's good yeh've a fella. What sort am I to be begrudging you a wee happy ending?'

'I can help you. I want to. You could stop being prostitute and –'

Alena reached across to Marina but was met with the batting of Marina's long, dirty nails against her wrist, her raised voice. 'Look at you, Miss High an' Mighty. Think yeh can judge me, eh? You owe me money.'

'Yes, that's why –'

Marina was up now, forcing herself across the table towards her. 'I gave you twenty to nick them shoes for me an' I never got them. Gi' me it.'

Alena sat back for a moment. She had the money. Knew she owed it, was proud to be able to give it.

Marina jabbed her shoulder. 'You've no idea the things I've tae do fer twenty pound. No idea.'

Alena took the notes and slammed them on the table. 'I have idea. I know very well.'

And then, heart pounding, she reached into her purse for coins to pay for her coffee. Marina had taken the notes and sat back, was trying to light a cigarette but shaking so badly that the lighter made two attempts before the tip burned orange. Alena finally found the coins and threw them on the table.

'What you are is not my fault. Is not my fault.'

She turned and pushed through the tourists, leering into windows, pointing to the neon 'peep show' signs, but even as she repeated it wasn't her fault over and over she saw the faces of girls who had trusted her and realised it was, it was all her fault.

7

After that, there was no peace. Not in long walks against the strong, gritty wind that blew through London and cooled a city on the brink. Not in Dave's arms or a full belly, or her music. She had felt guilty before, of course she had, but she had told herself over and over it wasn't her fault. Tricked. Forced. Abused. And when she had escaped, no, had been allowed to walk away, she had just wanted to survive. Every day became all about staying safe, about how to live and not hurt anyone, including herself.

She had allowed herself to take comfort in what had been done to her, what she had been made to do. Until now. Now, there could be no peace. Marina's furious, filthy fingernails, that smell that said she had given up and the sneaky whisper of a black eye, they all stayed with her, as though Marina was made up of all the other girls.

Away from Clapham, Soho and that cold toilet cubicle, Alena had wrapped herself in Dave, her job, in the people and sounds and smells of Hackney. She had hidden in a happiness she didn't deserve and now when she walked from door to door she wasn't pulling the trolley of newspapers behind her, she pulled all those girls. They dug nails into her flesh, bit her ankles, clawed at her hair to keep her back as she tried to walk her route. She smelt their cheap body spray covering the smell of unwanted men, heard their voices with that childish inflection and imagined, each day when she woke, the life being fucked out of the chubby hopeful faces she had betrayed.

The day she thought she saw the shape of Fedir hunched

in a doorway in his jogging bottoms, his face in the shadow but his hand holding a cigarette in that particular way he had, between forefinger and thumb, she left her trolley in the street and ran home. That evening, she lay on the shower floor, scalding water pouring down, and sobbed until she was dizzy and her eyelids were swollen half closed. When she came out Dave was sitting in the hallway outside the bathroom door; worried, pale and confused. He reached out to her and she went; he held her, he asked nothing but there was no safety there for Alena any more.

'I don't deserve.'

She repeated it until she felt his tears hit her face. Full of shame, she said nothing at all.

'I ask for more jobs but he says I don't need so much work. Is not his fault, Mr Scannell is nice man. His wife is not nice though. I think she hates me a little bit. Bitch. One day I don't need that job and I go back and I say to her –'

'Lena? What's got into you? She's an old woman. Why'd you need more work?'

'To earn some more money.'

'But we're doing fine, you'll exhaust yourself. What do you need money for?'

He reached across the table and took her hand gently; it was the day after she had locked herself in the bathroom. He thought of her bones as made of a brittle caramel, the kind they make those angel-hair cages from for putting around those fancy little cakes they sold on Bond Street. She pulled back and stuffed both her hands up inside her jumper. Instinctively he thought about the pale, smooth skin her palms would be touching.

'I, I say to you already, I can't explain.'

'Well, you know you don't have to do the job. If your boss,

or anyone, if they're giving you hassle, don't bother, we don't need it. Not really. We'd manage.'

'I need it, I like the money and things to do. I just wanted to have a bit more for . . .' She gave a little exasperated sound. 'I say I don't want to talk about it. He's not trouble, he gives me sweets still. He likes me. Is just no extra work right now.'

'Alright, well, you know you don't have to worry, that I'll look after you? Always.'

She shrugged, released her arms to push aside the chicken kofte that he'd brought home as a treat and looked out onto the top deck of the number 76 bus.

'We should shut the blinds. Everyone can see.'

'No, look, I've been on that before. It goes too fast. I've checked myself.'

She shrugged again.

'Here, look, I got you something.'

He tipped back in his chair and picked up a shiny red bag. She took it in her hands, her face blank, maybe a bit annoyed, and pulled out the box. In it was a little chocolate sausage dog. It had white chocolate spots and along its long body he'd got them to pipe 'Alena' in pink icing.

'What kind is this?' She turned it around in her hands, inspecting it. Still no smile.

'It's chocolate of course. Lena, you sure you're feeling OK?'

'I mean the dog. The name of it.'

'Dachshund – sausage dog my mum always called them.'

Then a softening, he saw her shoulder drop a little; she waggled it in front of her face but as she spoke he thought she would cry.

'Woof, woof. Is lovely. Very expensive though. I see this shop before when I come to meet you.'

'They gave me mates' rates. I . . . I wanted you to feel better.'

She gave a slow, ashen nod. 'I like dogs, you know. Not little white snappy dogs with brown tears leaking onto their fur; real ones. Big ones.'

She kept staring at the dog. He knew he was losing her. Yesterday, when he'd come home and heard her crying in the shower, when she wouldn't let him in to calm her like the other times, he'd known it was the beginning of losing her. And now, she kept looking at him like he was a mistake, a spill on the carpet or something she'd bought in the sales that she wanted to push to the back of the wardrobe. He felt winded. The present was stupid but he'd thought she'd love it. His old Alena would have.

'Sorry, Alena. Look, it's a daft present. I should have bought you flowers or a pair of earrings or . . . I just –'

'No, is good present. Thank you.' She began ripping at the plastic box with her teeth. 'I like it. I'll eat it now. Do you want some . . . ?' and then she lowered her hands heavily to the table, as though the sudden activity had exhausted her. 'I just feel . . .'

They both waited, eyes on the chocolate dog, the uneaten kebab; he saw the anxious twitch of her fingers on her wrist, knowing she had to give him something.

'Blue.'

'You feel blue, like sad?'

'Like sad but like horrible inside too. Like I shouldn't be with you.'

She was just on the other side of the table but he couldn't touch her, it was as though she was already leaving. Panic rose in his throat as acidic, sudden and unstoppable as vomit.

'Do you want us to break up? Is that it? Because –'

He was afraid to say another word but she saved him, reached across what had felt like the miles of the tabletop and put her hand on his arm. Her palm was cold and wet but it was her skin on his.

'No, please. Please. I mean like I shouldn't . . . like I am not good enough. I am just feeling bad. I promise. I will get better, I'll be better.'

'No, you're perfect. You're better than good enough, you don't need to change a thing. Jesus, there's not a day goes by when I don't wake up and thank God for having you. It's just that you seem so sad and, well . . .' He would say it, had to, though he felt himself edging over a cliff with no idea how far the drop was. '. . . you don't seem to want me to touch you at the moment. I mean, in bed.'

'So is about sex?' She pulled back. 'You're like all the other men and only think about your fucking dick.'

A sheer drop. He should have fucking known. She had her arms wrapped around herself again, staring with fierce eyes out of the window.

'Listen, no; I love you and part of that is fancying you and so, yeah, I want us to . . . but it's not the be-all and end-all, it's just that I was thinking that maybe you . . . didn't . . .' He looked out the window himself, a man from the tower block opposite was watering his single rose bush on the patch of grass outside his flat, later he'd be out to scatter scraps of bread for the pigeons from a Mothers Pride bag. 'It seems . . . I was thinking maybe you don't fancy me any more.'

He looked back and her face was gentle again, her eyes heavy with tears and, his heart thumped, she was shaking her head. 'No, no. Is . . . no.'

'No? No you don't then?'

He had to get out of there. He really was losing her. He didn't even know what he'd done, if it was about him, or he'd stopped being useful or maybe she saw that his life was too small. He pushed back his chair but his legs stayed still and then she was there, pushing her whole body against his, putting her cold hands to his face, on his shoulders, pulling him into her.

'No, no, I love you. I don't want you to go. I want to stay. Is just me, I'm blue. But I'll be better. Please, I love you, I do.'

As though the pieces of his body had flown back together, glued by her words, he was able to hold her, sit down again, pull her onto his lap. Arms circling each other he fed her the little chocolate dog. She bit the head off first and whispered, 'Now is just a sausage. No more dog.'

He laughed quietly, though he hadn't known he had a laugh in him, and held onto her. He'd just keep holding on until she came back.

Dave had taught her the phrase: London is your Oyster. After all those months of walking from Paddington to the Southbank Centre, where sometimes she could find a warm sofa in a quiet corner and close her eyes, or see a band for free in the ballroom and then walk along to Tate Modern where, one month, she had spent hours sitting under the huge, orange, artificial sun in the entrance hall. After all those months, she still enjoyed bleeping her card against the yellow circle.

She gave the bus driver a wide smile and a thank-you, and though he just stared straight ahead he nodded, which was more than they usually did. She didn't mind, it must be a horrible job, not like at home where they could decorate their bus, play their own music, had company in the money collector and snacks in easy reach.

She made her way past the squeeze of buggies and shopping bags and sat opposite a woman and her boy, knocking knees with them as she pushed herself along the rough material of the seat.

'Sorry, sorry.'

She was surprising Dave: a picnic, though it was almost too cold for one. She was bad, she was a bad girlfriend, but there was nothing she could do about it but try to be good. Be kind, smile, be polite, work hard, be sweet to him. She tasted blood and realised she had a healthy chunk of cuticle between her teeth. She would stop that too. She felt heavy, her arms and legs were tired, but it wasn't just that, everything seemed spoilt – like food that tastes delicious but you know will give you a stomach ache.

At night now, instead of spooning David's body under the duvet and reading one of her books, about shoes and chocolate and kissing, she had started to try and write things down. Dave looked over at the Cyrillic and would make a noise through his nose and rustle his paper impatiently beside her. Then she would turn and cradle the side of his head, his hot, soft ear in the palm of her hand.

'What?'

'Just that pad and paper and you slamming it shut every time I look over even though you know I can't read a word.'

'Is not secret. Well, it is, but is journal, is supposed to be secret.'

She couldn't bring herself to write the words though. She wrote the food they ate that day (toast, blackcurrant jam, Crunchie, fish fingers and tinned potatoes, spaghetti bolognese – David cooked – strawberry ice cream), she wrote what she watched on TV (*Doctors*, *Murder She Wrote*, *Home and Away*, *Hollyoaks*, *EastEnders*, half of *Crimewatch*, then I make him turn off) and what she did (morning shift, Tesco's, nothing), but she could not, even writing in her mother tongue, bring herself to write about the girls' faces flicking through her mind. It didn't make sense that not so long ago she was happy, not happy all the time but OK, and now she never could be. And Marina, she thought about her too, wondered if things were getting worse for her somewhere. The thoughts circled her mind like rats with their tails tangled until she felt eaten half alive. She wanted David but she couldn't reach out to him. Until one night when she realised that she was punishing him more than herself and he didn't deserve it.

So, no matter how little she wanted to be touched, how much it hurt to smile, to laugh and make jokes, she did it. She thought of how he'd taken her in and cared for her. She couldn't stop punishing herself but she wouldn't punish him too. And she couldn't leave. Because that would kill her and she had done so much just to survive. Alena swallowed her thoughts and looked out as London streaked past like a film set.

'Love, love?'

Alena looked up at the woman opposite.

'You're . . .' She nodded her head downwards. There was a bead of deep red liquid snaking down Alena's goose-pimpled leg. The woman had dusty-looking hair, thick mascara, a face that was too tired to be shocked but she stared nonetheless. Her boy looked over and then back at his mobile phone, his thumbs moving in a blur across the screen, the music on the headphones giving off a louder whym, whym, whym. Alena lifted her plastic bag.

'Ach! Is beetroot salad.'

'Oh, I thought . . .'

Alena shook her head, made a face. 'No. Is salad!'

The woman reached into her bag stuffed full with brown envelopes and bottles of tablets with peeling labels and, before Alena could protest, took out a stringy tissue and wiped the trickle away in a single strong swift motion, leaving not so much as a smear. She smiled at Alena, and in those well-worn creases Alena thought she saw all of the woman's life, then a weary wink before putting the beetroot-stained tissue in her bag again.

Alena smiled back and wondered why such a thing would make her eyes hurt. Her mother was why. She wouldn't let herself think about the unanswered postcards, the first sent days after she was let go and one a week since. She wouldn't think about the way her mother had seemed to be struggling the last year they were together, that she seemed to be crumbling away. Alena had thought it was money problems which, of course, she'd done nothing to ease despite the promises of being able to send money home from her new life. Perhaps she didn't want to reply, perhaps the postcards never reached her. She squeezed past the woman and boy again at the next stop and walked the rest of the way to David's shop. Three stops early, enough time to cry it all out and be smiling when she met him. She was being good, learning to be better for him even if she felt like shaving her own skin off.

No, no, no – even as the word ricocheted around inside her head her face was pulling itself into a hard smile. She was suddenly aware of the taste of coffee still on her tongue, how her limbs hung, the faraway noise of the buses and cars just outside the block and the chill of the hallway stairs goose-pimpling her arms.

She wanted to run back into the flat, to lock the door behind her. But then she'd be trapped and Dave would come home eventually and . . . instead she forced herself to stay focused on his face, those eyes too much to look at full glare. Alena looked at his hairline instead, his thick dark hair had started thinning even in this last year.

She had the thought, and it almost had her gurgling out a laugh, that perhaps he was just a trick of folded paper or light and shadow. The power of this thought moved her hand to him, to the arms which had once enclosed her, pressed her into another girl's mattress, that girl who wasn't this Alena, arms that had once led her through stations and airports, had beaten her and freed her. He grabbed her, and though she tried to pull away he held tight, and she worried about the bruises he would leave and how she would explain them.

In the second that followed her mind was a kaleidoscope, her thoughts the rattling pieces of its constantly changing picture. She realised she could scream out to the thick-armed kebab-meat-slicing brothers, but what could she say and why would they believe her? If she ran he would only come back. He knew where she lived. Which meant he knew where Dave lived. He looked desperate, so maybe nothing she did would matter. The final thought, as clear and cutting as a shard of glass, was that she had fooled him once and she could fool him again.

She kept her panicked eyes on him, his wide, cruel smile, she had no option but to keep her hand on his arm as he waited, with those burning eyes, for her to say the first word. The words were rolling in her mouth as she thought of Dave, of the way his mouth lay slightly open when he slept and the way he kissed her under her chin each morning, and she forced them out, gambled.

'Fedir. I cannot believe. Is so good to see you.'

His hand relaxed, then tightened again, and while his face grinned there was something there that scorched panic down her spine. He held his arms open now, that same expression on his face, and she was forced to take two steps towards his body, which smelt just as it always did of his father's cologne, cigarettes, his leather jacket. He pulled her into him, closed his arms around her, squeezed her face into his chest, pushed the breath from under her lungs. Still she kept the smile fixed on her face.

'Thank God I've found you. You disappear but I find you!'

He held her that way, her arms slack at her sides, until she thought her chest might explode from refusing to inhale his smell, his body. Then he pushed her back, hands tight on her shoulders, and kissed her on the mouth, a dry, violent, near-bite, a kiss that hurt her lips. 'Alena.'

'Fedir.' Her throat was so tight it almost whistled.

The smile dropped a moment. 'Your hair?'

She reached up to the red he had once known as blonde.

'I don't like it. I'll come in, yes? Is your apartment.'

She shook her head, forced herself to smile and would not look back at her front door.

'Why do you say this?'

'Is not mine, is . . . friend. I visit friend.'

He looked away and spat sharply onto the roughly carpeted steps; except for his thinning hair he almost looked younger than before, something to do with those eyes. Maybe he was thinner in the face. When he looked up his fake smile was gone and he grabbed her arm again, twisting the soft skin.

'Alena, why will you lie?'

Like an electric current through her body she realised her mistake and gasped for breath.

'I just stay here for a little while. A few days, a week. A visit, you know?'

He took her wrist and twisted it until she felt the spark of pain in the elbow joint, pushed her towards the flat door and stood while she unlocked it. Her hand was surprisingly steady. Nothing about the flat seemed real to her now he was there in it. He didn't look around but gave her wrist a sharp jerk once they were inside. She led him to the living room, worried he would mark her.

She was concentrating so hard on her legs and them not falling from under her, on making sure her feet made it to the living room, away from the bedroom with its double bed and still-rumpled sheets, the imagined smell of her and Dave, that she forgot to keep the sickening smile on her face. Then she would focus on keeping her face right, and she would stumble.

He sat on the sofa with his knees wide and took a half-bottle of vodka from inside his jacket. Alena had a woozy suspicion that this was a game. It was too unreal, as though a character from TV had suddenly appeared at her door. He looked strange, sitting there, waiting. He reached out to her, standing a few steps away, and gave her a tug that sent a jolt of pain up her arm and into the shoulder socket – 'Come on' – dragging her towards him just as he had over a year ago.

'No!'

It was a dry whisper of a word but she could have bitten her tongue for saying it. He knew where she lived. He was in her and Dave's home. Everything was going to end. The only important thing was protecting David and then, if she could, herself. Do nothing.

'You think I've come to take you back?'

She said nothing, looked him straight in the face. Do nothing. He made a sound from the back of his throat and looked towards the window.

'Get glasses then, stupid girl.'

At the kitchen counter, turned away from him, she made calculations. Dave wouldn't finish work until six so he wouldn't be home for three hours. She felt herself unwind a fraction. Fedir could do anything he wanted to her, as long as he was gone by the time Dave came back.

She returned with two odd glasses and a can of Diet Coke. 'In case you want to mix.'

Fedir unscrewed the cap with his teeth, poured them large measures. They sat quietly for a moment and Alena went to pour hers into the mouth of the Coke can, then thought better of it and poured an inch of swirling Coke into the vodka.

'It's too much like chemicals, vodka. How did you get here?'

Keep him talking. Stop it all from happening for a few minutes longer.

He nodded, lifted his drink but then put it down again. 'Tube to Islington and then train, Dalston Kingsland.'

She ignored the part of her which said she should do nothing. 'But I mean here, how did you know to . . .' She bit back the word 'find' just in time and muffled her almost-admission with a gulp of the vodka that burned right down to her stomach. '. . . where to come and get me?'

He shook his head, took a drink. He was older, older than the boy in tracksuit bottoms who loved *Top Gear*, but she was older than the girl who had watched *Friends* with him.

'Before I want to know from you, what happened to the phone I left you? I call, only the next day, and there wasn't nothing.'

'My bag got stolen. In a hostel.'

And this was true, and she'd been grateful for the loss of the phone, and yet here he was.

'So you wanted to find me?' She sucked another mouthful

of vodka through her teeth, felt it balloon in her stomach – she wasn't used to it. 'But I was so frightened Andriy would find me, he would kill me. I didn't know what to do so . . . I tried to forget about all of that before.'

'Did you forget?'

Alena thought of her eyes raw from lack of sleep, of Marina's filthy toenails, the faces of girls that someone was shuffling in her head like a pack of cards, and shook her head. Fedir poured more vodka and Alena sat. She felt calm but of course that was the vodka. She took a gulp, a few bubbles sparkling on her tongue, felt the rest of her numbing. They didn't speak again until they were halfway through the drinks.

'He almost kill me, you know?' He was pushing his finger into a cigarette burn on the arm of the sofa. 'I told him you ran.'

'He beat you?'

Fedir shot his head up, gave her a look. 'Only so much. He knows I could kill him. No, he locked me in my room and . . . there wasn't food. Or drink.'

'I'm sorry.' And for that single second, with her heart pumping acidic vodka, his too bright eyes on her, she meant it.

He shrugged. 'Anyway, was only a few days. I forgive him because now he is sick.'

'Andriy?'

'Yes, he is very sick. The business is stopping, nothing new in or out. And so I can come and find you.' He turned to her then, too close, and she could see his eyes full of water even from the other end of the sofa. She couldn't help it, she moved closer, wanted to comfort him somehow. 'He's in hospital, you see? Pancreatic cancer. Is the worst cancer for pain, you know?'

Still she couldn't bring herself to say anything, could not

allow herself to speak a word of sympathy for Andriy, feared if she opened her mouth it might actually smile.

'You live with a man here?'

Alena moved back abruptly and let out a giggle of nerves. 'What?'

'When I find you, I see.' That word 'find' again. 'I saw him leaving there. Not just today.'

'Yes . . . he . . . I sleep on here.' She hit the sofa cushion, felt blank from the drink, didn't think she could make her legs run anyway and willed herself to think. 'He's . . . a gay, homosexual.'

Fedir picked up a cushion, threw it hard in her face and bellowed, mouth gaping, his tongue bloated in its warm pink cave.

'You live with a batty boy?'

Alena let out another giggle; the man who lived with his pimp father was shocked. 'He is nice.'

Now Fedir was laughing harder, the laugh she remembered from watching *Friends* with him, loudest when the pet monkey was humping people's legs. 'I thought you had boyfriend. I think, if you have boyfriend, I will kill him. Or you, I don't decide yet.' He banged the table with his hand, still laughing hard.

Alena laughed along, shook her head, let her lungs scream for breath. Then the laughter stopped, reduced to the occasional heavy, interrupted breath and shake of the head.

'I want to fuck you, you know? Fuck you and that tight little Russian pussy like before, yes? When you liked it so good.' He reached across and clasped her hair in his fist. 'I don't like this hair on you.'

He pushed his hand down the waistband of her jeans as she wriggled backwards. She couldn't bear it, tasted bile on her tongue, and even as she was trying to escape she was also thinking how easy it would be just to lie back and open her legs to him again.

'Me too. I miss . . . you inside me. A real man. Oh! But I have my time.'

No further advance but no retreat either; he just stared at her with a cheated, furious face as though he would bite her and break the skin out of sheer frustration.

'Time?'

'My period.'

He moved his hands to her sweater and lifted it, pushed his face closer to her breasts. 'I don't mind. I cannot wait. I wait for too long because Miss Stupid lost her mobile. Now I won't –'

Alena lodged a foot on his thigh and pushed him back, just enough, not too much. 'I bleed so much. It hurts.' She kissed his hard resentful mouth. 'I want our first time not in that house to be special.' He shrugged and grabbed at a breast, squeezed it painfully with a petulant hand. 'I'll buy nice, sexy underwear. It will be so good to be with you again.'

He pushed his weight on her, forcing her legs apart anyway, scooped her breasts from the cups of her bra. 'You want to?'

She forced a laugh; her skin was ice cold but he, of course, was not thinking about her. 'Of course I want. You're the best. Soon, very soon.'

He sucked her nipple, and then pressed the full weight of himself against her, his tongue roaming her wide-open mouth, a distraction, as she slowly pulled down her jumper, and closed her legs to him. She got down on her knees, undid his belt and he twisted her hair in his fists. It was a delay not an escape, her time would come. Fedir was not a man who asked, and when he took, he took everything. When she was done, he buckled himself, swallowed the last of his and then her drink.

'I have to go to hospital for visiting. I'll see you tomorrow. I'll come to you after morning visit.'

'When? I mean, what time? . . . I like to cook you food.'

'Twelve sometime. Don't go anywhere. I can still get you or your –' he gave a short, mirthless laugh – 'batty boy!'

He took her hands in his and pressed his mouth, still damp with saliva from his gasping orgasm, to Alena's, his tongue slipping across her closed lips. She held the gag reflex until the door slammed and then she ran to the toilet and vomited.

She had to get out of that flat and once she was outside she could barely believe that there was still a bruised grey cloud not quite obscuring the sun above them, that the golden light was still brushing buildings and paving slabs. That the world outside was insolently unchanged.

In the space of an hour everything might as well have vanished. As she started walking, she couldn't think of anything beyond the primary-coloured tanks of prams rolling up the street, the mums in skinny jeans with lattes in their free hands, a pit bull staring mournfully at its owner and a young girl with a high ponytail and Puffa jacket shouting loudly into her phone, 'Oh my days! Fried chicken.' There was the painting of the owl on a brick wall that had made her want to save for a second-hand camera.

Before Fedir had come back she had felt part of this, a strange, wiry thread sewn through these pieces, delivering her news and smiles, a circle of stitches that led back to David, their home, their shared breath in the morning and each day beginning in safety and, at least until Marina, with happiness during those first blurry-eyed morning moments of realising he was next to her.

Now they were just lumps, these things and people, and she

was outcast, an exile, her mouth stinging from vodka-laced vomit, her throat aching from uncried tears and her heart racing in frustration. She needed to think, to make a plan and save everything, or, if she couldn't save everything, to save Dave.

Slack-shouldered in the doorway of a pub, she remembered his kiss and wiped her fingertips hard against her lips, then scratched across them with her fingernails dragging at the dry skin. She kept staring at the street until something, a grasping hand in the pit of her stomach, got her onto a 73 bus and towards the only thing she wanted: Dave. She stood in the aisle, swinging in time to the curve of the roads, willing her panic to quiet and her mind to work.

8

She couldn't bear to sleep next to David, see him so exposed, and she wouldn't let him make love to her, as though by not sharing herself with both men there wasn't really any betrayal. Instead she sat at the dark living-room window, drank cup after cup of coffee. And when her eyes were so tired that the lights were just long luminous streaks and her heart felt like it was swelling under her ribs, Dave came and carried her back to the room, kissed her lips and watched over her while she fell into a fractured sleep.

She reminded herself she had been through worse and for longer. That she must keep her head down, bide her time. Do nothing to make Dave suspicious or provoke Fedir. She tried to be grateful for small things, like knowing when Fedir would come. Later than eleven, after morning visiting, which meant she got to keep her job too. They had a few hours together, two mercifully quick fucks, before he went back to his father for evening visiting hours. That there had always been a few hours between Dave leaving her, craning his head inside the door for an extra kiss, and Fedir arriving, pushing himself mouth first through the door, his hands following to grab at her.

The first time, she rearranged the rooms, pulled out the sofa bed, brought the duvet through, scattered clothes and towels. She wouldn't allow herself to think about how long she'd be able to keep it all up for. She felt something steely coursing through her, some of the old Alena, she'd done worse, she could do it all again.

At the start, she'd been able to use the excuse of her period for a merciful six days, had conspicuously left her tampon box on top of the toilet. But on the seventh day she had realised he'd take it regardless and she'd lain back on the sofa, held her knees to her chest, the way he liked, and spoke the words he wanted to hear. With each jolt she had prayed Dave would never find out. After that, each afternoon, in the few hours between Fedir leaving and Dave coming home, she could wash and cry, open the windows and put her clothes into the washing machine.

But one day she was still leaning against the just-closed door, still had Fedir's wetness running down her thighs, when she heard Dave's key on the other side of the door.

It was only three steps to the bathroom but she only managed two before Dave was through the door.

'Who was that?'

Without thinking, she bunched the fabric of her skirt in her fists. 'What? Why are you home?'

'Power cut – we all got to go home early. Who was it then? That big bruiser on the stairs. He called me a batty boy. What the fuck? He sounded like one of your lot. Who is he then?'

He took one step forward but stopped a few steps short, as though keeping some distance would help him read her better. Alena was trying to work out if the flat smelt of sex, whether to meet his eyes, to release her hands from her skirt slowly and smile, maybe even squeeze out a laugh.

'Lena? What's going on?'

'Was . . . is just stranger. Looking for a Michael somebody. I send him away.' He was looking too close at her now. Bite before you're bitten: pure instinct. 'Anyway, what is meaning "one of my lot"? He wasn't even Russian. Unless you are jealous? What do you think about me, David?'

He took another step towards her and she took one back, trying to pull an offended face.

'No, Lena, it was just weird, that's all. He was half pissed and he called me that name and –'

She held up her hand in his face. 'What do you think? You think I'm a whore? If I'm near a man I fuck him, yes?'

'Oh my God! No, I don't think that, of course not. I was just wondering . . . I mean, you've been –'

But she could see, his face was soft again. He was sorry, he wanted to make it better. If only he could. Her tears came easily, they were right on schedule after all.

'Leave me alone.'

With that she stepped inside the bathroom and turned the lock. She heard the knocks, Dave's voice on the other side of the door.

'Alena? Lena, look, I'm sorry. This is stupid. Listen, I'm home early, let's just enjoy it. I'll make us dinner, we can go out for a coffee after.'

'Fuck off!' She was taking off all her clothes, turning the shower as hot as it would go.

Of course later she would eat with him. She'd let him think he was making it up to her. The water beat down on her chest and she promised herself and Dave she would make all of this up to him. Somehow she would.

Alena was falling to pieces and Tanya had given him shit all day. She'd spent the time whispering with the other girls and throwing 'what you looking at?' eyes at him until she got his attention, only to turn back to the group, rolling her eyes and proclaiming, 'Christ, he is like, such a stalker.' She'd told the girls he had a peephole to the women's toilets and Yvonne had called him in, told him she knew it was rubbish but that it was the law to speak to him about it. Dave walked down there with her. There was a hole in the ventilation but everyone knew it had been there for ever.

'Not to worry, ducks, we'll just get it taped up and stop those sharp little wagging tongues.'

He'd shaken his head, a lump in his throat. 'Yvonne, after all this time, you believe me, don't you?'

'Course, you're a little lamb, Davey, anyone can see that.'

'Then, I mean, can I file a complaint or something? Against Tanya? I don't want the other girls thinking I'm capable of something like that.'

Yvonne drew herself up, showing a roll of double chin, her lips pursed. 'Dave, why don't you leave well enough alone? Acting like a bully won't help matters. You should've just asked her out when you had the chance.'

'What? It's not like that. I'm the one being . . . well, you know. She just keeps getting at me all the time and she can't just spread lies. I have to work here for God's sake.'

But Yvonne wasn't listening, already bent at a funny angle to pull up her tights, stomach bulging, legs apart.

'Then work.' He could just see her lipsticked mouth under her sweat-darkened armpit. 'You're a big lad, Davey, no need to whinge. Besides –' she straightened, a light sheen of sweat on her upper lip, a little out of breath – 'Tanya's a good little salesgirl. And popular too. You won't win yourself any points by making a hash of this.'

So he finished the shift wondering whether he could go to an agency to get something else. When the bag check came he barely glanced into them. Tanya was last in the queue; she held her bag open, the tip of her tongue tracing the tips of her upper teeth, with a face that suggested she might be holding open something far more explicit than a pink patent clutch bag. The thought flickered – as bitchy as she was, how much easier Tanya would have been than Alena. He'd have known how to handle her; shallow but readable at least, no secrets there. And she was a looker; she knew it and so did he. And as though she read his mind as he put his hand in her bag to inspect it, she snapped it closed on his fingers and winked.

'Careful, Davey boy, mine bites.'

She couldn't, didn't dare, not be at home waiting, she was lucky enough that on weekends it was extended visiting hours and Andriy expected Fedir to stay, but she thought she might crumble under the weight of the lies she was telling, or forget which of her many faces she was meant to be wearing.

Andriy was getting worse not better and that made it easier, because for the first part of the visit Fedir would let her make him tea with a spoonful of jam, answer her questions in a tumbled, angry rush, stumbling over his words as he described the tubes and machines, the awful, excruciating pain. And she could just about find some sympathy, a kind word fuelled by the thought of the old man lying, as Fedir had described, in his own filth for a whole morning, developing oozing sores on his buttocks and the back of his legs. How, in Andriy's worst moments of agony, that thin, wet tongue now hung limp in his mouth, flopping from the side of his lips to be put right by the impatient, rough fingers of one of the 'fat, black bitches of nurses'.

Alena asked and asked, let Fedir tell her every detail, and it was this that enabled her to place a hand on his back, bring him a toilet roll when uncried tears made his nose run like a small boy's. Still, after he'd had the mother treatment, he expected the whore treatment too.

She made the choice at the beginning that it was safer inside than out; at least Dave would not be told about a man pawing at his girlfriend. She knew Fedir had to leave at four thirty to reach the hospital. She did what she could each visit to delay her inevitable fucking: headaches, elaborate lunches, even, the day after a particularly sickening visit, a very long, bad poem she said she'd written for him.

As ever a dumb animal, he was so willing to believe they were a couple, she almost thought she could keep the whole thing up, because she'd beaten him once. But he was a wounded dumb animal now, ready to lash out. He'd flown into a rage a few days before when he realised that it was twenty past four and he'd got no further than sucking a nipple.

'You are frigid bitch, you know? My father is sick and I come here to be with you. From now on, I want your legs wide open from the minute I'm through the door. You know, I take any girl, hundreds, and they lie down and enjoy it. From you I have to beg to suck a skinny little titty. Sometimes I think I'll cut you, you know? Cut your titties, cut your face, when I'm finished with you. Bitch.'

He'd slapped her – she was so grateful the skin was unbroken she barely noticed the burning handprint – then slammed the door as he left. The next day he arrived saying his father was not being moved from intensive care after all, brought a floppy pink bunny with flammable fur. It held an embroidered satin heart that said 'Love is . . .'. She took pleasure in taking a lighter to the rabbit in the park at the bottom of the road after he'd left. She watched the fur melt and the plastic whiskers twist and smoulder in the flame and thought it was worth the risk of neighbours thinking she was weird. And as she watched the flames she began to realise she had no option but to run and to try to carry Dave with her.

He always knew when she'd left the bed; even in his deepest sleep he noticed the loss of the smell of her, of the heat that rose from her body. It was those missing things that he noticed, rather than the creak of the bed or her collection of belts rattling on the door handle.

She'd been doing it a lot lately, sitting cross-legged on the table by the living-room window, the lights off, staring at the road outside, ripping off scraps of skin from around her fingers. The first time he'd approached so quietly, or maybe her thoughts were so noisy, that she hadn't even noticed him in the doorway and he'd had a few precious moments to look at her sitting, wrapped up in herself and his old bathrobe, hands around a mug of coffee, staring into the steady 2 a.m. traffic below, then across at the few lights that remained on in the tower blocks.

Her profile was sharp in a way he'd never noticed and when he couldn't stand to look any more, wanted to reach her, touch her, instead, she turned with a strange expression and the dropped mug splashed coffee up between them. She'd apologised and he'd carried her through to the bedroom, where she'd fallen into a restless sleep and he'd sat and watched over her until his eyes burned, trying, as had become his habit, to populate the suduko puzzle that was Alena – what went where to add up to what?

Tonight, though, he was tired. It had been almost a week and a half and she had stopped bothering to apologise, just stared at him with exhausted, bruised eyes and slid heavily from the table like an angry schoolkid caught smoking. He was shattered, he'd have to face Tanya the next day. He'd been thinking about things too, he'd started depending on this woman. A woman he hardly knew, without a passport or a past, who seemed fuller of holes than ever. He scratched at the bloodied rash that had crept across his wrist in the last few days.

'Alena? Come on.' He turned back towards the bedroom but she caught his wrist. 'Come on. You might want to stay up until it's time for your shift but I'm the one working all bloody day tomorrow.'

'I want to leave, David. I need to go somewhere else.'

He could tell she was serious, deadly, there was no sense in him arguing, but he was knackered and stressed and needed sleep, he couldn't talk about this now.

'What? Why? I'm doing my best for you, aren't I? To make you happy? I don't know what's happening to you but you've got to calm down. You'll feel better when you sleep. At least let me get you something from the chemist's tomorrow to help you do that, something herbal, then everything will seem better.'

'No. I'm not happy. I'll sleep when we're away from here. Please. It doesn't matter where we are.'

'We? So you want us both to just up sticks, take off? Come on, you're not talking sense.'

She'd pulled him to her then, spoke her next words with her mouth buried in his neck.

'Please. Please, David.'

He pulled away, held her at arm's distance, tried to ignore his frayed temper, tried to be patient.

'Maybe this is what you do, but look, you're not feeling well at the moment. You're not thinking right. I'll get you something to help you sleep, we'll talk about this in a few days properly when you're feeling better. Just a few days and then we'll really think about it. OK?'

'No, I need us to leave. Please.' She looked up at him now. 'I go without you if you don't come.'

His patience snapped, a white-hot scorched thing. 'So unless I agree to go, out of the blue with no explanation, you'll leave, will you? Find another fucking mug somewhere else? You know what? Fucking fine then.' He walked back to the bedroom, slammed the door and gathered the lion's share of the duvet around him. A few minutes later he felt the slight pressure of her getting in behind him, her cold, slim hand navigating between the quilt and his stomach.

'I'm sorry. We talk about in few days and I'll try to feel better, David.'

He put his hand on top of her hand curled around his torso.

'If you're really not happy I promise we'll talk about this properly. I promise.'

He wouldn't sleep now and he'd be woolly tomorrow, he'd say something to make himself seem like a twat and somehow Tanya would get wind and there'd be another whole day of her stinging at him like a vicious little mosquito with a taste for south London lads.

Alena was still awake too, he knew. The only sound was his breathing a bit heavier than usual, stoked by fear, maybe some residual temper, but he imagined that he could hear her eyelashes move through the air when she blinked, one of her hands squeeze the other's fingertips as she sometimes did, her tongue root out a raw patch on her gum.

When his mum was sick he imagined the cancer like round green lumps of jelly expanding inside her, latching onto textured bones and ballooning from smooth liver, coloured intestines. That's how he imagined this love, but it was red jelly, and it suckered around his heart, bubbled around his throat, took root in his belly, and as he fell asleep, his breath slowing, hand reaching for hers and pulling up her salty palm to kiss, he felt that red jelly stopping up his gullet but he was too tired to open his mouth.

She knew straight away. His neck all blotched up, the infected look of the whites of his eyes and that sweet petrol smell on his breath that she recognised from her father all too well as the evidence of a long drinking binge. He kissed her and bit her bottom lip, catching the dry skin, and she had to pull away from his hand between the legs of her jeans. She stepped back and he swayed. She gave a jolly-hollow laugh. 'Let's get you some tea! You always did like to drink, Fedir.'

She allowed herself just to get close enough to push him gently towards the sofa and went over to the kitchenette counter on the other side of the room. She stared at the kettle, finally filled it and switched it on. Go slow enough he might just pass out. Then he was beside her.

'He must go in a home.'

The kettle boiled on; during Alena's time in the flat it had never switched off by itself. Steam rose between them but she couldn't take her eyes off him.

'He will go in a home. Hospice they are calling, where people die. He took money for the business and didn't tell me. Sold it I mean, when I am supposed to do his business.' He shouted, then grabbed her chin. 'His son takes the business.' She was already half bent over the counter. 'I need to feel better.'

He moved his hand to the back of her neck and curled his fingers around it. She didn't move. Steam wet her face, she was trying to retreat, as she always did, to a small warm place inside where this wouldn't touch her. But she wasn't sure that place even really existed.

'I want to feel good. You owe me, like always.'

She thought he had said I own you. He slammed her head to the counter though she offered no resistance and held it painfully in place, all of the bones in her face aching, while he fumbled at her jeans with his other hand, pressed her face harder, closer than ever to the still-boiling kettle. It took her a moment to realise that the cold, sharp pain was the little knife, the only one they had, for vegetables, pressing at the soft nape of her neck. She thought she felt the warm trickle of her own blood.

'Fedir!'

'Do it for me.'

Her hands undid her buttons, though it felt like her fingers wouldn't work. She tried to move her head from the knife and he slammed her forehead down again, she felt a red-hot shock through her cheekbone. Except for that first horrific moment, it was fast, not too rough, later she would think he'd done it from pride not pleasure; he talked through it in a rush of words that she couldn't make out beyond the panting, beyond the distortion of snot and tears and grief. She concentrated on the burning of her cheek from the kettle, the part bruise, part burn she'd have to hide from Dave, and the tiny cut on her neck.

He finished, pulled himself from her sloppily and buttoned up. She stayed for a moment with her head on the counter, her cheek numb.

'Make tea, the kettle is dry.'

He went to the toilet and she pulled up her trousers, poured a glass of water and held the lip of the glass to her cheek, letting the cold water sting the rawness. When she turned round he was holding the tickets she'd bought the day before, a too-late delaying tactic. She had no option. They were late but they went up the road and watched *2 Fast 2 Furious* in the beautiful old art deco cinema, with red velvet curtains and seats. The same cinema she'd always wanted to go to with Dave. He held her limp hand in his hot sweaty one and squeezed it during the race scenes. Alena held a cold can of Coke to her cheek and said nothing.

Outside the cinema he kissed her.

'It was a good film. A good date.'

She gave a sharp laugh as he put his hands on her shoulders.

'I don't come for a while, I think. The hospice is in Kent and I have to show business.' It was too light outside and he was more sober now, playing the grown-up. He spoke quietly into her ear. 'But I meant it, I'll never stop. I'll give you more of today. You liked it, yes?'

She felt the fizz of something close to hysteria. He was serious, his eyes focused on her as though they'd just tried a new sexual position. He wanted her to say yes, he believed she would.

'I liked it?'

If he heard the upward slant of a question it didn't show on his face as he walked down towards Dalston Junction, turning once to give a high-handed wave like a mummy's boy off on a school trip and eager for a last glimpse of home.

Alena waited at the end of the street as usual and watched the big-haired, high-heeled girls leave one by one. Where before she saw fawns today she imagined them plump-chested birds, fluttering in groups, tweeting excitedly at the world around them and each other, acrylic fingernails as bright and sharp as feathers cutting at the air for emphasis. Her David, he was so good, decent, so painfully trusting. Save him, hurt herself; hurt herself and hurt him, or kill his hope that someone could love him, that someone thought he was the best person they knew.

Fingers gently pressing at her cheek she watched a tall girl, with a huge black beehive and amazing breasts, trail a finger down Dave's shirt front. Watched the rest of the coop turn to watch and laugh before the beehive walked off, rolling her hips, looking backwards at him.

And then he was there. Had she been less twisted, frantic, in herself, then she might have noticed that he was pale, waxy, that he looked up and smiled but his body was heavy. Still she ran towards him, the bumper of a black cab skimming the back of her calves, gave his chest a shove.

'What was that?'

'That was Tanya. I've told you she's been –'

'Why is she touching you?'

'She's winding me up but – Jesus, what happened to your face?'

'I slip on the stairs and . . .'

She never got to finish because then there were tears. And though she wanted to push him away, scream at him that he should never let another woman touch him like that, she clung to him, pushed her ribcage to his as though she were trying to hide inside him. And he sheltered her, brought his arms around her head.

Eventually she recovered, pulled the heels of her palms across her eyes and they started walking in silence through the noise of the city. They stopped at a fish-and-chip shop and he told her to wait where she was. Through the glass she watched him, sorting through the coins in the palm of his hand, sharing a bit of tired chit-chat with the older moustached man shovelling the chips into paper cones. Could she say the words? How could she begin to tell him who she really was? His Alena, filthy layer of lies after filthy layer of lies, something sticky, black, at the core at her.

He came out holding the cones of chips, vinegar dripping from the pointed bottom and splashing onto the pavement. She wasn't just hungry, she was starving. Those chips, the warmth, the filling of her mouth and her belly seemed like more comfort than she could have hoped for. He looked on as she stuffed them into her mouth. 'Yeah, that's it. Get some food inside you.'

She stuffed the hot chips into her mouth, burning the centre of her tongue, breathing out small gusts of steam as the vinegar teared her eyes. They slowed to a dawdle, letting tourists cluster around them and pass with tight, irritated faces. He attacked his own chips as hungrily as she did and she saw a little smile of enjoyment playing around his eyebrows. She'd never really noticed his eyebrows properly before, short and soft like a boy's.

Alena nodded, accidentally stabbed her tongue with the wooden fork in the effort to think. Think.

'I'm sorry I get upset . . .' She looked up at him; he had a smudge of ketchup at the side of his mouth and she licked her finger and wiped it away unthinkingly. '. . . but I want to talk to you about something big and I get nervous.'

He wasn't looking at her; he stared at the bottom of his cone, intent on getting out the last crispy bits in the tip.

'But chips make me braver.'

He didn't laugh; he looked closely at her, paused on her bruised cheek.

'I am sorry. I leave it for another time . . . better time.'

'No, come on. I'm being daft. And selfish too. I had a shit of a day, and Tanya, she . . .'

'She what?'

'Forget it. It's stupid. And of course you can always talk to me. Of course, Lena.'

'Sorry.'

'Come on, let's sit down.'

They laced their way through Soho Square, through the crowds smoking under heaters outside bars, buzzing with the possibility of the night ahead, some paying close attention to Dave until they spotted Alena holding his hand.

Alena felt short of breath, glad they were sitting on an out-of-the-way bench. The truth was battering behind her lips, a black balloon inflated with foulness that she couldn't bear for Dave to hear. In her chest she allowed four hard pumps of her raw, pained heart before she began speaking. After she'd finished, Dave looked hard at her.

'You didn't mention it again. I thought you'd changed your mind. So . . . why?'

'Because, because I want to see everywhere, not just London, someone say Manchester is good for jobs.'

He looked at her, shook his head. 'No, no, no, this doesn't make sense. You love Hackney, a lot more than I ever have too, and those museums, the markets. What's happened? Something to do with your face? Is it your boss's wife again? Or look, I mean, are you still worried about the girls at work, because that Tanya, she's just a –'

A flash of something filling her eye sockets. 'No, I just –'

'If your boss has been giving you a hard time, if anyone's laid a finger on you, I've told you, I'll –'

She put her hot hand on his face to quieten him. She felt the surge rise up but she couldn't cry. 'No, no, David. You said you would think about it. Listen, I just want to see a new place.

Why do we stay here? Is so expensive. We can have new start, the two of us.'

He shrugged, used a fingernail to scratch at the bark of a nearby tree.

'Then let's go. We pack, get on bus, we get new jobs.' She knew she was making it sound too hard, too new. 'And I want to live in bigger house, David. Outside London we can and maybe I can get a real job where people aren't so strict about visa. We can save up and go around the world, just like you always dream. We do it together.'

He looked at her, exhaled in one slow breath and nodded. 'Well, you did get me thinking about a change the other night; of job really, but maybe a fresh start, the two of us. I mean, things have felt rocky lately, and you're right, about getting a bigger place up north, it is cheaper.'

'Yes, yes, we'll have a big house, new jobs, we can find new places to go.'

He nodded again and she let the tears go because it all seemed so easy, because she almost believed her own fantasy, the big house, proper job and the plane ticket to somewhere even further away. She would go, take him with her, nothing else mattered. If Fedir found her again they would leave again, as long as she could take Dave. She stood, pulling her coat around her. He looked up at her.

'I hope those are happy tears? You'll never stop being a surprise. I'd no idea how much you wanted to leave. I mean, I could see that you weren't happy any more but I thought the other night was just . . . you should have said. And you're not in any trouble, Lena? Because if you are you can tell me and –' And she pressed her fingers to his mouth and shook her head. He took a deep breath, drummed his fists on his knees and nodded. 'So we're going to do it then?'

'Yes, yes. We should go. Take Tube and pack and we can get overnight bus maybe, or stay night in station, or no, we can leave in morning but early. I think it is long journey to Manchester.'

'What?'

'Is long way so we need to be out of house by early.'

She had her hand on his shoulder; she wanted to drag him up and all the way to the coach station.

'Alena, are you OK?'

'Fine. Am just . . . excited.'

'Listen, me too, but look.' He took her hand from his shoulder and tugged her down beside him. 'Sit a minute.' She sat heavily, scratchy panic filling her lungs with every breath. 'Alena. I want to do this, OK?'

She bit her cheeks, crossed her arms over her chest.

'But we have to give a month's notice on the flat to get back the deposit, we'll need that, and so I can get a reference from Yvonne. I should see if there's a security agency to get me work up there and if we book in advance we can get the train not the bus and you wouldn't want to leave Mr Scannell in the lurch, would you? I mean, I don't care if you do but –' He looked like he had more to say but didn't know how to. 'And I know, I know you're maybe just used to leaving suddenly and heading off but this way is best; it's a better start for us. A better fresh start.'

'I don't care. I want to go. Tonight or tomorrow early. Please.' The last word was barely a whisper but it might not have existed, she knew there was no way. He would come, but not yet, of course it made no sense to leave so suddenly. Unless you were frightened that everything would ignite and burn to ash in front of your eyes. Unless you had a knife to your back.

'What's up with you? You're worrying me.'

She wouldn't chance his worry, it was too close to suspicion. So she kissed him hard on the mouth. 'OK, OK. Four weeks?'

He was smiling now, unbuttoning his shirt collar like a lawyer on TV after a hard cross-examination, he looked happy. 'You know, it's funny because after the day I had, I was just thinking maybe you were right, maybe we should get away, that you were the only thing stopping me. Not stopping me, it was thinking of you that kept me in that job, so I could look after you and then you show up and –'

'Four weeks?' She said it louder than she meant to, caught herself, and tried to smile.

'Alena? Yeah. Four weeks, a month. Four weeks and we'll start somewhere new. I'll call the landlord tomorrow.' He moved round to her, and kissed the bridge of her nose, her upper lip, the tip of her chin. 'It'll fly by, I promise.'

Alena said nothing, she was willing Andriy to die in the night and keep Fedir busy with grief. As a guilty afterthought she wished his son dead too.

9

They caught the 344 most of the way. They were skint, skinter than when they had decided on the move. Manchester wasn't going to be as cheap as they'd thought but she'd been out every day before he was even up, doing what work she could in the early mornings so they could save something, sitting in the Internet cafe writing down the prices of flats to rent in the afternoons. They could afford Salford maybe, or just a room in a shared house, just for a start.

She'd managed to get an extra round for a week; the lad on that route was on his older brother's stag do in Magaluf. He was probably vomiting on a girl's high heels around the same time that Alena was slipping out of bed, tugging on her jeans and kneeling over Dave, kissing his forehead, breathing in his sleepy, sweaty smell.

On his way to work the day before he'd caught her coming back from a round, her pale smiling face framed against the bruise of the early-morning sky, an empty mug she'd taken her coffee in that morning dangling from her finger. He put his hands on her shoulders, stepped her gently away from the long damp piss-patch that ran up the wall, from the Spurs fans who'd packed out the pub opposite the night before, and kissed the hollows of her eyes.

She still wasn't sleeping but it seemed to matter less as the weeks went by. Maybe the work helped even, she was delivering leaflets in the evenings too, the boxes stacked up in the hallway along with a limp, deflated neon-yellow messenger bag, as though just the sight of the leaflets exhausted it.

'Have a rest now, eh? There's two slices left so have some tea and toast and then get some sleep. You look shattered.' Her eyebrows raised. 'Beautiful but knackered.'

She gave him a tired peck on the lips, the mug giving him a rap on the temple as she raised her arms to his face. By the piss-stained wall, her back from a shit job and him off to his, her kiss, her bitter breath on his face, felt like the best start to the day he could imagine.

So they were skint and they took the bus, buses, because they couldn't afford the Tube. But it didn't really matter how they got there. They had time, and she liked the bus, made them sit upstairs at the front and treated it like a trip out. She stared at everything as though she was on one of those open-top tourist buses, and he wondered how much she had and hadn't seen before.

'It is hairdresser's, you see? And it is called "It Will Grow Back"'

They shared that day's haul of sweets from Mr Scannell, fizzy cola bottles, white chocolate buttons with multicoloured speckles, foamy pink shrimps, till his teeth felt soft in his head. He'd given her some old magazines too and they put their feet up on the bus windowsill and flipped through the pages of *OK!* together. One of the weddings was already a divorce. Dalston, Islington, King's Cross, change.

He felt nervous, like he was taking her home to tea. She'd dressed nice for it, too; dressed nice for those three bus journeys and an afternoon in a drizzly cemetery; he loved her more for that. And she'd made them buy flowers, just a few bunches of cheap red tulips, 'Come on, we can't afford it. It doesn't matter. It's not like Mum didn't know a thing or two about being hard up.' But she'd insisted and now she cradled them in her arms as they wilted.

On the third bus, a single-decker from Putney, they stood so close together that he was afraid Alena would hear his heart thumping and read his dirty secrets like Morse code. Thump-thump, thump, thump-thump, thump. They passed the estate and he couldn't help but crane his neck, he could just see the Co-op, all done up green and shiny now, the old Co-op blue long forgotten.

Every stop he stared at the pensioners with their trolleys, the young mums squeezing on with angry faces, mucky pushchairs and muckier kids. He thought he recognised a few of them, maybe just from the Co-op, but they stared past him, took in Alena in her smart skirt and blouse, bright red hair, with a flick of interest and then stared into whatever space was free, faces blank.

'You're sad.'

She'd whispered it, the bus swaying her closer to him as it turned towards the Asda superstore, pushed her hand round to the small of his back and massaged it with a circular motion of her fingers. 'I understand, but I think your mum would like me.'

He put his face down towards the crown of her head – her hair smelt of coconut today – and hoped that his Morse code heartbeat wouldn't betray that his mum would not have liked her one little bit. Wouldn't have liked her jumble-sale clothes, strange accent, her bright patchily dyed hair, not to mention the shoplifting, the mystery past or the taking away of her son not just from Roehampton but all the way to Manchester. His mum, who'd never left Roehampton, except for a few trips to Southend and Great Yarmouth, would not have liked Alena at all. She'd liked Shelley; blonde and nicely dressed, one of the old estate lot, not asking for much but the usual, perfectly made up and entirely fucked up. But then he remembered that it didn't matter what his mum wanted. And he was incapable of not wanting Alena.

The cemetery, just beyond the Asda and back a bit from the dual carriageway, was filled with cheap flimsy tombstones covered in names he remembered, just, from his mum's gossip. *'Poor Maureen Yates kicked it. God rest her but, and I'm not being funny, what do you expect with a husband like that?'* Alena stood between the stones, clutching the drooping tulips, shivering in her thin skirt; he thought he could feel the ground rumble beneath them – his mum spinning in her grave probably, or maybe just a lorry transporting a slag pile. Alena put the flowers down gently.

'Pleased to meet you, Pat.'

He stared at the sparse patch of grass spread with the flowers. His mum loved him. She'd said it enough times. 'I just want you to be happy, love.'

He took Alena's cold fingers in his hand. 'That's enough. Let's go.'

He walked away without looking back. They went to the Asda cafe and had a cup of tea to warm up; shared a toastie.

'I'm ready.'

She looked up at him. Under the strip lights, sitting at the bright yellow table, she looked pale, thin and delicate as a petal. 'For what?'

'For our fresh start, Manchester, for us to be foreigners together.'

And Alena, cold and tired as she was, gave a laugh and bobbed her head. 'Well, thank God, Dave.' She held out the last piece of toastie to him, the yellow cheese oozing, 'We leave in five days. Then you will be a foreigner with a funny accent too.'

King's Cross, Islington, Dalston, home. He stopped her just before the piss stain, wanted to walk over the threshold and leave the day and its shitty cemetery, memories of Shelley and the estate behind them.

'Thank you.'

She didn't make a joke, or tell him she was cold and to hurry up with the keys. She looked like she was letting the words sink through her. 'It is me who thanks you. Dave, I have been wanting to –'

She opened her mouth but it was filled with the passing noise of a police siren and by the time it had gone she had dipped her head and started rummaging herself for the keys.

'I am freezing and starving to death.'

'Alena? What was it you were going to say?'

'What?' She kept her eyes on her bag. 'Is nothing. Come on, David, there's packing and we only have days now not weeks.'

It was like indigestion, or like his heart was trying to squeeze itself back up one of its own arteries. Something happened to his body when he looked at her. Her hair was longer now, to her jawline, and the screaming red colour she put through it, spattering the sink and one of his T-shirts, had been tamed a bit in the sun over the summer.

She was waiting at the end of the street like she had been every night since they'd decided to move. Sitting on the kerb, knees pressed together from the cold, the bottom of her face hidden by the open *Evening Standard*. He hadn't had her that long, so maybe it wasn't a surprise that she could still make his hands shake, that the fear of saying or doing the wrong thing would bubble up and make him hesitant.

He waited for the little bouncy ball in his chest to slow a bit, put his hands in his pockets to hide the shake and watched her turn the page, maybe tutting he thought. Then she closed the paper with a snap, folded it and held it over her head to shade her face from the bright, cold light. He couldn't see her eyes meet his but he saw the thin curve of a smile, a quick flash of those sharp teeth. His heart twisted, it was the way that her skinny jumble of legs and arms lengthened at the sight of him; she stretched herself, lowered the paper, smiled a proper wide-open smile and then looked away quickly. He walked down the road to her and started to cross, not looking left or right. He still couldn't take his eyes off her. It definitely wasn't indigestion.

He had noticed the changes in her but with a kind of distracted confusion; her new clinginess, meeting him at the end of his shift in all weathers, still not letting him touch her at night, the same question every single day about how many more days till they could leave, the tantrum when he said they should stay on an extra week in the flat as a favour to the landlord. The truth was he turned his face away, distracted, as though these new traits were a persistent fly. It was just a new part of the many parts of her that he couldn't, and might never, understand. He'd wonder later whether he could've changed everything just by stopping. Just by looking.

He thought maybe she was reacting, like him, to the change. That like his running it was her response to the fear and exhilaration of starting something new, just the two of them as a pair. He'd started running to work, through the backstreets, estates and big white houses with two cars in each driveway. Down the canal with the constant 'tring' of bicycle bells and out into the smog and grinding traffic of Old Street. He thought about a place that only belonged to them, that they'd arrive in together. No niggle that Shelley would suddenly appear on the doorstep or that one of the girls from the estate would suddenly get herself a well-off bloke and come swanning into the shop. Why Manchester? Why not, if he wasn't fussed? It was meant to be like London really, just a bit littler. He'd stretch his stinging muscles to snapping point on a bench, with a bronze of an old man reclining, by Bond Street, and make lists of all the things that made the move make sense: it would be cheaper, it was a fresh start, he could do his work anywhere, they could get a bigger place, Alena wanted to.

But on his gentle cool-down jogs towards work, leaning to the right from an over-stretched hamstring, he couldn't help but make the other list: once he went to Bognor on a school trip and he had been so homesick they'd had to send him back with one of the teaching assistants; he wouldn't be able to visit his mum any more, or, as he sometimes had before Alena, to catch the bus to Putney and go to where him, Shelley and his mum had watched the boat race on the Thames before everything turned to shit. He wouldn't be going if it wasn't for her, it was all for her, really. Still, he wasn't leaving much behind.

It was all so quick, and Alena, she kept trying to speed it up. She'd always been stubborn really; quietly, gently insistent about things, but never like this, never for herself, always on his back all the time and he kept wanting to ask, almost did, if Manchester was where she had been before him, before them. A bad taste rose up his throat and coated the inside of his mouth when the thought occurred to him that he was just carrying her up there to be taken away from him. Her drifting away these weeks, her pushing about the whole thing, just made him even more nervous.

But now, outside the shop, as she stood gently before him, letting his arms circle her, he felt the flutter of the dropped newspaper pages against his leg and she lifted her arms around his neck, pressed herself against him and said into his chest, as though she intended her voice to make its way past flesh and bone to the pounding, hurting muscle of his heart, 'I have missed you today,' and he forgot the arguments and worries and suspicions. He forgot everything but Alena, and succumbed to the uneasy comfort of wanting and needing only what is in your arms.

She was leaving the shop after dropping off the trolley, apologising again to Mr Scannell that she had to stop her round so soon, carrying the bag of chocolate buttons he'd given her and already steeling herself in case Fedir should suddenly decide to visit, when Mrs Scannell grabbed her arm.

'Hey, you.'

Alena had tried to force a smile at first, seeing Mrs Scannell's teeth, which showed she liked sugar as much as Alena, bared. Until she realised it wasn't a smile at all. Until she felt how hard the grip was. Until she saw the look in the woman's eyes, the same look she had every time they crossed paths.

'I've told him, you know.'

'Sorry? What?'

'I don't want your kind here. A foreigner, an immigrant. Taking jobs from our lads. The state of you, a grown woman delivering papers. If it was my choice the first thing I'd do is call in immigration – there's posters on all the buses, in case you hadn't noticed – it would only take one phone call to get them to come and check you out. And don't think I haven't seen you sniffing around my Albert –'

'What? Mr Scannell? No, I have boyfriend. David. I love

him. Is just job, good job! Besides, I'm leaving soon, you know, to go somewhere else and for record . . .' Alena pulled her arm away, forced herself to make eye contact with the woman. 'I am Polish, not an illegal. I bring my passport . . . maybe I explain to Mr Scannell if you want? Tell him you ask me about it?'

Mrs Scannell looked away and then attempted a hard, puckering smile.

'Oh, I know you're going away, it's all he's talked about, the idiot. Well, I'm no idiot. Off to steal another job from some young English lad who deserves it? You just leave my Albert alone, you've bothered him enough. And Polish, eh? Well, you might not be illegal but I'm not wrong about the foreign part.'

They stood facing each other. Alena wouldn't tell the old bitch that if she wasn't careful she'd take her husband just to spite her, that she didn't deserve a kind man like that, but she wouldn't run either. They stood facing each other until they heard the electronic sing song that told everyone the shop door was opening.

'Off you go then.'

With a flick of Mrs Scannell's fingers Alena was dismissed. She felt all of the English swear words she knew, a lot after walking the streets of Hackney, battering against her teeth and then thought of last week's wages and how they needed them.

'I understand, Mrs Scannell. Is just good job for me. And I go very soon, really.'

She walked away, tore open the chocolate buttons and shoved them in her mouth to stop her tears and smother the names she wanted to call that woman, all gathered and waiting in her mouth. She barely heard Mrs Scannell shouting after her.

It was three days until they were to catch the coach with what they could take packed into a giant suitcase and two laundry bags. Dave had so little, it made her feel less guilty, if not less dirtied, that he seemed to have hardly anything to leave behind either.

She was worn thin, felt that she was running a marathon, no, a double marathon, that the flesh was starting to peel from the soles of her feet and her shin bones would splinter through her wind-thinned skin from the weight of trying to get them away. To make them safe. Now she wanted things. Not just to be alive and safe, she wanted to wake up every day with Dave, for her stomach to ripen with his child one day, to be able to say, maybe one day, 'That's David, my husband.'

She knew him better now. Had been to the estate he grew up on, reminding her of her own tower block; she had never imagined such places existed in London before she'd arrived. Hackney had flats too, almost exactly the same, but there was something about his childhood estate that stank of the abandonment and disappointment of home.

She knew him by the thud of his heart when they went to his mum's grave, his badly masked worry about money and jobs. And now he felt almost heavier than she could bear. But she couldn't leave him behind. So she kept going, a matter of days and she could rest, they could have a life together.

She carried her leaflets from street to street, each time expecting to see Fedir, hurrying from door to door. She wanted to take a pill and wake up on the coach in three days' time with Dave next to her and Fedir, Andriy, the filth of her beginnings in London disappearing or at least folded up tight and buried in a dark secret place.

Dave only ran in the mornings but she was running all the time. She sustained herself on a diet of him, his kisses, his voice, his nearness. She sustained herself on promises, and silent deals and thoughts of three days' time. If she could make it to Manchester she would do anything, anything, more than she had done already to escape, and carry him with her.

10

He wouldn't have noticed if it hadn't been for her. They were watching *EastEnders*, the flat all packed up around them. Tomorrow they were going to take the TV to one of the shops down the road and sell it for what they could, but until then someone was having an affair with someone else's niece, Dave couldn't keep track, and Alena had wanted to see the end. They had the heating on full blast, she liked it that way, and he was in boxers and vest, hoping the pasta, tuna and onion that felt like it was lying on his stomach would start softening up, and moving downwards as gravity intended, and enjoying Alena's new habit of lying with her head on his lap, her long legs swinging off the end of the settee.

So between the racket in the Queen Vic, the pasta and Alena's long pale legs he wouldn't have noticed the smash of glass if she hadn't bolted upright, twisted her head in that strange animal way. She'd been nervy for weeks and he was just about to tell her that it was just the usual, 'Come on, lie down. It's kids; you've lived here long enough to –' But then he heard someone calling her name outside and still, idiot that he was, he might have thought it was just one of those things, except that she was so still, looked so broken, and then she started crying. Not her usual, full-bodied weeping but tears rolling quietly down her face, making a kind of whimpering sound.

'Alena, Alena, Alena.'

For a minute he just sat still; listened. In the Queen Vic someone got a gin and tonic in their face and someone else got a slap from a small, ring-heavy hand that left the slappee's earrings swinging back and forth in shock. And then he was up, standing over her.

'Who's that? Who's out there shouting your name?'

The tears kept rolling. She didn't answer, she stared at the screen and shook her head, tiny movements back and forth, back and forth.

'Alena?'

Two men calling for her; Fedir, Dave; she was hugging her knees now, trying to drown it all out.

'Why didn't he just ring the buzzer?'

'Because he is fucking idiot.'

She was shouting, still staring at the screen, her face wet now, her bottom teeth biting her upper lip, the voice outside screaming while they sat on the sofa.

'Alena, come on, you little frigid bitch, I come to see you. I'm coming up.'

Still Dave stared at her as though stuck; Alena stared at the screen, her body shaking.

'Alena, you slut! Bitch. You're nothing but a –'

He'd taken five steps already, shouting before he'd reached the window.

'Whoever you are, I'm going to fucking kill you. You hear me?'

'You are the fucking faggot?'

That bloke from the stairs, it was him.

'Fucking faggot and whore playing house. Alena sends out her bum fucker.'

'Who the fuck are you? Who are you?' He was pulling on his jeans, already thinking about getting two good punches in, that bastard's nose cracking like a boiled egg under his fist, the sound his skull would make as it smashed into the floor.

'I fucking kill you and the whore. Dirty bitch, prostitute bitch.'

How did he know where she lived? How did he know her name? Who the fuck was he? He bolted, he was going to murder him, but then Alena was throwing herself against him.

'Stop. You can't, he'll kill you. Or there are others, they will, please, I am . . . am so sorry, I am so sorry. Please don't.'

Later he would claim that he didn't know what he'd done. That she'd got that bruise the colour of a smear of mustard on her cheek some other way, but he remembered pushing her, and heard her cry out behind him as she hit the coffee table's sharp edge. But still she clung to his legs, and there was something about her desperation that spoke truth. He pushed her off, while that bloke kicked at the door now, he could hear the wood starting to crack.

'I'm giving you two minutes to fuck off out of it then I'm calling the police. You hear me? Two fucking minutes.'

The man kept kicking at the door, the hinges straining but holding. Then the noise stopped and there was a sound as if whoever he was had slumped down on the other side. Alena stood, walked to Dave and tried to put her hand on his chest, then withdrew it at the last moment. Her eyes dark, serious.

'Please, David. Just let me go.'

Adrenalin drained from him and he wanted to sleep. He wanted to go back to ten minutes ago, take her to bed, listen to her nattering about flats and jobs in Manchester as he fell asleep. She was pulling on her shoes and coat now, sobbing as she searched for her bag. They said nothing but the TV said, 'She's always been a bad un. I knew she hadn't changed. Trollop. Common trollop is what she is.'

He switched it off. 'Are you OK?' He had no idea why he was asking that. 'Lena, who the fuck is he? He's the one from before. What the fuck's happening here?'

She was crying harder now, her breath shuddering, her eyes starting to sting; red and swollen. She shook her head. 'No.'

'No what?'

He felt his temper rise. She couldn't just brush him off. She took everything from him, he was prepared to give her everything. He beat down the instinct to smash her open like a piggy bank and find out what was inside. He was frightened of what she made him capable of, just standing there with her bag dangling from her shoulder, not enough breaths between sobs, snot collecting on her upper lip. He spoke quietly, stood as still as he could in the centre of the room, afraid that his voice or a sudden movement would give away how close he was to forcing all her secrets out of her.

'Did you sleep with him? Is that why he's here? I mean, he's been here before, hasn't he?'

She looked up at him now, her face crumpled; still she said nothing.

'Not before, I mean if he's an ex-boyfriend, I mean.' His voice cracked, strangled by what he was about to say. 'I mean since you've been with me, since you lived here, has he touched you? Have you let him?'

She covered her face with her arms, putting them around her as though to protect herself. It was a whine, clogged by tears and a too-tight throat, but he could just make it out.

'I have to go to him and take him away. For both of us. Please, I promise I explain everything later. No more lies or pretending. I just –'

The knocking started again, slower, sullen. He walked over and gripped her arms, stared into her face as she tried to turn it away from him.

'Lies? Pretending? You'll explain right now what the fuck's going on here. Right now.'

She pulled away. 'Wait for me. I'll come back later tonight and I promise I'll tell everything.'

She was already in the hallway; he stood under the bare bulb, unable to move. He felt dizzy.

'Alena?'

She took one last look at him, wiped her face with her palms. 'I'm sorry. Wait. I promise I make this better.'

And then she was gone and all he could hear were muffled voices, one angry, one cajoling, moving further and further away.

He was drunk enough to be malleable. So drunk, the smell of a long day drinking lying sweetly on his skin, that he didn't notice her crying as she pressed her body and then her face up to his, her lips to his. So drunk that she simply had to cradle his balls through his trousers, whisper into his ear, her voice distorted with tears, for him to follow her downstairs. Every step another away from danger, away from Dave coming to harm. Every step another away from the only thing she had wanted to live for.

Outside the block the night air, the lights and noise of the traffic, seemed to wake him and he stopped, pulled at her arm. Alena could see Dave's hunched outline at the window above.

'No, I want to fuck. We tell batty boy go out. I want it.'

He reached and grabbed at her breast and she had no choice but to allow it. He was pulling her backwards now, his fingers gouging at her soft skin, and, looking up at the window one last time, realising she had little left to gamble, she leaned in and whispered in Fedir's ear.

'You silly man. Where do you think I will live? An illegal with no job? Where will we fuck then? Be a good boy and take me for a drink. You want another drink, yes?'

She stroked his hardness through his jeans and he grabbed

her head with both hands and kissed her, biting her lips, filling her mouth with his boozy breath, his tongue, and then he was under her control again and she led him away by the hand.

'Come on.' She glanced back but the window was empty.

They went to a narrow corridor of an Irish bar. Alena tried to resist drinking, thinking of having to face Dave later; but then thinking of facing Dave made her drain her glass dry and ask for another big drink. Fedir started a fight at the bar that ended with a glass being thrown and her dragging him out while he shouted: 'Look at my beautiful bitch. What have you guys got, eh? You think I know fuck nothing, well, I'm telling you I know fuck all.'

He took her in an alley beside the pub. Wobbly, messy, the freezing cold wall scraping her skin, not quick enough and so close to the street that anyone could see. Alena the whore exposed in every way possible. When he stopped a taxi afterwards, his flies still undone, she waited until he got in, slammed the door and waved like that had always been the plan. She thought he might try something, but he was already sliding sideways, his eyes half closed.

When she finally made it home, her emotions strangely still and silent, the door to the flat was wide open and she knew that Dave was gone. She walked into the living room, sat down and stayed there with her knees tucked up, kneecaps digging into her chin. She was thirsty, her tongue thick in her mouth, but she still sat. She turned the TV back on and stared at the changing faces on the screen. Her thoughts crackled with a sort of white static, a pitch so high that she was only aware of it because of a soft vibration running across her skull.

She could go to the tap and drink straight from it. If she wanted she could make a cup of tea. For a moment, the idea that even when everything had shattered she could still go and have tea, eat a biscuit, roused her, lowered the pitch and set her brain circling the idea of Fedir coming back, of him hurting Dave or Dave hurting him, of her being hurt, of where Dave was, what she could possibly tell Dave, of whether she could – and then it retreated to the same high pitch that itched her scalp. So she stayed sitting.

And that is where she woke, not realising she'd fallen asleep, and heard the door and then she ran from the sofa, in time for the bedroom door to slam in her face. She could smell it though, the thick sweet boozy smell, could hear it in the sounds on the other side of the door, his anger and clumsy steps filling the flat which had only been filled with his absence earlier.

She should have left then. Left with the clothes on her back, because she could feel his fury melting the walls between them. She should have left before, when Fedir first showed up. But she hadn't and now she didn't either. Instead, she slid down the door and listened until she sensed a thick, black sleep fall over him. She had escaped Russia and then a monster, two monsters, somehow she had found Dave and she had almost got them away. Surely she could escape Fedir and get them away to Manchester, when he was sober in the morning, when he had slept it off.

She took his winter coat and lay down on the sofa, pushed her arms the wrong way into the black sleeves and pulled the collar up to cover her lips and nose. She thought she could smell him, a cold winter day, his wanting her still. I can get him again. And with that she fell into a thin, dreamless sleep.

But there was no sleeping it off. He was gone again the next morning before she woke from her suffocating, sweaty sleep. She followed her own advice and did nothing. Against every instinct she stayed still. Let Fedir come back, let Dave hate her, let him smash her face in with a drunken fist, let the walls fall upon her and break her bones. She wouldn't leave.

She found the cold, steely part of her that she'd spent so long trying to rid herself of and used it not to give up. She washed the sheets and hung them over doors to dry. She made a stew, chopping the piles of vegetables minutely into matchsticks.

She got on her hands and knees and scrubbed the floorboards, wiped the skirting boards of their downy grey fur. She folded their clothes and balled up their socks, dipped newspaper into vinegar and squeaked it across the windows, used her fingernails to get at the black mush on the ledge of the shower door.

Finally, she cleaned herself, showered with the hot tap full on and just a trickle of cold and turned her face right up to the scalding water, she pushed the flannel inside her with her fingers again and again, until she felt swollen shut with soreness. She felt filthy.

Still, neither of them came. She listened to the sirens, screams, the travelling music of the London night. She ate a packet of biscuits and drank tea. She watched an episode of *Home and Away* and wondered who between Fedir and Dave would win a fight; London versus Ukraine, Good versus Bad. She consoled herself with the thought of Dave's running, how fit he was, while Fedir never exercised, and then got down on her knees and vomited up tinny, lumpy liquid, remembering that David would likely be drunk and Fedir, the pig, would never come alone. When she heard the key clacking, drunkenly at the door, she stayed where she was. She smelt of vomit and couldn't bear to see the way he might look at her.

11

Who knows how many more days she would have had to wait for Fedir to return or Dave to sober up, to be thrown out of the flat, to be punished in some way. In the end the punishment came from neither of them, or at least she didn't think so. Of course she'd thought about it before, the possibility, when she was looking for jobs and saying day after day to people, looking at her feet, 'I have lost passport.' When Mrs Scannell talked about all of those posters on the buses.

Or even before that, when the police did their circuits of Paddington, right by the public toilets, she knew that at any moment one could become curious and they could take her aside, ask a few questions.

Somehow, though, she imagined that having a proper flat, her sort-of job and more than just a rucksack's worth of clothing would protect her. That there would be a solicitor or a charitable agency she could go to. Maybe it would be like the overdue electric bill Dave had had and she would get a red letter and then perhaps a cold, frightening phone call. But they came at lunchtime, as she was heating up a can of soup. There were four of them and they allowed her to pack her things into a thin grey bin bag but she wasn't allowed to leave a note for Dave who would be out drinking or running, the only two things he'd done since Fedir had shown up – drink up a hangover, run it off and then drink up another.

At the centre she got her phone call. It went to voicemail and her message came out in a long rattling gush.

And then the phone beeped as though she'd been cut off.

She chose to believe the message space had run out. The centre was a prison, with bars and gates and guards. In fact it was worse than a prison. Who wanted to invest in people who were being sent back home?

At Heathrow she was walked through with one of the guards to her 'escort' already waiting on the departures side. Holidaymakers in shorts, premature orange suntans and baseball caps stared at her as though she was a criminal. She supposed she actually was. Her punishment, losing what she needed most, returning to Russia and to her mother, if her mother was still there, but hoping that with Andriy gone – surely, she thought, gone by now – Fedir would be too cowardly, too lazy to find her. Or that, she saw clearly now, Fedir and Andriy had never had reach beyond their small pocket of London, their lice-infested, local haunts.

In all this time she had heard nothing from her mother, had had no reply to any of those carefully chosen postcards. Nothing. The thought crawled across her skin and she scratched at her collarbone, leaving a deep pink mark.

How would she explain her absence? Her lack of contact for that first year? She could always lose herself in Moscow, become another faceless worker, doing a poorly paid job, to keep the wealthy in lattes, clean Jeeps, shining, perfumed toilet bowls.

A pair of grubby trainers stepped towards her. Lank hair, lumpen coat, tracksuit bagging at the knees and elbows and an embarrassed look floating around her puffy features, specks of dry mascara under her eyes.

'Alena? I'm taking you home.'

'Excited to be going home, I expect?'

Idiot. Alena had rattled off a string of meaningless but

complicated Russian words, summoning as many tongue rolls as she could manage. The frumpy woman had just smiled weakly, shaken her head and rummaged in her bag for a mint. She didn't offer Alena one though she had a full packet.

They sat two guards in front of her and that woman beside her. One of the guards was ancient and the other so fat he had to put his hands to his belly to squeeze himself into his seat. She clearly wasn't considered high-risk, though that didn't stop the fat one dangling handcuffs in Alena's face.

'Any trouble. Any.'

The plane journey was boring – there was no movie – and Alena just stared at the seat in front, ignoring the businessman on her right who kept 'accidentally' nudging her breast with his elbow during his many forays into his cheap briefcase with its combination lock, and which when she peered inside contained only a browning banana and a copy of the *Sun* newspaper. The woman did wordsearches and sucked her pen throughout, *thisk, thisk, thisk,* while she looked for the words, voicing the first few letters, 'th, th, th', in between sucks. After the first hour sitting with her eyes shut and one particularly lingering breast nudge, she opened her eyes and said as loudly as she could: 'You are both ignorant as horseshit.' She jabbed the back of one of the guards' seats. 'Them too. No, in fact, horseshit has more purpose.'

But because she said it in Russian they both just looked at her and the woman piped up: 'Sorry about this. Deportee. You know, she's being deported. I thought I had a good one today to be honest but they do get like this.'

And the man gave Alena a look, as though she might be capable of doing the things he'd read in his newspaper that immigrants do and asked the steward if he could swap seats. The guard with the handcuffs snored through the incident. Then

Alena only had to put up with the woman and her wordsearches and contented herself with pretending to sleep and sprawling into the woman's personal space; a small victory.

As soon as they got to the airport the woman queued to hand over Alena and the documents to the immigration guard. She chewed at her thumbnail and Alena spent the time getting used to Russia again; all the flat colours – greys, beiges – and then bright splashes of blocky colour – reds and blues and yellows. Her fellow Russians so neat and trim and organised with their little leather travelling bags hung across their bodies. Standing patiently, unsmiling, whole families spreading out across the five queues and then signalling each other over if their queue moved the quickest.

Alena wondered if maybe the woman was afraid they would not take her back, that she'd be stuck with this strange, surly girl. She wondered if that had ever happened, but she wouldn't break her silence to ask. Certainly, the passport guard looked unimpressed as the woman slid over the papers along with her own passport and started babbling. 'Just returning one of your girls to you! Now normally, how it works, is I give you these and then you go get someone and I leave her in your care. This is my bit, just get her onto the plane and off again, onto home soil as it were, or in this case I think we could say the Motherland.'

He stared hard at the woman with a clear air of 'who gives a fuck about you?', while she gave him a small, nervous cluck of a laugh, . He did not open the passport or touch the papers for several moments, and as the queue got more restless behind them, the woman's brisk busybody demeanour slowly vanished. Alena shared the very slightest of smiles with the guard. He jerked his head towards her.

'You're with her?'

'Yes, please just look over the papers and get whoever it is so I can get her off my back.'

The woman's head swivelled between the two of them, red-faced and pop-eyed. Another small triumph, at least until the guard read the papers and then treated Alena to a particularly contemptuous curl of his lip before summoning another guard and refusing to meet her eye again.

They only questioned her for three hours; far less than she'd expected. That was how long it took to open a savings account in most banks; Russians and their bureaucracy – one way to keep people employed, she supposed. It was an elderly woman, her matronly chest nestled within her tent-like blazer, her lipstick a shade of coral which Alena now realised was particular to Russia, and a dull red hair colour that fought violently against the blotched skin that spoke of lonely nights in front of the television with a bottle of vodka and a big greasy bag of pastries.

The questioning was easy really, she just told the truth, up to a certain point: tricked, deceived; that she had put her trust in someone but there had been no job and no money, homelessness and then some lowly work; frightened and unsure of what would happen if she tried to get help or come home. The woman stubbed out her cigarette, took a sip of her tea. She must have seen hundreds like Alena with the same story. Certainly, as it unravelled, you could see her leaning back, taking fewer and fewer notes, taking more interest in the clock, with its sombre ticks that seemed to get further apart as the hours passed.

'But why not, I always say, why not go to the Russian Embassy? It is there to protect people like you, a little Russia for you to go to.'

'Because I was worried that I had a student visa and that I

might be in trouble.' Alena bit her lip, forced herself to think of her mother, Dave, trying to dredge up some feeling because the truth was she was beyond giving a shit. It was expected though, so she blinked out a few tears. 'Am I in trouble?' The woman's eyebrows were raised, she hunched forward. This was a right or wrong answer game and Alena could only guess; she spoke slowly, gauging the woman's reaction. The woman sat back heavily, gave a brief approving nod.

'I don't see why we need to make this a problem for you. Let's just say . . .' She pulled out a pen and started filling out a four-page, densely printed form with a quick practised hand. She had matched her nail varnish to her lipstick, this enormous woman who must be over sixty if she was a day. 'Let's just say, overstayed visa, yes?'

Alena nodded and wondered if this woman could be one of the many who must look the other way, or stamp documents without reading them, or talk in code to get people to agree to lies without ever asking them to. One of the many people who must get girls out of the country and into places they would never wish to be. The woman looked up as though she felt the sudden chill in the room.

'You understand you won't go back to Britain? You won't be granted a visa again.'

'I understand, I don't care. It is nowhere – why go away when I can be in Russia, the greatest country of all?'

Alena spoke as if someone had pulled a string in her back, and even though it sounded absurd to her, the woman gave her first smile and nodded emphatically before going back to her paperwork. Right answer again, Alena, right answer again.

12

The doorstep of his mum's old flat. Though he didn't realise it at first. All he felt was his cold damp trousers and an empty bottle of whiskey rocking back and forth in the freezing morning wind. The estate was quiet, it felt like the hour when only the night-shift workers would be coming back, maybe the odd cleaner heading out. He raised himself up, he was cold and brittle right down to his bones and his body felt worthless to him; he could leave it, and its piss-stained clothes, right there without a backward glance. But he was stuck with it, just like he was stuck with the thudding headache that would become searing pain at the back of his skull when the booze wore off, but that didn't stop him from checking the bottle at his feet for any last dregs.

He turned his face from the door, thought how his mum would be if she could see him now; as much as she had liked a drink, she kept her dignity. Even when she'd been betrayed, let down and left, she'd never shown herself up like this.

He still had his wallet – only a few quid in it but his card was in there. Since he'd been drinking at the Cavendish, and railing at anyone who wanted to listen, that he had his wallet and all of his teeth was a miracle in itself.

He walked to Putney, the long way across the Heath, avoiding dog walkers, grateful that he was at least wearing black jeans. Lots to be grateful for, Davey boy. As he walked he searched for clues of the previous night; memories like a TV programme you'd only half been watching a month ago.

He remembered he'd gone to a Wetherspoons and got talking

to a Malaysian air-conditioning salesman. He remembered them raising one of those Wetherspoons cheap doubles and calling all women bitches before they were thrown out. There was a Tube journey to Putney, talking shit to a girl who had tears in her eyes and her rushing to get off, away from him and his sloshing can. Then nothing until he was at the Cavendish, the estate's roughest pub, holding his bottle of whiskey, demanding a glass and some ice, saying he'd pay the same as a pint for it. Fucking idiot. He wanted to lie down on the grass and not wake up.

In the McDonald's disabled toilets he rinsed his trousers in the sink, his legs as best he could, and dried them both under the hand dryer for what felt like an age, the deep, loud noise hitting him like a cleaver through meat.

He just needed to get home, home at least for another day or two. Maybe he could get another week or two on the flat. Then what? And no job either. Then what? He squeezed the still-wet jeans up his thighs, took a painful look in the mirror and then started his walk along the river back home.

He'd deliberately left his phone uncharged. Left it there when it skidded under the bed one night, and it was only because he needed the landlord's number that he finally charged it. Three missed calls, that was all, and only one message. Her voice already sounding like it was in a foreign country, already too far to be reached. 'David, the immigration have come and took me away, they say I am on fast track but I don't know what this means. When I ask how long that is nobody is saying. Was probably that fucking old bitch, Mrs Scannell, I told you she . . . Listen to me, I'm at Colnbrook, they say is near Heathrow. You can come visit if you can call first. Please come. Please, if you even –' And then that steely voice telling him the day, the time of the message, that mechanical voice telling him it was already far too late. That by doing nothing, by pissing his days away, he'd done something awful.

He closed the door on the home that had made and broken him, filled with shadows of her. Ones that he might have wanted to remember: her legs on the windowsill; watching her through the shower door, her hip, then her breasts and then her mouth appearing as she wiped circles in the steamy glass. And the ones he couldn't bear to remember: her banging on the door and begging him to answer her; the shrill, silent way she'd said nothing when that drunken fuck had shown up. He changed his mind, he didn't want any of them good or bad. He found a shitty place on the Gumtree website, no deposit, no interview, no pictures, just show up and move in. But Tooting Broadway was far from east London and close to the shopping centre where he'd found agency work. He walked his circles mindlessly around the shopping-centre floor, thumbs in his waistband like a man twice his age, avoiding the treacherous cord from the floor-buffing machine and gaggles of kids in hoodies: he wasn't being paid enough. He took another job at nights, sitting on the front desk of a shining black glass tower in Docklands where the lights were always on for the bankers who struggled out at 2 a.m. and a few worse-for-wear ones arriving at 4 a.m. looking to lay their heads on a desk for a couple of hours. Docklands was far out but he usually got a bit of shut-eye, and then more at home.

He'd pissed away what little savings he'd had, and everything else for that matter. Now he needed to start scrabbling it back somehow. So, when his calves burned, when acid rose up in his throat from eating whatever was in the melting black plastic tray he'd plonked in the microwave, when he felt raw with exhaustion and had three more hours of looping the beautifully buffed shopping-centre floor, he forced himself to remember why: pay your dues, take your medicine, Davey.

On his day off he stayed in his room at the top of the bedbug-ridden house and looked out at a bench where the local winos sat and screamed, swigged and scammed. One night they set fire to one of the women's long greasy grey hair. Dave ran down but when he got there she was lying on her back, laughing about it, still clutching her can of cider, while the two other drunks laughed along with her. Every time he fancied a nice cold beer one look at them turned him right off.

So he did it, put up with the bugs in the mattress, the squelch of the carpet outside the shower, the smell of pot, the techno, the rants from Reggie (who'd just separated from his wife), the acrid smoke from the cooking of the seven Indonesians who slept shoulder to shoulder in the living room, and the middle-aged, watery-eyed Maureen, a not very successful masseuse.

'I could do you if you like, David?' She'd placed a wavering hand over his. 'Discounted, or no, no, I mean free.'

She gave a laugh which pealed up and then disappeared to nothing.

He kept himself in his room. A little box where he paced, planned, did his sums again and again on the backs of envelopes or that day's *Standard*, watched the shoppers in and out of the Sainsbury's across the road and played his game; through the grime of the window he judged the fall of their shoulders, their walk, the shopping they carried, who came along with them or, more to the point, who didn't. The game was whether they were happier or sadder than him: happier, sadder, sadder, Jesus, even sadder, happier, happier. It was a twisted 'play your cards right' and Dave had no idea if it made him feel better or worse.

13

She had thought she'd be left to find her own way back but she was given a plane ticket by the government and 5,000 roubles for 'resettlement'. It seemed ridiculous to her, and she wasn't ready, but the woman brought her noodle soup, a slice of solid white bread, tea, a brown holdall to replace the bin bag and a large padded peach coat with a ripped lining. Lost, never to be found again. That bag, that coat and Alena were meant for each other.

Still, this was the woman being decent and Alena felt suddenly guilty. Life taught people, and caught people, making mistakes – who knew that better than her? She was allowed to stay in the interview room until her flight was due and she was glad of that, to be away from the crowds outside, the reunited and torn apart, the insistent babble and constant feeding she'd forgotten about.

She wasn't ready. The woman had taken off her blazer, slipped off her lace-up shoes and was reading the newspaper. Alena tried to rattle the spoon on the bottom of the bowl as little as possible as she scooped up the noodles, the puckered, grey-looking peas. A mouthful of that coarse bread and she could not be anywhere else.

'I'm not ready.'

Though the words hit the table and reached up to the strip lighting for a moment she thought the woman wouldn't respond. The paper stayed firmly up between them and then slowly, reluctantly, it was lowered. The woman's mouth a grim coral line. She shrugged, heaved her body up, reached into her pocket and produced a small foil-wrapped chocolate, warm and misshapen from the heat and weight of her body, and handed it to Alena. Then the paper rose again and Alena read of a university dormitory arson attack, a war criminal's murder in a Moscow playground in broad daylight, a scandal about a contract for new pavements. Her eyes were unaccustomed to the letters, her mind unaccustomed to her home.

She went straight there. She got the train from the airport and a bus. How old everything seemed, the bus's powder-blue paintwork, its dusty pink curtains, the football pennants hung in the windows and five gas cylinders on the roof. How colourless the other passengers were: bad plastic shoes, shadows under dark eyes; hard make-up, harder faces. A man at the front drank beer from a label-less plastic bottle, gold cross dangling against a stained white vest under his coat, his stubby fingernails occasionally scratching his red cold-blasted neck.

A woman at the back shouted that she needed to get off and her note was passed down the aisle from hand to hand; none of the passengers looked at one another but the money got to the front. Then the driver's hand emerged, a woman's, Alena was surprised to see, with beautiful red nails and a giant plastic pearl ring. The passenger's change was passed back to her in coins before she got off down the back steps, pulling her piebald fur coat around her, pausing for a moment on the street as though the still-cold air had turned her to ice, then moving, slowly, slowly in her high-heeled boots, across the shining surface of the road.

It was like the set of a film of your life that someone else has made, everything replicated but with slight inconsistencies. Where was the stray wolf-like dog that would lie outside the cafe barking ferociously until you gave it a scrap? Why were the taxi drivers not hanging around the pancake kiosk? A minimart had replaced the chemist. A door that had been red was now painted blue, but a spray-painted flower remained in the cold of the Siberian winter and there was the bank, and the furniture store her mother liked to go and browse in, stroking her rough hands against the smooth wood.

Her pulse quickened and she felt the shock of icy cold in her marrow. She had once thought that facing her good, honest mother's face would be the worst thing possible, that her mother would not allow her to cross the threshold. Now she wished for that cruelty, for a release of the pain.

She walked the back way feeling like an impostor, a stranger who had stumbled upon a short cut. The wooden beams of the block were flaking away; two hot summers and another cold winter – was it any wonder? The bottom door was open, the lock broken as it often was, and she walked into the lobby. The same smell: garlic, urine and bleach, graffiti up the walls, 'fuckdepolice'. Idiots, they wouldn't even know what it was they were writing in English. Of course the lift was broken and so she climbed the nine flights; at each floor she said a silent prayer that none of her neighbours would emerge, coddled in their winter clothes and complacency, full of curiosity, those wagging tongues.

The colour of the door had changed and she felt tears swell in her chest at the thought of her mother painting, holding the base of her sore back every time she dipped the brush. Alena had always loved that colour of green, maybe her mother did it to cheer herself up or to welcome her back home. Maybe as a memorial.

Alena banged twice with the edge of her fist on the metal door. She could hear a television and then the door opened, a bright light sparking up the lobby. He had glasses, a moustache, on his hip he held a beefy little boy, in a woollen bonnet and

Spider-Man pyjamas. He frowned, moved back, brought a hand to the child's head. Alena didn't know what she looked like, but she guessed she didn't look like good news.

'Yes?'

Alena shook her head and started moving backwards. When she reached the top of the stairs, she fled.

She walked away with the wind whistling through her new coat. They were strangers, that coat and her, so she had no way of knowing which special part to hug, to wrap round her body to stop the chill. And she was used, now, to the biting cold, and the flurry of snow, stinging needles against her skin. Of course she feared the worst. It could have been done. Andriy had the money, and it would be forgotten by the police as though her mother's life was only an awkward planning application, a regulation to be sidestepped with enough roubles. But after she had escaped Andriy's house she had convinced herself there was no profit for them in hurting her mother, or indeed even finding her.

But if that was true, then where was she? And why did she find herself blind with panic when she struggled to remember which bus would take her to the only place she could then think of going?

On the main street she expected to be stopped by people. Alena! My God, is that you? But she looked at herself, in her strange clothes, imagined how her face, her hair, had changed, and took comfort. Still, she wished that Agnetha would be in town that day, that she would see Alena and run a few steps in that childlike way of hers and put a cold hand to Alena's cheek. For a moment Alena stopped walking, unsure of which way to go, but then she thought of Agnetha's strict father, so free with his fists and protective of his little princess, of taking her tumble of clothes and shame to the doorstep of their beautiful, unhappy home, and instead she kept walking in the direction she'd started out for. She'd learned to trust her instinct even when she could trust nothing else.

Down the alley she saw new graffiti, more than she remembered, ice-cream wrappers tumbling through the snow, cigarette ends and crumpled beer cans half buried. Some things do not change. She knocked on the peeling door of the cafe. There were muffled noises on the other side and then a Middle Eastern man opened up, wiping his long thin hands on his dirty apron. Alena thought she might have to run again but he gave her a shy smile, a bob of his head with it, and instead she found her tongue.

'I was hoping . . . I wanted to know . . .' She gave a short laugh because as nervous as she was, she suddenly found it hard to use her mother tongue again, it seemed to want to revert to the broken English she had struggled with for so long. The man gave a wider smile until she forced the words out. 'Is Henka here? She and her son Mikhail, they used to live here, and I was wondering –'

'Yes, yes, yes.'

She stepped into the kitchen that smelled of hot fat, scorched onion, male sweat. She knew to go upstairs but he put a hand on her arm and so she dropped her bag and waited while he made a tray with two fried mince-filled buns, *pirozhki*, and two cups of tea. Then he took her bag on his shoulder, handed her the tray and they climbed the grimy stairs together. So it happened that when Mikhail's mother, Henka, opened the door in a fug of hair-spray and cigarette smoke, Alena stood with offerings and she had to hug her across the tray, those enormous breasts resting on the meat buns, being steamed by the mugs of tea.

Henka left in a flurry of apologies and exclamations, a clatter of heels, as she smeared gloss over her lip-linered mouth and told

Alena to just look in the fridge, and for God's sake, choose something else to wear.

After Henka had gone, Alena hadn't wanted to rummage through her wardrobe, wasn't sure that there would be anything she'd be comfortable wearing anyway, but she went and had a shower, changed into some red jeans and a grey sweater from her bag, then lay on the sofa. She'd had her first kiss with Mikhail on that sofa, now with one creaking arm pulling away from the seat, it was where Henka had shown her how to put on mascara and where they had sat, all three of them in a row, watching TV and eating sunflower seeds, building a mountain of husks on the glass table in front of them.

After their awkward embrace on the doorstep Henka had scooted her in and then put the tray down. Her hair had changed – long, platinum-blonde, styled in a ponytail – but the fake-tanned face was the same, and the fake eyelashes, false nails, false boobs. There was very little of Henka now that was as God intended except her good heart and the roll of fat around her waist she got from loving *pirozhki* a little too much. She was manic as ever, as though she were off to stop the meltdown of a nuclear reactor rather than open a small clothes kiosk in the indoor market. She had grabbed a bite of one of the buns, rooted in her bag, given Alena's arms a squeeze, rooted, chewed, looked up at Alena, a blur of movement.

'This I cannot believe! But, my flower, I have to open the shop. Will you be OK? You can come too? No, you're tired, of course. We have a new supervisor and I don't want to be fined for opening late. He's new, from Moscow, some cousin of someone else's, and well – But you don't want to hear this. You'll stay here, ah, sugar, stay here and eat and –' she paused for a moment to look at Alena's clothes – 'really, for God's sake, go through my wardrobe.'

Alena had stood still and smiled faintly as Henka had whirred around her, upending and repacking her bag, rummaging in one drawer and then another, taking a bite out of the other bun, the first left haphazardly balanced on top of her handbag. She had walked over to Alena and given her a few sticky, lip-glossed kisses. 'Little Alena, you look tired but you're home.'

Finally Alena had found the courage to ask, just as Henka was turning the key to unlock the door.

'My mother? I went but . . .'

And for three seconds Henka had stood still, staring at Alena's face. And then she had squeezed her arm again. 'Of course! Poor girl. I am sorry, of course. But your mother is alive and well looked after. She is just . . . Dementia. Do you understand? It seemed to be so quick no one realised and then, well, it just wasn't safe for her to be by herself.'

Alena could hardly take the news, wanted Henka a-buzz again to distract her.

'But . . . how? She was only in her sixties.'

'She's in a home, out towards Irkutsk.'

And Alena had stood for a moment while Henka looked at her face, then they'd hugged, Henka checked her watch, brought her hands to her head and smacked another hard kiss on Alena's cheek.

'Later, we'll talk later. Now, sleep, eat whatever there is, and please, please use my wardrobe.'

Then she had gone, in a clomping stumble of heels down the stairs, a flash of platinum ponytail and a raised hand to the cook in the cafe. Alena was left standing in a place of her childhood, the too-loud silence of the flat drowned out by the even louder insistence of her own conscience.

Alena was still sleeping when the clack of heels woke her up. Henka lit a cigarette, threw the pack to Alena and started unpacking her shopping.

'I didn't get a fine but that man, honestly, Alena! He comes sniffing around and then you have to offer him tea and he'll finger the stock, lingering over the bra-and-panty sets, I know his sort. From Moscow, did I mention that? Go on, you don't be shy with me, take a cigarette.'

'I've stopped smoking actually, a year or so now.'

Henka paused to give her a disapproving look and then returned to the bags. 'Anyway, if he thinks he's getting anything out of me but what he's owed, and by that I mean rent, then he's a bigger idiot than that face of his suggests. Honestly, Alena, "Fine figure you've there, you'd never believe you'd a grown son."'

Alena jumped in. 'How's he doing, Mikhail?'

'You know that boy, born golden, he works in St Petersburg now.'

'That's wonderful, I'm so pleased for –' And without warning Alena crumpled, her face slick with tears in seconds, and Henka clicked over, making mother-hen noises.

'Darling, darling, I am so sorry, what sort of silly woman am I? Of course you want to know about everyone, you want to know about your mama, and Mikhail, and I want to know where you went, of course I do.' Her fingers rubbed Alena's back, nails snagging her sweater. 'Honestly, I don't know why I'm babbling on, it's just a shock, everyone thought . . . well, I mean not everyone, but we knew your mama hadn't heard from you and that so-called friend of hers, the one that took you there, that stuck-up Chanel handbag bitch, she disappeared off the face of the earth. Your mama, she tried everything to track you both down, spent days on the telephone, but by then she was already starting to –' Henka took a breath and smoothed her blouse down. 'I'll make dinner. I think we have a lot to talk about. But before I say anything else let me say, as I should have when I very first saw you, welcome home, Alena, you've been missed.'

Three months. Three months of the two jobs, the Tooting room and the windows that froze up on the inside, rat droppings on the kitchen counter and his fucked-up housemates. Three months of the junkies outside and watching the endless, miserable plod, plod, plod of plastic-bag-laden shoppers.

He was thinner now, and stronger, walked with his head held a bit higher when he did his rounds, but inside he was still shrinking away at the thought of what he had done, what he had thrown away in a few days of fury. He was saving; saved every penny from his second job, kept the notes rolled up in a jam jar inside a bag at the back of his wardrobe. He knew it was stupid, to take them out of the bank and keep them in a house, especially a house like his, but it was part of his ritual. Every night he scattered the fluttering notes on the bed and counted them, the musty, salty smell of the money rising up as he put them in piles of one hundred. And the more of the duvet he covered, the closer he was. While he counted he wondered if she was working herself, fooled himself into believing that she might have her own pile of crumpled notes, that she might also roll onto her stomach at night, press her face into the mattress and try to remember his warmth beside her.

But he was conning himself. He'd heard nothing from her,

though he checked in with Tahir, his old landlord, to see about mail; he'd even paid for a redirection at the post office. Not a word and he didn't blame her one bit.

Liqueur chocolates shaped like little wine bottles, a ridiculous gift, but Alena had remembered one Christmas morning and her mother biting off the bottle necks pretending to guzzle the booze and how they'd laughed together. The crowded bus and the sense that strangers were sharing something too personal in riding along with her, were what put her in mind of that trip to the Roehampton graveyard. She was visiting her own mother's resting place, a thought that curled around her skull, as missing Dave remained the same ache in her bones.

The place was better than she expected; a converted school, its pale green front pretty against the stark winter sky, it had rich dark wooden floors and lots of light. If she worked hard she could imagine noise and energy, fresh young lives in the corridors. Except that it was so warm, the sort of stale, slow heat that brings to mind spoiled meat. It was so hot that coming in from the bitter wind outside made her fingers and cheeks itch, that she gulped at the air thick with the smell of bleach and old cabbage. Though there was some reassurance in that odour because it was closer to what she expected.

Her mother was in a common room filled with strange, bright Ikea-looking sofas and a few old school tables, notches carved into the edges by former pupils. A huge TV on the wall showed Putin out hunting, bare-chested and black-eyed, laughing with the reporters. Her mother sat at one of the tables beside a fruit bowl, staring at the television. She looked so old. She looked beautiful too, almost peaceful in the cold wash of winter light from the window.

'She hasn't had a very good few days, I'm afraid. Like most, she has good days then bad, she can be perfectly normal sometimes but she often has a patch of days like this. I'm very sorry. It's not you, it wouldn't be a good day for her to see anyone.' The nurse was no more than seventeen, and though she smelt a little of beer from the night before, really did look regretful. 'Perhaps you could come some other day? If you call before we can tell you how she is, whether she's having a good day?'

And Alena had wanted to say, 'I'm not just anyone' or 'What have you done to my mama?' or 'Do you know how far I've had to travel to get to this stinking room and I don't mean the four-hour bus journey either?' but just then her mother looked up, her brown eyes bright, seemingly sharper than ever, and Alena walked quickly across the room, the speed drawing attention in a place so used to the aching slow of life there.

'Mama. Mama, I –'

She stood in front of her mother but couldn't look at her face; instead, she focused on the sweet ripe smell of the fruit bowl making her throat tighten. She put down the little box of bright liqueurs.

'Mama, I –' Her mother looked up sharply, stared and then turned her head away, searching for the nurse as though Alena was a mad person she must not acknowledge or be drawn into the madness herself. 'I'm home. I came home.'

'Nurse? Can you take this girl to whoever she's looking for?'

'Mama?'

'This is very usual. Lots of them do it. It's nothing to do with you, don't worry. It's a symptom.' Alena hadn't noticed the nurse beside her, a patch of blistering pimples on her chin. Her mother spoke directly to the nurse, this time in the strict voice Alena knew well from her teens.

'Really, if you can just take her to wherever she's meant to be. I was just watching the news actually and this is quite inconvenient. I'm sure someone's waiting for her, please take her there.'

The nurse laughed, shook her head, and the girl's easy understanding, so far from her own shock at hearing her mother refer to her as a stranger, made Alena want to push the nurse aside, tell her to fuck off away from her mother.

'Don't you worry, Vera, the news will be on later too. Now this is . . . ?'

She turned to Alena, who could have wept.

'Alena. I'm her daughter.'

'Now Alena has travelled a long way just to have a chat with someone here. You'll let her sit with you for a while, won't you? Maybe you could watch the news together?'

Her mother shrugged, fixed her attention on the television again. Alena took a deep breath, fought the urge to leave the room.

'I'm very tired – could I just sit with you for a little while? We don't even have to talk.'

Her mother didn't take her eyes from the screen but she laid a hand on the chair beside her and Alena sat down.

'Thank you.'

The nurse gave Alena a little pat on the shoulder and wandered off to another table. Alena wanted to turn her mother towards her, was desperate for her to see some of her own face in the younger woman in front of her, to gain even a flicker of recognition, but she kept her eyes on the screen.

'Are they kind to you here? You look well.'

'Please. You're welcome to sit awhile but would you mind being quiet while I'm watching this?'

'OK, Mama.'

Then her mother looked at her for just moment, a small

smile drifting over her features, a kindness she remembered. Her mother laid her hand on Alena's.

'You're confused, I think. You really must be tired.'

'OK, OK. You're right, I must be confused, but I'm here now.'

Alena put her hand up to stop the nurse from approaching, bent to her bag and pulled out a small tube of hand cream. She squeezed a white blob onto her palm and then rubbed it into her own hands just as she had watched her mother do from when she was a girl, first between the fingers, then smoothed over the backs of her hands, massaged in circles up the wrists.

'Would you like some too?'

Her mother didn't look at her but, with an air of resignation and someone used to being cared for, allowed Alena to gently push up the sleeves of her cardigan, to smooth the cream into the skin and bones of her hands and arms. She didn't react to the tear splashes and Alena wondered if they felt warm on her skin.

'Beautiful hands.' It was a distracted statement and Alena didn't know whose she meant.

'Yes, yes, you always had beautiful hands. You said that was one of the things Father loved.'

Her mother snatched back her arms and then took hold of Alena's wrist.

'You. You have beautiful hands.'

'Yes, they're the same. See?'

Her mother frowned and then her upright posture collapsed as though all the air had left her body.

'You. You are . . .'

Tears dripped onto her own wrist. A mother's tears, warm on skin.

14

If he'd had any friends, they might have talked him out of it. Told him that they did have postcards, stamps, the Internet in Russia these days. And all Dave had was the name of a village with too many 'isk' sounds that he couldn't even pronounce properly and no idea if she'd even have gone back there.

He found it on Google Maps, a dot in that giant expanse of Russia. He'd log on at the Somali Internet cafe on his day off, with the same hunched posture as if he was looking at porn, and just stare at the dot where Alena might be right now. People, anyone in fact, would have tried to tell him he was being daft, worse than daft. If him and Deano had still been speaking he would have tried to rough him out of it. 'Come on, mate, I know you liked her but there's so many girls like her out there. What about this? – we get an easyJet, go to Prague and hammer it. And girls like that, that short-skirted ice-queen type who're always up for it after a few drinks, they're ten a penny out there. Come on, what have you got to lose?'

And Dave would have thumped him, a good, satisfying full-contact fist to his greasy nose, like he should have done all those years ago, and would've replied that the whole point was he had nothing to lose. And, he might have added that Alena was one in a million, not ten a fucking penny.

Dave tripped over the floor-buffer cable and Sue, the buffer queen, yanked the cable back. 'Look out, sunshine, too much daydreaming, that's your trouble.' It didn't matter what anyone else thought; he was going. He'd find her, make it right. He'd buy the tickets tonight and in six weeks he wouldn't be walking in circles, he'd be moving across a country, towards Alena, or at least towards knowing he couldn't find her, that that was it, and then, at last, this constant thirst would cease.

There was a method to it. Hands grabbing just the right amount of slimy ham, dry pale yellow grated cheese, slices of mushroom, throwing them onto the circle of pale batter and rolling it all at exactly the point the pancake would be golden underneath; the dollop of sour cream, ice-cream scoop of Russian salad and, if she liked the customer, a sprig of dill.

Of course, in the beginning she had produced inedible lumps, undercooked, overfilled and bursting forth, a stodgy fat babushka of a pancake. Now, a few months into the job she liked to think her pancakes were homely, well-kept wives, the dill a dash of lipstick dabbed on before leaving the house. There was a lot of time to think during the day.

It wasn't the cold that had got to her in the first months she'd been home, since that was a typically brutal Siberian winter. She knew to layer up, even against Henka's advice. 'You look like a sack of potatoes. They'll mistake you, put you in the chipper and then throw you into the deep-fat fryer, you'll be served up with a shawarma. At least borrow my nice pair of fur-lined boots, the ones with the heel? With legs like yours, Alena, you need that heel, trust me.'

It wasn't even the job that she found so hard. She was grateful for it and to Henka, who had had to consent to dinner and an under-the-table grope at Tex's Wild West Restaurant with the Muscovite Market Manager to get Alena in the back door when there were other, less notorious, girls queuing patiently for the job. No, what hurt, even after everything, were the lingering eyes of the people she once knew, school friends mainly, if she would ever have called them that, now wives and mothers, stopping by to pick over her bones.

'London not for you then? And have you been up to see your poor mother in that place?'

Alena would shrug, take care and pride in the pancake she served them, as their eyes roamed over her face, her sweater-swaddled body, looking for clues; she satisfied herself that at least they would never see her charred insides. She visited her mother every few weeks, and though she thought it would be less painful in time, it never was. It was actually even more so on the days when her mother recognised her. Still, spring would arrive and they would walk together in the grounds so her mother could see the green shoots signalling the sunshine to come. In between visits, they spoke on the telephone, Alena standing by the busy main road, pushing herself into the corner of the pissy-smelling booth to get away from the blare of traffic, picking at stickers advertising live webchats with schoolgirls.

'Mama? It's Alena.'

'Who?'

'Alena, Mama, I came home. I'm home, remember? I'm going to come and visit next Monday.'

'Who did you want to speak with? Perhaps this is a wrong number, they're always getting me to the telephone for no good reason at all.'

Her close friends had gone of course, her best friend, Agnetha, her old boyfriend, Mikhail, to the bigger cities, to jobs. She cried in Henka's arms after she'd heard Agnetha had been working for a bank in London all this time. It was only the people left behind who visited her little plywood shack that stood right next door to country children sitting in the cold selling whatever they had from the farm, those 'friends', who wanted to watch the high and mighty Alena make pancakes and turn her eyes away from their gaze.

The women all had children who hooked their little fingers over the ledge while their mothers stared at Alena with a sort of hunger that Alena didn't think would be filled by pancakes. Once or twice they invited her for coffee and she shook her head, smiling '*Nyet*', explained she was staying with a friend and had promised to cook dinner.

Instead, at the end of each shift, she would pull down the hatch, lock the freezing padlock, and walk along the main street to the river as fast as she could, working up a winter sweat that would cool icy on her skin as she stared at the frozen water, unmoving, rippled and pitted as a gash of scar tissue. She would pull Henka's fur coat to her, try to squeeze some extra warmth from her sweaters and stand silent and alone; almost peaceful. She looked at the river, teeth chattering, and reminded it, and herself, that all winters do pass in time.

He worked out that, between his plastic-tray dinners and knackering jobs, he'd saved just over three grand and he jumped. That's how he thought of it, on the bus to Oxford Street, banging the end of a rolled-up newspaper against his knee. He was jumping and he didn't care what happened after that.

He'd been on those websites, the ones meant for kids on gap years who were going out to pickle their livers in vodka and cop off with each other in those international Irish pubs that sold Guinness and pie and mash; the sort of place he'd wanted to go to himself back when he was planning his own big adventure.

This was a different adventure though. Those sites weren't

meant for someone chasing his last chance but they had told him about this place, above a New Look that he thought used to be a C&A. The website was old, had that home-made look about it, and the office wasn't much better, just a shitty room with a cheap, maybe free from a newspaper, map of Russia pinned up and a single desk that looked like it was from a skip. And it wasn't a kid in a beanie with too many stamps in his passport and no savings who ushered him in but a short squat balding cockney, 'East End original, Kent now', with blurry sea-green tattoos up his arms and the sort of polo-shirt and gold-chain combination that Dave hadn't seen since the early days on the estate. The man held out his gold-sovereign-ringed hand. 'Sit down, sit down.'

Dave, still with the *Metro* curled in his fingers, cast about until he found a fold-out stool and sat down on it gently, sure its tinny legs would buckle. It looked like this office was just packed up into a suitcase each day and carted home on the train. Still, he was here now and this bloke and his operation had obviously been here for a while too, so he waited for him to take the reins.

'Name's Tony.'

'Dave.'

'So where to, I mean obviously Russia, but *where*, for how long and why, it's the same question I always ask, why Russia?'

This was all delivered in a rapid cockney rattle. Dave scratched the back of his head, rubbed his palms on his jeans. 'Siberia, I mean just outside Irkutsk.' He mangled the name and Tony chuckled and nodded his head. 'I'm not sure how long, a month? Maybe three. I mean, does that ever happen? Do they ever let you stay that long?'

'It's Russia, so everything can and does happen.' Tony motioned Dave to carry on.

'Um, my girlfriend, I mean my ex-girlfriend, she lives there. I mean, I think that's where . . .'

His voice faltered, but Tony gave a slow nod. Dave saw what might have been a Union Jack bulging just beneath his elbow and remembered that this bloke was a bloke like him, just from another estate.

'She had . . .' Again, words failed him, but in that little room, with the low thrumming noise of the Oxford Street traffic outside, he squared his shoulders. 'She had visa issues and she had to go back, she's from there, Siberia, I mean, I think so because it was all so –'

And as quickly as all that had rushed out he went quiet, afraid there would be tears or he'd tell this Tony, this bloke he didn't know, who he wouldn't buy a second-hand car from, the whole ugly story. But Tony was still nodding, his fingers tented.

'Do you want to know how I got into this business?'

Dave actually didn't give a shit and couldn't see what it had to do with him, or Alena, or the £800 burning a hole in his pocket, but he nodded.

'I met this amazing woman, Dina, on the Internet, one of them sites that everyone looks down their noses at but what's so bad about two people from different backgrounds getting to know each other? Two people looking for the same things finding a way to get them? Ignorant I always think it is, plain and simple. Anyway, I couldn't get her over here by hook or by crook. We had a few holidays and then she couldn't get another visa and we tried for months, and I know you'll think I'm a wally, but I just kept sending over more and more cash, I was a pub landlord then. She was always saying, I just need to give some money to this one, or that one. Anyway, a month went by and I didn't hear a word –' he held up his hand for emphasis, milked his dramatic pause – 'and I was in bits. Everyone was saying to me you've been had you have. A "sting" they called it. And then one day I get a call and she's only at Heathrow waiting for the coach to Victoria. We're married with three kids now. Five of us in a two-bedroom council place in Kent because they keep giving the big places in London to them asylum seekers, refugee-types, but the point is –' against all of Dave's expectations Tony's hand reached out across the desk and landed on top of his own – 'I believe in love.'

Dave sat back; it was more than he had needed to know, and he was ashamed that a part of him wanted to say, 'I'm nothing like you. This wasn't the Internet, she never asked anything of me, she got a paper round for God's sake,' but instead he cleared his throat, gave the sort of charming smile he used to give before Shelley and everything else on the estate.

'I'm happy for you. So you can help then?'

Tony banged his hands on the desk that threatened to re-flat-pack itself.

'Help? Me and my missus have been doing this for years now, I could probably have you two married before you get on the plane. What do you want?'

Dave took out the list he'd written on the back of an envelope with a stubby betting-shop pen.

'Visa, as long as I can get. Accommodation, for Moscow at least, and plane, or I was thinking maybe train tickets out to Siberia. Whatever's cheapest, I don't mind how rough it is, I just . . .' Even after Tony's expansive story, it hurt him to say this last bit, drummed in from his mum that even if you had 2p in your purse and a single tin of soup in your cupboard you should still act as though your pocket was stuffed with twenties. 'Well, I've saved a bit but I'm not sure I've enough, especially if I need to stay for a while.'

Tony sat back and smiled discreetly, the discretion of someone who'd been in the same boat, Dave hoped, and not the sort of discretion of someone who'd happily flog you a cut-and-shut second-hand motor and wave as you drove off.

'I can sort it all, Dave, and this one is close to my heart so there's no management fee.'

Dave shook his hand and then thought all the way home about how it was probably sales patter, that he'd been swindled at the first hurdle, but when he went to collect everything, including his passport and a three-month visa, he saw it was a third less than all the websites had said it would be and Dave understood why he was in that shitty office and a council house in Kent.

He didn't need to pack much. He thought he'd need jumpers, a fleece, maybe thick-soled hiking boots, but he read it was sometimes so hot in Moscow that it was plagued by the drifting black smoke of forest fires and instead packed a spare pair of trainers, shorts, T-shirts, a nice shirt and trousers, thinking that there might be a reason to celebrate. Maybe.

Alena had bought him that shirt, said it brought out the grey in his eyes, like rainwater, she said. Funny how he'd thought her eyes were like tap water, and she thought his were rainwater, it should have been the opposite really. Or something more romantic, a stormy sea, but that wouldn't have been true; ever since he first looked into her eyes what he'd seen was decent, clear and everyday wonderful as tap water.

In the end he took his rucksack half full, the one that had travelled with him in the last ten years though never where he hoped it would: that honeymoon in Southend, to Shelley's, Hackney and then Tooting and now, finally doing his 'big trip', to Russia, hopefully to Alena, either way to some peace, the end of it all. And at that thought he stopped balling socks and rolling his T-shirts into thick sausages, lining up toothbrush and toothpaste. He sat still in his shitty little room and looked out at Tooting; with its cars beeping, gaggles of girls at the ATM taking out tenners for shots in Wetherspoons, the old bent-over woman with a light plastic bag of shopping, a single loaf of bread or a pint of milk, just enough to get her out of the house, a younger woman, her beautiful orange sari flapping in the grimy city air, swinging a child between her and her husband, the small boy's feet making a glorious, joyful sweep across the zebra crossing.

Dave packed the last of his stuff and prayed to the pulse of the city, his city. He asked for its blessing, that he might leave and come home again. And, after months apart, come home with Alena.

15

Of course he'd been to airports before, to Heathrow, once to Gatwick on a school trip when they'd let them put their school bags on one end of the luggage belt and run to collect them at the other end. It was probably then that the idea of travelling had stuck with him. Another time was to Luton for a Club Med 18–30 thing all the lads did for Deano's twenty-first but they'd got lathered on cans on the coach there and spent the rest of the time in the airport pub doing Jager Bombs so it was all a bit blurry. He mainly remembered the taste of an undercooked fried breakfast on his tongue and Ricky throwing up into a bin in the too-bright departures lounge, the awful blistering sunburn after the first day by the pool.

Now, though, it was just him and his bag and City Airport wasn't really a proper airport. It was a giant doctor's waiting room full of businessmen and women, all sitting with their briefcases, some sweaty-faced and hunched over laptops probably with screens full of numbers, their expressions fixed as though they were waiting for a particularly invasive procedure. There was one stag do, wolfing down baguettes in the Pret A Manger, all wearing slogan T-shirts: Mr Fruity, Mr Hung, Mr Wouldn't Waste Your Time, and a few holidaymakers in thin bright clothes looking for the duty-free they'd never find.

Dave went straight to departures, hoped to hell that Tony's cheap-looking, Monopoly money visa pasted into one of his passport's pages was legit. The queue moved quickly since the airport staff's job was to make sure all those very important business people made their meetings in Zurich, Brussels, Amsterdam or Paris.

Unfortunately, the couple one down from him didn't

understand about those important meetings but you could see they couldn't help it. The husband was about sixty, tall and thin, with a shiny bald head and a face that looked like it had never smiled. The woman, shorter and rounded, had had a shampoo and set done specially, and they were both dressed up in their Sunday best; her in a pastel trouser suit and him in a pale blue shirt and nice trousers. Like his mum, Dave thought, the sort who'd wear their best clothes for the travelling even though it was only ever a coach. You could tell they hadn't much money, they were worried about being made a show of.

The boarding passes had tickets with bar codes that you had to scan to get through the barrier but the woman didn't understand. The guard kept shouting, 'Madam, just hold it against it, just hold it against it.'

And her husband kept trying to guide her hand by the wrist towards it but she stood frozen. Her husband had a loud voice, too loud as though he, or perhaps she, was deaf, and he was shouting, not unkindly, just like it was the only way she'd understand. 'Hold it, just like I did, hold it against it.'

And then the guard started shouting at him. 'Sir, if you can just come through now. Madam. Just. Press. It.'

And behind Dave he felt a tsunami of disdain, tutting, snappy checking of watches that pushed sharp elbows into other passengers' personal space, the whole seething snake of the queue going sour. The woman could feel it too.

Of course, when they finally reached the metal detectors they had coins, nail clippers, metal belt buckles and key rings galore. A female guard with a hand-held metal detector scanned it over the woman while she looked at her husband horrified.

'Madam, just lift your hands up from your sides.'

The woman lifted her arms and then lowered them again

before the metal detector could cross the undersides. She did that five times, until the guard was laughing kindly and saying, 'Madam, just keep them up, OK? Keep them up until I say put them down.'

And her husband, looking worried for her, like he wanted to take her away back on a bus to wherever they'd come from, shouted. 'Up, Maureen. You've to keep 'em up.'

Dave wanted to walk over, hold her wrists gently and talk to her quietly, turn her away from all the impatient stares, the huffy twitching and expensive shoes clicking off importantly to other queues. He was sure he could have made her understand. After the sole inspection, which took another ten minutes, her husband put his hand gently on her shoulder, tilted his head into hers and said something Dave couldn't hear.

She wandered off barefoot, shoes dangling from her fingers, looking like she'd been assaulted, and as Dave went through, quick as a whistle, he consoled himself thinking of the all-inclusive resort they were on their way to, how that woman would stretch out her legs and catch the sun and have a glass of sangria too many. She'd come back brown as a nut, with souvenirs for the grandkids and her waistband a bit tighter from the all-you-can-eat buffets.

When Dave was planning his big trip, he'd always imagined flying, somehow his imagination always combined the taking off with a countdown, with a rocket being launched. All he remembered from last time was that he'd fallen asleep almost straight away and one of the lads had written 'knob' on his forehead in biro. Now, tucked into his seat, he felt this was just a clean, characterless little bubble of possibility. You sat in a seat you were told to sit in, ate what you were given, from the little compartments, icy cubes of melon and spongy omelette. There was even a little light to tell you when you could piss and when you couldn't. Just the blue sky outside, clouds that looked solid and not a thing you could do about anything even if you wanted to.

The only other non-business passenger was a girl with frizzy hair and glasses, wearing friendship bracelets made of coloured string. She had a journal open and, from across the aisle, Dave could see that every entry started with 'Je suis' but that was all the French he knew. No, actually he could've told her his name and told her he resided in Putney, asked her how she was, whether she had a dog, but he stayed quiet, watched her chewing on a sodden clump of string at her wrist.

Leaning back, staring at the sky, his food sitting on his full stomach, he could almost make himself believe he was going off to a happy ending. That he would find her, she would forgive him and then there would be no secrets. Then, like a bad omen, the turbulence started, the girl's pen made an angry gash on the page, a steward's hand slipped and a stream of steaming coffee spilled on the floor. Dave, reaching to help with the coffee pot, upended his tray and the little pots and cartons and square dishes went scattering.

The steward looked down at Dave struggling to pick everything up; he was too tanned but it made his teeth look nice and white; he looked young, younger than Dave. 'Really, sir, there's no need. The seat belt sign is on.'

And he bustled off to seat-belt himself in. The turbulence lasted the entire journey, the passengers being jostled and thrown about and the stewards running around with panicked smiles. When they touched down everyone applauded and Dave told himself there was no such thing as a bad omen and that he should just be grateful he didn't have 'knob' written on his head this time.

His guidebook had said he needed to fill out a form but when he walked towards the island with the little forms and pens that he just knew wouldn't work, he was ordered back into the queue by a young kid in uniform, collar tight above his bobbing Adam's apple. It was just a string of spat-out Russian words but Dave understood an order when he heard one, even when it was from someone with blackheads and a birth certificate ten years newer than his own.

At the counter someone older, but with that same expression, gave Dave's visa a quick snapping stamp and with a bored look told him to pass through. Tony had seen him right. Three months. One way or another, three months was enough.

The first thing he saw was a booze shop. There was something mesmerising about all those bottles of vodka lined up, more versions than you could imagine, that made Dave want to go inside; bottles with just slightly different shapes and different-coloured labels, all looking crystal clear, healthy almost. Two-thirds of the shop was vodka; this would have been Shelley's dream destination, though it was the Canaries she always spoke about.

The arrivals area was lined by a tight crush of relatives holding small bunches of bright flowers, and oily-mouthed, sharp-eyed taxi drivers. The relatives stood silent with the barest of smiles, all the little girls had intricate plaits and ponytails, adorned with miniature top hats or flowers, and glum faces. The whole thing put him in mind of a dog show somehow. The taxi drivers' eyes flicked over him in a way that made him slide his hand over to his wallet and decide to catch the train into the city after all. Dave, though he felt nothing like it, smiled, as though this were his own personal welcoming committee, and walked out into the overwhelming grey of Moscow airport.

He tried to take out 200,000 roubles like a dolt, 4,000 quid, and his heart was thumping from worrying about his card being refused. Then he did his sums and felt like an idiot, doubting he'd make it out of the airport, let alone right across Russia. He withdrew 7,000 roubles not sure how long it would last him. Tony had said Moscow was pricey.

'I'm not going to lie to you, Dave, the prices in Moscow, they'll blow your socks off. But you'll just have a day there and then you'll be on your way and you'll want a proper bed for the night, a hot shower before the plane the next day.'

'Couldn't I take the train? I mean, it's meant to be great, isn't it? And –' he had looked down at his hands – 'I thought it might give me a chance to get myself together, get used to being there and everything. You know, before I see her. Sort out everything in my head.'

Tony had nodded, picked up and set down his mug again.

'Dave, it's up to you. I mean, well, I don't know how you've left things with this girl, and I'll be honest with you, it's about the same price to go by plane. But you're right about flying, you'll be stepping right into the thick of it all, and I'm telling you, Dave – Russia? Culture shock –' he'd sing-sung those two last words – 'but with the train, right enough, you get a few days to gather yourself, get used to everything. Some experience too. So, it's up to you, what do you think?'

And though Dave knew he didn't need to gather himself, he'd planned exactly what he wanted to say, he decided on the train, maybe because there was a little part of him that was still that kid who'd wanted to see the world and maybe because he also knew how she would respond and that he might be glad of those few days beforehand just watching Russia roll by, when at least he still had hope.

16

The way into the city was like different pictures all sliced up and taped back together, birch trees and farmland, high-rise blocks with bits peeling off them like giant sunburn, factories belching from fat chimneys. And then there was Moscow, with its tall grey buildings, greyer for the sultry dusk behind them, their tiny lit windows like crushed glass. As the chill of the train's air conditioning crept up his arms he caught himself thinking that this didn't feel like a friendly city. He saw himself in the window: a ghost floating on top of rows of electric generators, coils and pipes, and his face looking scared as shit. Some great adventurer he was. He'd never have made it to the other side of the world.

The Metro was amazing though. All wood and marble and sculptures, glittering glass mosaics showing rosy-cheeked children waving red flags and workmen with blue eyes and chiselled jaws. Trying to buy a ticket from the woman behind the counter was the first problem, she was sixty-five if she was a day, with frizzy yellow hair and a bright pink lipstick setting off her jowly face. She was a misery alright, and even more so when she realised Dave couldn't speak a word of Russian.

She kept saying something to him and as she did a queue grew and he felt it shift behind him like a single thing. Stupid tourist, it seemed to push forward and say, idiot Englishman. Eventually someone walked to the front of the queue, took Dave's wallet out of his hand and slid another 100-rouble note into the metal bowl at the bottom of the window and then pushed the wallet back into Dave's hand. The man didn't look at Dave, simply walked back to his place, and the woman, straight-faced as though nothing of any interest had happened, slid his Metro card through the window without making eye contact. Dave said a halting Russian thank-you and walked off towards the barriers with the hard eye of the station policeman, in a too-wide hat, on him the whole way.

Nothing was in English, nothing. Even the letters that should have been familiar looked the same. It was like a code he hadn't learned, even though he had spent hours in his little room mouthing the letters, joining them up, making baby-like gurgles and twisting his tongue around sounds that made him spit. The heat, his tiredness, the idea that he'd only been in City Airport a few hours ago, made it all seem a bit like a bad dream as he teetered on the escalator, his backpack rocking him. At the bottom there was a little glass booth with another uniformed grandma inside it, this time with red lipstick and a jaunty little grey cap. They don't say that in the guidebooks, do they? Moscow Metro, powered by women who look like your nan. He sidestepped the flow of foot traffic and knocked on the glass booth, tried to conjure the word he'd learned onto his tongue.

'Pashalsta?'

She turned and, seeing his smile – he never usually smiled this much – her own mouth broke out into a wide smile, a tooth missing from the bottom row, her eyes hidden behind a woolly clump of over-mascaraed eyelashes. Dave held the scrap of paper up to the booth window, damp from where he'd been clutching it. She took out her reading glasses and looked at the paper where Dave had written the backwards 'N' and 3, the odd curves, in the hand of a three-year-old. She nodded and made her fingers into two small legs walking downstairs, motioned left and then held up three fingers and then two and Dave, because she was obviously trying hard, replied, 'Da, da, da,' bowed his thank-you and then lumbered off with no idea where to go.

It took him an hour and a half and two journeys back on himself but eventually the penny-sweet-coloured lines brought him to his station and then up the steps past the violinist and into a street that smelt of pancakes with the shining dome of churches in the night and kids sitting around passing two-litre bottles of beer.

The last thing he thought as he settled himself into the creak of bed in his tiny room that night was how funny it was that McDonald's tasted exactly the same. Then he thought that he wouldn't tell Alena his first Russian food had been a Big Mac.

The main thing he felt was stupid. As he mugged and gurned, held up his fingers for numbers and made sign language for water, mimicked milking a cow to a hard-faced woman who, when she finally understood, gave a small quiver of the lips that might have been a smile.

He bought apples and oranges from a woman's cart by the Metro station, her hair covered in a maroon scarf, five gold upper teeth set off by her dark olive skin. He'd seen her the night before, during that hungry, dreamlike walk to the McDonald's next to a church. She'd been sitting outside her stall with a friend, their wide bottoms squeezed into red chairs meant for toddlers. They'd sat silently, looking up at the moon behind the gold dome of the church, her friend swigging from a can of lager and the fruit woman, still with a tray of berries on her knee, tucking into an ice-cream cone.

Now she gave him a gilded smile, charged him practically nothing, pressed a free polystyrene cup of tiny wild strawberries into his hands and motioned for him to eat them. For some reason it embarrassed him and, when he tried to push a note into her hand, she looked at him sharply, then turned away from him and shook her head. She didn't look round again, busied herself with brushing dirt from a pile of beetroots with a paint-brush until Dave mangled out a thank-you and walked away feeling that he had behaved badly. He wanted to go back and explain, joke about it in the way he would've in Dalston market. Somehow he'd managed to turn a gesture of kindness into something awry, and those sweet strawberries rolled about his mouth like tiny bitter pills. He'd never felt more of an idiot.

The main station was the colour of mint-choc-chip ice cream. He went through the metal detectors, avoided the eye of the police German shepherd, lips itching about its teeth, and bustled past the families with bags and bags of luggage. People had laundry bags bigger than Dave had ever witnessed, large enough to serve as a small house for a child. Even in Hackney, where laundry bags were an unofficial community mascot, he had seen nothing like it. He saw some of the travellers had cardboard boxes, filled with rabbits and kittens, fastened with bungee cords to suitcases on wheels.

Like the Metro stations, this building was hewn from marble and wood, old-fashioned lights covering everything in a creamy light. It reminded Dave of a Mayfair hotel he'd once worked in, before they realised he had no class. The difference was that here it looked like they'd decided to put up the local estate in their fancy hotel. All those boxes and bags, neat and tidy but well-worn clothes, and too much gold jewellery. The women were in plastic shoes and matching plastic nails, too much make-up over grubby travel-tired skin, the men swigging lager and children getting their arses smacked when they got too hopped up on the chocolate cakes and giant packets of crisps that their parents kept giving them.

In fact it wasn't like that hotel at all; it reminded Dave of those films when big buildings are used by refugees sheltering from some sort of disaster. And there was Dave, fitting right in, a refugee from his own disaster.

He started working his way through the kiosks, buying boiled eggs, sweaty, cling-film-wrapped slices of bread and salami, tomatoes and the strange bumpy cucumbers they sold. Like everyone else he jostled his way through the narrow doors of the identical kiosks and bought a different thing in each one, as though this were part of the trip, a tour or a ritual. He bought bags of crisps and more dusty oranges. Twice the women motioned to the fridge with beer and vodka and Dave shook his head.

He looked at the kids running about and bought little packets of jelly sweets and a big bag of M&M's. Finally he sat on his rucksack and ate a Russian Magnum, picking off the chocolate bit by bit to get to the ice cream, watching the giant digital clock count down. Tick, tick, tick. At least he was moving, getting closer to whatever he'd find on the other side of Russia. He experienced a woozy feeling, as though he'd climbed to the top of some scaffolding without realising how high it was. He noticed his heart was thumping for every second that passed. He'd been right, he needed this journey to sort himself out.

He was working the ice-cream stick between his teeth, letting the wood splinters scrape his gums, when he saw the child crying. In this crowd a kid crying wasn't anything you paused to look at, except this one was wandering in circles, his panicked eyes batting around. The more he circled, the less his eyes fell on what they were looking for. He was maybe three or four, with dark hair and brown eyes, a skinny body in combats and a once white T-shirt that showed the round of his belly. He cried more, brought his hand up to his head and rubbed his shaved scalp with his palm and kept moving. Not circles now, but jagged little tracks back and forth through the crowd. What could Dave do? He couldn't even speak to him.

There were police a few metres away and an older smart-looking woman with a wheely suitcase, not laundry bag, who stopped him. She asked him something and the little boy struggled words out, looked behind him. She was a grandmother herself maybe, but she was unsmiling, kept her hand on her suitcase handle. She pointed to the police and the boy looked at them then back at her, his chest heaving, and then, rubbing his knuckles at his eyes, went and stood in front of the police, two, one clearly more senior in one of those cartoonishly wide-brimmed hats.

The boy stood two feet away from them and now Dave saw he had tears running down his face and he was having trouble speaking. The senior policeman looked down at him with a small distant smile on his face, asked the boy another question, a quiet one, and the boy looked around, shook his head, and just when the policemen were talking to each other and Dave realised his mouth was full of splinters from the ice-cream stick, they walked away from the boy in a slow amble. The boy, startled for a moment from his tears, stood and watched them go. The older woman stood by her bags, shrugged and looked away as the young boy blinked, started crying again and scrubbing his scalp with fresh distress.

Dave struggled himself and his backpack up. He was just wondering how to say 'Where's your mum?' in sign language, and how badly it would turn out for him if he thumped the stupid hat off that fat lazy arsehole of a policeman's head, when the boy's hand was snatched by a tall woman in the tightest jeans

Dave had ever seen. The boy gave a half-second beautiful smile then, arm first, legs following and his eyes looking, still perplexed, at the policeman's back, he was dragged away in a flurry of what Dave assumed was the Russian equivalent of 'Wait till you get home, I was worried sick, what's wrong with you, running off, I can't turn my back for a second.'

The final minute ticked over and Dave's platform came up on the board. The crowd surged as though they didn't all have tickets, as though it was the last train out of town. Somewhere in the crush a woman held a newborn to her chest and dragged a laundry bag behind her, so Dave stayed still until she passed, then he hefted the laundry bag up onto his shoulder and gave her a smile and one of the shallow bows he'd become used to doing.

He was close to tears. Everything was just getting to him, piling up and covering his mouth and nose; that little lost boy and then that woman and her baby, her cheap yellow sandals, the dried brown smear of blood across the top of her foot where they cut in, and her shy, too-grateful smile though he had done nothing but carry a bag a few metres. Then his attendant, *provodnista* he'd read they called them, he'd never seen anything like it. A mahogany tan, white-blonde wig, lips heavy with gloss half a centimetre outside her lips, her breasts crushed into a bra meant for a teenage girl, lumpen legs encased in shiny tan tights, her belly concertinaed twice by her uniform.

She stood by what he thought was his carriage. He smiled his smile, the one he'd used to crack the rock-hard hearts of tired women since he was a teenager, the one that had made his name in the Co-op and then with Yvonne at the shop. And though he'd admit it didn't have the hundred per cent success it used to he'd never seen it hit a brick wall like this one. She snatched the ticket, asked for his passport and, as he tried to get at it, his arms strung with the many plastic bags of his station shopping spree, his rucksack like a burning boulder on his back, she rolled her eyes and said something to two young lads in their army uniforms. The uniforms had the cheap ill-fitting look of fancy dress, and the boys laughed loud and enthusiastically, breathing kebab-and-beer gusts over his shoulder as he fumbled for his passport. Once she'd inspected it very, very closely, she shoved it back. He tried to ask where he should go but she just waved him through; Dave felt the sharp flick of her nails on his bare arms.

The train was old-fashioned and strange but somehow it was all a bit like he'd seen it before too. He was in berth 11, up on top, in compartment 13. His home for the next four days. Four narrow beds, two stacked on top of each other on either side with a little table by a window in the middle. On each bed there was a neatly rolled mattress, thick blanket, a greying pillow with the spines of feathers sticking out. There were pink suitcases piled up in the little space between the beds. A grandma sat on the bed under his, seventies at least he thought, wearing a kerchief, with skin it was impossible to imagine as having once been smooth, and a small girl of about seven with enormous bunches, so long she was sitting on the ends of them, and a serious little face, a tiny, pursed mouth. They looked up at him and then back to the colouring book on the grandma's lap.

Dave stood in the doorway, wondering if he should offer to move the bags for them – poor love, she probably couldn't do it herself – there was a luggage space above the door. He motioned towards the suitcases, eyebrows up, and reached for one, about to motion hoisting them, when the grandma looked up, pulled her granddaughter closer to her and started repeating, while waving her hands, '*Nyet, nyet, nyet, nyet.*'

She did it in such a traumatised way that Dave held his hands in an 'I surrender' gesture, until, after a particularly long and uncomfortable stare from the girl's pale eyes and a disgruntled shake of the woman's head, they turned back to their colouring. After a few minutes of standing there, being barged as people in the corridor pushed past his backpack, he found the latch to release a tiny three-rung ladder and squeezed his pack and then himself up onto the narrow bed, his knees gouging his cheese-and-salami sandwiches as he slid on the spray of plastic bags.

By now people from the rest of the carriage's compartments were wandering up and down the aisle, which was carpeted in what seemed to be the giant equivalent of one of those rotating hand towels. Dave sweated, hunched over, his crown scraping and bumping the ceiling, and finally managed to shove his pack away into the space above the door. He hung his warm, misshapen groceries from a hook, unrolled his thin stained mattress and the itchy blanket. When he took off his boots the strong smell of his hot feet guffed up the carriage and though he couldn't see them he imagined the girl and grandma below looking at each other, in the shade of their bunk, with the resignation of people who have to spend four days with an idiot foreigner and his overripe feet.

Dave put on another pair of socks to suffocate the worst of it but by then he could feel the heavy bags of his eyes, that thickness in his throat that meant he was close to tears. He turned to face the wooden wall, away from the curious eyes in the corridor, the occasional snatches of conversation between them and the grandma. He tucked his knees up as much as he could until the bulk of him pushed against the safety railing. And finally the train, a giant arthritic animal waking and stretching, shunted and jerked itself from the platform.

It was a pathetic way to be leaving Moscow but still he kept his eyes closed and imagined that he was back in Hackney, in their bed with the dip in the middle, the sheets always covered in crumbs. Alena was behind him but it was too hot to cuddle she'd said, though he felt her weight next to him and the clicking noises she'd sometimes make with her tongue when she was sleeping. He tried to remember her smell but could only think of the scent of burnt bacon and for some reason that comforted him. He imagined that bed, that he'd wake up with Alena every day of his life, that they would still fight, he'd never know all of her secrets, she'd never be a better cook, but there wouldn't be any memory of that night of shouting and smashed glass, of her begging him for help and him turning away from her, or the sick hung-over feeling in the pit of his stomach when he realised what he'd done.

For a few seconds he was there, he could feel the bare skin of her back warming his just a few inches away, felt that he could roll back and her small body would shore him up.

'*Billyet.*'

He felt the sharp prod of those nails on his jeans leg and then a heavy square plastic bag thrown on top of him. He pulled himself up. He was getting pissed off with this – she must've seen he was resting; whether she understood or not he was going to tell her a few things about the customer always being right or at least not a total mug. But when he sat himself up as far as he could and pushed aside the plastic-wrapped sheets, he saw that the *provodnista*'s wig was squint and that there was something sick, bloated, underneath the sheen of dark tan. She wasn't a well woman. Dave recognised it easily enough.

He took a deep breath, handed over his ticket and then she motioned him down from the bunk. Once he had contorted himself onto the floor below, he watched as she made up his bed for him in quick practised movements, and chattered with the girl and grandma, shaking her head. She gave him a nod and clasped both her hands under her ear, pushing the wig further to the right. 'Sleep, sleep.'

Dave smiled at her, said thank you, and he saw the smallest smile in return; an embarrassed tilt of her head, a hairline fracture in her hardness. She looked like a teenager hoping to please but wanting everyone to think anything but. A touch more sure of himself, he tried again to smile at the grandma but she kept her eyes fixed on the passing trees and her granddaughter stared baldly at him, her face unreadable, the wispy end of one pigtail between her lips.

He went for a walk, did eight steps before he got to the end of the carriage. At both ends were toilets, all stainless steel that looked like they were from the 1950s, spotlessly clean – they even had a 'cappuccino' scented air-freshener – except for a filthy rag thrown on the floor. The toilet flushed with a pedal that opened a metal flap onto the rails and Dave apologised to the people of suburban Moscow as he watched his sizeable turd ricochet off the rails. The toilets didn't have taps, just a metal nozzle you pushed up to release the water, but Dave wouldn't learn this until two days into the trip. Too embarrassed to ask, he just ran his hands around the droplets left in the metal sink and hoped he wouldn't get dysentery before he could see Alena.

Outside the *provodnista*'s little office – a room with a chair, table, a bunch of lopsided plastic poppies and stacks of packet noodles and bags of crisps – was the samovar. He'd read about these but it wasn't fancy like he'd expected. It was just complicated, all nozzles and tubes, a thermostat, a lever to turn for hot water. It made him think of an old time machine, or of *Charlie and the Chocolate Factory* that his mum used to read him, the machine that churned out magic gobstoppers in gusts of steam. As he filled his travel mug and added his sachet of 'all-in-one' tea that smelt vaguely of baby sick, he wondered what his mum would've made of all this: the *provodnista*, the solemn children, her Davey all the way out here chasing after a foreign girl he barely knew.

'Stuck up, the lot of them, you'd think they were living somewhere fancy, not practically Third World. No wonder it was called the flaming Cold War, I'm frozen through just from the looks of them, ice queens and then some. And that one, running the train, using them rags as bathmats and putting on her airs and graces in a Wonderbra and enough make-up to sink a battleship. If she thinks my Dave's head will be turned by a few hospital corners she's another thing coming. And don't you worry, I know this is just a phase, isn't it? This Alena girl's turned him besotted but she's not his sort really, is she? Not like Shelley, a good girl from the estate; what would I ever have to chat about with that foreign one? And all those charity-shop clothes and her temper, those tears. Not for my Davey. No, he'll come home soon enough. What's he want with a place like that, a girl like that, when he could be back here?'

Dave turned away from the blur of his reflection, and the temptation of those thoughts, in the wide belly of the samovar. His mum wasn't there though, it was just him and the shadow of Alena he was chasing, that he'd been chasing since that very first day. And as he walked his way along the giant hand towel, stepped over kids crouched over card games and swerved around people walking to the toilet with bowls of grimy cucumbers to wash and children's potties to empty, he realised that the sore, raw place of missing that his mum had once occupied now belonged to that girl with the charity-shop clothes, temper and gentleness in equal measures.

He imagined that feeling of missing a machine inside him, maybe a small version of that samovar, except this one was constantly pumping and steaming away, the thermostat needle jumping side to side. He thought that if he couldn't find her, or worse, if he could find her but she turned him away, it would explode in his chest, splintering his bones and puncturing his soft lungs, and he would be full of shrapnel, whistling with holes of grief every time he took a breath for the rest of his sorry life.

He was ready to climb back up to his bunk, turn himself to the wall. He needed to succumb to a small, silent, self-indulgent cry. But back in the cabin the table groaned under the weight of a loaf of bread, a block of white cheese, sausage, tomatoes, boiled eggs, pink wafer biscuits and chocolates in gold plastic wrappers. The woman and girl sat side by side in front of the table staring out of the window. When Dave walked in the grandma pushed forward the girl who said, in halting English, 'You name is?'

'David.'

She gave a wide smile, turned to her grandma and rattled off a sentence with a heavily accented Dav-yeed in it, and the old woman, who he now noticed had a dress with an extra panel sewn in in long hand-stitches and slippers with the toe taped to the sole, nodded and smiled a gappy smile that made her loose skin collapse on itself, and motioned to the empty bed opposite the table.

'Dav-yeed, Dav-yeed.'

She put her palm upturned towards the table and then brought the tips of her fingers to her bottom lip.

So Dave sat opposite her and said thank you and when it

became clear that he wouldn't help himself the woman cut small portions of each item of food and handed a piece to Dave and then to the girl who sat snugly beside him. The three of them watched the dusk behind the birch trees, the only sounds their chewing, the blunt knife scraping through the thick bread until the woman made a noise with her tongue and said, her palm upturned this time towards the window, 'Russia.'

He nodded, the woman nodded in return and the little girl's arm snaked through Dave's to steal a shiny wrapped chocolate from the table.

17

They'd given up riffling through the back pages of his book to try and exchange phrases. It had tiny print and pages thin as a Bible's. It was the weight of, and about as useful as, a brick, though it claimed to be the ultimate guide for savvy travellers. Maybe the problem was that Dave wasn't savvy, no matter how many travel books he'd read. Again, he wondered how he would have managed on that big trip of his.

The old woman and her granddaughter had got off in Omsk, a good word Dave had rolled around his tongue a few times. They'd finally let Dave touch their cases and he'd piled them all up by the train door under the approving eye of the *provodnista*. He needed that approval after she'd caught him chucking a few inches of Cupa Soup down the samovar drain; people had pushed their heads out of their compartments to see who was getting a tongue lashing and then looked at each other, shaking their heads as Dave had stood, head bowed, trying to mop the lumpy bits with the sleeve of his jumper.

Before she left, the grandmother had packaged up the last of the biscuits, sweets, a few tea bags, and given them to Dave, clasping both his hands. When he offered the little girl a chocolate bar he'd bought specially at a station to give her, the grandma kept pulling her finger across her throat. Here we go, thought Dave, thinking of her panic over the cases, but actually he understood, as she gently chopped her straightened hand up her chest: she was saying the girl was full up.

She was a good sort, proud and too polite to take anything

in return for all she'd offered him. He'd become attached to her, her soft white hair and the tiny brush that she'd get out before clasping small, thin sections into bright children's clips. She doted on the little girl and anyone could see, from the hand-stitched clothes, the fall of her shoulders, the skin no more cared for than a muddied plastic bag, that she'd never been doted on herself.

The girl still just stared at him, but Dave thought she was just curious. When the train door opened onto the platform they were met by the girl's father, a short beer-bellied man in a vest, chain, tattoos, his ginger skinhead and wide grin setting him apart from the other miserable faces on the platform. After Dave had helped them off with the cases the father came and gave Dave, not a handshake as he'd expected, but a hug with thumps to the back that could have saved a choking man. The woman insisted on waiting for the train to depart and waved him off like a long-lost son; the little girl still stared at him, unsmiling, with her arms at her side, until they couldn't be seen any longer, leaving just the bright pink spot of their caravan of luggage on the grey platform.

So now he found himself opposite his new companion. Another woman, which made Dave grateful. He'd been to the buffet carriage – his mum would have loved it there, with proper paper napkins folded in swan shapes, fake flowers in vases, big plastic-coated menus, wine glasses on the table and nothing on the menu but beer, vodka, nuts and crisps. That visit made him realise he wasn't interested in sharing with a bloke. He'd watched them, both young and older, get slowly, silently and efficiently hammered, nibbling on nuts. The visible relief when they cracked the can.

But from Omsk this woman and him had the whole compartment. It was hard to tell but he thought she was in her fifties, about his mum's age really. She was fat, not just a bit overweight, but massively, well beyond the help of Weight Watchers or a Davina McCall DVD, in the way that makes it hard to decipher a body under the folds of flesh. She wore prints, a loose floral blouse on top, stretchy stripy trousers on her bottom half. Her face was heavily made up, and even Dave, who didn't think about those things, thought Shelley's Avon round was wasted in Roehampton. She could have made a killing here.

He would find out her name was Nina, after a lot of thumping of his chest and saying Dave, Dave, Dave. She smiled a wide eager-to-please smile, with plenty of gold teeth, nodded emphatically but took a while to respond and say her name. If he tried to use a Russian phrase from the guidebook she nodded and nodded again, smiled, and when they realised that they didn't understand one another, would look out of the window embarrassed and holding her girth.

But eventually they relaxed into each other. Dave slept while she did her wordsearches, and read her magazines. He'd step out into the corridor and come back in to find a faintly cheesy smell wafting and her brushing her long black hair straight in order to twist it back up into the bun. She didn't want to share food, which was a bit of a relief after being force-fed for the last couple of days, but it took her a while to realise he wasn't fussed. So when he went out for his walk on the platforms during their stops, to buy an ice cream from one of the old women carrying them in laundry bags, or watch the pastel sky slide behind another station coloured like a block of Neapolitan itself, he would come back to find her hurriedly wrapping up whatever she'd been eating, brushing crumbs from her front with a guilty smile.

In the end Dave bought a large flat pasty thing and ate it

without offering her a piece and they were able to settle into a comfortable understanding. So now they sat with their own foods scattered across the table, picking away. Dave did fast double beats with his hand on his chest.

'Love.' He made his fingers walk through the air. 'I'm going across Russia to find love. No, no, I mean to find *my* love, my girlfriend.'

At this her bun wobbled and she nodded, a flash of gold, a few extra chins.

'Girlfriend.'

They all knew those words, girlfriend, boyfriend. He leaned forward.

'At least she was my girlfriend. She always had her secrets but we've both made mistakes and now we'll fix them. Together. I mean, you can't ignore it, can you? Love. Or the fact I'm going right across Russia, across the world even, for her? And I'd stay here, I mean if that's what she wanted and I was able to, I'd learn the language and all that, but she always said she loved London, I mean better than Russia. No offence. So I mean, I'm just hoping . . .'

He trailed off. Even though Nina was smiling encouragingly he knew he was speaking to himself. She reclined on the seat, her mug, in one of the glass-and-metal holders that the *provodnista* gave out, sinking into her stomach, her bun pushed forward by the pillow behind her head. She was obviously enjoying the chat though. Dave took a drink of his Coke, warm and flat from sitting by the window.

'So the plan is . . . well, there's no plan really, except to find her. I know the town where she lives. I mean, I know where she used to live.' He looked away now, out of the window and into the trees, the occasional flash of blistering blue sky, sprays of lilac flowers that seemed to be the only thing that grew by the rails. 'And I can see, of course I can, how hard it's going to be, but I just need a few bits of luck. And I'm due that. No, that sounds ungrateful, I don't mean I'm owed it, meeting her was the best luck ever, but still, I'm asking for a bit more. I'm not a lucky sort really though, not really.'

The Coke, and probably the fish-flavoured crisps, the pastry, the ice cream and chocolate and cling-film-wrapped pancakes bought from one of the platforms, had made his stomach bloat, acid rise up in his chest. He slid lower into the seat, stared hard at the unchanging scenery, though he could feel the woman's eyes still on him. Saying it out loud, even to someone who couldn't understand, made him realise what a fool he was being. That he should just get off next stop and go home. The woman, with considerable effort that made Dave look even harder at the window, turned on her side, reached across and gave his knee a pat, still smiling.

'Lucky. Lucky.'

And Dave smiled back, he couldn't not in the face of those gold hip-hop gnashers, the purple eyeshadow and fingertip-shaped streaks of red on the cheeks, but he shook his head. 'No, not really. Just for one summer, a few months. Then, I was lucky.'

The woman stopped smiling and looked at Dave and then bent to a carrier bag. When she sat up, she was red in the face and Dave thought that cheesy smell was stronger. In her hand was a brown banana, just a few yellow splotches along its flaccid length.

'Eat.'

What else could Dave do but fill his mouth with the sweet, soft, fizzing flesh and say thank you while the woman watched every bite with a mixture of loss and pride? He was still lucky enough to recognise an act of real kindness when he was offered one.

The Who filled the Lada and the cab driver, smelling of booze and a night sleeping in his battered leather jacket, tapped the steering wheel along to the music and looked at Dave, sitting beside him, to see if he was happy too. It was 6.30 a.m. and Dave had just arrived in Alena's home town.

'You see? I listen to this when young.'

He didn't know this song but he nodded and the man looked back at the road happy. It looked like he might burst into song. Dave stared out at the streets; he certainly wasn't in Moscow any more. The buildings were either part demolished old wooden houses, like something out of *Little House on the Prairie*, or huge tower blocks. The tower blocks were a bit like his own but so much older, built with concrete and ancient wood; clothes hung in front of their windows, some had scraggy plants put out. He supposed it was a homely sign but they looked ragged.

He knew he was being mad to hope he'd see Alena straight away, there was no one on the streets, except one or two people, faces covered by umbrellas to protect themselves from the fine film of early-morning drizzle. Dave examined a pair of legs, but the calves weren't round enough, they'd never delivered free papers to half of Hackney. The song had changed and he could see his driver looking over at him, could almost feel the rusty wheels creaking as he tried to come up with something to say.

'You see, it is . . .' He nodded a few times out of the window and then took his hands off the wheel to flutter his fingers in the international sign for rain. Dave pulled his eyes away from the street.

'Raining, yes.'

'Yes, yes, yes, yes.'

The driver said it fast as though Dave had interrupted his flow of thought, as though that word had been on the tip of his tongue, but then his eyes shone and he smiled wider again, pleased with himself.

'Like London always.'

And Dave gave a small laugh, no more than a slight coughing noise, which was all he felt he could manage. It was his nerves or maybe this place, how run-down it looked; would she really have come back to a town like this?

'Yes, most of the time, mate.' Then, realising, 'You speak good English.'

The driver took this as his moment to speak and turned down the volume on the song's guitar solo.

'At home I learn.' He got redder in the face. Dave worried that the effort of dredging up the English words might take the car off-road, that or the two beer cans rattling at his feet. Not that he was judging of course. 'But is hard because I don't . . .'

'Practise?'

'*Da*. Yes, yes. Practise. Here –' God help them, he'd taken his hands off the wheel again to point around and to look at Dave to make sure he was nodding along. 'Here . . .'

'This town?'

'Yes, yes, yes, yes. This town was –' he clapped his hands together, then kept them clasped tight – 'closed.'

'Closed?'

'No visitor.'

'Right.'

'No leave.'

'No one could leave. Yeah, I read something about that.'

He shook his head for a good minute while his face worked

away at coming up with the words, the car filled with those long eerie guitar chords and they turned onto an estate of those tower blocks.

'*Da, da, da*. Hard to leave and come back.'

The driver's head lowered a little into the collar of his jacket. He breathed heavily and then turned up the volume again. Dave knew the town had been closed already. Just like a TV programme he thought, everyone stuck in one town, everyone dying to get out and everyone afraid to say so. He thought of the way a streak of gossip could paint his estate in lies in an afternoon and then multiplied that by the size of a whole town where everyone was trapped and seething. He wouldn't work out what this meant for Alena, wouldn't try yet. Maybe he'd get the chance to ask her.

They stayed quiet for the rest of the ride, deeper and deeper into the estate. When 'Seeker' came on the driver's mood seemed to lift; he looked round at Dave and slapped his palm on his thigh. 'Best.'

'Yeah, probably. Mate, we are going to the Hostel Sputnik, aren't we? Sput-nik?'

'*Da, da, da*. Sputnik. *Da*.'

And with a sharp turn, which threatened to lift the left side even of the bulky green Lada, they pulled up outside a tower block, a play park with shattered bottles to one side of the entrance, a mountain of split-open bin bags to the other.

'Sputnik?'

'*Da*, Sputnik.'

The driver motioned Dave out of his side of the car and into the grey morning. Dave's stomach twisted a bit. He'd heard all sorts. Tony had warned him: 'The time you want to be really careful is coming and going. Cause everyone knows you've got everything on you. And don't bother going to the police either, not unless you want to get a kicking and then a fine for the pleasure.'

He looked around. The driver seemed harmless, friendly even. Dave could have had him easily. Unless this was where his mates came out, big bruisers like those muscly sculptures they had all over the place. Maybe they'd be swinging a hammer and sickle each. The driver walked over to the door to the flats and Dave assessed his situation. It was deserted, he could run but not that far with his rucksack and that had his passport in it. Should he just get it done with now, while the bloke seemed to be wandering about waiting, do a runner?

'Come.'

Dave picked up his rucksack and walked over. There, by the door, which Dave now noticed said 'Fuck Off' in a looping spray paint, in English too, was a sign saying 'Hostel Sputnik'.

The driver was looking at him closely now, smiling. 'Sputnik. Sputnik.'

He was so relieved he wasn't about to be mugged it didn't even register he'd travelled thousands of miles and spent over a thousand pounds to end up on a worse estate than Roehampton. He reached into his jeans and handed the bloke a few notes, he didn't care what he took, but the driver pocketed the top two and handed the rest back with a shake of his head. Dave decided that since he wasn't having seven shades of shit kicked out of him this might be his lucky day. He fingered his wallet. It was the only photo he had of her, one of a photo-booth strip of four, Alena on his lap, but pouting into the camera, a strip of sunburn down her nose. Dave tried a grin but his lower jaw felt like jelly as he turned back to the driver. 'Girlfriend. Lives here? Do you know her? Have you seen her?' But the door was already closed, the car reversing and Dave was left standing alone, surrounded by the desolate tower blocks, holding the picture and with no idea how to start trying to find a person who probably wasn't there anyway.

Top berth again, this time of Ikea bunk beds. The room was shared by two Russian students, one beefy, the other a scrawny little lad, both in their early twenties and speaking no English, and a bearded Canadian. The Russians worked studiously all day and night, bent topless over their laptops, swigging black tea, and later beer, out of plastic bottles battered from reuse. Beefy wore a small gold cross that tangled in his dark chest hair. The Canadian stayed mostly silent, reading a block of thin, fluttery pages with a ripped cover that claimed it was *The Life and Times of Stalin*. Occasionally he would swap hands, rotate a wrist.

He'd wanted to go looking straight away but he'd lain down for a few minutes and woke hours later, sweating, his heart thumping as though his body suspected he'd just missed Alena somehow. He looked at the photo again, considered showing his room-mates, and then tucked it back into his wallet. Sick to his stomach with cowardice, he had a feeling like he was stranded in this strange town and was already messing things up. Eventually he washed his face, looked at himself in the mirror and thought it wouldn't be such a bad thing if Alena never saw him again after all. Then he walked out into the still, hot air of the evening.

He walked and walked, peering in cafes and restaurants. He wandered the grounds of the university until a guard started following seven paces behind him. He tried an indoor market selling everything from bras to golden plaits of cheese. His ankles started shouting at him to stop, and his head told him he'd have to ask someone, show the picture, but each time he tried to his hand shook so badly he couldn't get it out of his wallet and he gave up.

He thought he saw her once, through the window of a dark, tunnel-like bookshop, a slim white hand brushing red hair up and away from the back of her neck. All the breath left him; he was rooted to his spot and ashamed to find, when the girl did turn and she had wide lips, a nose too long and narrow, that he was crying quietly as people moved around him on the pavement.

After that, exhausted, panicked and wanting to get straight on the train back home, he walked through the town to the supermarket on the edge of the estate. Even though he knew how much Russians enjoyed their food he expected a dusty, sparse shop selling the usual stuff. Instead it was filled with everything you'd get at a normal supermarket, only it was nicer; wider aisles, more of any one product than you'd ever need, eight types of cottage cheese, every kind of chocolate bar. It was only because of the Europop and the pack of lean dogs huddled together outside licking their paws that you'd ever guess it was Siberia.

He bought crisps, an apple, some cottage cheese with apricot jam, a six-pack of Coca-Cola and two slabs of chocolate with a picture of a ballerina on the wrapper. He could have almost been at home, if he blurred his eyes at the writing and closed his ears to the nonsense sounds around him. But he wouldn't do that, because any woman pushing a trolley, or dragging at a child's arm, stacking a shelf with Russian Heinz ketchup could have been his Alena. He realised he was terrified of not finding her and almost as terrified that he would. He fingered the picture in his pocket, pushed the edge of it under his nail. Tomorrow, he'd do better. He'd show the picture. He'd ask about and put up with the hard, suspicious stares, the feeling of his heart swelling to bursting and then deflating again at every Alena false alarm.

He went and sat on the scorched, scratchy piece of grass outside with his food. The dogs did nothing, just flicked their tails in his direction and flared their dry black nostrils when he opened the bag of crisps. And there they sat together, all of them with nowhere else to go.

18

The smell of ammonia made Alena's eyes water. She kicked off her sandals, went to the tap and put her mouth to it; the cleanest water in all of Siberia, right from Lake Olkhon. She felt woozy. The cold water stung her teeth and focused her a little.

'There's shawarma, Alena. In the oven. I couldn't eat it, the heat. At lunchtime I went down to the fountain and dangled my legs in it and ate an ice cream, just like a kid again.'

Henka craned her head, covered in cling film, to speak with Alena. She was in her underwear, the bright peach lace digging into her softer older woman's flesh, her feet on the table with a nub of cotton wool between each toe. Alena said nothing, she was trying to act normal, as normal as she was those days at least. She took a spoon from the draining board, opened the fridge, took out a jar of sauerkraut and went to sit with Henka on the sofa. Henka slung her legs over Alena's, the smell of cocoa butter mixing with the ammonia.

'How was it today? Are you sure you're OK? In the heat of that shack? Because you know if you need to stop we'll manage, you've spent more than enough time making pancakes now, a clever girl like you. There's always a way.'

Alena gulped down her mouthful of cold cabbage but her throat felt swollen, she could hear her breath shuddering inside her, as though it was hurtling up and down her windpipe. She swallowed again, bit her lip, tried to ignore the dizzy sensation in her limbs.

'It's fine. I gave the kids from the flower stall your cookies today. They were so excited they jumped about like kangaroos for the rest of the day. You probably shouldn't send them again though – their grandmother had a face like a cat's arse over it.'

Her voice sounded so normal.

'No, Alena, that's just what her face is like.' She hoisted her legs from Alena's, looked at the clock. 'Change the channel if you like, lie down, take off your dress, I need to wash this out.'

Alena did as she was told and flicked through the channels, car chase, soap opera, news, but she could still hear Henka shouting over the running water.

'You won't come tonight? It might be good for you? Lily said she could get you in free and that salsa is meant to be good . . . You're not going to meet a nice man with your lips clamped around a spoon of sauerkraut and –'

She didn't understand that the sound was coming from her at first. A pitiful whining, followed by deep moans from deep in her belly, she didn't realise she had curled herself into a ball, that her open mouth was dripping saliva onto her knees. Then Henka was there, towel only half covering her, hair dripping warmly, wetly, onto Alena's face. She knelt by the younger woman and cradled her head under one arm.

'What? What? Poor thing. What an earth? You tell me. Tell me now.'

'He's here.'

'What? Who's here? Alena, come on now, you're not making sense.'

'I saw him today. On a bus. Just the side of his face but I know. I think so. I think he's come for me.'

'Who, Alena? Alena? Acht, it could have been anyone. You poor girl. You're overtired is all, no wonder. But don't you worry, you're safe here, do you hear? This is your home and we'll protect you and you're safe. No one can hurt you.'

Alena raised her head, her face shiny with snot, sweat and tears she hadn't known were there to cry.

'He won't hurt me. He loves me.'

She sat cross-legged and watched the children with their heels kicking against the ponies' flanks. The ponies, their thick dirty manes twined with neon plastic flowers, ankles garlanded with satin ruffles, hardly seemed to notice, and neither did the tiny, pinch-faced girl, maybe nine, with skin a colour between tanned and dirty, who led them round by a pink harness. Beside her the carousel played a song so loudly it made her breastbone vibrate, *boom, boom, boom, let me hear you say wayoo, wayoo*, but soon it would switch to some nineties ballad and she could just sit quietly. Wait.

Beside her a girl sat on her boyfriend's lap, holding a rose. He was all dressed up and Alena could smell his aftershave. He rubbed his hands up and down the girl's white satin jeans, whispered into her ear, and she giggled, flicked the head of the rose at his nose in chastisement. Alena took another sip of her minty bright green slush drink, the only thing that was cold enough to refresh her in the heat. She crunched the ice until the tips of her teeth stung, breathed in the smell of cooking meat, horseshit and the boy's aftershave.

She had this idea that if she sat for long enough, here, right in the middle of the park, the traditional meeting point for lovers, beside the stalls, fairground and the garlanded ponies, ice-cream and shawarma stands, that he would come. Dave would come to the same place she had come with her friends and giggled about boys, and later, where Mikhail had taken her and bought her a pony ride though she was far too old for such things. Where she had sometimes taken her mother and they would drink a small beer each, stretching out their legs in front of them.

She had a sudden memory, like a smell drifting by, of her mother just after her father had passed, sitting under a tree, her face to the sun but the leaves above them mottling her face with shadow, and if you looked you could see her cheeks shining with the grief of loss. Alena pulled her feet closer to her centre. Perhaps her mother had already been deteriorating then, perhaps if Alena had noticed she could have got help sooner, slowed things down. Perhaps, perhaps not, but it is hard to live with the knowledge of certain things, let alone a knowledge that allowed you to imagine you could have done something to change things, to help someone you love.

She wondered again if she should look for him, but somehow doing nothing seemed better to her. He had come this far, he would find her. The couple were kissing, not deep, open-mouthed kisses but small snapping pecks that, she saw when she turned her head for a moment, created a string of spit between their mouths, his hand rubbing the white satin of her leg more rhythmically, more urgently. But Alena would stay. Her straw gurgled and they looked around and she gave a raise of her eyebrows and then remembered herself how it was to be in love, to want to kiss someone and not care about saliva, or who was sitting next to you, or how much aftershave he was wearing, and gave them a smile.

'Sorry.'

She would wait until the night came and cooled the sweat on her skin, until her backside hurt from the bench, until there was no one left in the park except one lone child, up too late, taking a final pony ride. Then, the rest of the strong-shouldered, hungry-looking children would mount their garlanded ponies and ride them single file from the park up the main street to their estate. She stayed and waited for Dave to appear as if by magic from Hackney, in his English clothes with his accent that people wouldn't know was London proper. She would wait until he walked through the park, slowly and quietly as he always did, as though hanging back from an invisible crowd. The last child would fall from its horse and wail, the father would shout at the other overtired child holding the reins, who shrugged, expressionless, staring right into his face. She would do nothing but wait. She could wait. And then she would send him home again. She could, she would, send him home again.

19

There was a roar of laughter from the end of the table and Dave's head shot up as he watched his young hostel-mates clap their arms around each other's shoulders and smack each other's stomachs so the thin material of the shirts carefully ironed in their room stuck to the sweat of their bodies.

Scrawny stood, searching for something in his pocket, swaying backwards and forwards like a lamp post in a strong wind, his wide slack smile showing a gold back tooth. He pulled out a handful of notes, a few coins tumbled to the concrete floor and he stared at them for a moment in surprise as his beefy companion turned to laugh with Dave.

Dave reached into his pocket and pulled out a handful of roubles, scratching himself on the rough edge of the table, though it didn't quite earn the name of table since it was nothing but a square of plywood balancing on two drums of cooking oil, and stretched across with the coins.

Taking the coins, Scrawny tripped his way over to the karaoke machine that stood by the chiller cabinet filled with beers, cling-film-covered meats and cheeses. Dave had already had three Cokes and now his stomach felt tight, his gullet blown up like one of those long thin balloons. Luckily, in this place burping was considered not only OK but essential.

Scrawny made several passes at the coin slot of the karaoke machine before the owner, an old woman, discarded her bag of crisps and put it in for him with a tired, indulgent smile.

Dave wondered if this was where they always came, this

shack in the middle of the train station car park, one wall made of plastic sheeting, the other three of corrugated metal, with only one real table and the rest built from whatever flat surface they could find, the pictures and statues of the Virgin Mary slotted in among the packets of soup, crisps and chocolate, plastic bottles of vodka.

Dave was glad of the invite though, as he'd sat and watched them get drunker and drunker in the dorm room after ironing their shirts. Applying the same diligence and focus they had to their studies all week, they passed the bottle between them and sat, unsmiling, side by side on an upper bunk. Half a bottle down, their features melted a bit and they got the girl who ran the reception desk and spoke English to invite him out. Fuck it, why not? He was done. He'd looked in every shop, every place he could think of. A whole week on buses and foot, awful disappointing day after awful disappointing day. He'd even found the guts to show her photo to anyone who looked like they might be friendly, which was almost no one.

He was done in, with no idea what to do next. And now he was in this metal shack watching the kid murder a Russian version of what sounded like Roxette, wondering whether he was alright to leave them or if he should try and get them into a taxi with him.

He saw the outline before she walked in. A hulking, backlit shape looming up beside him until the sheeting was pulled back and there was a blonde girl, rucksack on back. The scattering of people at other tables glanced at her, expressionless, and then turned their attention back to each other or to Scrawny, his eyes clenched shut to better deliver a scrotum-tighteningly-high chorus.

Dave kept looking. Her hair was pulled back, she had a face

he recognised from the younger ones in the shoe shop, part scared of everything, part *but I won't be letting you know it*. Dave tried to guess where she was from but it was to hard to tell. She took her backpack off by bending over and swinging her whole body around till it landed with a thump on the floor. Then she walked to the bar, head high, and ordered a Diet Coke in a nice posh English accent. The owner looked up and shook her head, unsmiling.

'*Nyet*.'

'Oh, um, OK, ah . . . *kafye see moloko*?'

The owner shrugged but reached, still sitting, to hit the kettle switch, tore open the sachet with her teeth and poured it into the plastic cup. When she sat down and pulled out her *Lonely Planet*, Dave turned round.

'You'll regret that.'

She looked up, shook her head, put on a tough face.

'I said you'll regret that.'

She splayed the book face down on the table. 'Jesus, sorry, I thought you were with them.'

She jerked her head towards Scrawny and Beefy who were now swaying in each other's arms while giving the bar their rendition of Celine Dion.

'I am.'

'No, I mean I thought you were Russian.'

'Right. No, they're my hostel-mates. I'm from London. You?'

'Farnham, in Surrey? Travelling solo. You on the Trans-Sib too? Can you believe their night trains leave at 2 a.m.? I honestly thought I was going to be found macheted in someone's boot getting down here. Just hailing any car and offering to pay them for a ride? My mum would have a fucking fit!' She laughed, took a sip of her coffee, made a face and put it down. 'So are you going east or west?'

'Neither. I'm stuck here for a bit. But I came from Moscow.'

'What would you be stuck here for?'

Dave jerked his head towards his sweating, howling companions. 'I think it's their local.'

'No, I mean in this shit-heap town. I can't wait to get to Mongolia now, better still Japan where I can get some healthy food and people actually, you know, smile at each other.'

Dave looked up at the two of them gurning into each other's faces but said nothing about it not being each other that the Russians had a problem with.

'Not what you hoped?'

'No, I mean it's, like, quite fascinating.' She lowered her voice. 'No democracy, everyone totally materially obsessed, newspapers just printing whatever that halfwit Putin wants them to say. It's hard to believe this was once a revolutionary country. I'm glad I came, I just can't wait to leave.'

Dave took a sip of his Coke. Thought of his old shop with its menagerie, false nails clicking against the till screen, women buying hundreds of pounds' worth of shoes that they could barely walk in.

'It's not so different from home.'

The girl looked down at her hands and then quickly over towards the twosome now at the bar sharing a family-size bag of Lay's crisps, shoving handfuls in. Dave worried he'd embarrassed her.

'I'm here for my girlfriend.'

She tore her eyes away from the crisp carnage. 'What? Sorry?'

'I'm here to see my girlfriend.'

'Cool – is she studying here or something?'

'No, she's from here, this is where she grew up.'

She nodded, making a face he couldn't quite work out,

maybe thinking about how she'd just slagged off his girlfriend's home town.

'So . . . is she working tonight, or out with the girls or something?'

'No, she doesn't know I'm here yet.'

And there was a cold look, he felt it fall on him like a blue light. A slight tension in her shoulders, her eyes trying to go a bit deeper to see if he was a stalker or a nutter. He didn't shy away from that look, he was starting to wonder himself anyway, but he didn't want to freak her out; she was already in a shack at a train station at 1 a.m.

'I mean, it's a surprise. She's out of town for the weekend so I thought I'd be waiting when she got back.'

Shoulders loosened, the smile came back and she tilted her head to one side, gave a big smile.

'That is so romantic. Is it a long-distance thing then?'

Scrawny and Beefy had started wandering over to the table now, crisp crumbs on their chins, shirts unbuttoned, Beefy showing his impressive mass of chest hair. Dave gave them fifteen minutes more of drinking before they'd be impossible to get home, taxi or not.

'Yeah, you could say that.'

'She must be beautiful. They just are here, aren't they, the girls? So skinny and those great cheekbones.'

Scrawny was sitting next to the girl now, leaning in, head bobbing, eyes half closed, having an animated conversation with her in Russian whether she could understand it or not. Dave reached into his wallet and gave the girl the picture of Alena.

'But isn't that the pancake girl?' He could tell from her face that he'd failed the stalker and nutter test. 'You think she's out of town?'

At which point Scrawny grabbed the picture from the girl's hand and brought it to his face, putting his arm round the girl, who, seeing how the night was going to go, was already trying to struggle her pack on.

'What?'

'Nothing, just . . . whatever's going on, I hope you guys work it out.'

'What? What do you mean, whatever's going on?'

Dave took the picture back while she shrugged off Scrawny.

'Nothing. Look. Forget it. I've got to get some stuff for the journey.'

She had the stranded expression of someone who's been pulled into a domestic, something too intimate, that she would've run from if she hadn't been lumbered with that massive backpack.

'Hey, hold on a minute. Just –'

But Scrawny was pulling him over towards the karaoke box in the corner, playing Billy Joel. She left through the plastic sheeting across the doorway and she was nowhere to be seen once he'd disentangled himself. Dave stood in the darkness of the car park; he wasn't done looking yet.

It scared him how easily he could have missed her, just gone home believing she'd never come back here, or even that she'd lied about where she'd grown up. And of course he'd walked past the market before but he'd never ventured beyond the first line of falling apart stalls with blaring pop music, it had seemed so unwelcoming; the make-do shacks, so many of the people working were whole families in cheap, grubby clothes, selling vegetables and fruit with the dirt of their farms still on them. Or the grandmas, selling little plastic bags of radishes and cucumbers from their handbags or honey in anything from coffee jars to shampoo bottles. He supposed they were the Roehampton Estate people of Siberia, but there was something about the way they talked quietly with each other, and the way their eyes scanned him quickly up and down, that made him think that maybe it was harder being at the thin end of the wedge here, even if you did have a bit of land.

So he'd never been in beyond those first stalls, and if he only had he could have found her, just like that. Days of wandering around, and after enough knockbacks too scared to show the picture, just staring at faces looking for hers, the sun smacking at the top of his head, and he might have found her in his first week, on the first day even.

The cafe was at the top of one of the fancier shopping arcades and looked right down onto the market. He'd been here on his second night but he'd sat on the other side, staring the wrong way across the town while he froze under the air conditioning and stuffed down gluey carbonara with a five-quid pot of tea. He hadn't been back because it had started to fill up with a young, shouty crowd, in a way they reminded him of the skinny-jeaned kids back in Hackney, and he'd been a bit put off by the full-wall murals of blonde twins in latex bras and buttockless trousers.

Now, he sat in a booth covered in sticky fake green leather, sipping slowly on a Coke. That's how he'd spotted the stand, next to a flower seller, with its big hand-painted sign with a picture of an orange rolled-up pancake.

He'd been seated by a sweet-looking aproned waitress, who smiled as she practised her awkward English, though he was barely listening. He had already started watching her. Her hair was lighter he thought, maybe from the sun or because she didn't dye it at home. She smiled sometimes, and he was able to imagine, by her quick efficient movements as the late-lunchtime queue shrank, that she was happy in her job. He couldn't make out what she was wearing, just the clash of yellow against the tawny brown of her hair. So he just sat and watched, sipping his Coke, afraid that if he took his eyes off her she'd quit or get sacked, just disappear into the jumbled market and he would never find her again.

'Can you like anything else?'

The waitress held her hand up to her mouth when she spoke, as though covering it would mask any mistakes.

'Yeah, actually.' Dave turned back to the window. 'That stall, the pancake one? What time does it close?'

'Pancake?'

'Yes.'

She bent over the menu and ran a finger down the list. 'Is here.'

'No, that one, the stall. Does it close at night?'

She smiled shyly, shrugged and motioned to another waitress nearby who came over.

'Can I help you?'

'Yes, thanks, I just want to know, that pancake stand there, what time does it shut?'

'The market closes at . . . ah . . . seven o'clock.'

'And the stalls?'

'Yes, all market.'

Dave had taken a breath as they both stood in front of him, hands clasped against their aprons. They were probably only a bit younger than Alena.

'Do you know the girl who works there? Alena?'

The older girl spoke rapid-fire to the younger one, who

replied even faster, saying the word Alena and using her hands to gesture towards him. Now they looked at him differently, part fascination, part as if they couldn't wait to get away. The older one wasn't smiling any more. '*Nyet.*'

'Really? Because you said a lot just then.'

'*Nyet.*' Harder this time.

Dave looked at his watch. Twenty past six. 'Right, just the bill then, thanks.'

They turned and continued their whispered conversation, glancing back at him, but Dave didn't notice. He was watching the bob of Alena's head, the strong quick movements of her arms.

She slammed down the lid of each of the Tupperware boxes with the heel of her hand, then hauled them into the fridge. It had been five days since she had sat with Henka, still dripping in her towel, and told her all about Dave, a little about Fedir who she said was a boyfriend, a bad, cruel boyfriend, but certainly nothing about Andriy. Of course Henka had heard the rumours, the same rumours Alena saw written all over people's faces when they came and bought their lunch from her, so maybe Henka guessed something of who Fedir was. But if she did, she didn't pry, she made tea and brought out a large chocolate bar, as though a full belly would help Alena tell her everything. Perhaps she was right.

As Henka had got dressed Alena had continued to tell her story, for the first time since she'd got back. She didn't cry at the bad parts, instead she cried when she described the little chocolate dog Dave had brought home to her, or the time he had found a Russian cafe in Primrose Hill and splashed out when she said she missed borscht, how he came with her when he could at the weekends and they delivered papers together, talking the whole way, racing up tower-block stairs, stopping for ice creams and kisses.

'They have tower blocks there?'

'They have everything like we do, good and bad.'

By the time she had finished Henka was in her red dress applying another coat of mascara, ready for salsa class.

'And he's come for you. So romantic, like a film! Shall I ask people to look for him? You know Lily knows everyone, she's a foghorn, if anyone can –'

'He'll find me by himself. And then I'll send him away.'

Henka turned, the mascara wand frozen against her lashes. 'What?'

'I'll send him away, Henka. You must see why.'

Now, slamming the chiller door closed and pulling down the plywood cover over the stall's opening hatch, she wondered if maybe it had all been a stupid mistake, that she had just been overtired the day she glimpsed him. She was sick of the feeling of waiting, her skin prickling as though she was being watched, of Henka rushing towards her every night asking if he had come, that she thought she'd seen someone with that bloodless British skin at the supermarket and all he had bought was a packet of biscuits.

Alena went back into the shack, took off her oversized T-shirt and apron and reached for the dress Henka had given her, a yellow summer dress; a kaftan Henka had called it, pulling it from a dusty suitcase that hadn't been opened since the seventies, 'but it's nice and cool in this heat'.

She picked up her bag. Tonight she wouldn't go to the park and wait like a madwoman, she would go home, take a shower and have a cry, eat the fried potatoes she'd been dreaming of all day. She might go downstairs to the cafe and play chess with

Amir, and she would give up on waiting because five days was enough for him to have come if he was properly looking. Even if he hadn't been, five days was enough. She slung her bag onto her shoulder.

'Are you going home soon?'

The old woman at the flower stall closed one eye in a lazy wink and shrugged one shoulder.

'Right, well, goodnight, see you tomorrow.'

But the old woman was rising, squeezing her lumpy knees as she rose from the stool. She bent to a bucket near to her and drew out a small bunch of lavender, held together at the stem with red twine. She held it to Alena, who hesitated. The old woman brought the bunch to her nose and then jerked it towards Alena.

Alena took the flowers and fumbled in her bag for some coins but the woman was already back down on her stool, head up towards the sky, eyes closed.

Alena made her way through the stalls, already shut or being packed up, held the lavender bunch to her nose and said her goodbyes. She would have let him go. She would have sent him away. She'd only wanted to see him just once more, to undo in some way the ugliness between them. To see his face and wish him a happy life, tell him he was a good man even though he didn't realise it.

The smell of the lavender, her disappointment, the tears behind her eyes made her woozy and she stopped for a moment to calm herself. When she looked up, there he was, as though she had conjured him. But it was him, head bent, shoulders down, pale as a sheet of paper, waiting patiently for her.

He'd imagined it of course. In his mind it usually went one of two ways: she ran into his arms and he spun her around promising they'd never be apart, just like in the films that his mum and Shelley used to enjoy so much; in the other version she saw him and walked the other way, he caught up with her, begging her for a moment, and she turned round and slapped him before telling him that he was dead to her, just like in the soaps his mum and Shelley used to like so much.

In all the time he'd spent thinking about the moment they saw each other again, while walking circles in the Wandsworth shopping centre, dropping off during his office night shift, on hot Russian trains while he refused yet another snack from his cabin-mate, he never imagined that she would see him and walk towards him with a calm, sad smile on her face and that the first words he'd say to her would be, 'Is that a kaftan?'

Alena looked shocked and then laughed; she was right in front of him, just a step away. Her hair was longer, she'd stopped dyeing it, but it was still red at the ends, and she wore less make-up, which was what maybe made her face look a bit rounder, or maybe that was the pancakes; she'd always loved her grub. She didn't answer his question though.

'David.'

And then he remembered himself and thought to take that last step to her, he just wanted to touch her wrist, or her hair, though he knew he had no right to, but there was something about where she had placed herself, a step back from him, and how she held her body that stopped him, so instead he told the truth.

'I missed you.'

'I miss you too.' She looked behind her at the market. 'Is strange to see you here.'

'I just can't believe you're right in front of me. You . . . don't seem very surprised.'

'Is small town. I thought I saw you and then I thought I was going mad.'

'Right. So you were just waiting for me to show up.'

'I didn't know.'

They stood for a moment. Dave smiled and then looked down at the ground. He had no idea what to say or what to do now. She seemed so calm, so out of reach.

'Do you want to go somewhere? I mean, we can talk, I came all this way and . . .'

He stopped and looked at her. She was different, and it wasn't anything to do with the hair or the giant eighties dress she was wearing.

'Of course. Let's go.'

And, just like every other time, she walked off ahead of him, weaving through the crowd, occasionally twisting her head back to see he was OK and following.

20

She led him slowly, seemingly towards the park, but instead she stopped shy of it at Orange, a fast-food cafe filled with teens sharing bowls of fries and watching MTV. He caught up with her, and she lowered her gaze. The hardest thing, she realised, was that being with him was so familiar, that it would be so easy to raise a hand to his face or lean up and kiss his clammy, pale cheek. He looked so done in that she wanted to comfort him, but wouldn't risk touching him.

'This is where you want to go, Lena?'

He was scanning the tables of large, loud groups of kids and the pictures of red-headed twins on the walls. Alena agreed that they were strange, ugly pictures, all pale skin and freckles and crooked teeth. No one could work out why they were there.

'Just for a drink? I work all day.'

'Sure, sure, of course, I mean, I don't mind, it's just . . . you guys put up some weird pictures in your cafes.'

She pushed open the door and the smell of grease hit them. Dave placed a hand on the base of her back and before she realised what she was doing she had pressed back into the warmth of his palm. Then she took two small quick steps to get away.

'I get the drinks, go sit.'

And she saw the hurt on his face at her sharpness.

She brought the drinks back: Diet Coke for her, Coke for him. She put them down carefully and then slid into the booth, loosening her dress around her as she did. He was staring at her, half smiling, still pale with worry. There was too much, too much to say, too much between them to cover over a polystyrene cup of Coke sitting at a plastic table. He reached out for her hand but somehow lost heart so that he was only holding the very tips of her fingers, his thumb smoothing the dome of her nails. She took her hand away under the guise of picking up her drink.

'It's strange to see you. How long have you been here?'

'In Russia? A week and a half now. I flew to Moscow and then caught the train. Do you know the train takes four days?'

'Did the *provodnista* give you trouble?'

'Yeah, at first she did actually.'

'Yes, I do journey from here to Moscow before I go to London. The *provodnista* is very nasty, using Hoover when everybody sleeps.'

They shared a smile but the words in her mouth were like clay. All the things she could be saying and she was chatting like he was a stranger on a train platform.

'Do you like it?'

'Not Moscow, but here, yeah, a bit more. I'm staying in a hostel on an estate. The first thing that wakes you up is the sound of kids in the little park downstairs. But that's not really the point, I mean me liking it, because the only reason I came . . .'

She couldn't bear to look at him, his leaning, his confused face, because it wasn't going like he thought it would, though she couldn't imagine what he thought would happen.

'Lena? Lena, I came here for you.' He'd raised his voice slightly and a group of kids looked over and then laughed between themselves. 'Ignore them. Kids. Listen, I would have come sooner, I saved for months and came here to find you because –'

A thought occurred to her. 'How? How would you find me? How did you know I would come here?'

'Because you told me. Do you remember? You told me how your mum bought a little chicken coop and a chicken to keep on her balcony but that there was a cousin-in-law of a town official in the flat below who didn't like it and a week later the coop and chicken were gone again. And I said that sounded pretty harsh and you said your town was no worse than anywhere else in Russia and I asked you which town and you said.'

'I don't remember.'

'I do. I remember everything you ever told me. Everything you ever gave me about yourself, I kept. And I didn't know you'd come here. How could I? But I thought . . .' He looked at his hands folded in front of him on the table. 'I thought I had to try because if I didn't I'd never forgive myself.'

Alena looked back up at the screen, that old music video: schoolgirls in the rain kissing. At the table next to them the teens had started throwing fries at each other. 'Thank you for coming so far. I miss you.'

He reached forward and took her whole hand this time, holding it tightly. 'But I'm here now.'

Alena looked at him. She would give him away. She would send him away. 'Come with me.'

She stood and walked out without looking behind at him, through the door and out into the heat of the evening.

This time Alena didn't walk ahead; instead she walked shoulder to shoulder with him so he had to twist his head all the way to see her. He tried to work out what was different, or maybe this was just how she had always been in her own town, surrounded by her own language; a sureness that he didn't recognise and a heavy determination in the way she stared ahead, occasionally angling them out of the way of another person on the road. He was nervous, so nervous it felt like the blood coursing around in his forearms was made of electric sparks. It had been OK, in the cafe, but when she stood up he felt thrown again, he couldn't tell what she was feeling, and everything she was doing and saying made no sense when you added them up together.

She said she missed him but she didn't want him to touch her, she didn't send him away but she didn't seem to want him there either. She was treating him like an annoying cousin she was begrudgingly showing around town. And because he couldn't get a fix on what was happening he didn't know what to say, his mind was at such a high pitch of nervousness that he just walked quickly along with her, turning his head, pretending to look at one building or another while he tried to remember everything he could about this different, new Alena.

They walked the main road of the town, a long street he'd walked plenty of times before because he was sure of how to get back to the hostel from there. It took an hour and a half to go from end to end but they'd started two-thirds of the way. He didn't know where they were going.

'So, where to?' He hated the way it sounded like they'd only just met.

'Is secret.'

And for a moment he was back with her on a Hackney city street and she was taking them to a little community garden she'd found. Once they'd reached the garden she'd produced a sausage roll for him from her pocket and they had wandered around, her stroking the leaves and petals of the plants while he read out the names, making her laugh by attempting the Latin words in his Roehampton tongue never made for any other language. But now he looked closer and there was only a slight smile there. Back then she had beamed at him.

He wasn't sure he could stand it; it was worse than the waiting and the not knowing. Being here with her, close enough to hold her and tell her that he was sorry but that he could be better, surely him being here proved that, but somehow he couldn't speak the words. He wanted to tell her, she'd come to him and then he'd come to her and wouldn't that mean that they had a new chance, that it was possible to begin again? He opened his mouth. 'Do you want an ice cream?'

She shrugged, which he took as a yes, so they stopped at a place with giant plastic penguins outside. She picked a long, thin, stick-shaped choc ice wrapped in gold foil and emblazoned with a sickle and hammer, and Dave, because he'd suggested it, though he was sure his stomach couldn't take it, picked a Magnum. The Russians loved their Magnums.

Somehow eating that ice cream made everything seem a bit more normal, them walking side by side not touching, not talking really, until eventually Alena pointed over to a large building.

'The university, very good one.'

And Dave, because he forgot himself, or maybe because he thought the rules were different between them in Russia, asked, 'Did you go there?' She gave him a look that he couldn't quite read, mostly because she had a speck of melting chocolate on her chin and it reminded him so much of that smear of pickle when they first met.

'So tell me how you came here.'

'I told you. You mentioned the name to me, and then I thought it was worth a chance, because I had nothing when you left and . . .' He'd stopped but then a babushka's wheeled shopping trolley snapped at the backs of his ankles and he had to keep walking, talking to her at that awkward twisted angle. '. . . and if nothing else I wanted to say I was sorry. So sorry for not listening to you and just, just fucking it all up.'

And then he did stop because he was frightened he would cry or maybe start shouting, he could feel something rising up in him, and then her small hand was in his, holding it tightly, and when she spoke to him in a strong quiet voice, her English was so jumbled he wondered if she was as confused as he was.

'It's OK about that. You don't have to talk. Not about that – wait for longer and we'll talk. I meant about money and getting here and how you come to the market to find me.'

She kept tight hold of his hand and they kept walking up the gentle hills of the main road while Dave told her about leaving Hackney and going to Tooting.

'You left Hackney?'

And for the first time he could see distress on her face.

'Yeah, I needed a cheaper place and everything reminded me of you. I kept thinking you were going to come in after your round and curl up with me to watch telly on the sofa.'

She squeezed his hand but said nothing. And he continued telling her about the little room in Tooting, the mental flatmates and his jobs, how he thought about her all the time, every single minute; how when he got to the town he'd nearly given up on finding her, how people were so cold, and no one would even look at his photo never mind help him. And how, when he'd been ready to admit she wasn't there he met this English girl who'd acted a bit weird and made him think, maybe he should keep looking.

'Ponytail? Smiling all of the time? She came to stall every day. We talk about London.'

'Yeah, that was her.'

Again she said nothing. And now they were at the end of the main street, looking towards a park. Dave hadn't been up this way, it was a deserted stretch, but he'd looked at the map long enough to know the River Om curled around here which was why the main street suddenly stopped. Somehow he felt like the end of that road was the end of his chance and he stopped and turned to face her; she stepped back but he kept their clasped hands as an anchor between them.

'I've come for you. I don't mind what we do after this but I love you and I want you. And I know I've let you down and that I don't have much to offer but I swear, I swear it, Lena, give me a chance and I'll never let you down again.'

Her hand dropped from his, she turned away and he reached out for her shoulder.

'Lena, I'll ask you nothing about that bloke. I don't need to know. I just want to know you and I'll ask you nothing else, I swear it.'

'But you need to know. I need you to ask.'

People outside a beer stall had stopped to stare at the foreigner harassing one of their girls and so Alena smiled round to them in a stiff, fuck-off and mind-your-own-business way, and nodded her head towards the park. As she walked she looked down at her feet. 'We'll go here. It is my favourite place. Except for Hackney.'

And Dave would have laughed but he could barely see from uncried tears, cars going by, the different language filling up his ears, and the sun, relentless, beating down on his back. He simply followed her as he always had.

Just as they crossed the road the music started from inside the trees. A sad, choral arrangement that could put a chill in even the hottest summer evening. They had put speakers among the small forest of straight, thin birch trees that stretched on either side of the monument, so as you walked through your ears filled with the mournful music and you had no option but to focus on the giant statue in the centre.

'What's that?'

Alena hadn't thought how strange the music would seem, ghostly, as though coming from nowhere.

'Is part of monument to remember soldiers. Come see.'

The statue was fifty metres high. She still thought it was one of the most beautiful things she had ever seen: a woman, her bent head covered in a kerchief, saying goodbye to a soldier, perhaps her son or lover, their heads bowed towards each other in grief as she pressed a flower towards his chest. On either side of the path leading up to the statue were rows of walls with the names of fallen soldiers embossed into the weather-beaten bronze. Alena couldn't remember how many times she'd stroked her fingers across them, imagined in doing so she was offering comfort to someone. A game, but a game she still played while Dave wandered around beside her.

'Why carnations?'

'What?'

He nodded to the flowers laid on top of the walls of names, bleached of colour and brittle from the sun.

'I don't know. It just is.'

He walked off and stood at the foot of the statue, in its shadow, looking up at their endless, painful goodbye, and Alena realised why she had brought him here, though she hadn't known it until now. She'd thought she just wanted to go somewhere calm, that she'd felt bad about taking him to the loud, ugly Orange cafe. But now she understood, she wanted to give him something, even if it meant she could never come here again without that small bird of grief that nested in her ribs fluttering away at the memory.

'Come on, down here.'

They walked behind the statue and Alena turned to see his reaction. Below them was the vast River Om. A fattened black-brown vein weaving through the sun-scorched plains before them. It was one of the few places in town where you could look into the horizon and see only horizon, no buildings. Down by the river a four-wheel drive, from there the size of a matchbox, whinnied trying to get off the banks and onto the road. On the gentle slope that led down to the river, girls in bikinis lay on blankets in the long parched grass; a tinny radio played a pop song against the backdrop of the cicadas. Alena could smell the girls' sun cream.

'I've never walked up this far.'

She nodded and walked them towards a bench. 'Tourists never do but it's in the books. I came here in winter, you know. When I miss you so badly I want to drink myself to death or else just stop.'

'Stop?'

'Just stop. I look out at the river – it freezes in winter; there was no one here and I come and sit on this bench. There were two reasons why I keep going. One reason is I keep thinking something will happen when the river starts moving again.'

'What was the other reason?'

But she just shook her head and so he reached up to her face and brought the round of his palm to her jaw.

'I've never heard you like this before, Lena. You're, I don't know, you're . . .'

She turned her head away. 'You don't know me, David. I

want you to know you are very good and you make, no . . . you were making me happy.'

'Lena, I –'

'No, now I will tell all the things you never ask me and you will be quiet. And then you will go home again.'

'No way, I'm not going home, and I don't need to know anything about –'

But Alena was too far in now. She fixed her eyes on the panicked darting shadows of field mice in the undergrowth of the grass, flitting one way and then the other, seemingly with no one end in sight.

'I begin and say that my father died because he drink a lot. And because he drink a lot he upset people in this town, important people, and because he upset them he can't get jobs and we were very poor. Even ten years ago this town was very different. It's still poor, maybe you see, but then if some people are upset with you there were no jobs even. Do you understand?'

'Yeah, of course I understand. You know where I grew up and that it was just me and my mum too.'

He reached for her hand and she moved it, slowly but carefully, away. She wouldn't look at him.

'Is not the same. There is no government grants and hardly any paying for people without jobs. Sometimes, my mother and I, we work, mostly not. I think if I learn English I get good job. I study all of the time and get good grades. Some girls, they go to London and work only as waitress and send home money and I think that is what will be same when I go.'

She felt a little sick and moved her eyes to the slow ooze of the river, a boat the size of a fingernail making painfully slow progress along it.

'But the woman who takes me to London was not a good

woman. And maybe I was stupid. And my mother too, or maybe my mother wasn't stupid at all, I don't know. She is sick now, in a home with dementia, and I won't know. I go to see her and it is breaking my heart. David . . .' She chanced a look at him, his brow furrowed, his face pale and sweating, and turned away. '. . . do you know that there are girls who come to London and no one ever sees them again? They become prostitute, because people make them?'

'Alena.' He reached out for her and this time she allowed it because she was afraid that without his strong hand over hers, the other gripped around her forearm, she would slide from the bench.

'No, this is not what happens to me, because I am a lucky one. That is what they say, Alena is a lucky one. Old man, he makes me his girlfriend. He . . . does things to me. I live in house with him, an old witch housekeeper, his son. He makes me find girls like me to make prostitute, at airports and train stations, and I help them, son and father, capture them because girls trust me.'

Alena tasted the salt on her lips before she knew she was crying. Her voice stayed low, calm, even.

'I hate myself but I cannot go because of my mother, being frightened for her. And I have nowhere to go. Soon the son comes to me at night when the father doesn't want me. I always think he will let me go.'

Now Dave let go of her arm, put his head in his hands.

'That night? That was him? I would have killed him.'

She didn't listen, felt only the absence of his touch and reminded herself to get used to it.

'But I . . . I hate myself and one day I stop. Then the son, Fedir is his name, he does, he lets me go. So you see, then he thinks he owns me.'

Her breath shuddered, she cursed the plaintive pitch of her voice, stopped to breathe.

'I live on the streets. I sleep in disabled toilets until you find me. Until you catch me that day. I was stealing for another woman. A prostitute too. I think maybe she is probably dead now.'

Dave turned away and shook his head. Alena wiped her slick cheeks with the palm of her hand.

'I want you to know at first I need you and somewhere safe and then I really did love. Then Fedir found me. I keep thinking he will go away or we can leave but he keeps coming.' She turned then and tried to lift his face to her but he shook her off. 'I want to protect you and try to get us to Manchester. I should have been leaving you but I couldn't. And then Fedir, he . . . takes me when he wants. Do you understand?'

Down on the hill someone shook a white sheet into the air, a bright gash against the dark river; behind them the cold music in the trees started up again. Dave straightened, his face a dark mask; he reached out and held her upper arms. He didn't say anything and she stared right into his face; fury and hurt and a rawness; an awful, just born rawness. And then he started to speak. It was no more than a tight whisper from the back of his throat.

'How do you wake up every day having lived that way?'

Something cold passed across her body, a steel she'd long forgotten, cold under her skin.

'Me? How can I live that way? How could you? With your own secrets buried so deep. You think I am so stupid I don't see the black bruises under your skin?'

'We're not talking about me. This is about you. Or us. None of that matters. This is it now, you and me, we're both here. We found each other for a reason.'

And though she knew it wouldn't make any difference she

spoke the words, and they emerged like small slivers of ice from between her lips.

'We are talking about you. Tell me.'

Even as drunk as he was he knew. The sprawl of her arms and legs, a stepped-on insect, and then the pained low, slow laugh that strangled itself into sobs as she realised, too. That sloppy grin replaced by a feral, animal sound echoing from the cold, earthy-smelling block's walls, bringing that old battleaxe Doreen and her scabby-faced junkie son Shaun scurrying from the bottom flat, pecking about like pigeons after a few crumbs of drama and emotion.

They looked on, breathing hard through their mouths, as the blackish finger spread, reaching out from Shelley's body like an oil leak. And then she shouted for Dave to 'do something for fuck's sake, you pig, look at what you've done', and he simply stood, still swaying from the booze, at the top of the stairs, hands in his pockets and a strange deep chuckle gargling up his throat.

Later, when Shelley was all cleaned up, inside and out, a scrape they'd called it, necessary after the seven-month mark, they returned to the flat. In silence they stood as she made herself a drink, slicing open the joint of her ring finger while cutting the lemon; she watched the blood drip and then licked it away, gave a taunt of a smile, a trace of red still on her lower lip and upper teeth, with her eyes full of panic. Dave, still silent, wrapped a greasy tea towel around her fingers.

'Look it's nothing, just a little nick.'

She lashed at his face, scratched at his chest, tore at the neck of the T-shirt he was wearing.

'You filth, you fucking bastard, you did this to me. You wanted this. Filth. You fucking killed our baby and you killed me too. Filth.'

He'd waited. Waited until she had cried herself out, slept, and was slicing the lemon again, wincing as the juice hit the raw, open wound, and then he'd left. Filth that he was.

It was the hands in pockets, the chuckle, the leaving. Shaun and Doreen telling any who would listen about him 'just standing there, weird look on his face, you know, don't you? When you just see the look on someone's face.' That's what gave people the right to go about saying he was a wife-beater, a drunk, a murderer of his own child. The same people he'd known all his life, who came and drank the free bar dry at their wedding reception and cheered Dave on as he'd run from block to block of the estate.

Just as the news of the benefit fraud inspector's car parked outside Nightingale block, or the *Friends* box sets off the back of a lorry up for grabs, the story spread. Passed, hand to hand and mouth to mouth, along the queue at Greggs bakery, waiting for the 214, paying the provvie woman. And, of course, when the hollow-eyed Avon lady went door to door, selling her own story as well as face masks and collagen lip gloss, not a scrap of anything on herself to cover her own tired eyes and grey complexion, the empty spare flesh around her middle.

'I don't even want to talk about it. I really don't. But people should know, who we're living with. What he's capable of. I don't know, it was his mum I think, turned him funny. I said to him, not in my flat, not on this estate any more, you're not welcome. Poor Pat, she'd turn in her grave. I'm just a wreck, I'm in pieces, but what can I do? Keep going, that's it.'

He stayed at the Co-op until he realised. Realised the smell of stale booze on his skin and the shake of his hands gave them more ammunition. The manager took him aside, told him they were 'cutting back' on security, that he should lie low for a while. Dave stayed on the estate longer than you'd imagine a man would, surrounded by whispers, disgusted looks that soaked into him like the cold, wet, hopeless morning. Blokes always getting up into his face, barging at his shoulders and jabbing at his chest. He hadn't realised how popular Shelley was. He took a few beatings, an eye swollen shut, a cracked rib, enough of a kicking for it to hurt when he took a piss.

Deano's nana, a tiny woman who click-clacked about with the help of two walking sticks, had taken him in, and he stayed in sight of his mum's old flat, sleeping in Deano's football-poster-covered childhood bedroom, while he was in Ibiza.

'Davey, I've known you since you were missing the potty and shitting on my doorstep and I know a pack of lies when I hear them. Still, you've got to feel for her, poor woman. You'll never know what it's like, the pain of losing a child. The worst thing in the world.'

And he filled his mouth with a Rich Tea biscuit and stared at *Countdown* on the telly and didn't say that he'd lost a parent and a child and that he knew full well.

Shelley went door to door, from cup of tea to cup of tea, soaking up attention and squeezing out her misery as though she was leaving that black stain on each of their carpets. He couldn't forgive her, no matter how much she'd suffered. For not being able to stop drinking, for being criminally fucked up even when she'd had everything she wanted at the expense of everything he'd wanted, for not keeping herself, and their baby, safe. For making him the patsy.

He had sat with her that night, matched her drink for drink and hadn't said a word. He'd even brought the bottle home himself and hadn't tried to remind her she was trying to 'be good'. Because he was suffocating and wanted a drink himself, knowing full well that one would turn into half the bottle. He didn't blame her but he couldn't forgive her either. So he let her turn him into a monster, took it silently, drunkenly, numbly, lost everything he had, because he'd never forgive himself either.

'You drinking too? With her? You could have looked after her. You should have. That's why you had no one when you met me.'

'You had no one either.'

She said nothing and he stood, walked over to the verge. One of the sunbathing girls craned her neck to take a good look at him.

'I'm not proud of it, Alena, but there was nothing I could have done either way, even if I hadn't been drinking with her. She couldn't help herself. I wasn't the one that was pregnant.'

As he spoke he took slight steps closer towards the edge, away from her and away from the things she was saying to his back. Hiding his face because he knew it wasn't true. 'I paid the price. I lost everything.'

He was crying now, she thought, his shoulders and head fallen, his hand at his face. She stood quietly and walked away, watching his back, afraid that if he turned she would need to hold him and make him feel better and then she would be lost again. He stayed where he was and she took one last look and then turned her own back to his.

He found her on the other side of the statue, saw her pale dress billowing out in the breeze and, with the sun behind her, the small but unmistakably ripe, round shape of her pregnancy, so obvious now. For a moment, the time it took for the sun to disappear behind a cloud and emerge again, he almost walked away. The music had stopped, the only sound a child shouting somewhere in the distance. He walked to her, put his hand gently against the back of her neck, and she turned, her face red, blotched from her own tears.

'Yeah.'

'Yes?'

'I am to blame. But your story, well, Alena, it wasn't your fault. You poor girl. I don't know how you start to live with something like that. But we'll find a way, you and me. But if we just give up then it's . . . it's stamping on what we've been given. I mean, it's . . . we can't undo stuff. We just can't. God knows, I've wished I could. But can't you see that giving up when you've got this and those girls haven't is the worst thing you could do? And me, I don't know how many chances I'm allowed but I'm trying to do good here. I could be good for you if I had the chance.'

She had no more talk, no more fight. Instead she took his hand and placed it to her stomach. She had practised saying the words. 'This is not your baby.'

He moved his hand away, looked behind him. He stepped back, nodding heavily, and she could see it: all the determination, all his big words deserting him, as though they alone had been holding up his body. Alena stepped away. It was done.

But then his hand was on her arm and he was pulling her back to him. Not too roughly but as though he couldn't bear to, and couldn't stand not to. They stood under the shadow of the statue's grieving goodbye, heads close together, breath ragged. Dave placed his hand back on her stomach, as gently as if he were cradling a new, very fragile egg. The music began again.

'OK.'

Alena put her hand over his and began to cry, a sobbing that shook her whole body while he held her up, the shedding of something she hadn't fully known she was carrying.

'OK?'

And he held her to him, as tight as he dared, another man's child drumming its thumb-sized feet against his ribs.

'OK.'

ACKNOWLEDGEMENTS

There are so many people who helped me make *Thirst* the book it is. First and foremost my thanks go to my brilliant agent Juliet Pickering and my outrageously clever editor Becky Hardie. There aren't just words – without their tireless support, insight and hard work this book would not exist. Both helped me to bring Dave and Alena truly to life and I can't say how grateful I am for that.

Huge thanks also go to: Carol, Melis, Louise and all at the Blake Friedmann Literary Agency and to Clara, Susannah, Parisa and all at Chatto and Vintage – I've never felt in safer or smarter hands. To my dearest friends and earliest readers, Susanna and Levia – thank you for starting out on this road with me and sticking with it. Thank yous go to Jen and Kerry who both provided me with happy homes to write in, Meg, the Green Carnation Crew (Uli, Simon, Chris, Clayton, Chris and Sarah) and as ever the Ostrove-Pounds and Bennetts for both making me part of their families.

Thirst was developed with support from the National Lottery through an Arts Council England grant which enabled me to travel across Russia in Dave's footsteps and I also received invaluable support from Spread the Word.

Finally, thank you to my beautiful godchildren Xander and Zarla for adventures already had and those still to come.